Rebecca .... now swelled to include five beautiful grandchildren, lives in Salt Lake City, Utah, in the land of the Rocky Mountains. With canyons and high alpine meadows full of wildflowers, she never runs out of places to explore. They, plus her favourite vacation spots in Europe, often end up as backgrounds for her romance novels, because writing is her passion, along with her family and church.

Rebecca loves to hear from readers. If you wish to e-mail her, please visit her website, www.cleanromances.com.

Award-winning author **Jules Bennett** is no stranger to romance—she met her husband when she was only fourteen. After dating through high school, the two married. He encouraged her to chase her dream of becoming an author. Jules has now published nearly thirty novels. She and her husband are living their own happily-ever-after while raising two girls. Jules loves to hear from readers through her website, www.julesbennett.com, her Facebook fan page or on Twitter.

Helen Lacey grew up reading *Black Beauty, Anne of Green Gables* and *Little House on the Prairie*. These childhood classics inspired her to write her first book when she was seven years old, a story about a girl and her horse. She continued to write, with the dream of one day being a published author, and writing for Mills & Boon True Love is the realisation of that dream. She loves creating stories about strong heroes with a soft heart and heroines who get their happily-ever-after. For more about Helen, visit her website, www.helenlacey. com.

WITHDRAWN

A Bride by Summer

REBECCA WINTERS
JULES BENNETT
HELEN LACEY

MILLS & BOON

First Published in Great Britain 2018
by Mills & Boon, an imprint of HarperCollins*Publishers*
1 London Bridge Street, London, SE1 9GF

A BRIDE BY SUMMER © 2018 Harlequin Books S. A.

The Texas Ranger's Bride © 2015 Rebecca Winters
From Best Friend To Bride © 2015 Jules Bennett
Once Upon A Bride © 2014 Helen Lacey

ISBN: 978-0-263-26867-6

05-0718

MIX
Paper from
responsible sources
FSC™ C007454

This book is produced from independently certified FSC™
paper to ensure responsible forest management.

For more information visit: www.harpercollins.co.uk/green

Printed and bound in Spain
by CPI, Barcelona

THE TEXAS RANGER'S BRIDE

REBECCA WINTERS

Dedicated to Christopher R. Russell,
a military warrior from Texas who has
become a cherished friend.
This is for you, Sarg.

Chapter One

"This is Tammy White and you're listening to Hill Country Cowboy Radio broadcasting from Bandera, Texas, the Cowboy Capital of the World!

"Oh boy, have we got a lineup for you on this Labor Day weekend, including the star of the Bandera Rodeo, Kellie Parrish from Austin, Texas, our state's hopeful to win the National Barrel Racing Championship in Las Vegas come December. She'll be our guest in the second segment of our show.

"Now hear this. All you cowgirls out there, listen up and hold on to your Stetsons because we have some jaw-dropping, gorgeous, bronco-busting, homegrown cowboys in studio. But that's not the best part. They're four of our famous, legendary Texas Rangers, the pride of the great state of Texas! I've asked my buddy Mel from the fire department to be on hand in case I go into cardiac arrest. It's not every day I'm surrounded by such hunky men. They're not only easy on the eyes, but they wear the star and put their lives on the line every day to protect us.

"Welcome, gentlemen. How come we're so lucky

that four of you were willing to be interviewed? Judging by the way you were laughing when you came into the booth, does it mean you're good friends both on and off duty?"

The men all looked at Cy. Their captain in the Austin office had asked him to be the spokesman for this interview. None of them wanted to do it, but the boss insisted it was important for the Rangers to have a positive public presence. Cy had to cowboy up.

"Yup. The four of us share a very unique bond."

"We want to hear all about it, but first why don't you introduce yourselves and tell us where you're from?"

"Sure. I'm Cyril Vance and call Dripping Springs home." Kit took his turn next. "Ranger Miles Saunders from Marble Falls." Vic followed. "Ranger Stephen Malone. I grew up in Blanco." Cy nodded to Luckey on the other side of Vic. "I'm Ranger James Davis from Austin."

"Ladies, it's too bad this isn't television! You'd eat your hearts out if you were sitting where I am. Through the Hill Country grapevine the station learned that a lot of Rangers are in Bandera to help celebrate Jack Hays Days. You'll see them riding their horses in tomorrow morning's parade. It would be hard to believe that anyone in the state of Texas doesn't know the name Jack Hays. But just in case you don't, we want to hear from you why the name of Jack Hays stirs the hearts of every Texan, particularly those of the Rangers."

"I'll take this," Vic volunteered. "When Sam Houston was reelected to the presidency in December 1841, he recognized the effectiveness of the Rangers. And on

January 29, 1842, he approved a law that officially provided for a company of mounted men to 'act as Rangers.' As a result, 150 Rangers under Captain John Coffee 'Jack' Hays were assigned to protect the southern and western portions of the Texas frontier. Houston's foresight in this decision proved successful in helping to repel the Mexican invasions of 1842, as well as shielding the white settlers against Indian attacks over the next three years."

Vic turned to Kit. "You tell the rest."

"Be happy to. Jack Hays was responsible for improving the quality of recruitments and initiating tough training programs for the new Rangers, as well as initiating an esprit de corps within his command.

"The Paterson Colt six-shooters had just been invented and Captain Hays and his men were fortunate to be armed with these weapons instead of single shotguns. When the Comanche attacked Captain Hays and his company of forty in Bandera Pass in 1842, they were defeated."

"Gentlemen? I found a quote from Walter Prescott Webb, a twentieth-century US historian who said, 'Their enemies were pretty good…the Texas Rangers had to be better.' Do you Rangers still use those old six-shooters? If not, what kind of weapons do you carry?"

Luckey spoke up. "We use a variety that includes the .357-caliber SIG Sauer, the .45-caliber Colt automatic, the SIG Sauer P226 pistol, the Ruger mini-14 automatic rifle and the Remington 12-gauge shotgun."

"There are dozens of questions I want to ask, but

since you're pressed for time, why don't you tell our listeners why the four of you are particularly close?"

Cy nodded. "When I joined the Rangers, I didn't know any of the men in the company. On my application, I'd mentioned that I was a descendant of one of the men in Captain Jack Hays's company of forty. During my interview with our captain at company H, he told me there were three other Rangers in our company who could also trace their ancestry back to the original company of forty."

"Wow!"

"Wow is right. He got the four of us together. The rest was history."

"Imagine that. What a remarkable coincidence! You guys are the real thing. It's in your genes. Kind of gives you gooseflesh."

Kit chuckled. "That's one way of putting it. I can't remember a time when I didn't want to be a Texas Ranger. The pride my family felt for our heritage was instilled in me."

"It looks like none of you could escape your destiny."

Luckey grinned. "We wouldn't want to."

"I heard a rumor that everyone at Ranger headquarters has nicknamed you four 'the Sons of the Forty.' That's heady stuff."

"We don't mind," Vic stated. "But it gives us a lot to live up to."

"I'd say you're doing a spectacular job. According to your captain, the governor of our state gave you citations six months ago for your capture of a drug cartel

ring on the most-wanted list. Do the four of you always work together on a case?"

Cy shook his head. "No. It's a very rare occurrence that we have an opportunity to do something big together, but we help each other out from time to time. Each case is different."

"Cowboys and cowgirls? Our station is honored that these Texan heroes have taken time out of their busy lives to let us know a little bit more about them. I have it on good report from your captain that the Sons of the Forty will be leading other Rangers on horseback from all over the state in the parade tomorrow. That will be the chance for you ladies to feast your eyes on the best of the best! Thank you for coming in. It's been a Hill Country thrill for me and everyone listening."

"Thank *you*," they said in a collective voice.

KELLIE GOT OUT of her truck in front of the radio station, pressed for time. She'd just driven in from Amarillo over three hundred miles away, where she'd made a decent time in the rodeo the night before. But it wasn't the low score she'd wanted. The fact that she didn't get the best time had little to do with her skill or her horse's.

Since she'd been on a five-state, pro rodeo racing circuit over the past five weeks, she'd been deeply unsettled by a guy who'd been following her from venue to venue among Montana, Oregon, Utah, New Mexico and Texas.

He'd come up to her after her win in Pendleton, Oregon, and asked her out on a date. She told him she was married in order to put him off. When she drove

to Utah for the Eagle Mountain Rodeo, there he was again while she was brushing down her horse after her event. He was hoping she'd changed her mind and would go out with him.

She warned him that if he ever came near her again, she'd call the police. At the same time she signaled to her horse handler, Cody. He walked over to find out what was wrong and the stalker took off.

Cody was taking care of her horse Starburst, the one she'd brought on this circuit along with her champion palomino, Trixie, who was the best horse Kellie had ever owned. Trixie had helped her get to the Pro National Rodeo Finals, which were held in December. It was only three months away and she didn't need any kind of problems that would cause her to lose focus.

The stalker had so frightened her, she'd stuck with her rodeo buddies for the rest of the night. Later on in Albuquerque, New Mexico, she found a note on her truck window that said she couldn't avoid him forever and accused her of lying about being married. That told her this man had mental problems, and that put her on edge. She kept the note to show the police.

Afraid this wacko might turn up in Amarillo, she'd bunked with her good friend Sally, who was married to Manny Florez, one of the bull riders in the rodeo. Cody stayed with her horses and looked after them.

After one more rodeo tomorrow night in Bandera, she would drive straight to her parents' ranch in Austin instead of going home to her town house. Together they'd go to the police. But right now she needed to get

through this radio show and then put her horse through some exercises.

She'd left the animal in the horse trailer at the RV park on the outskirts of town with Sally and her husband. For the time being they were her protection.

Trying to conquer her fear of the man stalking her, she headed toward the entrance of the radio station and collided with the first of a group of tall, jean-clad men in Stetsons and cowboy boots coming out the door.

"Oh—I'm sorry." She stepped back, shocked by a dart of male awareness that passed through her at the contact. "I didn't see where I was going."

"No problem, Ms. Parrish." His eyes were a piercing midnight blue. "Good luck at the rodeo tomorrow evening. We'll be rooting for you." He tipped his white hat to her.

"Thank you," she murmured as they headed to a van in the parking area.

Kellie had met hundreds of cowboys in all shapes and sizes over her years pursuing her dream to get to the Finals. She'd dated quite a few, nothing serious. But these four were exceptionally good-looking. The man she'd brushed against had momentarily caused the breath to freeze in her lungs. Why hadn't *he* been the one to ask her out on a date in Oregon? She might have been a fool and said yes without knowing anything about him.

Stunned by her immediate attraction, she hurried inside the building afraid she was late. The receptionist told her to walk straight back to the broadcast booth.

"Oh, good. I'm glad you're here. We're on a station break. I'm Tammy White. You're even more beautiful

in person. Thanks for doing the show. You're one of our state's biggest celebrities."

"Maybe with a few rodeo fans."

"You're too modest. Your appearance here is making my day."

"Thanks, Tammy." Kellie shook hands with her and sat down. "I barely got here in time."

"I don't suppose you bumped into the Sons of the Forty while you were on your way in here?"

Kellie blinked. "I actually did bump into one of them. Wait—aren't they the Texas Rangers who brought down a drug cartel recently? It was all over the news."

"Yup. You had the luck of getting to see them up close and personal." *Up close and personal is right.* "I swear if I weren't married…" Kellie knew exactly what she meant. The man with the deep blue eyes was a Texas Ranger!

Kellie couldn't believe it, except that she could. With his rock-hard physique and rugged features, he looked as if he could handle anything. Come to think of it, he had been wearing a badge over his Western shirt pocket. But she'd been so mesmerized by his male charisma, nothing much else registered.

"Okay, Kellie. We'll be live in seven seconds. Ready?"

"No. I'm no good behind a microphone." Her mind was still on the striking Ranger. Her body hadn't stopped tingling with sensation.

"Don't worry. Leave it all to me. This is going to be fun."

It would be fun if it weren't for the menace lurking

somewhere out there. Thank heaven for Sally and her husband, who were letting her stay in their trailer with them tonight and tomorrow night. Monday morning she'd take off at dawn.

She couldn't get back home fast enough to tell her parents what had been happening and go to the police. Kellie had put off telling them about this, hoping the man would give it up, because she didn't want her folks worrying about her. But she'd gotten a call in the middle of the night last night, which was the last straw. Her stalker was potentially dangerous, and that terrified her.

CY'S CAPTAIN, TJ HORTON, walked into his office Monday morning. The veteran Ranger now sported a head of gray hair, but he still looked tough enough to take on any fugitive and win. "It's good you're back."

"I'm just finishing up some paperwork on my last case."

"I've got a new one I'd like you to look over. It just came up. Come on into my office."

"Sure." He followed him down the hall. The captain told him to shut the door and take a seat. Cy could tell something was up.

TJ sat back in his swivel chair with his hands behind his head and smiled at him. "You men did the department proud over the weekend. I listened to your contribution on Hill Country Cowboy Radio. Whether you liked it or not—" nope, none of them liked it "—she made you guys out as the poster boys of the department. You're now known as the Famous Four. I thought that might happen, but good publicity never hurts in an age

when law enforcement takes a lot of unfair hits. The favor you did for me personally was much appreciated."

"Anything to help, sir."

"I heard a *but* in there. Next year I'll pick another bunch to carry the flag."

"That's a relief."

TJ chuckled, but then leaned forward with a serious expression. "The police turned over a case to our office this morning. It's high profile and the victim could be in serious danger. Because the case has crossed state lines, they feel our department is better equipped to deal with it. I'd like your take on this one." He handed him a folder.

Cy nodded and opened it. The name Kellie Parrish leaped out at him. *She* was the person in danger?

With her silvery-gold hair and cornflower-blue eyes, the barrel racer was a knockout. Under other circumstances he would have liked to hang around the radio station and listen to her interview. She'd been on his mind ever since he'd seen her a few days ago.

He scanned the folder's contents. She was being pursued by a stalker. He'd followed Ms. Parrish across her latest five-state racing schedule. She'd given the lieutenant a description of the man and a typewritten note he'd left on her truck windshield.

The most alarming aspect of the case was the fact that this stalker had phoned her cell phone as recently as the middle of Friday night. She'd been asleep in her friend's trailer in Bandera before driving to Austin this morning. Terrified, she'd gathered her parents and come straight to police headquarters.

Cy let out a low whistle. "I met her coming in the radio station as we were leaving on Friday. We watched her perform at the rodeo Saturday night. She had the second-best time."

"That's not only an amazing coincidence, but fortuitous. It isn't often you already have prior knowledge of the victim, so you understand what kind of threat she's been living with."

Especially when he'd found her incredibly attractive.

The hairs lifted on the back of his neck. Cy couldn't remember the last time he'd had this strong a feeling for a woman in passing. Because of the stress of the job, he didn't have much time for dating and hadn't been out with anyone for at least four months. After watching Ms. Parrish's performance at the rodeo, he'd admired her skill and found himself wondering how to go about getting to know her better. Not in his wildest dreams had he thought it would happen like this.

TJ kept on talking. "The police chief told me her parents met her at the station. They're well-heeled ranchers from southeast Austin who are demanding protection for their daughter and are willing to pay for it. Ms. Parrish is a prominent athlete. I've already ruled out a possible kidnapping scheme with a plan to collect a ransom or she would likely have been abducted at her first stop in Montana. Her parents want her to quit the rodeo circuit and stay with them until this lowlife is caught. She's their only child."

Cy got it. Ms. Parrish was their precious baby.

He shifted his attention from the file to his boss. "If you could have seen the way she rides, you'd know

she would never agree to that." Even under so much stress, she'd put in a terrific time at the Bandera Rodeo. "Otherwise, I'm certain she would have quit the circuit in Pendleton when he first showed up and returned to Austin to contact the police. Several of her competitors headed for the championship in Las Vegas were also in Bandera competing. My bet is on her winning the whole thing."

TJ shook his head. "In order for that to happen, she would need full-time bodyguards on the circuit with her. Her parents can afford it. I'll call them now and ask them to bring her back to headquarters so you can talk to her. When you've got a feel for what you're dealing with, let me know how you want to handle this case."

"TJ? Send her in to me first. Then I'll talk to her folks." Parents had their own ideas about what should be done. It simplified things to talk to the victim without anyone else in the room. "I'll let you know when I want them to join us."

His boss nodded in understanding.

"Until they arrive I'll dig up some more background information on her. I'd better get to it." Cy got to his feet and headed for his own office. He'd start with the personal information listed on her website and go from there. Uncanny how he'd already planned to look at her site when he got the chance, just to learn more about her.

"Let's see what turns up on you, Ms. Parrish."

He typed it in and sat back. Seconds later, there she was astride her palomino, lying low over her horse as it was racing straight down the alley. Pure poetry.

Kellie Parrish
Born: Austin, Texas, on February 14, 1990
Residence: Austin, Texas
Dad: Bronco Parrish—3-time NFR Bull Rider Champion
Mom: Nadine Parrish—Barrel Racer Finals 4 times
Horses: Smokey, Walnut, Miss Pandora, Crackers, Farley,
Starburst, Trixie
Joined Pro Rodeo at age 11
Total Earnings: $2,103,775
Wrangler NFR Qualification: 10
College National Finals Qualification: 2
National High School Rodeo Finals Qualifications: 4
Pro Wrangler Finals winner, Oklahoma City, OK: 3
Women's Pro Rodeo Association member

Cy read her blog, keeping track of the dates of the entries for July and August. She'd archived her previous blogs. Her ardent fans wanted to know all about her. How come she wasn't married yet? Did she have a boyfriend?

She'd answered that she preferred to keep her private life private, but she was friendly and encouraging to those trying to become barrel racers themselves. She urged them to click to her online clinic for pointers. That woman was so busy, Cy didn't know how she had time to breathe.

She'd put her rodeo schedule for the season on a separate page. There were links to the WPR Association and all the social media accounts. In other words, her life was pretty well an open book and prime fodder for

the degenerate who'd targeted her. Talk about a sitting duck! A gorgeous one.

His eyes went back to her personal stats. The questions some of the commentors asked about her personal life had grabbed his attention. Some of them might have been sent by the stalker. An idea on how to handle this case had started to form in his mind. He reached for the phone to arrange for their department's sketch artist to be on hand when she came in. They needed a picture to run through the criminal database, which could access the files from every state in the union to come up with a match.

There was no telling how long the creep had been stalking other women or when his sick fantasy about Ms. Parrish had started. She'd been traveling the circuit for a number of years. He could have seen her anywhere at any time. But he'd approached her for the first time in Oregon only four weeks ago. Cy would start there.

In case this man was a serial stalker or worse, he wanted a list of every known stalking incident in the Pendleton area in the past year. While he waited for the Parrish family to arrive at headquarters, he put through a call to the Pendleton police department. He asked them to fax him the names of stalking victims and their descriptions of the men menacing them, whether their cases had been solved or were still open. One of those descriptions might match up with the man Kellie Parrish had described.

Restless, Cy went to the cubbyhole down the hall they called a lunchroom and poured himself a cup of

coffee while he waited. He had dozens of questions to ask. Vic walked in on him. Their eyes met.

"Guess who's in the boss's office."

His pulse raced for no good reason. *She's here.* Kellie Parrish had made an impact on all the guys. "I already know. A stalker's after her."

His friend's black brows shot up. "You got the case?" Cy smiled. "How come that never happens to me?" Vic poured himself some coffee. "If you need help…"

"Thanks. I'll let you know." Cy took his mug back to his office.

Before long, TJ appeared at the door with her. She was probably five foot seven without her cowboy boots. "I believe you two have already met. Ms. Parrish? Meet one of our agents, Cyril Vance."

Cy got to his feet and shook her hand. "It's a pleasure to meet you again, Ms. Parrish, even if it is under harrowing circumstances."

Fear had darkened the blue of her eyes. "I hope you forgive me for bumping into one of the Sons of the Forty. I'm the one who's honored." TJ had disappeared.

"Please sit down."

"Thank you." She'd dressed in jeans and a creamy-colored Western shirt. Beneath the overhead light, her neck-length wavy hair had that silvery-gold metallic sheen he found stunning. So were her face and the rest of her curvaceous figure. Absolutely stunning.

"Can I get you coffee or a soft drink?"

"Neither, thanks."

"I'm going to record our conversation if that's all right with you."

"Of course."

"I have the notes taken by the police. It says here this stalker last contacted you by phoning in the middle of the night."

"Yes. That was Friday," she said, tight-lipped. "I don't know how he knew my cell number."

"How many people have you given it to?"

"My parents, closest friends, my cousin Heidi and of course my horse handler, Cody."

"Tell me about him."

"He's been my closest horse friend since middle school. We've both had our dreams. I was going to win the PRO Finals Rodeo this year and teach barrel racing. He was going to help me and then run a stud farm. Cody is engaged and plans to get married after Finals."

He nodded. "When you fill out forms of any kind, do you list it as your contact number?"

"No. It's not written anywhere. I always give out my parents' number. No…wait. I did give my cell phone number to a friend, Olivia Brown, who works at the Women's Pro Rodeo Association in Colorado Springs, Colorado. She used to ride with our Blue Bonnet Posse, but her husband was transferred to Colorado Springs, so she got a job with the rodeo association there."

"I'll want to talk to her. Now I'll need a list of your friends and cousin, and their phone numbers. Here's some paper."

"All right." She got right to work. When she'd finished, she looked up.

He took the list from her. "Thank you. What did the stalker say on the phone?"

She bit her lip. "'You lied about having a husband. Don't you know it's not nice to lie?' Then he hung up."

"Was there just the one call that night?" She nodded. "Now let's talk about everything that happened the first time this man made contact with you."

She shuddered visibly. "It was right after the barrel-racing event and awards. I was in the process of removing the saddle from Trixie when I heard an unfamiliar male voice from behind call me by my first name. I turned around to discover a total stranger invading my space. A lot of guys have approached me over the years wanting a date, so it wasn't unusual."

Cy could believe it.

"I don't mean to sound full of myself. It's just part of what goes on during the racing circuit, and I've always taken it in good fun before turning them down. But this was different. He came too close. After telling him no, he just stood there with a smile that made my stomach churn. Something about him wasn't right."

"Could you tell if he'd been drinking?"

"No. I couldn't smell alcohol. I was holding the saddle in front of me with both hands and I told him I was married, hoping he'd get the message and go away. When he calmly told me to prove it, I would have thrown the saddle at him and called security, but a couple of friends happened to walk over and he disappeared. I didn't see him again until I drove to Utah for the next rodeo at Eagle Mountain a week later."

"You drive a truck and horse trailer?"

"Yes. I live in the trailer while I'm on the road. My

horse handler drives his own truck and trailer carrying one of my other horses."

"Do you own a car?"

She nodded. "A four-door white Toyota sedan. I keep it at the condo when I'm gone."

"Do you own or rent?"

"Rent. After I leave the rodeo circuit, I'll be buying my own place."

"Where's the parking?"

"The double-car garage is in back, but there's parking in front."

"Is it in a complex?"

"It's a two-story town house with neighbors on either side of me."

Cy paused long enough to buzz the artist to come to his office, and then he turned to her. "We need a picture of this man. Without a photograph we'll have to rely on your eyes. Our department artist has a singular gift."

She clasped her hands together. "All right."

"While we wait for him, I want you to think back. Before Pendleton, have you ever had the slightest suspicion that someone had targeted you?"

"No. Never."

That sounded final. Jim showed up at the door with a sketch pad and electric eraser pencil. "Come on in, Jim. Ms. Parrish, our state's reigning barrel-racing champion, is being stalked. Let's see what you can work up."

"Sure." He sat in the chair next to Kellie, eyeing her in male appreciation. "It's a privilege to meet you, Ms. Parrish. We'll start with a sketch. I could use the computer, but a sketch can tell you things the computer

can't. Don't get nervous or frustrated. You may think this won't work, but in three out of ten cases a culprit has been caught through a sketch. I'll work from the eyes on out. Shall we get started?"

She nodded and answered one question after another while he sketched. They worked together while he refined his drawing.

Cy asked her for a more thorough description while Jim was working.

"He looks like the guy next door. You know, someone's brother. Maybe late twenties. Kind of lean. Okaylooking. Nutty-brown hair that curls. Short-cropped. Maybe five-ten, but he was wearing cowboy boots. Weighs probably 150 to 160 pounds. Brown eyes. He wore jeans and a different pullover the second time I saw him."

Jim kept working at the sketch and showed her what he'd done. She said, "His nose was a little thinner." After fixing it he asked her to take another look. "What do you think?"

"You truly do have a gift. It's remarkably accurate."

"We try."

Cy took the drawing from him. The guy bore a superficial resemblance to Ted Bundy, the serial killer from several decades back, but he kept the observation to himself. "That's great work, Jim. We'll go with this to put in the Integrated Automated Fingerprint Identification System. Thank you."

"You're welcome." He turned to Kellie. "All bets are on you winning the championship in December."

"Thank you so much."

"If anyone can catch him, Ranger Vance can. See you, Cy."

When Jim left the office, she looked at Cy. "You're called Cy?"

"Short for Cyril." *Don't get sidetracked.* "Your next rodeo is in South Dakota in two weeks, but I understand your parents want you to quit the circuit."

"Yes, but since we talked with the police, Dad has told me he'll hire some bodyguards for me so I can continue to compete."

Cy shook his head. "That won't work. We want to draw out this stalker and arrest him. He'll know if you have people protecting you. That will change the way he has to operate. It will hinder our efforts and prolong the time you're forced to live in terror."

Her eyes clouded. "I don't want to give up competition, not when I'm so close to the Finals in December. Isn't there another way?"

Yes, but he didn't know if she'd consider it. He knew her parents would raise objections.

"There's always another way. If you'll excuse me for a moment, I'll be right back." He left the office and headed for TJ's, knocking on the open door.

His boss's head lifted. "Come on in."

Cy shut the door and sat down. "Where are her parents?"

"In the reception area. Have you got an angle on this case yet?"

He nodded and brought him up-to-date. Then he told him his idea. TJ didn't say anything at first. That didn't surprise Cy. "I know it's unconventional."

"Unconventional? Hell, Cy. It's unorthodox and unheard-of in this department."

"But it could work. This way she could continue winning rodeos."

Another few minutes passed before TJ said, "I'll admit it's brilliant. You realize the two of you will be walking a very thin line."

Yup. Cy knew exactly what he meant and he wasn't talking about the culprit. "I'll need another Ranger working with me. Whoever you can spare."

His eyes squinted. "You think she'll agree?"

"Probably not, but it's worth finding out. She's had the world championship in her sights since she was eleven years old. If she says no, then I'll know I was wrong to think she'd do anything to achieve her goal."

He nodded slowly. "All right. You bring her in here and I'll send for her parents. She doesn't need their permission, but they'll have to be in on this from the start or it won't work. I'll make sure all three of them are fingerprinted before they leave the building today."

"Right."

Chapter Two

Cy's plan was bold. But no matter how many ways he could think of to attack the problem, he kept coming back to his first idea.

"Ms. Parrish?" he spoke to her from the doorway. She got to her feet. "If you'll come with me, we're going to meet in the captain's office with your folks."

They walked down the hall, where Cy met Kellie's parents. She took after her father in height and coloring. From her mother she'd inherited her good looks and figure. He shook their hands.

TJ invited everyone to sit down. "Ranger Vance has looked at every aspect of this case and has come up with a strategy. Every so often our Rangers plan a sting and go undercover. It's a very effective way to flush out a criminal. Your daughter's case presents a challenge because no one wants to see her quit the barrel-racing circuit when she's so close to winning the championship in Las Vegas." He glanced at Cy. "Tell them your thinking."

Cy got to his feet. "You could hire bodyguards. But it would probably cause the culprit to stay away for a

time, not *go* away. We want this stalker to be put away permanently, and ASAP. The best thing to do is flush him out."

"That makes sense to me," her father said.

"What if he's followed me here to this office?" Kellie sounded anxious, but was still keeping her composure. Cy admired her for that.

"I'm sure he's done that and a lot of other things. He knows where you and your parents live. He knows your rodeo schedule, your phone number. He knows your routine and enjoys frightening you. But we're going to turn the tables on him and produce the husband he doesn't believe exists."

Those blue eyes rounded in shock.

"A husband is different from a bodyguard who goes with you everywhere. A husband and wife have their moments of separation. While I'm not with you, one of my team will be guarding you from a distance.

"To set this up, you'll announce your secret through your blog. I've read through it. Your fans have pressed you over and over again to reveal if there's a special man in your life. After telling them all this time that your life is private, you're going to tell them that you recently married a cowboy. Furthermore you are looking forward to a long honeymoon after the Finals in Las Vegas.

"By putting the announcement out on the internet, it will prove to the world you are telling the truth. Of course, this stalker still won't believe you because you've been his fantasy for a long time and he doesn't live in anyone's reality but his own. I still have yet to

discover if he's a psychotic who has lost all connection to his world, or a psychopath with a serious mental disorder. But in either case he'll be enraged when he reads your blog.

"I can assure you he's been reading it for as long as he's been stalking you, and so far there's been no mention of a husband. He thinks he's safe. I have no doubt that some of the people making comments about your personal life on your blog have come from this lowlife."

At that observation she paled.

"It will torture him that you really could be married. He thinks he knows everything about you and won't be able to stand the fact that he could be wrong. That will bring him out of lurk mode. When he does that, it will be his big mistake.

"We have no idea of his place of birth or where he lives. He could be from Austin and followed you all the way to Oregon to begin his reign of terror. You can be sure he has already cased your condo and your parents' ranch and knows every move you make. The Pendleton police are sending me a list of stalking victims in the Pendleton area in case there's a way to link him to your case.

"If he'd wanted to kidnap you to compel your parents to pay a ransom, it would have already happened. So we can conclude money is not his motive. Though you didn't see him in Albuquerque, we know he was out there somewhere putting a note on your windshield and phoning you in the middle of the night in Bandera. According to your schedule, you have another rodeo in South Dakota in two weeks. For the time being I imag-

ine you'll be training here in Austin every day until you leave. He's probably planning to do something to you while you're not on the road. Remember—he feels invincible."

When she heard Cy's assessment of the situation, he noticed she'd lowered her head, causing the strands of her molten hair to catch the light from overhead.

"So far you've had your handler and other people around while you've been taking care of your horses. But he'll assume you'll be alone in your condo part of the time for the next two weeks. The beauty of this plan is that when he comes after you, I'll be there watching for him. When he makes his move, he'll discover your husband on the premises. Do you have any questions?"

Now was the time for Kellie to tell him she couldn't go along with his plan. He held his breath, waiting for her parents to voice their objections. Instead, her mother looked at her daughter with an anxious expression.

"His plan sounds solid, but how do you feel about it, honey?"

He watched Kellie nervously moisten her lips. "I'm thankful I won't have to be alone." She looked up at Cy. "Even if it means everyone will think I'm married, I want that disgusting creature caught." Her voice shook.

TJ sent Cy a silent message. *I'll be damned.*

"Before you go home with your parents, I'll need your key to the condo and your phone, Ms. Parrish."

"All right." Her hands trembled as she rummaged in her purse for those items and handed them to him.

"What's the code to get into the garage?" She told him. "Keep your mailbox key."

"Oh. Okay."

He looked at his watch. "Give me six hours, then all of you come to the condo with any luggage you took on the road and I'll let you in. Pick up your mail on the way in, but don't go through it. Act as normally as you can. We'll talk details inside your condo so we're all tuned in to the same channel."

Kellie's father shook Cy's hand again. "Our daughter didn't tell us what had been happening to her until this morning. It's a nightmarish situation and we're very grateful that you're willing to take her case. We'll all be praying this plan works."

"Thank you for helping her," Kellie's mother said with tears in her eyes.

"It's our job and I'm happy to do it. I'll see you later."

He watched Kellie walk out with them. Cy knew in his gut that this stalker didn't want money. He wanted to do her harm. She'd said he looked as if he was in his late twenties. He wondered how many women before Kellie had already been terrorized by him. The stalker fit the general profile for a predator who was usually from eighteen to thirty.

After they left TJ's office, Cy turned to his boss. "Her condo is in West Austin. I'm going to need help to set things up before they arrive."

"This is a high-priority case. Vic just finished a case and is in the building right now. I'll ask him to assist you before assigning him a new case."

Nothing could have pleased him more. "Thanks, TJ." There wasn't a lot of time. They'd have to assemble a team fast.

Not long after he'd returned to his office to send the artist's sketch to the database, Vic walked in. "I'm all yours." He planted himself on a corner of the desk. "That stint on the radio must have put the boss in a good mood."

"It was so important to him, he actually went along with my plan."

"Which is?"

"Outrageous, but Ms. Parrish agreed to it, too, rather than leave the circuit. She wants to win that championship. I figured she would put her desire to achieve her lifelong goal over her fear of this stalker. We're going to pretend to be married so I can protect her day and night."

"What?" Vic's black eyes narrowed. He got to his feet. "You're kidding me."

Cy gave his friend a sharp look. "Can you think of a better way to get the job done?"

They'd known each other a long time. "Hell, no. It's genius, but—"

"But it doesn't hurt that she's a beautiful woman, right?" He couldn't help but read his friend's mind. "I've examined my motives and have decided that even if she were someone else, it wouldn't make a difference. She's been working her whole life to achieve her goal. For her to quit now would be the end of her dreams, not only for this year, but maybe forever. Anyone with her kind of skill and drive deserves all the help she can get."

"I agree with you."

"This guy is a creep who's been tormenting her for a month. She told him she was married so he'd leave her

alone. All that did was fan the flames, so I've decided it's time she produced a husband. I want to catch this stalker, Vic, and believe this is the best way to capture his attention and nab him."

"Where do you want to start?"

"We'll get a surveillance team set up in the van to monitor her when I can't be with her." Cy handed him the sketch.

Vic studied it for a minute. "You know who he looks like?"

"Yup, but let's not go there. In case he's camped out by her condo, you and I will impersonate roofers so we can get in around the back of the building through her garage without him suspecting anything. I want to lift any fingerprints we can find. We'll rig the interior with a camera. Let's move."

He folded her list of names and numbers and put it into his pocket. The note she'd given the police needed to go down to the lab. He already had a list a mile long of things to be done before she arrived with her parents. They'd need wedding rings.

KELLIE CHECKED HER watch as her father drove them to the front of her condo in her parents' Volvo sedan. Six thirty p.m. She still couldn't believe what she'd agreed to. She and the striking Texas Ranger had to pretend to be married starting tonight!

What have I done? She closed her eyes. *You've done what's necessary to survive.*

"Come on, honey. Let's go in and have dinner. You haven't eaten all day."

"I couldn't." But her parents had insisted on picking up some barbecue for all of them.

She hadn't had an appetite since this first started. As for sleep… Nothing seemed real. That monster could have been following them from the ranch. She almost expected him to suddenly appear at the mailbox.

The normal number of bills had stacked up. She put the mail into her purse before getting back in the car. Her mom had been over to her condo several times this past month to water her plants and make sure everything was all right. Thank goodness the Ranger would find her house clean and in good shape. There were times when it looked a mess.

She eyed the condo. No one would know the secret it was holding. If everything had gone as planned, then the Ranger was inside. A vision of the way he'd looked when she'd bumped into him in Bandera was indelibly impressed in her mind. He was a man whose aura gave the impression he could deal with anything or one. Her pulse raced at the realization they would be spending time together.

Kellie got out of the car and hurried up the front steps ahead of her parents. He must have heard them because he opened the door to let them in.

"Hi." His deep voice filtered through to her insides.

Kellie looked up at him. "Hi." He'd changed into a dark blue sport shirt and jeans. His eyes matched his shirt. Outside the radio station, he'd been wearing his white Stetson. But in his office as well as now, the light in the living room illuminated the sun-bleached tips of his wavy light brown hair.

Her mother was carrying the food. "I've brought dinner for all of us."

The Ranger smiled and took the bag from her. "Thank you, Mrs. Parrish. How did you know I'm starving?"

The way the corners of his eyes crinkled sent a surprising curl of warmth through Kellie, who put her purse on a chair. While he and her mother went to the kitchen, she turned to help her father carry her bags upstairs to the bedroom. That was when she saw that another couch had been added to the living room. Everything had been rearranged so it would fit.

As they passed the guest bedroom upstairs, she saw some of the Ranger's things on the bed. She avoided her father's eyes and continued to her room.

"Are you okay, Kellie?"

"I don't know what I am yet, but knowing this Ranger is here to protect me is all that's helping keep my sanity right now."

Her dad gave her a big hug. "I'm relieved, too. The captain told me Ranger Vance was one of the men who brought down the drug cartel earlier in the year. He says there's no one better, and I believe him. Come on. Let's go back down and hear what this Ranger has to say."

Kellie nodded. "I'll be there in a minute." She needed to pull herself together.

He kissed her forehead and left. She took time to freshen up in the bathroom before joining everyone at the dining room table. When the Ranger saw her, he stood. "I'm sure it's strange for you to feel like a guest in your own home."

"I'm too thankful you're here to think about it."

He sat back down. "These ribs are delicious. Thank you. I work better on a full stomach. Tonight I'm going to help your daughter draft her marriage announcement message for her blog. By ten it will be out on the internet. As her parents, you'll be bombarded with questions from everyone who knows you. I want you to tell them that Kellie and I met on the circuit. It was love at first sight and we couldn't stand to wait, so we were privately married before her rodeo performance in Montana.

"Tell people there will be a wedding reception for us at the ranch in December, after Finals. Don't say any more or any less. We'll worry about explanations after this stalker is caught."

This is really happening. She eyed her parents, who agreed to do exactly as he said. He had a way of instilling confidence and trust.

He looked at them. "From here on out, Kellie is going to do what she would do if there were no threat. The three of you will carry on with your lives while I work behind the scenes. No one is to know about this case except the four of us and my team."

"Sally and Cody know a man was bothering me."

"I talked with both of them earlier in the day. They won't be telling anyone about this."

Kellie's father thanked him again. "I think it's time we left the two of you alone so you can get on with your plans. Come on, Nadine."

They both got up from the table. Kellie jumped up to hug them. "I'll call you all the time so you're not worried."

"We love you, honey."

"We do," her father said in a gruff voice and gave her a bear hug. "Do everything the Ranger says."

"I promise." She walked them to the front door. "I love you. Thank you for being the best parents on earth."

"I won't let anything happen to her," the Ranger assured them before they left the condo. The conviction in his voice prevented Kellie from breaking down.

Kellie shut the door and hurried past him to clear the table. He helped put everything in the waste bin while she wiped down the top. "If you want to get started on the blog piece, we can do it here."

"Sounds good, but let's sit down for a minute and lay the groundwork."

She nodded and followed his suggestion. He sat across from her. "First of all, I'd like you to call me Cy and I'll call you Kellie. Next, we need to make this real." He reached in his shirt pocket and set three rings on the table. After putting the larger gold band on the ring finger of his left hand, he said, "Go ahead and see if they fit."

With trembling fingers, she picked up the engagement ring with a beautiful one-carat diamond. She slid it on and it was a surprisingly good fit. So was the gold wedding band. The moment was surreal.

"How do they feel, Mrs. Vance?"

Her head flew back. Their gazes fused for a moment. *It feels too natural.* "Fine."

"Will they bother you when you ride?"

She blinked. "No. My right hand does most of the work."

"Good. Let's discuss the living arrangements. I plan

to sleep downstairs and had the team bring over a hide-a-bed couch. If you don't mind, I'll use the half bath on this floor, but I'll shower upstairs when you're not here. For the time being I'll use the guest room to store my clothes and equipment."

In the next breath he pulled a pair of latex gloves from his back pocket and put them on.

"Why don't you bring me the mail? I'll go through it in case this stalker has sent you a message to frighten you further."

At the thought, her body broke out in a cold sweat. Kellie went into the living room to get her purse and brought it to the table. After she opened it, he reached inside and took out the bills.

He went through the pile one piece at a time. "Let me know if you see something odd."

She shook her head. "It's the usual bills and ads."

He kept going. When he came to a *Cowboy Times* magazine, he held it up by the spine. Two cards fell out along with a three-by-five white envelope. He picked up the letter. There was no return name or address. Her name and address had been typed on the front. "This was postmarked from Austin on the same day he approached you in Eagle Mountain."

Kellie felt her stomach drop while she watched him open it. He spread out the eight-by-ten piece of folded paper. The word *liar* jumped out at them in big letters. She gasped. The stalker had cut them out of some magazine and had glued them on.

"This is going to the forensics lab. It's my opinion that over the years this man has had a string of bro-

ken relationships, maybe a failed marriage, and feels betrayed. He has no friends or anyone he's emotionally connected to. Every time he finds a new target, he convinces himself it's love. When nothing works out, he goes into a rage because every woman turns out to be a liar."

"I wonder how many other women he's done this to."

"Who knows, but it stops with you. I noticed you have a laptop upstairs. Why don't you bring it down and we'll get started on your announcement?"

"I'll be right back." When she brought it down a minute later, she noticed he'd put the letter in a plastic bag and had discarded the gloves. He'd also produced a laptop she'd seen lying on the hide-a-bed.

"I'd like to access more of your archives while you work on what you want to say."

"I'll send them to your computer." He gave her his address.

They worked side by side. She wrote something, then deleted it and started again. After several attempts she got into the blog-writing mode and allowed herself to go with the flow.

"How's it coming?" His deep voice broke the silence, but it continued to resonate inside her.

"It's almost there. I'll send you a copy in a minute to see what you think. After I've denied any involvement with a man, it's going to have to be convincing." She read over what she'd written so far.

Hi, all my faithful rodeo fans out there! I'm back from my last rodeo in Bandera, Texas, and won't be com-

peting until two weeks from now in Rapid City, South Dakota, where I'll start out my Midwest circuit. My times have been up and down lately. But that's because something thrilling has happened to me in my personal life.

So many times you've asked me if I have a boyfriend or if I plan to get married one day. I've always said that my love life was private. But I can't keep quiet about this any longer. I did find the man of my dreams while I've been on the rodeo circuit. It was love at first sight for this gorgeous hunk of a cowboy. He's bigger than life to me and my hero in more ways than one.

We decided we couldn't stand to wait to get married until Finals in December. So we tied the knot in a private ceremony before my competition in Pendleton, Oregon. I'm so happy to be his wife, I go around in a daze. It's little wonder I've been unable to concentrate. Trixie thinks I'm a little crazy, bless her heart. It's a miracle she puts up with me and knows how to kill the cans in spite of me.

All of you know I always had a rule that I wouldn't allow a man to throw me off my game while I was riding the circuit. No distractions for me. No siree. But I hadn't met my husband when I said that. The second I looked into his eyes, my world changed in an instant. He's the prince I dreamed about when I was a little girl. He's the great man I'd hoped to meet while traveling the circuit around this great country of the USA.

We'll have a wedding reception after Finals. I'll post some pictures. You'll all swoon when you see him!

PS: Of course I want to win the championship, but

winning the love of my husband surpasses all else. I'm the luckiest cowgirl on the planet and grateful for all of you who constantly send me your support. Long live the rodeo!

Kellie saved the file and pushed the send button. In order to make her blog convincing, she'd had to put her heart into it. But while she waited for his opinion, heat crept into her cheeks. "I just sent you the announcement. While you check it for changes, I'll get a cola. Would you like one?"

"Sure. Thanks."

"Let me know what you think," she said and left the room.

Cy OPENED THE file and started to read. His heart thudded when he came to the lines "The second I looked into his eyes, my world changed in an instant. He's bigger than life to me and my hero in more ways than one." The more he read, the harder his heart pounded.

"What do you think?" She put a cold can of cola in front of him. "I know it's probably too much, but I realize this has to convince my readers."

He opened his drink and swallowed half of it in one go. "I agree it's over-the-top, but it sounds like it came from the heart. When that creep reads this, it will push his buttons to the limit. The only correction is to delete Pendleton and put in Glasgow, Montana. That was your event before you left for Oregon. We don't want him to think his appearance in Pendleton had anything to do with the timing of your marriage."

She pulled the laptop in front of her and made the change. "I should have thought of that." Kellie smiled at him. "That's why you're one of the Sons of the Forty! Okay. It's done."

"Go ahead and post it. Now we wait. I wouldn't be surprised if your fans respond in droves and overload your website."

Cy finished off his drink and got up from the table to toss it in the wastebasket. He'd left her phone on the counter and brought it to her. "I checked your phone. The only call you received in the middle of the night came from a throwaway phone and couldn't be traced. I want you to continue to answer your phone.

"I've set it up with an app so you can record an incoming call. I'll walk you through this. It's easy." He pulled his own cell phone from his shirt pocket. "I'll call you. After you've answered, press Four and it will start recording. Ready?"

"Yes."

He pressed the digit that had programmed her number. She let it ring three times, then clicked on. "Hello?"

Cy nodded, letting her know to press the number four digit.

"Hi, Kellie. Did you just get back from Bandera?"

"I drove in this morning."

"How's Trixie?"

"She's at the ranch getting some TLC."

"I bet you wish you were with her."

"Tomorrow I'll drive out there and we'll go for a ride."

"Sounds fun. Talk to you later."

He held the phone away from his ear. "Now click End Call. The recording is downloaded to your iPhone and displayed on the screen. Tap the recording icon to listen. You can also trim the recording as needed by dragging the edge of the file on the screen."

She followed his directions and suddenly they heard their conversation while seeing it at the same time. A natural smile broke out on her lips. Good grief, she was beautiful. "Technology is amazing."

"In your case it's crucial. I want every word recorded when he phones you again."

"Do you think he'll try soon?"

Cy nodded. "If I don't miss my guess, he won't be able to hold back, not after what you've put on your blog."

"I'm afraid to talk to him." He noticed her shiver. "I don't think I'll be able to sleep tonight."

"Tell you what. Why don't you go upstairs and get ready for bed? Then come down here to sleep on the couch for tonight. I'll be nearby on the other couch. If he calls, I'll be right here. Try to get him to talk about why he thought you were lying to him. Anything he says could give us a clue about him."

"You wouldn't mind? I'm behaving like a baby."

"You're behaving like a woman who's being stalked. But I admire you for not giving in to your fear. That's what he wants. He's been watching you for a month if not longer and still doesn't believe you're married. But the blog entry will force him to reveal himself. The phone allows him a voice connection to you. Keep him on long enough for our voice experts to analyze it."

"What do you mean?"

"Vocal oscillations convey so much about the speaker. But more important, our experts will be able to tell if he's a Texan. A Texas accent stands apart from the rest of the South in that it has a twist that is a blending of the major features of the Deep South and Upper South."

"I didn't know that."

He nodded. "The drawl of the Lower South has more influence in East Texas, while the 'twang' of the Upper South has left a greater imprint on West Texas. In South Texas, particularly, the Spanish and Mexican characteristics are heavily combined with that of the others. Once we get a recording of his voice to the experts, they can tell us if he's from here or another state or region entirely. If we can pinpoint where he's from, it could be a great help."

"Then I'll try to keep him on the phone. Excuse me while I run upstairs to get ready."

"Take your time. We've got all night."

Cy planned to stay in the clothes he was wearing. Tomorrow he'd shower and change while she was out at her parents' ranch.

While she was upstairs, he sat down to see if there were any responses to her blog yet. A low whistle escaped when he counted seventy responses already. He scrolled through each one. When he came to the end, he was satisfied none of them was her stalker. It was touching to read how much her fans cared about her and appreciated her help through her online rodeo tips. But they were all excited about her marriage.

He opened up the archives. There were literally hun-

dreds of entries on her blog site. It amazed him. She was definitely a star in her own right and an obvious favorite. He knew she had dozens of awards, but she didn't keep them here. Probably at the ranch. One thing he knew about her already. There wasn't a narcissistic bone in her lovely body.

While he read through a few more entries, she padded into the kitchen in bare feet wearing a blue robe. Beneath it she wore pajamas with Texas Longhorns on them. She'd brought down a blanket and pillow.

Cy had to be careful not to stare. "I take it you're a football fan."

"These are from my parents last Christmas."

"My dad gave me a pair of the same pajamas two years ago." They both laughed.

As she came closer, her smile faded. "Has that lunatic sent a response yet?"

"No. But you now have four hundred hits. Your eager fans want pictures and don't want to wait until December."

Without saying anything, Kellie walked into the living room and lay down on the couch, propping up her pillow and covering herself with the blanket. Cy checked his watch. It was ten to eleven. He picked up her cell phone and put it on the coffee table in front of her.

Once he'd made up the hide-a-bed, he went back to the dining room for her laptop. After turning off the overhead lights, he turned on a lamp in the living room and sat down next to it so he could continue to read the responses as they came in.

"When are *you* going to sleep?"

He liked it that she was concerned enough to ask and flicked her a glance. "Don't worry about me."

She sat up. Her disheveled hair gleamed in the soft light. "I don't know how to begin to thank you for what you're doing for me."

"It's my job."

"A horrible one," she said in a shaky voice. "Every day on the news you hear about some stalking victim found in a landfill—"

"Don't go there." Cy stopped her cold. "Nothing's going to happen to you."

"But who protects *you*?"

He smiled to himself. "I have a team that backs me up. My buddy Vic, one of the men you saw coming out of the radio station with me, is helping on your case."

She lay back down. "You're all remarkable."

"Save your thanks until after we've caught him."

Chapter Three

Kellie had no doubt he'd get the job done, but Cy Vance was too modest for words. That was part of the charm of the man who was growing on her with every passing second. His rugged profile stood out in the lamplight. He'd stretched out in the chair with his hard-muscled legs crossed at the ankles.

She'd been around cowboys all her life. Some of them were more attractive than others. Some had great builds. Others were loaded with talent in the arena. Still others had engaging personalities. But this Texas Ranger had all of those qualities and more. He'd been put together in such a way no one could compare to him.

Impatient with herself for concentrating on the attractive Ranger, she turned over so she faced the back of the sofa. She needed sleep. Desperately. Knowing he was right across the room from her gave her a sense of comfort she hadn't felt since her first encounter with the stalker. How unbelievable was it that the Ranger she'd bumped into in Bandera had come into her life at the most precarious moment of her existence?

When her cell phone suddenly rang, she jerked upright. Kellie flung herself around, staring at her phone in terror.

"It's all right." Cy's deep voice was reassuring. "What does the caller ID say?"

She took a shaky breath. "It's my best friend, Kathie."

"Go ahead and talk to her. Put it on speaker."

Kellie reached for it and clicked on. "Kathie?"

"Hi! I know it's late, but I had to call you. Good grief, Kellie. Is it really true that you're married?"

Her gaze locked with Cy's. "Yes. How did you hear?"

"Patty told me she read it on your blog tonight. How come you didn't tell me?"

Oh dear. Kellie heard the hurt in her voice. Now for the lie… But this lie was going to save her life and it took away her guilt. "It happened while I was on the circuit and there was no time." That part was true. "Look, Kathie. It's a long story and—"

"And your husband wants your attention. Is he right there?"

At that remark Cy's eyes smiled. Kellie felt a fever coming on. "Yes. We just got in from Bandera. I'll tell you all about it later."

"He must really be something for you to get married so fast you didn't even have your parents there."

"W-we couldn't bear to wait any longer."

"Whoa. I'll hang up now, but I expect a detailed report later. You know what I mean."

Embarrassment brought the heat in waves. "Thanks for calling. We'll talk soon. I promise." She clicked off and put the phone back on the coffee table.

Cy closed the laptop and put it on the floor. He leaned forward with his hands clasped between his knees. "Kathie is one of the names on the list you gave me. Who is she?"

"My best friend in our group. Sally, my other friend, is a part of it, too."

"What group is that?"

"There are about thirty of us who ride for pleasure, but serve as volunteers in case of any kind of local emergency."

His brows lifted. "Do you have a name?"

"We're the Blue Bonnet Posse."

"That's right. You mentioned one of your friends from the group who moved to Colorado Springs. Come to think of it, I have heard of the posse. Weren't you the ones who found that autistic child who'd wandered away from home last year?"

"That one, and a lost Boy Scout. The police department calls our leader when they need volunteers to do a search in the outskirts of Austin."

"No doubt you're kept busy. Those lucky parents must be indebted to you. I'm impressed."

"It's our job." She echoed his earlier words to her.

"Touché." He reached down and pulled off his cowboy boots. She watched him turn out the lamp and stretch out on the hide-a-bed. It couldn't be that comfortable, and he hadn't even changed. He lay on his back with his hands behind his head.

She forced herself to look away. But no sooner had she curled on her side hoping to fall asleep than the

phone rang again. Still petrified, but less startled this time, she reached for the phone.

"Put the speaker on," Cy reminded her.

She nodded. It was her father and she clicked on. "Hi, Dad. I've got the phone on speaker."

"Forgive me for calling this late, but your mom and I want to make certain you're all right."

Her gaze drifted to Cy. "I'm fine. Really. The news is out. Kathie just called me."

"We got a call from your cousin Heidi. She read your blog and couldn't believe it."

"I know this is going to come as a shock to everyone who knows me."

"They care about you. It's a tribute to the wonderful woman you are."

"Spoken like a biased parent."

"We love you, Kellie." His voice sounded gruff with emotion. "Tell that Ranger we can't thank him enough."

She looked at Cy's silhouette in the semidarkness. "He knows how you feel. All I do is thank him."

"We're expecting you for lunch. Good night, honey."

"You get a good sleep, Dad. Cy is keeping me perfectly safe. Love you." She hung up the phone and hugged her pillow.

The next time she had cognizance of her surroundings, she heard the phone ringing. Immediately her adrenaline brought her to a sitting position. The second she realized there was no name on the caller ID, she felt bile rise in her throat. Cy had already hunkered down at the coffee table, urging her to pick up and press the recording app.

Her body shook as she reached for the phone. Doing as Cy asked, she clicked on. "Hello?"

"I knew you got home today. How did you like my letter?"

Her eyes closed tightly. "How did you get my phone and address?"

"That was easy as skinning a cat."

She shuddered. "What do you want? I told you I'm married."

"I saw what you wrote on your blog. You think I'd believe that crap? You're a liar!" He shouted the last word.

"You think I'd lie to all my fans and friends? If that's true, then why do you keep phoning a liar?"

"Because you deserve to be taught a lesson you'll never forget."

"Did your girlfriend lie to you?"

"They all lie. When I get through with you, you'll wish you'd never been born, Kellie girl."

"My husband's going to have a lot to say about that."

"Liar, liar, liar, liar, liar, liar!" The line went dead.

Kellie was trembling so hard she dropped the phone. Cy retrieved it and clicked on the recorded conversation. She'd forgotten to put on the speakerphone. His jaw hardened as he listened to the recording.

"That was rage we heard just now. He's afraid you might be telling the truth. You handled him perfectly and kept him on long enough to record his voice patterns. I'll be going into headquarters tomorrow. I'll drop off the letter at the forensics lab and take your phone to our voice expert to see what he can do with it."

He checked his watch. "It's only four in the morning.

Why don't you go up to your bed? If he phones again, I'll let it ring. You need more sleep."

"What about you?"

"I'm fine."

"Even if you aren't, you'd never tell me. Thank you." She grabbed her pillow and blanket before going upstairs.

CY HAD SPOKEN prophetic words. The phone rang every half hour until eight on Tuesday morning. Then it stopped. He made breakfast with the groceries he and Vic had bought yesterday. While he devoured eggs and bacon, he phoned Vic on his phone. His friend answered before the second ring.

"What's up?"

"The stalker phoned her at four this morning. We were able to get a decent recording. When I'm back in the office, I'll have the lab analyze it. I'm headed there as soon as she leaves for her parents' ranch. I assume she'll be gone most of the day."

"The team will take turns monitoring her."

"Good. Where did you leave a car for me?"

"Walk down the alley behind the town houses to the corner. It's a Subaru parked in front of the third house on the right with a for-sale sign. The key is in the usual place."

"Do you think the lab has the results on the fingerprints we lifted yesterday?"

"Maybe. Stan said they'd hurry it."

"With all the bases covered, let's hope this nut case makes his move soon."

"Did you get any sleep last night?"

"Afraid not, but I will today after I get back from the lab. Kellie will probably be gone most of the day. I'll tell her to call me when she's coming back."

"You can level with me," he said in a quiet voice. "How's it going?"

He took a deep breath. "The easy answer is, nothing's going on that shouldn't."

Just then Kellie came walking into the kitchen dressed in Levi's jeans and a short-sleeved yellow blouse. She was a vision and he lost his train of thought.

"Cy? Are you still with me?"

"Yeah."

"I was just saying I can't wait to hear your difficult answer."

Neither could Cy, but this was pure business and that was the way it would stay. "Got to go. Thanks for your help. I'll catch up with you later at the office." He clicked off and stood to greet her. "Good morning. How do you feel?"

"Thanks to you I was able to go right to sleep."

"That's good news."

"But I bet you didn't get a wink." Her eyes had filled with concern.

"I'll make up for it later. Sit down and I'll serve you breakfast."

"I could smell the bacon. I should have gotten up to do it. Fixing food for me isn't your job."

"But you need more sleep than I do after what you've been through this last month." He put a plate of food

in front of her and poured coffee for both of them before sitting down.

"Thank you, Cy." She ate a piece of bacon. "Yum. Crisp, just the way I like it. Were there any more phone calls from him after I went to bed?"

Cy eyed her directly. "He rang on the half hour eight times. I let it ring every time. Your marriage announcement has set him off, exactly the reaction I'd counted on."

"Did he leave messages on the voice mail?" There was a tremor in her voice.

"Yes, but you don't need to hear them. I'm taking your laptop and phone into the lab today, but I'll bring them back." The stalker probably had a stack of prepaid phone cards, but there might be a time when he had to use a pay phone that could be traced.

Her brows furrowed. "You think they're too awful for me to hear?"

"No. They were more of the same. He was ranting like before."

She sat back in the chair. "Then you really didn't get any sleep."

"I'll catch up today while you're at the ranch. Someone on the team will be monitoring you every time you leave your condo. A member of the crew will follow you. If you have any concerns, call me on your parents' phone. This is my cell number." He wrote it on the paper napkin.

"While I clean up the kitchen, I'd like you to get on your laptop. Post a new message on your blog. Say that you've read the messages and you're overwhelmed by all the good wishes. Then start to read any messages

that have come since last night. I'm curious to see if he's posted anything. It's my hope he's so angry he might explode and give himself away."

As he cleared the table, she reached for her laptop and opened her blog file. "I don't believe it! Hundreds more messages have been added since last night."

"That's not surprising. Your online tips about barrel racing have won you a loyal audience. Everyone's intrigued about your new relationship."

She lifted her eyes to him. Along with her silver-gold hair, her eyes were a deeper blue this morning and dazzled him. "The fans want to hear about *you*, not me. If they knew you were one of the Sons of the Forty, they'd go crazy and you'd be forced to go into the witness protection program."

With those words his pulse sped up. "Hiding out with you is virtually the same thing."

He loaded the dishwasher. Cy had been a bachelor for so long in his own house, he was used to doing his own cooking and housekeeping. He felt right at home in her kitchen. "Why don't you start reading and see if there's a message that strikes a different chord with you?"

"It'll take me some time."

If they'd met under different circumstances, nothing would have pleased him more than to have whole days and nights with her with no life-threatening issue to deal with. But he had a case to solve and needed to get to headquarters pronto. As he was finishing up, he heard her cry out in alarm.

"What did you read?" He walked over to the table and stood behind her so he could see what had disturbed

her. In looking over her shoulder, he could breathe in her fragrance from the shower.

"It's this one sent at eight twenty this morning."

"That's when the phone calls stopped. Read what it says."

"'I bet you're making it up that you have a husband. Why do you enjoy being a tease? No one would watch you in the rodeo if they knew you were such a liar.'" She let out a quiet gasp.

Without thinking, Cy put his hands on the back of her chair. He could tell she was trembling. "I'm going to stop him, Kellie. This morning he made his biggest mistake so far by posting this message on the blog. When I'm at the office, we'll trace it to its source. With every misstep, we're closer to catching him."

She nodded without turning around. He quickly removed his hands and walked over to the kitchen counter where he'd put her phone. He heard her chair legs scrape the tile and turned in her direction.

"I know you're anxious to get going, Cy. I'll run upstairs for my purse and leave for the ranch."

"I'll walk you out to the garage." While he waited for her, he put her phone in his pocket.

The door to the garage was located at the other end of the kitchen. He unlocked it and turned on the garage light where her white Toyota sedan stood parked. He and Vic had checked it for fingerprints yesterday.

When she came out, he opened the driver's side door for her. Once she was inside, he asked her for the remote. "I need it to get in and out with my own car. I'll let you in when you come back from the ranch."

Her eyes played over him as she handed it to him. "Where is it?"

"Parked around the block. Try to enjoy the day, Kellie. You'll be constantly watched. Call me from your parents' when you're ready to come home."

"I will. Have a good day yourself. Be careful," she whispered.

He took a quick breath. "You don't have to worry about me."

"But I do, and I *will*."

It had been a long time since a woman he cared about had been concerned about him. Her unexpected smile revealed the spirit inside her that had dominated her life and made her a champion. He admired her passion for life.

As she started the engine, he pressed the remote so the garage door would open. After she'd backed out, he retrieved his phone and alerted the surveillance team that she was leaving the condo.

Once he couldn't see her, he hurried inside for her laptop and the bagged letter. After he had everything he needed, he left through the garage, closed it with the remote and walked down the alley to the end. Eight-foot-high heavy-duty vinyl privacy fencing ran the length of the alley to separate the backyards of another set of town houses. It was a gorgeous September day, probably sixty-five degrees out.

He found the SUV and took off for headquarters. On the way to his office he stopped by the lab to leave Kellie's phone and laptop plus the letter. Stan came

out to talk to him. "TJ said this is high priority. I'll get working on everything now and give you a ring later."

"Thanks, Stan. I need you to do something else for me. I want Rafe to analyze this stalker's voice and see what he can figure out."

"I'll ask him to work on it now and take a late lunch."

"I'd appreciate that. I don't see Janene. When she comes in, ask her to find out the IP for the person who sent Ms. Parrish the message on her blog. I've flagged it."

"Sure. I'll put it on her desk."

"Thanks. See you later."

Cy took off for his office upstairs. On the way down the hall, Vic saw him and called him into his office. "I've been waiting for you. I've got stuff to show you that will blow your mind. Look what the database brought up from the sketch you entered."

Intrigued by Vic's excitement, Cy grabbed a chair and sat next to him. "Thirty-two matches came up on the computer."

"Is there one from Oregon?"

"No."

"My first hunch was wrong, then," Cy muttered. "How about Utah, Montana, New Mexico or Texas?"

"None of those states."

Damn.

"Give me a second. I'm refining these for exact similarities."

Cy watched the screen. They both made sounds when two faces came up. After studying them he exclaimed,

"They're the same person with different rap sheets. How in the hell did that happen?"

Dean Linton Michaels, aliases Dan Linton, Dan Michaels, Michael Linton, Mick Linton, Delinn Michael, twenty-eight, latest known address in Flossmoor, Illinois, is wanted for the murder of two women. The first account is for the stalking and strangulation of a twenty-four-year-old woman, Lucinda Rosen, in Chicago, Illinois. The second account a year later is for the stalking and strangulation of a nineteen-year-old woman, Mary Ferrera, in Memphis, Tennessee. Charges include Aggravated Kidnapping, Unlawful Flight to Avoid Prosecution, Aggravated Sexual Assault. No. 10 on the FBI's most wanted list.

Vic darted him a glance before he scrolled down. "Take a look at this rap sheet."

Lines marred Cy's features as he found himself looking at what appeared to be the exact same man. This one had longer hair.

Andrew Dunham, aliases Denny Andrew, Andy Dunham, Drew Denning, Donny, twenty-eight, latest known address in New Orleans, Louisiana, is wanted for First-Degree Murder in the stalking and strangulation death of a twenty-three-year-old woman in Charleston, South Carolina, thirteen months ago. Charges include Aggravated Kidnapping, Unlawful Flight to Avoid Prosecution, Aggravated Sexual Assault.

Cy shook his head. "It's amazing how closely these two men resemble the sketch. There has to be a mistake since both pictures have to be the same person. Three murders in three years. Kellie needs to see these pictures. If he's the same man and the one she can identify... Let's get on the phone to the agents working those cases while we figure this out."

Over the next two hours they held phone conferences with the FBI agents from Illinois, Tennessee and South Carolina. In all three instances, the agents praised the Rangers for their detective work on Kellie's case and pledged their help.

After Cy's last call, he waited until Vic got off the phone. "I've sent both sets of fingerprints to Stan to verify if it's the same man. They say every person has a double somewhere in the world."

"I wonder if that's really true," Vic murmured.

"Who knows? I need to learn as much as I can before I show Kellie these photos. Even though the artist was able to find us a match, maybe he only bears a superficial resemblance to the man she saw." He printed out both photos. After folding them, he put them in his pocket. "Want to go down to the lab with me?"

Vic jumped up. "Try to keep me away."

When they entered the lab, Stan told them to come around to the table where he was working. They passed Rafe's office. He looked up. "I'm working on this voice analysis. Give me until tomorrow."

"Sure."

They moved toward Stan.

"You got some good prints lifted from the condo and

the car," he said. "Several belong to the victim, and several others belong to the mother. One partial print you lifted from one of the buttons of the keypad for the garage doesn't match anyone's."

Cy eyed Vic. "That's interesting. Maybe we'll find the person who left it. Right now we've got a new puzzle for you to solve. I just sent you the photos and fingerprints of two wanted fugitives who appear to be the same man from the IAFIS data base. But if they're the same man, why didn't the computer pick it up?"

"Let me see." Stan pulled up the information on the computer.

"Their cases have been built from two different areas of the country with different names. Their photos closely match Jim's sketch of the man stalking Kellie. How long will it take you to determine if both pictures are of the same man?"

"Give me a few minutes and I'll check right now." He put both sets of prints up on the screen and used his loupe and counter. He examined them for a while, and then his head came up. "Well, what do you know? Those men aren't the same person. This is a case of identical twins, but as you know there's no such thing as identical fingerprints."

Cy sucked in his breath. "That means both brothers are killers."

Vic looked equally stunned.

"It happens," Stan murmured. "Come close and I'll show you." He pointed to the subtle differences. "Fingerprints are not entirely a genetic characteristic. They are a part of a 'phenotype,' which means they are deter-

mined by the interaction of an individual's genes and the intrauterine environment. One fetus in the womb has different hormonal levels, nutrition, blood pressure, position and growth rate of the fingers at the end of the first trimester.

"Minor differences in fingerprints arise from random local events during fetal development. The genes determine the general characteristics of the patterns of fingerprints. However, inside the uterus, finger tissue comes in contact with the amniotic fluid, other parts of the fetus and the uterus.

"Some experts point out, for example, that touching amniotic fluid during the six to thirteen weeks of pregnancy significantly changes the patterns of a fetus's fingerprints.

"Overall, identical twins' fingerprints tend to be similar, but there always will be subtle differences making even their fingerprints unique. That's why there was no match."

Cy unconsciously furrowed his hair with his fingers. He felt the same as years ago when his chest had been stomped on by a bull. "If one of these twin brothers was the man who'd targeted Kellie, how am I going to tell her there are two of them? Hell, Vic. What if they work together and committed all three murders?"

"Maybe that's why the letter in her mailbox had been posted by the one brother here in Austin four days ago while the other brother trailed her all the way home from Oregon."

He eyed Vic. "The murders of the three women were committed a year apart at different places, making it

possible that they'd worked in tandem." Cy's body broke out in a cold sweat.

Vic clapped his shoulder. "Take it easy. I know where your thoughts are headed, but it's too early in the process to go there. Like you said, maybe she'll say these photos don't look enough like the man who harassed her in Pendleton to make a definite identification. We know mug shots as well as sketches can be deceiving."

"Yeah. I know," he said in a wooden voice. He turned to Stan. "Do you think that partial print from her condo is substantial enough for you to detect if it matches one of these fingerprints?"

"That will take some time. I'll see what I can do with it."

"Thanks, Stan. Give me a ring no matter what you find. I'll be up in my office for a while longer."

"I'll go with you." Vic walked out of the lab with him.

In the space of a few minutes, Cy felt the full weight of this case to protect Kellie. During his career as a Ranger, he'd never been personally involved like this before. As the captain had warned him, this was a different kind of case for Cy. *You two will be walking a very thin line.*

Cy had no idea he could feel this gutted over the gravity of her situation. He couldn't think of her as just any woman who needed help. His feelings were more complicated than that, but he had an obligation to keep this situation straightforward. Yes, he was attracted to her and admired her great talent, but he couldn't allow that to interfere with his judgment and work ethic.

When they reached his office, Vic looked at him and said, "Go home, Cy. You haven't slept for twenty-four hours and won't be any good on this case without sleep."

"You're right. I'll leave now." He glanced at his watch. It was one thirty. "Kellie will be coming home this evening. I want to be there when she drives in. Thanks for everything, Vic."

"Hey—just doing my job."

"You do a lot more than that, and now I've got another favor to ask."

"Anything."

"Pick up her phone from Stan when he's done with it. I'll get it from you later."

"What's your next move?"

"If Kellie identifies this man as the one who approached her, I'm going to fly to Colorado Springs early in the morning and take her with me. She said she gave her cell-phone number to a friend of hers who works in the office of the Women's Pro Rodeo Association. The stalker had to get her cell phone number from someone.

"I checked out her friends and horse handler while we were at the town house yesterday. They haven't given her phone number to anyone, so I'm going to check out a hunch. We'll be back by evening at the latest. Keep a close eye on her place while we're gone."

"Will do."

"Thanks, Vic."

Cy left the building and hurried out to the car. He couldn't get to Kellie's town house fast enough. Once he'd parked in the garage, he rushed through the house to the upstairs bathroom for a shower and shave. After putting

on a clean pair of jeans and a T-shirt in the guest bedroom, he felt better. All he needed now was some food.

He ate a couple of peanut-butter sandwiches and drank half a quart of milk. After putting his phone on the floor next to him, he collapsed on the hide-a-bed. He'd catch a couple of hours before she phoned. Cy had her garage-door opener and would have to let her in.

It felt as if he'd barely sacked out when his phone rang. He reached down for it and saw that his mother was on the line. In the midst of everything, he'd forgotten to tell his family that he'd gone undercover on a new case and wouldn't be available for a while.

That wasn't like him to let something so important slide. As he lay there, he realized he needed to get his act together in a hurry. Biting the bullet, he clicked on.

"Hi, Mom. How are you and Dad?"

"We're fine, darling. The point is, how are you?"

"I'm well, but I'm on a new case and have gone undercover."

"Oh, Cyril—we never see you anymore."

He knew his mother worried about the career he'd chosen, and she never failed to complain about it. But right now he didn't give her the chance.

"Sorry about that, but it's the nature of the job. I promise I'll leave messages to let you know I'm all right."

"I guess that means you can't come to the engagement party we're planning for Beth and Tom on Sunday night."

"I wish I could, but I'll have to wait to see them after this case is solved." He had to solve it. "Give everyone my love. I promise to call you soon."

Cy hung up and lay back again, letting out a heavy sigh. His sister was marrying Thomas Adamson in six weeks. He was an up-and-coming attorney in the law firm Cy's great-grandfather had established in Dripping Springs. Cy was meant to join the business, but law had never held any interest for him. He preferred law enforcement.

After high school, he'd gone the rounds with his father more times than he could count. To make matters worse, halfway through college he'd broken his engagement to a young woman whom his parents really wanted him to marry. He wasn't anyone's favorite son.

Cy fell back to sleep until the phone rang again. A look at the caller ID showed Bronco Parrish. It was Kellie's father. She was calling from the ranch. He clicked on and said hello.

"Hi" came her slightly breathless greeting.

"Are you coming home now?"

"Yes. I'll be there in ten minutes."

"I'll be waiting and open the garage door for you."

"Thank you. See you soon."

It was a long ten minutes. Unable to stand it any longer, he hurried through the house to the garage and opened it while he waited for her. His pulse picked up speed when he saw her drive in next to his Subaru SUV and turn off the engine. She got out of the car and walked toward him with a look that led him to believe she was relieved to see him.

He was relieved, too. Night had already fallen.

Chapter Four

"How's Trixie?" Cy asked after Kellie walked past him into the kitchen.

"Happy to be home. We had a good ride."

He shut and locked the door. "Have you eaten dinner?"

She swung around. "Yes." Her eyes searched his. "Any news yet?"

"Why don't we sit at the table? I have something to show you."

Kellie swallowed hard and sank down onto the nearest chair. He sat opposite her and pulled a paper out of his pocket. "The sketch Jim made was run through the IAFIS criminal database. This is what resulted."

He unfolded it and placed it in front of her. Her gasp filled the kitchen's interior. "That's the man! But his hair is longer here and he looks a little thinner than I remember."

Cy pulled out another paper and unfolded it. The second he put it in front of her, she jumped to her feet. "This one is exactly like I described to you and the artist. His hair is short here."

"There's no doubt in your mind?"

She stared at him. "I'm positive both photos are of the same man who approached me in Pendleton."

"That's all I need to know."

Kellie sat back down again. The photos had caused the blood in her veins to chill.

"We can thank God you came into the police station yesterday before anything happened to you."

Her hand went to her mouth. "It's the same man, so why are there different sets of names for him?"

He pocketed the papers. "It turns out they are identical twins."

She could hardly breathe. *"Twin murderers?"*

"I suspect they work together, but the FBI agents I spoke to didn't realize it until the forensics lab discovered that their prints weren't exactly the same. It would explain why you could receive a letter postmarked from Austin at the same time he approached you in Eagle Mountain."

Kellie buried her face in her hands, trying to comprehend it. The next thing she knew, he'd put a cup of coffee in front of her. "Drink this. You need it."

She took a deep breath and sat back in the chair. "Thank you." For a few minutes she sipped the hot liquid while she tried to absorb what she'd just learned.

"Tomorrow morning I'd like you to fly to Colorado Springs with me. Your friends have sworn they've never given out your cell-phone number to a soul. But if your friend at the Women's Pro Rodeo Association has put your number into the computer, that may explain where these men got it."

"You mean they hacked their computer?"

"I don't know. That's what I want to find out. You've been with that association for several years. These men know your rodeo schedule. Your name is on file with them. I'm curious to know if your friend kept your cell phone number to herself or put it in the computer, never thinking about it. Maybe she even saw him."

Kellie thought back. "When I gave it to her, she knew never to give it to anyone else."

"That was before she moved. Chances are she didn't put it in the system, but I need to find out."

She marveled at the way his mind worked. "What are you thinking?"

He leaned back in the chair drinking his coffee. "These stalkers are cunning. In order to talk to you, the one who approached you had to have done his home-work. What you put on your website about belonging to the Women's Pro Rodeo Association might have given him an idea I want to explore."

Kellie had a feeling he hadn't told her everything. "What time do you want to leave?"

"At 5:30 a.m. We have a 7:00 a.m. flight. If we get our business done fast, you'll be back here in time to put your horse through some maneuvers before eve-ning. This will be our first venture in public as a mar-ried couple, so we'll behave as man and wife when we reach Colorado."

Man and wife. A tremor ran through her body. He'd anticipated every question and had answered them be-fore she could even think.

"Then I'm going to get ready for bed now."

"Before you go upstairs, I want you to walk out to the mailbox and bring in any mail you find. Don't worry. One of the team will be watching you. I'll be waiting by the front door."

She got this sick feeling in her stomach over the idea that the stalker might have been near her condo today. Reaching in her purse for her keys, she left the town house and took the short walk to retrieve her smattering of mail from the box.

After she returned, she walked over to the table and put it down. There were three ads, a catalog of home decor furnishings and a five-by-seven white envelope with nothing written on the front. When she saw that it didn't have a stamp, she froze.

"When does your mail normally come?"

"Between two and three."

"The stalker may have come after to slip this into your box."

"You think he had a key?"

"These criminals are professionals and have tools, but we're going to find out."

Cy put on gloves and picked it up. After opening the flap, he pulled out a black-and-white glossy photograph of Kellie taken in a beauty salon. She was sitting in a chair with a drape around her neck. Her head had been cut out and it fell on the table. The word *liar* had been printed on the back of it.

"I don't believe it!"

He gave her a probing glance. "Where was this taken?"

"At a beauty salon here in Austin where I go to get my hair styled."

"How long ago?"

"Right before I left for Montana, about five and a half weeks ago."

"You're sure about the timing?"

"Yes. Normally I wear cowboy boots all the time and I always get my hair done later in the day. But that particular morning I had an early appointment and I put on those sandals before I left for the salon because I was in a hurry."

"What time was your appointment?"

"Eight thirty in the morning."

"Do you remember the date?"

"It was a Wednesday. I had to leave right after to make it to Glasgow in time for the rodeo on Saturday, August 2."

"That meant you were in the salon on July 30. How big is the place?"

"It does a lot of business. The Blue Gardenia is on Third Street downtown."

"I've heard of it. Do men get their hair cut and styled there, too?"

"Yes." She shuddered. "That means he was in there watching me. He probably has dozens of pictures of me. It's sickening and depraved."

"Stay strong, Kellie. We're going to catch him."

A moan escaped her. "What about his twin?"

When she looked at him, the dark blue of his eyes seemed to have turned black. "Him, too. Go on up to bed and set your alarm. We'll leave for the airport at

five thirty. Before we walk out the door, I'll turn on the camera over the kitchen door on the garage side."

"You think he'll come while we're gone?"

"I'm not sure."

He obviously had more work to do she wasn't privy to, so she got up from the table. "I don't know how to thank you for what you're doing. Your life is in danger, too."

"But this is my job. One I like, though no one in my family does."

"What did they want you to be?"

"An attorney like my father and his father and his father before him."

So Cy was the lone wolf... His own person. She liked that about him very much.

"When this whole ghastly ordeal is over, I'll tell your family personally that you have the undying gratitude from me and my family for coming to my rescue."

His intense gaze continued to hold hers. "That's nice to hear. Now try to get some sleep and leave the worrying to me."

THE SECOND SHE disappeared upstairs, Cy phoned the crew in the surveillance van. "Lyle? The stalker put an envelope in Kellie's mailbox today. There are eight tenants using that box. Did anyone approach it you can't identify?"

"Yes. A woman with dark brown hair. I checked with the landlord of the property. He's never seen her."

A *woman.* "Strange. What time did the camera record it?"

"Four twenty."

That was after the mail had been delivered. "Send me a picture."

"There are three of them. Doing it right now."

As they came through his phone, he studied them. The person was dressed in a woman's business suit with low heels. She would be the same height Kellie had described for the stalker. Any view of the face gave only a partial glimpse. The lab could magnify the images for a better look.

"Lyle? Send these to forensics for enlargements."

"Will do."

"Tomorrow I'll be in Colorado Springs part of the day with Ms. Parrish. That'll give the stalker time to case the town house. He may try to get in to find out if a man lives here with her. Maybe the stalker's twin will show up, too. It's possible they dress in drag part of the time. Keep me posted."

"Sure thing."

Cy ended the call and phoned Vic. "It's possible one of the twins has been dressing up as a woman. I'm sending you the photos taken by Ms. Parrish's mailbox. Go over to the Blue Gardenia beauty salon on Third Street when it opens tomorrow. Show these pictures to everyone who works there. I'm curious if one of the employees can identify our stalker, who likely used his phone camera to take a picture of Kellie getting a haircut." Cy gave him the time and date. "If you get any information from one of the workers at the salon, let me know.

"Then I want you to call around to the places where you can buy a wig. Take those mug shots with you.

The photograph taken of Kellie was snapped almost six weeks ago. See if our stalker purchased one or two wigs in different colors during the month of July and get a copy of the receipt. It's a long shot, but do what you can."

"I'll try everything including places that sell theatrical makeup. He could have posed as an actor needing makeup and a wig."

"Exactly. Thanks, Vic."

"When will you get back from Colorado Springs tomorrow?"

"I'm not sure. Kellie needs to exercise her horses, so I'll drive her to her parents' after we get off the plane. But I'll phone you."

On Wednesday morning Kellie got out of the rental car and walked alongside Cy as they entered the building that housed the WPRA in Colorado Springs. She welcomed the warm seventy-nine-degree temperature. Conscious she was playing a part as Cy's new wife, she'd worn a flirty skirt and dressy blouse with high heels to play up her feminine side. It felt good to put on something besides jeans and cowboy boots.

"May I help you?"

"I'm here to see a friend who works here," Kellie told the attractive, twentyish-looking receptionist who hadn't taken her eyes off Cy from the moment they'd walked in the foyer. In a business suit and tie, he'd drawn the attention from a lot of women during their flight.

"Her name is Olivia Brown." Kellie prodded the younger woman in case she hadn't heard her the first time.

"Oh, sure. She's the one who moved here from Texas and works in the membership auditor's office. I'll ring her. You know? You kind of sound like her."

Kellie happened to glance at Cy, who was smiling at her rather than the receptionist. Even his eyes smiled, sending a charge of electricity through her body.

"Olivia wants to know your name."

Gathering her wits, she said, "Tell her it's a friend from the Blue Bonnet Posse."

The receptionist passed it on and suddenly red-haired Olivia came running down the east hallway. "Kellie!" she called out and ran up to give her a hug. "I can't believe it!" She turned to the girl at the desk. "Janie? This is the very famous Kellie Parrish! She's going to win the barrel-racing championship at Finals in Las Vegas this December."

"Wow." Janie's eyes had rounded in surprise.

"One could hope," Kellie murmured in an aside.

"Who's the stud?" Olivia whispered.

Kellie's heart was palpitating out of her chest. "I'd like you to meet my new husband, Cyril Vance."

"You got *married*?" Her voice came out more like a squeak.

"We did," Cy said and shook her hand.

"I announced it on my blog."

"Let me see." Olivia grabbed Kellie's left hand, then whistled. "Gorgeous." She looked up. "I haven't had a chance to read it yet. Oh, how wonderful. Congratulations!" She hugged her again. "Come on down to my office. I'm dying to know what brings you two here. If

you're on your honeymoon, I can't figure out how come I'm lucky enough to deserve a visit."

Cy cupped Kellie's elbow and squeezed it as they followed Olivia down the hall.

"Come on in and sit down. Do you two want coffee or soda?"

"Nothing, Olivia. We ate before coming here, but thank you. There's a specific reason why we're here. I'll let Cy explain. My husband is a Texas Ranger working on a case that involves me."

After a five-minute explanation, there were no more smiles coming from Olivia. He showed her a paper that included both mug shots. "These men are identical twins. Do you recognize either of them?"

"No. I've never seen them."

"Do me a favor and show this to everyone who works here. If they've seen them, phone me immediately." He wrote his work number on the paper. "If one of these men had come around here, it could have been as far back as a year ago."

"I'll do it today." She looked at Kellie. "You poor thing. I'm ill over what you've just told me. Let me get into the records on the computer. I always update the information on a file when rodeo results come in. I've been here eighteen months. If I added your cell phone, I don't remember doing it."

"Does everyone on the staff have equal access to the files?"

"No. Only certain of us have the password to get into them." She opened the file.

Kellie wasn't aware she'd been holding her breath

until Olivia looked at them with a pained expression on her face. "Oh no—I *did* put your number in next to your parents' number. I remember now. I put it there for me, never dreaming anyone would ever see this file but me."

"Please don't worry about it, Olivia."

"It could be a blessing in disguise." A somber look had stolen over Cy's features. "Do you know the company that cleans this building?"

"Yes. It's called Grayson Janitorial Services."

"When do they clean?"

"At night after nine."

Kellie turned to him. "You think the stalker pretended to be a janitorial worker and got into the computer?"

"Maybe. If he's cyber savvy, it's a distinct possibility he broke in." His gaze swerved to Olivia. "We're going to go there now and talk to the owner."

"Let me give you the address." Olivia looked it up on the computer and wrote it down on some scratch paper to give to him.

"Thank you. Before we leave, I need one more piece of information. What company services your computers?"

"It's Standard Computer Services."

"We'll find it. Thank you, Olivia. Your help has been invaluable."

"I wish I could have helped you more. I pray you catch that stalker. It's too horrible."

"Cy is keeping me sane," Kellie confessed. "Give my best to your husband. We'll talk soon." They hugged

once more before Cy escorted her out of the room and down the hall to the entrance.

"Good luck!" Janie called out. "I hope you win."

"Thank you."

They walked outside and Cy helped her into their rented Buick sedan. Using the Google mapping system, they drove across town to Grayson Janitorial.

Kellie glanced at Cy. "I know Olivia was upset that she'd put my cell number in the database."

"As I said, if this helps me trace the stalker's steps, it could uncover valuable information. It's like putting a puzzle together. Every piece I find forms the picture. If I'm on the wrong trail, we'll head over to Standard Computer Services. Maybe they sent out a technician to the WPRA who resembles our stalker."

Once Cy had parked the car, he took her arm and they entered the business. The store was filled with janitorial supplies. He flashed his credentials in front of the man at the counter.

"I need to speak to the owner."

"Just a minute." The man made a phone call. "A Texas Ranger is out here needing to talk to you."

When he hung up, he told them to walk around the counter and through the closed door to the back office. The middle-aged owner got up from his seat behind the desk and shook their hands. Cy wasted no time pulling out another paper and showing it to the owner.

"Have you ever hired either of these men to work for you? It could have been as far back as six months to a year ago. I'm following up a lead on a case. I un-

derstand your company cleans the offices of the WPR Association."

"That's right." The other man studied the mug shots before shaking his head. "I'm the only person who hires and assigns the work for my employees. I've never seen these men."

"What if one of your employees took a friend along while he or she worked?"

"That's against the rules, but I'll talk to my crews. Can I keep this paper?"

"I want you to. I'll write my work number on it in case you have information for me. Thank you."

Cy put an arm around Kellie's back as they left the office. It felt so natural, she didn't think about it until they'd reached the car. While he looked up the address for the computer company on his phone, she glanced at the striking man behind the wheel. She wondered if he could be aware of her in the same way she was of him. When she'd introduced him as her husband to Olivia, she'd felt a sense of pride. *Because you're attracted to him, Kellie, and you're getting too comfortable around him.*

He started the car and drove to another part of the city, where he parked in the lot next to the building reserved for Standard Computer Services.

"Cy? If you want, I'll wait here while you go inside."

His head turned to her, impaling her with those dark blue eyes. "Until I arrest the stalker, I'm not letting you out of my sight."

The way he said it caused a shiver to run through her body. "I just thought—"

"It's my job to keep you safe," he broke in. "I brought you to Colorado to introduce me to Olivia. There's no way I'd leave you sitting alone in this car."

Of course he wouldn't! A killer was after her.

She undid the seat belt and got out of the car before he could come around to help her. For a minute she'd been so concentrated on him and so worried he sensed her attraction to him, she'd said something that had probably made him question her mental capacities. *Get a grip, Kellie.*

He accompanied her inside the building. When he made inquiries, one of the guys working the counter showed them to the manager's office. It was like déjà vu. After introductions, Cy asked the manager to search through their work orders for the WPR Association going back a year.

"This will take me a minute."

"That's all right. I want you to be thorough." While they waited, Cy pulled another paper out of his pocket.

"It looks like we've sent our technicians out there four different times."

"Tell me the dates."

Kellie heard him mention January, April, June and July.

"Do you send one technician at a time?"

"Almost always."

Cy handed him the paper. "Have either of these men worked for your company within the last year? Take your time."

The manager took it from him. Within seconds he looked up at Cy. "This one with the longer hair. His

name was Denny Denham." Kellie let out a soft gasp. "He applied for work in April, but only stayed until the end of June."

"Denny Denham has many aliases. He's on the FBI's most wanted list and killed a woman." The manager dropped his jaw in shock.

Kellie's heart thudded painfully. Cy's hunch had paid off. At this point she was in awe of his genius.

"Why did he quit?"

"He said his mother was in a hospital in Michigan and needed him."

"Was he a good tech?"

"Very good. I didn't like losing him."

"Was he the tech sent to the WPRA offices on any of the dates you gave me while he was still working for you?"

"I'll have to go through the signed receipts. It'll take me a few minutes."

"Go ahead."

Cy flashed Kellie a smile meant to encourage her that they were on the right track. He could have no idea of the emotions that smile stirred up inside her.

The manager looked at Cy. "Denny signed the work order for June 20. It was right after that he had to quit work."

The set of Cy's hard jaw spoke volumes. "I want to see his application."

"I'll print it out."

Cy took the paper and stood to shake the manager's hand. "You've been very helpful on this case. Thank you."

The manager still looked dazed as they left the office. Once in the car, Cy started the engine. "I've got everything I came for. We'll head back to Austin in time for you to get in some training with your horses. En route to the airport would you like to stop for a hamburger at a drive-through?"

"That sounds good."

"I got lucky today. That always gives me an appetite."

"It's not luck, Cy. You're brilliant. Didn't you want to study his work application before we left?"

"I'll pore over it with Vic after we get back. It'll be filled with lies, but maybe there'll be something in it that will be valuable to the agents working on the other murder cases."

She stared out the window. "That poor manager looked shattered. Surely he did a background check."

"I have no doubt of it. The trouble with criminals is that they're human beings just like everyone, and for most of the time they drift in and out of the shadows without anyone realizing it until it's too late."

Kellie's gratitude for Cy and all he was doing caused her throat to swell. "I'll never be able to thank you enough, and don't tell me it's nothing."

A low chuckle came out of him. "I wasn't going to. Since taking your case, I've become a husband. I never dreamed it was such a responsibility."

"You're probably sorry you got involved to this extent."

"I wouldn't have done it if it wasn't exactly what I felt needed to be done."

"But I feel guilty because it makes it difficult for you to have a personal life."

"Don't worry about that. I've had a personal life and barely escaped getting married."

Her head swung toward him. "Seriously?"

He nodded. "Her name was Eileen Richards. We were engaged, but it didn't feel right to me and I broke it off."

"How long ago?"

"I was twenty-one and halfway through undergraduate school."

Kellie imagined he was in his early thirties now. "That's young."

"Yup. But my parents and her parents were all for it. As I told you before, they had my life planned out to be an attorney. To everyone's displeasure, once I'd said goodbye to her, I left school and signed up with the Austin police department. I discovered I didn't want to defend criminals, I wanted to catch them."

"Thank heaven," she whispered. "How long have you been a Ranger?"

"Almost three years and I've never regretted my decision. To answer your next question, Eileen is married to a successful businessman. According to my mother, she's expecting her second child, and I couldn't be happier about it."

Neither could Kellie.

Once they'd eaten a quick lunch, they dropped off the rental car and caught their flight back to Austin. They walked to the short-term parking for Cy's car and headed for her parents' ranch.

"We made good time, Cy. It's only four o'clock."

"That's why I wanted to get away early this morning."

She gave him directions and soon he'd pulled up in front of their ranch house. "Would you like to come in? I know my parents would like to talk to you."

"Another time and I will, but I've still got a lot of business to do. Don't forget that one of the crew always keeps you in his sights."

"I know. I'll ask my parents to drive me to the town house tonight."

"Give me a call. I'll be waiting for you."

He had no idea what that meant to her, but he was probably tired of hearing it and she could tell he was anxious to leave. She climbed out of the car and hurried to the front door. Opening it, she called out, "Mom?"

"In the kitchen, darling."

Kellie wheeled around and waved to Cy. He waved back and drove off. She stared after him, wishing she didn't feel strange when his car disappeared. As if she'd lost something.

Her mom gave her a hug. "You're back earlier than I would have expected."

She took a deep breath. "Cy accomplished what he needed. Where's dad?"

"He's out in the pasture, but he'll be back by six."

"Then I'll have enough time to do some training drills with Trixie before dinner."

Her mother followed her up the stairs to her old bedroom. "What happened today?"

Kellie walked over to the dresser where she kept

her older clothes and pulled out a top and some jeans. "He found out how the stalker got my cell-phone number." While she changed outfits, she told her mom everything. "He's so amazing, I couldn't believe it. Talk about methodical. His mind works differently than the average person's.

"I found out his parents wanted him to go into law, but he broke his engagement to this girl and left college to join the Austin police department. He knew what he wanted and went after it. Now he's a Texas Ranger." She stared at her mom. "He can be formidable, but it's cloaked in sophistication. He told me he was going to catch this stalker."

Her mother eyed her pensively. "You believe in him."

"Utterly. He's incredible. I've never met anyone like him."

"No. Neither have I. Your cousin wants to hear all about him."

Kellie nodded. "I'll call her tonight when I get back to the town house. Has anyone else phoned?"

"Yes. Besides many of your friends, news of your marriage has prompted the *Statesman* and the *Chronicle* to get in touch with you for a story and a photo op. Even Tammy White from Hill Country Cowboy Radio is asking for another interview. She said you were a dark horse for pretending that you didn't know Cyril Vance when you were already married to the gorgeous Texas Ranger."

Heat crept into her face. "What did you tell everyone?"

"That you'd get in touch with them when you had time."

"Thanks, Mom. You're an angel." She pulled on a pair of cowboy boots she kept in her closet. "I've got to get out there so Trixie won't think I've abandoned her. See you in a little while."

She flew out of the room and down the stairs. Once she left the house, she ran all the way to the barn. But her thoughts weren't on Trixie. They were concentrated on the man who'd be at the town house later tonight to let her in. She found she was breathless just thinking about it.

Chapter Five

Pleased to discover that Vic was already at the town house, Cy drove into the garage, anxious for them to share information. His friend was dressed in the roofer uniform he'd worn the other day. He'd parked the roofing truck near the end of the alley.

"You got back earlier than I'd thought," Vic said as Cy entered the kitchen.

"That's because I found the information I wanted." He removed his jacket and tie and laid them over one of the chair backs, then he grabbed a soda from the fridge. "Do you want a cola?"

"Sure." They both took a long drink. "I brought Kellie's phone back, but she'll have to wait for her laptop," Vic informed him.

He saw it lying on the table. "Good. She'll be glad to have it." Cy reached for it and checked the messages. The stalker had sent three more. He put on the speakerphone so Vic could hear them, too. It was more of the same enraged vitriol.

Cy swallowed more of his drink. "I have news. Kellie's friend put her cell-phone number in the WPR As-

sociation's database. After some searching I discovered that a Denny Denham worked for Standard Computer Services as a tech in Colorado Springs starting in April of this year. He was called out on a problem at WPRA and signed the work order June 20. After that, he quit his job on the excuse he needed to be with his sick mother in Michigan."

Vic's whistle sang throughout the kitchen. "I talked to Rafe. Get this. He said the voice on Kellie's phone meets the criteria for a person from Virginia Beach or Charleston, South Carolina."

"A long way from Texas," Cy mused aloud. "Charleston's the place where one of the victims was killed."

"Yup. The minute I heard that, I started a search of all identical twin boys born in both the Virginia Beach area and the Charleston area over the time period I've estimated. I'm waiting for them to get back to me."

"You do great work. At this point I'm wondering where these killers saw Kellie and decided to target her. Until now they've operated in the other half of the US."

"You'll figure it out. In the meantime Stan told me that he couldn't get a good read on the half fingerprint from the garage-door pad."

Cy's eyes closed for a minute. "That was a long shot. Did the woman show up at the mailbox today?"

"No. Nothing went on around the town house. It's a waiting game now."

"I'm pretty sure he'll break in one of these nights, possibly even tonight after he sees Kellie's parents drop her off. I'll be waiting for him."

"Or them," Vic added. "The crew will cover the front of the condo. I'll be out in back."

"Any news on the IP address of the email sent to Kellie?"

Vic shook his head. "Janene's still working on the source. Tor hidden services mask their locations behind layers of routing. But she got into a site called 'hangman' and discovered the owner had left the administrative account open with no password. She logged in and is still digging around. As soon as I hear from her, I'll let you know."

"Good." Cy reached into his pocket and pulled out the paper from the computer services company. "This is the application the stalker filled out to get hired for work at the computer company."

They sat down at the table to study it. Cy let out a harsh laugh. "Look at that reference. As I told Kellie, it's full of lies. Two years at another computer company in Omaha, Nebraska, before he moved to Colorado Springs?"

"I'll call the number and see who answers." Vic pulled out his cell phone and tried it, then put the phone to Cy's ear. "You may have reached this recording in error. You can try again or call your operator." Vic hung up.

Cy rubbed his eyes with the palms of his hands. "No doubt he used his brother, who set up a phony address and phone to send the referral. These killers get around, Vic. They've got money to operate. Most likely smash-and-grab stuff, unless they're living off a family

death benefit of some kind. I'll email this to the agents on the East Coast."

"Depending on what goes on here tonight, I'll track things down tomorrow." Vic checked his watch. "Tell you what. I'm going to leave to get me a bite to eat. But I'll let you know when I'm back for the rest of the night."

"I can't do this without you." Cy walked him to the back door. After Vic left, he phoned TJ to check in and catch him up on the latest.

"If two of them break in, you may need more backup."

"Vic and the crew have us covered."

"I'll put two more Rangers on alert anyway," his boss said before Cy heard the click.

A second later his phone rang. The caller ID said Nadine, Kellie's mother. He picked up. "Kellie?"

"Hi." The small tremor in her voice brought out his protective instincts.

"Is all well with you and your horses?"

"They're in fine form." She'd ignored his question about herself. The tension had to be getting to her. "I just wanted you to know my parents are driving me home now. We should be there in five minutes."

"Good. Before you come in the house, check your mailbox."

"I will. See you soon." She hung up.

He got up from the table and walked into the living room while he prepared himself for what might happen tonight. If the stalker suspected Kellie had been telling the truth about a husband, he might lie low so she would think the menace had gone away. But neither he nor his

twin would ever go away. One thing about a sociopath. Once he'd fixated on his victim, he'd dog her to the bitter end no matter how long it took. With two sociopaths working together, they were a lethal combination.

He ground his teeth, hoping both of them showed up. Once they were taken down, Kellie could get on with her life. So could he...

While he was trying to imagine what that would be like now that he'd met her, he heard her key in the lock. In order not to frighten her, he moved to the kitchen so she'd see him when she walked in. After she locked the door behind her, she turned around.

He noticed she was wearing her riding clothes and boots. Kellie's eyes flew to his. She held up a couple of catalogs. "This was all I found in the box." She put them on the kitchen table.

Cy thumbed through them, but there was no envelope hiding inside the pages. He looked up. "Have you eaten dinner?"

"Ages ago."

"Why don't you sit down and tell me what's wrong? Did something happen you need to talk to me about?"

Her chin lifted. "What's wrong is that you're putting your life on the line for me," she said in a voice shaking with emotion.

He cocked his head. "Would you rather someone else were doing this job? It can be arranged."

"No!" she cried out. "No," she said in a softer tone and looked away. "That isn't what I meant at all."

"Then what *did* you mean?" came his deep, almost-seductive voice.

She folded her arms to her waist. "Situations like this shouldn't happen to anyone, but I know they do. Horrible things happen all the time, all over the world, and a handful of men and women like you are courageous enough to make the bad people go away. There isn't a way to repay you for what you have to face twenty-four hours a day in order to protect someone like me."

Cy put his hands on one of the chair backs. "I get my payment every time I lock up a criminal and throw away the key. There's no satisfaction like it."

"Then you're an amazing breed of man."

"That's exactly what I was thinking about you when I saw you perform in Bandera. Only a few exceptional women have the patience and the skills to work year in and year out to thrill the thousands of people who can only dream about what you do on your horse. The heart of a champion is inside you. All I could do watching you at the rodeo was sit back and marvel."

She eyed him with a frank stare. "What you do and what I do aren't comparable, but I appreciate the compliment."

"It was heartfelt."

"You enjoy the rodeo?"

"All my life."

Her eyes lit up. "Really?"

"I love it. Growing up we had horses and always went to the rodeo. I still keep my horse on my parents' small ranch and ride when I have time. Like most of my friends when I was young, I thought it would be fun to try bull riding and calf roping. But our pitiful attempts that ended in pain and suffering let me know it takes

a lot more than just wanting to do it. You know…like possessing the skill, like being born to it, like having the guts to go at it again and again."

Her chuckle delighted him. "That's my father."

"Some of us have it. Some of us don't."

"Instead, you face a terrifying human enemy with no thought for your own life."

Cy laughed. "Don't be deceived. I give a lot of thought to my own life, believe me."

Her smile slowly faded. "I've given a lot of thought to your life, Ranger Vance. Please take care of yourself." The throb in her voice resonated inside him. "It's almost ten o'clock. Unless you need me for anything, I'm going to go upstairs."

He reached for her phone and handed it to her. "You can have this back. Forensics got what they needed from it, but they still have your laptop. I've removed all the messages."

She gripped it. "Did they find a voice match?"

"Yes."

"A Texan accent?"

"No. The stalker sounds like certain people who live in either Virginia Beach or Charleston, South Carolina."

Kellie's surprise over the news caused her to groan. "Charleston was the place where he killed one of his victims."

"Listen to me, Kellie. If I have anything to do with it, there won't be any more."

She nodded. "As I told my mother earlier today, I believe in you. Now I'm going to call some of my friends who left messages with my mom."

"After you do that, turn the ringer off. If the stalker intends on calling you tonight, I don't want you bothered by him. You need sleep."

A pained expression broke out on her face. "What are you going to do?"

"Coordinate with my backup crew."

She slid him an anxious glance. "You think something might happen tonight?"

He watched a nerve throbbing at the base of her throat. Cy was determined to make her fear go away. "If not tonight, perhaps tomorrow night or the next. Either way we'll be ready."

"Then I'll say good-night."

"If you need me, phone me. But by no means come downstairs until I let you know it's all right."

"Okay." She held his gaze for a moment longer before she went upstairs. Soon after, Cy's phone rang. It was Vic.

"I'm walking down the alley to the garage."

"I'll open it."

"Did you know the boss has supplied extra backup?"

"He told me."

"Chris and Jose will be in a taxi in the alley. Lyle and the rest of the crew are in place."

"Good. We're set. This is the window of time the stalker has been waiting for. I'm counting on his making a move any night this week. Next week he knows she'll be leaving for Colorado. If he thinks she could be married, he's got to find out and get rid of her husband before he takes her off someplace and strangles her. He'll need his brother."

"Yup."

"See you in a minute."

Cy hung up and went out to the garage. He lifted the door partway. In less than a minute, Vic came crouching in before Cy lowered it. They both walked through the garage and kitchen to the living room.

"Has Kellie gone to bed?"

"As far as I know."

"How's she handling it?"

"The woman is tough. I'm beginning to understand why she's such a fierce competitor in the arena. That's the only reason this setup is working."

"I think it's more a case of the right two people being thrown together."

Cy knew where his friend was going with that remark, but now wasn't the time. "The thing I keep wondering about is why this pervert targeted Kellie specifically. Her beauty provides one obvious answer. But there's more to it than that. Nothing we've learned so far, not even after collaborating with the FBI agents back east, has shed any light. I'm trying to find the missing link."

"Maybe it will have to come after we catch them."

"You're right." He glanced at Vic. "What do you say we do this in shifts? I'll take the first watch." He fixed the hide-a-bed so Vic could stretch out when he was ready. "Since we know there's no side or back door to this place, my hunch is he'll come in through the garage with a device to let himself in the door into the kitchen."

Vic nodded. "That makes the most sense. The fence isn't that high. He'll be able to scale it easily. I did a pa-

trol of the town houses on the other side of the alley. The tenants don't have garages and park their cars in covered parking across their street. If someone wanted to hide out, they'd have to jump the fence from this alley into one of the backyards and wait so they wouldn't be seen."

After talking strategy for a while, Vic lay down. Cy turned out all the lights in the condo before going into the kitchen. He took out his .357-caliber SIG Sauer and put it on the table. After pouring himself a hot mug of coffee, he sat down in front of his laptop in the dark. Time to catch up on the paperwork for Kellie's case while he could still remember times and details of their trip to Colorado.

Once he'd finished, he went back to Kellie's website and scrolled through her scheduled events, starting with the first rodeo of this year. To his shock he discovered she'd entered the Salem, Virginia, Annual Stampede on January 9. His adrenaline surged.

She'd gone back east!

Cy should have thought about that before now, but he'd been so concentrated on the months since the stalker had appeared, only now had he started to explore all the possibilities.

After consulting a Virginia map, he saw that Salem was on the opposite side of the state from Virginia Beach.

He scrolled down quickly. More shocks. She'd ridden in the Walterboro, South Carolina, Rodeo two weeks after leaving Virginia. Cy looked up the South Carolina map. Walterboro was only forty minutes away from *Charleston*.

Were the stalkers born in Charleston? Did they call it home when they weren't victimizing women? Vic was still waiting to hear back on the identical twins most likely born there or the Virginia Beach area. His friend was asleep, so Cy would have to wait to discuss the idea with him later.

Needing to do something with all the energy flooding his system, he kept scrolling for more information. On the first weekend of February she rode in the Chatsworth, Georgia, Rodeo. Mid-February she entered the rodeo in Memphis, Tennessee, where another murder had taken place.

In March she'd participated in rodeos throughout the Midwest before returning to Austin via a rodeo in Hampton, Arkansas, and another one in Fort Worth, Texas. But his mind kept going back to the Walterboro Rodeo.

If for some reason the stalkers had gone to the rodeo that night, they would have seen Kellie, who had the best time during the performance that night. That might have been the place they first decided she'd be their next target.

Unless—and it was a big *unless*—they were born in Walterboro or the surrounding area. Were Cy's thoughts leaping to improbable conclusions because of the voice match Rafe had found? Could he rely on such a science to provide answers?

Impatient with himself for wanting to find Kellie's stalker so badly he was starting to cross that line TJ had warned him about, he got up to pace the kitchen. He didn't want to take the time to fix another pot of cof-

fee, so he opted for a soda from the fridge. No sooner had he sat down again than his phone rang. It was ten to three. A check of the caller ID told him it was Jose.

"What's going on?"

"I've got my night-vision goggles trained on a masked figure wearing a dark pullover and pants walking in the alley toward you. Can't tell if it's a man or a woman."

"Don't do anything. Let's see what happens, then close in." He hung up and called to Vic, who sprang off the couch and joined him. "Jose has spotted someone in a mask walking in the alley in this direction."

Vic nodded and drew out his weapon. While he hunkered under the table, where he had a direct view of the doorway, Cy flattened himself against the wall on the other side of the door.

They remained in position ten long minutes before Cy heard the sweet telltale sound of someone picking the lock, probably with a paper clip and tension wrench. If Kellie hadn't gone to the police, the scenario happening to her now would have ended her life. As he geared up for the takedown, a rush such as he'd never known took over.

All of a sudden the door opened. Cy came at the killer from behind and put a headlock on him, forcing him to the floor. The stalker let go with a stream of venom while he fought with the strength of a man high on drugs. Cy felt him bite his arm. It took Vic's help to subdue him long enough to handcuff his hands behind his back and ankle cuff him.

Cy rolled his body over and pulled the mask off his head. There was the face of the man in the picture with

the longer hair. He leaned over him. "Surprise, Denny, or whoever the hell you are. Was it Donny, Andy or Drew who strangled the woman in Charleston? I'm the husband you and your twin didn't think existed. You're under arrest for the stalking of Kellie Parrish."

By now Vic was on the phone to the rest of the crew. Within seconds Kellie's town house was filled with agents. Cy took the greatest pleasure in reading him his Miranda rights before he was hauled out to the van.

THE SOUNDS OF men's raised voices had brought Kellie awake. She shot out of bed and dressed quickly in a top and jeans. Cy had told her not to go downstairs. But whatever had been going on below, she couldn't stay up here and not know what was happening. She hurried out of her bedroom and flew down the stairs straight into Cy's arms.

He must have been on his way up to her because he caught her to him, hugging her hard before he held her away from him. "We caught the twin with the longer hair, Kellie. For the sake of practicality, we'll call him Denny. In time we'll catch his brother and you'll never have to be afraid again."

The information he relayed filled her with such relief, she could barely find words. "If anything had happened to you…" Her voice sounded raw.

"Nothing did."

"That's not true. There's blood on your forearm."

"He bit me."

"Let me see." She pushed the sleeve of his shirt up

to his elbow. "You need to go to the ER for stitches and a tetanus shot. You could be infected already."

"The bleeding has stopped. I'll take care of it later. Right now we need to talk." He ushered her over to the couch, where they could sit.

The warmth of his body stayed with her. "I know what you're going to tell me. This isn't over yet."

"No, it isn't." In the soft lamplight, his chiseled jaw stood out in stark relief. "We don't know if his brother was watching what went down here tonight from a distance, or if Denny planned to kidnap you and take you to his brother at another location. What we *do* know is that when the brother we'll call Dan realizes Denny has been arrested or isn't around anymore, his rage will escalate and he'll come after you himself to finish the job. Dan is the one who approached you in Pendleton."

Kellie kneaded her hands. "When he finds out you exist—maybe he believes it now—his hatred toward you is what frightens me."

He gave her arm a squeeze. "Nothing's going to happen to either one of us. Why don't you go upstairs and phone your parents? Tell them that one of the brothers is now in custody, and we're hoping to catch the other one soon. It will be a great relief to them."

"I know." She looked into his eyes. "Are you going to get your arm looked at now?"

"I'll do it after I run by headquarters. Vic will stay here while I'm gone so you'll be safe. I want you to go back to bed and we'll see each other tomorrow."

"It already is tomorrow."

His lips twitched. When he did that, her heart skipped a beat. "So it is."

"Cy?"

"What is it?"

Terrified she might give in to the impulse to kiss him and humiliate herself, she got up from the couch. "Thank you. There should be a better way to tell you how I feel, but I can't think what it is. Please get that arm examined." Before she blubbered all over the place, she left the living room and hurried up the stairs.

She wished she could go with him, but that was ridiculous. He was a Ranger and had business to take care of. He'd just taken down one of the FBI's most wanted criminals. Cy had done his job and needed to finish up.

Kellie sank down on the side of her bed. The trouble was, she'd come to look at him as someone much more than an officer of the law. They'd agreed to a fictional marriage to trap the killers, but tonight she didn't feel like a fictional character.

You'd like to be his real wife. Admit it, Kellie.

Appalled by the admission, and shocked that her feelings could run this deep so quickly, she phoned her parents. They were thankful Cy seemed to have accomplished a miracle so fast, and both were overcome with emotions. After they hung up, she got into bed, hoping she could fall asleep. When the phone rang again, she was surprised to discover it was already seven thirty.

She glanced at the screen on her cell, but there was no accompanying ID.

It was the stalker. He'd left a message. She listened to it.

"You're still lying about having a husband. I saw the police drag my brother out of your garage to their van. You're all going to be so sorry for what you've done. Just wait and see what I've got planned."

He'd been watching the whole time.

She phoned Cy immediately, but it went to his voice mail. She told him about the stalker's message before hanging up.

At this point she was wide-awake. The man who'd invaded her space in Pendleton was still out there, and now it was Cy who wouldn't be safe. Her fear for him was greater than ever.

While she waited for him to call back, she showered and washed her hair. After a quick blow-dry, she put on jeans and a plum-colored cotton sweater. Once she'd pulled on her cowboy boots, she was ready for the day.

As she went downstairs, her phone rang. She checked the caller ID. It was Cy!

With a racing pulse, Kellie clicked on and heard "Good morning."

"The same to you. Did you get any sleep?"

"A little. How about you?"

"Don't worry about me. I heard your message. It means he was hiding behind the fence. Don't leave the town house. I'll be over as soon as I can." She heard the click.

Kellie put the phone on the counter. She needed something to do and started to fix breakfast. In case he hadn't eaten yet, she made enough for both of them. Before long she heard the garage door lifting and ran to open the kitchen door for him.

He levered himself from his car wearing a brown Western shirt and jeans. Kellie had a hard time keeping her eyes off his hard-muscled physique. As he came inside, she could smell his soap from the shower and noticed he was clean shaven. Those deep blue eyes zeroed in on her. His piercing gaze sent warmth through her body. "Something smells good."

Yes, it does. That's you.

"It was my turn to fix breakfast for us. Sit down at the table and I'll serve you."

"I won't say no. I'm starving."

"Since I know you haven't had any sleep in twenty-four hours, you need food to keep you going." She got them started on eggs and bacon, topping it off with toast and coffee.

"This is delicious. Thank you."

"You're welcome. Let me look at the bite on your arm."

He flashed her a lazy smile before rolling up his sleeve. She was relieved to see a dressing had covered it. "I told you I watch out for myself."

"I'm glad you had a doctor look at it."

He rolled the sleeve back down. They were both being polite, but it was like trying to avoid the elephant in the room. He eyed her over the rim of his coffee mug. The gold wedding band on his ring finger gleamed in the overhead light, bringing her straight to the point.

"Cy? We have to talk about our situation."

"Agreed. You go first."

She took a deep breath. "That call this morning made me realize that you and I don't have to pretend

to be married any longer. The whole point was to flush out the stalker. Now that he's been arrested and his brother watched what went on—probably from behind the fence—there's no more need for you to stay here.

"Last night my dad said he's going to hire some bodyguards for me as soon as tomorrow. In the meantime I'll let the landlord know I'm moving to my parents' ranch, so my condo will be available for a new renter. That will free you to get on with other Ranger work. We have no idea when the stalker will strike again, let alone when he'll be caught. It could take a long time and you're needed for other important cases."

When Cy didn't say anything, she drank more of her coffee. "It's fortunate that no one knows your name, so no explanations are necessary. After the second brother is arrested, then I'll post the truth about the twin brothers on my blog and explain that the fake marriage was announced to lay a trap that worked brilliantly."

Starting to get unnerved by his silence, she took the rings off her finger and put them on the table. "Take these back to headquarters along with any equipment you've left here. And please thank the other men in your crew for protecting me. They'll never know how grateful I am."

He went on drinking his coffee. Why didn't he say something?

Since they'd finished eating, she got up and cleared the table before putting the dishes in the dishwasher.

"Kellie? If you've said everything you wanted to say, come and sit down while I tell you what I'd prefer to see happen, but it's up to you."

What did he mean? The hairs on her neck started to prickle as she did his bidding.

"I was in a meeting early this morning with the captain. I'm still assigned to your case until it's solved. There's no work more important for the department than for me to put away another killer on the list of America's most wanted. Though we've caught one killer, his twin is on the loose and more dangerous to you than ever.

"Since he knows his brother has been arrested, he's angrier than ever. Until he makes his move, and I expect it will be sooner than later, it'll make my job easier if we stay married so *I* can be your bodyguard. At this point I want us to be visible like any married couple. It will taunt him so much, he'll make a mistake. That's what I'll be waiting for. But if you'd rather your father hired bodyguards who would take turns living here, our department will provide backup. The decision is yours."

Kellie didn't need to think. His suggestion thrilled her so much she could hardly find words. But how to tell him without giving herself away?

"Since you already have a plan, let's not deviate from it now."

She struggled for breath. "Only if you're sure."

"Give me your hand." When she extended her arm, he put the rings in her palm. "Put these back on."

Her heart started to run away with her. Not only because of his touch, but because it meant she wouldn't have to say goodbye to him. Not yet anyway…

"Now, if you don't mind, I'm going to stretch out on the hide-a-bed and get some sleep. To put your mind at

ease, Lyle and the crew are outside and will remain on watch until tomorrow."

He got up from the table. "Later today we'll drive out to your parents' ranch and go riding together. I want to watch the famous Kellie Parrish in action. When our stalker phones again, and I know he will, let him leave messages and I'll listen to them later."

And with that, she watched him leave the kitchen, feeling more comforted than ever that her Texas Ranger was here.

Chapter Six

Cy walked into the living room, where he took off his cowboy boots. When he'd proposed that Kellie announce their marriage on her blog, he'd thought she would never agree to it. But she went along with the plan and had her parents' blessing.

Just now he'd assumed she'd put the brakes on this latest strategy. To his astonishment, it didn't happen.

Who knew how long the case might go on. Cy did know exactly how his family was going to react when he told them that he and Kellie were pretending to be man and wife. They were worried he'd never get married and continually tried to line him up with a promising match. The party for his sister coming up on Sunday was another excuse for his parents to introduce him to a new woman.

Because of his undercover role as Kellie's husband, any matchmaking on their part would have to be put on hold. They'd be forced to give up trying to manage his love life while he was still working on her case. Nothing would frustrate them more. Or please him more. In

fact he was tempted to take her to the party with him on Sunday.

What was today? Thursday? Was it only last Friday when they'd collided outside the radio station in Bandera? Since she'd come into his world, he'd lost track of time. How could it be that already he couldn't comprehend his life without her?

With a relieved sigh, he stretched out on the bed and turned on his side facing the wall. His body felt as if it weighed a thousand pounds, but the capture of Denny Denham had done a lot to lighten his mood. He could actually go to sleep knowing that when he woke up, he'd be with Kellie, who wasn't going anywhere without him. Later today they'd go riding together. He could hardly wait.

The next time he was cognizant of his surroundings, it was four thirty in the afternoon. He'd been sleeping on his stomach. When he turned over, there she was on the couch across from him, curled up with a book. Their eyes met. Hers were smiling.

Uh-oh. "If I snored, don't tell me about it."

"It will be my secret. But I want to know who Sylvia is."

Cy started to chuckle and sat up. "I don't believe it."

"Believe what?" She smiled broadly, illuminating his world. "It seems you've been carrying around a secret. A little while ago you muttered something like, 'Dammit. Where are you, Sylvia?'"

He couldn't hold back his laughter and moved his pillow so she could see his gun. "*That* is Sylvia."

She put the book down. "You call your gun Sylvia?"

"Yup. She goes everywhere I go, but sometimes when I'm dreaming, I find myself looking for her."

Laughter burst out of Kellie. "You gave it a woman's name. Why not a man's?"

"That's an interesting question. I really don't know."

"Was Sylvia an old girlfriend?"

"No such luck," he teased. "When I was a little boy, my father took me to the barbershop in Dripping Springs for my haircuts. The older man had a picture of his wife, who'd died, on the wall. He called her Sylvia. I guess it stuck in my mind to come out later. Some of my colleagues give their weapons a name."

She nodded. "Just like some pilots name their planes. My grandfather had an old car he called Elvira."

Curious, he asked, "Did you name all your horses?"

Kellie let out a sigh. "No, but one day I'd love it if Trixie gave birth to a little filly I could name and raise."

She could have been talking with the same kind of love she would have for her own baby. He wondered what plans she had for the future. "How long do you intend to compete?"

"After the Finals in December, I'm quitting the circuit. It's a demanding life and I've already been in it so long."

That was news to him. "What will you do?"

"This is a low-cost rental. I've been saving all my earnings and plan to buy a small ranch where I can run my own business of training future barrel racers. I have my eye on several properties that have been put out on the market. That way I can be involved with the rodeo, but on the other end."

He sucked in his breath, marveling over her ambition. "From the amount of fans who flood your website for training tips, I have no doubt you'll be so busy you'll have to turn some away."

"All in good time, I hope."

Enjoying this too much, Cy sat up and pulled on his cowboy boots before he got to his feet. He stared down at her. "Speaking of your website, I happened to look at your schedule before Montana and noticed you competed in rodeos back east."

"Yes. As I told you, Sally's husband, Manny, is a bull rider and we decided to enter those rodeos for points. It was also a fun vacation."

Cy rubbed the side of his jaw. "Since the stalkers were operating in the East, it occurred to me one of them would have seen you perform, possibly in Virginia or more likely in South Carolina. We know Charleston was one of the murder scenes. Since Walterboro is only forty minutes away, I'm thinking he might have gone to that rodeo and decided you were his next victim."

"I had the best time in the ratings that night," she murmured.

"The spotlight was on you. It makes perfect sense. We hope to pinpoint the exact location of their births in one of those two areas. It's possible they maintained a home there."

A delicate frown marred her brows. "To think they might have been following me since January…"

"While Dan tracked you all the way until he showed up in Oregon, his brother broke into the files at the WPRA and obtained your cell-phone number. But re-

member that there's only one of them now and I'm going to catch him. Excuse me for a minute while I freshen up, then we'll leave for your parents' ranch."

He put the gun in his side-waist holster. After making the bed, he left the living room and went upstairs to the guest bedroom. He shut the door and phoned Vic, who picked up on the second ring. "I wondered when I'd hear from you."

"I was catching up on some sleep."

"Which plan did Kellie go with?" Vic had been in on the meeting with TJ.

Cy stopped pacing. "I gave her a choice."

"And?"

"We're going to carry on as we have been."

"In other words she doesn't want anyone else being her bodyguard. Between you and me, the captain's worried you're going to lose your focus."

His jaw hardened. "Is that what you think, too?"

"It doesn't matter what I think."

"The hell it doesn't!"

"Honestly?" Vic questioned. "I've worked with you for three years and trust you with my life. If you think your plan is the best way to keep her safe and catch this predator, I back you all the way."

"Thanks, Vic. I'm going to need your help."

"You've got it."

"We're leaving for her parents' ranch in a few minutes so she can exercise her horses. The crew will be watching the condo while we're gone."

"While you do that I'm going to see if I can get any information out of our prisoner."

"If he talks, it'll be lies."

"Yup. But coming down off his latest fix, he might make a mistake that could be valuable. I'll catch up with you later. Watch your back, Cy."

"Always."

He clicked off and reached for his Stetson.

CY DROVE THEM up to the barn. Kellie got out and headed for the entrance. Cy followed and they walked over to the first stall. "Trixie? I want you to meet a very important person." Kellie's palomino nickered and her ears pointed. "This is Cy. He's going to ride Paladin while we do some circles."

Clearly Cy was no stranger around horses as he rubbed her nose and forelock. "I watched you perform in Bandera, Trixie. You're a champion just like your owner." Her horse nudged him in the chest, causing him to smile at Kellie. When he did that, she forgot where she was or what she was doing.

They moved to the next stall. "This is Paladin, one of Dad's geldings. He's a big bay who loves a good ride. *And* he likes Trixie. When they're out in the pasture, he follows her around."

Cy's eyes gleamed. "I can see why. She's a beauty. Who says romance doesn't exist among our four-legged friends?"

"The only trouble is, he can be annoying and she runs from him."

He burst into that rich male laughter she loved so much. "So she likes her independence."

"At times. But then there are others and she rests her head on his neck."

"Sounds like a mercurial female. I'll do my best to control him."

This close to Cy, darts of awareness shot through her body. Together they picked out their saddles and bridles, then carried them to the stalls. Kellie heard a nicker from another stall.

"Starburst? I haven't forgotten you, but it's not your turn."

A grin broke out on Cy's face. "You talk to them like they're human."

"To tell the truth, I like them better than a lot of humans."

"Amen to that."

Before long they were both mounted. One glance at the gorgeous male astride the bay and she was in danger of melting on the spot. The only way she could describe her condition was that she was in a state of euphoria being with him like this.

He was a natural on a horse and took firm command of Paladin, yet displayed a gentleness that won Kellie's respect and admiration. She decided he could do anything. They rode out to the pasture as if this was something he did every day. Though she hadn't seen him ride in the Bandera parade, she could imagine him with the other three Rangers carrying the flag.

After riding some distance, she headed for the outdoor arena. Cy followed at a slower pace and pulled to a stop. Her pulse raced because he was watching her.

Once inside, Kellie began her routine and made per-

fect circles with Trixie, always using a little inside leg. She made certain her horse's back feet went in the same track as her front feet. After a few minutes she walked her around, then changed to a trot so she could stand in the stirrups to build up the strength in her legs.

To transition from high speed to stops was part of the routine. So was the exercise of backing up, then calling to her horse to stop. While Kellie was building up her own leg muscles, the exercises were helping Trixie strengthen her hindquarters.

Finally she led her over to the fence and did a few more stops, causing Trixie to use her back hocks and stifles. The routine built the vital control necessary for barrel racing. "Good girl," she called to her horse and patted her neck.

In the background she could hear clapping. When she looked over her shoulder, she saw Cy on Paladin, walking toward them. Beneath his white cowboy hat, his dark blue eyes traveled over her, filling her with warmth. "I wouldn't have missed that expert performance for anything."

"Did you hear that, Trixie? Such high praise coming from one of our famous Texas Rangers." To cover her emotions, she gave her horse another couple of loving pats. "I think you've had a good enough workout for today. It's going to be dark pretty soon. Let's head back to the barn." She glanced at Cy. "I try not to overdo it with her. It's important I make an effort to change her daily routine. Tomorrow I'll work with Starburst for a while."

They rode back in companionable silence. After wa-

tering the horses, they put them to bed. On their way out to the car, he asked about her parents.

"They're so thankful you caught one of the stalkers, they decided to attend an important dinner tonight. Otherwise they'd be here to ask you to stay for dinner. But let's go inside anyway to freshen up before we leave for the condo."

In a few minutes they went back to his car. He helped her in and got behind the wheel. "I'm in the mood for a good meal. Have you ever eaten at the Watering Hole? It's only a few miles from here."

He was finally asking her to do something a couple would do, but she couldn't consider this a date in any sense of the word. Cy was hungry and needed to eat. Somehow Kellie had to rein in her thoughts that were growing out of control.

They'd been thrown together because of a life-threatening situation and nothing more. But it was getting harder and harder to remain objective when she was so attracted to him. *It's more than attraction, Kellie. A lot more.*

"I've been there many times," she answered. "Their charbroiled steak is the best in Austin."

"That was easy."

Yes. Way too easy. She was under the Ranger's spell.

Luckily it was the kind of restaurant where you could come as you were. The place was always crowded. While they waited in the lounge area to be called to their table, Anita Wall, one of the women in the Blue Bonnet Posse, made a beeline for Kellie and gave her a

hug. "It's so good to see you. I heard you got married. You've got to introduce me."

This was what happened when you went out in public. "Anita Wall? Meet my husband, Cy Vance."

Her married friend and mother looked up at Cy and did a triple take. Kellie couldn't blame her. The man was too striking.

"How do you do?" She shook his hand. "We've all wondered who the man was to snag our star." Her gaze swerved to Kellie before she whispered in her ear, "Now I understand. Wow, wow, wow."

While Kellie tried not to react, Cy asked, "Are you here alone?"

"No. I'm with some friends."

"You're welcome to join us."

She shook her head. "I wouldn't dream of intruding on you honeymooners, but thank you for the invitation." She gave Kellie one more hug. "Call me when you have time to talk."

"I will. It's wonderful to see you, Anita."

To her relief the hostess called their number and Cy escorted her to their table. Once their order was taken, Cy sat back, smiling at her. "Every friend of yours I've met lights up when they see you."

"Every friend of mine can't stop staring when they meet you," she countered before she realized what she'd said. Heat rose to her face. "They'd all be shocked and horrified if they knew what the real reason was for our being together. For your sake I hope the stalker makes another move soon."

"But not for yours?"

She lowered her head. "That came out wrong. Even if this is the career you've chosen, it has to be harrowing for you while you're forced to bide your time waiting for the next opportunity to present itself."

Their food came. Once they were alone again he said, "You have that turned around. You're the one being tortured mentally and emotionally." He cut into his steak. "Some victims would fall apart at a time like this, but not you. Your courage makes my job a lot easier to handle." So saying, he started eating.

"That's because you have a facility for calming me down. It's a gift, Ranger Vance."

Before she broke into grateful tears, she dug into her meal. They ate without talking. When she turned down dessert, he left some bills with the receipt and ushered her out of the restaurant to his car.

As they drove out of the parking lot, she turned to him. "I want to pay you for my share of the dinner. I don't expect the taxpayers of our state to take care of my bill."

"Didn't you notice that I paid cash for our dinner? It's from my paycheck. Any allowance I get as part of the job, I'm issued a credit card for that account. Tonight was my personal treat, if you like."

Kellie liked it too much. "Thank you. That dinner was delicious."

"I agree. Before this case is closed, I might just treat you again."

He got a chuckle out of her.

"That's better. I know you feel like this is the never-ending story, but it will be over before long. Our stalker

Dan is beside himself without his brother. His need to kill again is stronger than ever because they didn't get the job done. In his desperation to finish what they started, he'll reveal himself in some way and that will be his downfall."

"If you say it, then I know it's true."

"I'm touched by your faith in me. How would you like to go to a family party with me on Sunday night?"

The question caught her off guard. "But they'll all think we're married—"

"They know I'm on a case."

"Do your parents realize you're protecting me?"

"Because I'm undercover, they'll figure it out. The point is, my sister is getting married and the parents are inviting a few people over to celebrate the coming event. Because of my job I've been absent from too many family gatherings as it is and would prefer not to miss this one. But I can't leave you alone. Starting tomorrow we won't have backup from the department unless I ask for it. If you don't want to go, we won't."

She bit her lip. "I can see you need a babysitter for me, one armed with a weapon."

"It's all right. Don't give it another thought."

After what he'd just told her? *Ha.* Kellie eyed his arresting profile. "How many sisters do you have?"

"Just Beth, short for Elizabeth."

"Do you have brothers?"

"No. I'm the only one."

"Well, far be it from me to keep you from a party this important. If I had no siblings except one brother,

I know I'd want him there for the most important moment in my life."

Cy looked over at her. "It *is* the biggest thing in her life. I knew I could count on you," he said in a satisfied tone.

Emotional bribery that fed on her guilt went a long way to persuade her. He had no idea how hard this would be on her. They weren't engaged, and she couldn't count on seeing him again after he'd caught the killer. But there was another part of her that was crazy with excitement to go out with him, even if she understood the true reason for being in his company.

They pulled into the garage and he shut off the engine. "Let me have your car keys for a minute." She rummaged in her purse for them. After she handed them to him, he got out and inspected her Toyota, including the trunk. "Okay," he called to her. She started to get out. "But let me go in the condo first."

That was right. While she could forget everything but the joy of being with him, his radar was on alert every second. Kellie waited by the door until he'd turned on lights and told her she could come in. She entered and locked it. They were home for the night, snug and secure.

Despite the menace still lurking out there, she'd never been happier in her life. There was only one reason why, and that reason was walking around, all six foot two of rip-cord-strong Texas Ranger with dark blue eyes and handsome features to die for.

When she thought of Anita and the look on her face

when she saw Cy, Kellie feared it was the same smitten look she'd been walking around with since Bandera.

"Vic brought your laptop back." At the sound of his deep voice, she swung around and saw it on the kitchen table. "The lab has finished with it. Feel free to check your emails and your blog site. Add whatever comes to mind."

The mention of it reminded Kellie of her phone. She'd turned off the ringer. Thank heaven Cy was here. In his presence she wasn't frightened to see who'd called.

After getting it out of her purse, she walked into the living room and sank down on the couch. While Cy was upstairs, she checked her cell. Five messages had been left. One from Cody, who was verifying their trip plans to Rapid City, South Dakota, for the rodeo. She'd call him back. Four came from friends. There was one text message. It came from... *Trixie?*

Kellie felt sick. When she checked it, there was a picture with the text. She pressed on it and saw herself and Cy in his car as they were backing out of her garage. The text read, Plan to say goodbye to your husband, Kellie girl. It'll be payment for my brother. Then I'm going after your horse. Don't forget your turn is coming.

"Cy—" she cried out in panic. Within seconds he came down the stairs. "Look at this! He's a maniac! He's threatening to kill you and my horse!" She handed him her phone so he could see everything.

Without thinking about it, Cy sat down and put his arm around her shoulders to comfort her. He'd been wondering when she'd break down. All this time she'd

been so brave, but the threat accompanying the photo of her horse had been the tipping point for her. It was too much. She burrowed into his neck and sobbed.

He brushed the hair away from her cheek. "Awful as this is, it means he's ready to spring into action. But don't worry. Two of the agency's men dressed like local ranch hands are guarding your horses around the clock."

She blinked. "All this time?"

"Yes."

"Oh, thank heaven."

"The stalker doesn't have much more time before you leave for the rodeo next week. I'm convinced he's going to make his move soon. I'll be ready for him," he murmured, pressing kisses to her brow.

One minute she was clinging to him. In the next instant she raised her head to reveal a tear-sodden face. He brushed the moisture from her cheeks with his thumb.

"I—I'm sorry I fell apart like that," she stammered. "How embarrassing."

Cy heard the words, but their lips were only an inch apart, distracting him from his duty to protect her. All that registered was her warmth and beauty, seducing him into wanting a taste of her. It was wrong to give in to his desire, but he'd passed a threshold where chemistry had taken over. He could no more stop what was happening than he could prevent himself from being swept into a vortex.

When his mouth closed over hers, he heard a small moan, then she was giving him access as if she couldn't stop herself, either. For a minute he forgot everything while the wonder of her response had taken hold. One

kiss became another and another until it all merged into a growing need that had set them on fire.

He'd never known this kind of ecstasy before, not even with his fiancée. Maybe it was because of the danger surrounding them that the experience of holding and kissing her had surpassed any pleasure he'd known with the few women from his past.

Kellie was exciting from the way she looked, talked, walked, rode a horse and fought her fear. Her smile dazzled him. Her lust for life—her plans for life—thrilled him almost as much as her touch, almost as much as the feel of her body molded to his.

Caught up in a frenzy of giving and taking, Cy unexpectedly heard a familiar voice come into his head. *You realize the two of you will be walking a very thin line.*

Stunned by how far he'd gotten carried away, he lifted his mouth from hers with reluctance. Somehow he managed to let her go and got to his feet. He cleared his throat and stood there with his hands on his hips while he attempted to get his breathing under control. "That wasn't supposed to happen, Kellie. I apologize for betraying your trust, but you have my solemn oath it won't happen again."

She looked up at him through clear blue eyes dominating a flushed face. "It takes two, Ranger Vance. I was right there with you and crossed a line I swore I wouldn't. But I'll tell you this. I enjoyed it."

An honest woman. He smiled, loving her candor. "It was even more exciting for me than watching you round the third can in Bandera and fly straight down the alley."

After running his hands through her hair, Cy could see he'd disheveled it. She smoothed a few strands off her forehead. "It's past my bedtime, so I'll say good-night."

"I need to keep your phone," he said before she reached for it. Kellie nodded, then stood up and hurried out of the living room.

No sooner had she disappeared up the stairs than Vic called. Cy pulled out his phone and clicked on. "Did you get in to interrogate our prisoner?"

"Yes, but he's not going to give up any information. These guys are real pros, but I have other news you need to see and sent it to your email. I sent the same email to the agents back east who are working on this case."

"How soon can you get here?"

"I'm walking toward the front of Kellie's town house now."

"I'll let you in."

In a few minutes they sat at the kitchen table. Cy handed him Kellie's phone. "Take a look at the message from the sender named Trixie. Dan took a picture of me and Kellie in the car backing out of the garage earlier today."

Vic studied the photo and read the text. He shot Cy a glance. "The loss of his twin has unhinged him."

"Yup. He's starting to take daring risks and is damn good at knowing how to terrorize Kellie. I assume he's armed with a rifle in order to take care of me and Trixie. Then he'll go back to his preferred method to kill Kellie."

"We've got to find him quick."

"Did Janene ever track down that IP address?"

"No. It has her stumped for the moment, but I've received information on the identical-twin birth records from both cities."

"I want to see those, but first let's talk about the photo. Dan was obviously hiding behind the fence this afternoon in order to take it. No doubt he was hidden in the same place when we took his brother out to the van. I'm thinking he's using one of the town houses."

"So am I," Vic broke in. "I'll phone TJ right now to get us a warrant."

They could read each other's minds. "We'll need backup so we can do a thorough search of every town house on this street and the town houses on the other side of the alley. Our lunatic is hiding out here somewhere ready to strike. We need to nab him fast."

"Agreed."

While Vic got on the phone with their captain, Cy opened the email Vic had sent. He studied the statistics for identical twin boys born in hospitals in 1986 when the populations of both areas were smaller. The sum from both cities equaled ten sets, six from Charleston, four from Virginia Beach. Hopefully, the agents at the other end could track down the parents from birth records and make an ID that would help them form a correct profile of the brothers.

Vic ended the call. "TJ's getting the warrant as we speak. He's sending Luckey to guard Kellie so you and I can do the search with the crew. As soon as he gets here, we'll start."

Cy's thoughts were whirling. "I need to tell Kellie

about the change in plans." Since he had her phone, he needed to tell her in person. "Be right back." He got out of the chair and hurried up the stairs with her cell phone.

"Kellie?" he called to her before rapping on her door.

"Yes?" she answered immediately.

"I have to leave for a little while with Vic. But I won't go until Luckey gets here. He's one of my closest friends in the Rangers."

"One of the Sons of the Forty, you mean?"

"Yes. He'll guard you with his life."

"I don't doubt it."

"I'm leaving your phone on the floor outside your door in case you need it. If the stalker calls, let it ring through to your voice mail. I've just put Luckey's phone number in your list of contacts. He'll answer if you call him. Try to go back to sleep if you can, and I'll see you in the morning."

"Be careful, Cy."

He took a deep breath. "Always."

Chapter Seven

I have to leave for a little while with Vic.

Kellie could only imagine what that meant. Instead of lying there shuddering in fear for Cy, she threw back the covers and slid off the bed to get her phone. When she opened her door, she saw her cell but couldn't hear voices downstairs.

Something important was going on and he wanted her out of it, yet he always put her needs first. She believed he was so dedicated, he'd treat any person he was guarding with the same kind of care. That was the problem. Kellie wanted to mean much more to him.

When they'd kissed earlier, she'd never wanted them to stop. She couldn't blame all of it on hormones. This man was different. She was different when she was with him. Kellie had dated a lot of guys over the years, but something had changed when she'd first looked into Cy's startling dark blue eyes.

She picked up her phone and went back into the bedroom. If only there were someone she could talk to about this, but her feelings were too private to divulge even to her family or closest friends. She'd known Cy

for only a week. Anyone she confided in would smile and tell her it was natural that a man and woman thrown together in a dangerous situation would grab a little comfort that went along with the hero worship. But in the long run it couldn't be taken seriously.

As she walked over to the bed, more questions ran through her mind. What would it be like to be married to a Texas Ranger? To know that every time he left for work, he was facing danger head-on? When he didn't get home on time, or was involved in a stakeout that kept him away for days at a time, how would she be able to handle it?

Judging by the tension gripping her body right now, she already had the answer to her question. She wouldn't be able to cope. To love Cy meant she would never be at ease when he was out of her sight.

Kellie's mom didn't worry when her husband left the house. She knew he'd walk in at the end of the day and come find her wherever she was. Barring a natural disaster or an unforeseen accident, her mom didn't have to be concerned that she might never see her husband alive again.

Like her mom, Kellie had grown up knowing their husband and father would always be in their lives. She'd never given it a thought. But she did now...

With a tortured sigh, Kellie turned off her phone and lay back, praying this threat to her life would be over soon. If the stalker were caught before she had to leave for South Dakota, she would end her association with Cy cold turkey. That was the only way to deal with her

feelings. They never had to see each other again and she could concentrate on getting ready for Finals.

Tomorrow she'd talk to the real-estate agent helping her find the right property to buy. So far she hadn't found the exact thing she wanted. Maybe something else had just been listed on the market. Whether something turned up or not, she'd go on her last four-state circuit of rodeos starting with South Dakota, then Wyoming, Colorado and Oklahoma.

After that she'd come home for three more rodeos in Texas before she left for Las Vegas. Once Finals were over, she'd buy a place to get her new training business started. With the decision made about Cy, she turned on her side. But her mind wouldn't shut off. Being in his arms, being kissed with such hunger, had changed her.

Upset with herself, she turned on the other side. When sleep didn't come, she slid out of bed to get her laptop off the table. The latest scores of her competitors would be listed. Cynthia Lyman from Tombstone, Arizona, was the barrel racer to beat. She'd made the most money for the year, and her last winning time was 13.77.

Kellie needed to do better than that in order to come in first. Her time in Bandera was 14.10. Though she came in second, it wasn't good enough. Once she reached Las Vegas, she'd be competing for ten nights and had to nail those barrels with consistently low scores in the 13s. Focus was everything.

After reading the latest news, she went to her blog. Once she'd thanked people in a general message after reading the latest entries, she posted her schedule of

events for the next seven weeks and promised to add to her blog between each rodeo.

Eventually she grew tired and put her laptop on the floor before succumbing to sleep. When morning came, she was surprised to discover she'd slept in until nine. She couldn't remember the last time she'd done that. Emotional exhaustion had to account for it.

Was Cy back?

With her heart in her throat, she showered and dressed in riding clothes and boots. She ran a brush through her hair and put on lipstick before hurrying downstairs.

"Good morning, Ms. Parrish."

Her spirits plummeted to see a dark blond Ranger wearing a polo shirt and jeans seated at the table with his laptop while he drank coffee. He was a close friend of Cy's.

"Good morning. You must be Luckey."

"That's right."

"I take it C—Ranger Vance hasn't come home yet."

"Nope. He's still out working."

She bit her lip. "Have you heard from him?"

"Not yet."

Good grief. What was wrong with her? He wasn't about to discuss Ranger business with her. "I'm going to make breakfast. Would you like some?"

"Sounds good."

"Cy loves bacon and eggs." Cy's name rattled off her tongue. She could have kicked herself for using it.

Luckey's brown eyes smiled. "I think that's an all-around favorite." He didn't miss a thing. Of course he

didn't. He was one of the Famous Four she'd heard mention of on the news.

"Good." She got to work and whipped up some biscuits to go with them. Before long they sat across the table from each other while they ate.

"If I'd known that house-sitting Cy's wife was going to come with these perks, I'd volunteer more often."

She shook her head. "Once he catches the stalker, he probably won't be able to live down this fake marriage."

"Cy's a brilliant tactician. That fake marriage caught the first stalker before any of us could blink. It won't be long before he brings the other one into custody. In case you weren't aware, the captain gave the assignment to him because he knew he was the right man for the job."

Kellie knew that already.

"However, I'd like you to know that any of us would have been happy to take your case on after watching you in the Bandera Rodeo."

Luckey was a charmer and very attractive. "You could have no idea how grateful I am for all your help." She got up to pour him another cup of coffee. "I happen to know you were on watch all night long and must be exhausted. If you want to stretch out on the hide-a-bed in the living room, please go ahead while I wash the dishes."

He didn't get up. "If I lie down, then I'll go to sleep. That's a no-no on the job. I'm better off sitting here talking to you."

While she loaded the dishwasher, she asked the first question to pop into her head. "What made you go into law enforcement?"

"I wanted to be a Texas Ranger from the first time I saw a troop of them riding their horses in an Austin parade. I was just a little guy. When I told my dad, he said that we in the Davis family descended from a real Texas Ranger living back in the 1800s. After he showed me my great-great-grandfather's picture, that did it. I was going to be just like him."

"That's a darling story."

His chuckle filled the kitchen.

"Are you married, Luckey?"

"Divorced."

Kellie frowned. "I'm sorry. I shouldn't have asked."

"It's all right. My ex-wife didn't find my occupation darling."

No. She wouldn't. No woman *would* who wanted her husband with her every night of her life. "But if she married you—"

"She thought she could handle it."

With that response, Kellie felt as if someone had just walked over her grave.

He cocked his head. "How come you're not married?"

"I've been too busy chasing a dream."

"And thrilling crowds," he added.

Her mouth broke into a smile. "You're full of it, Ranger Davis."

"I couldn't agree more" came a familiar male voice from the living room. She lifted her eyes in time to see Cy, who walked into the kitchen looking wonderful even though he was tired and needed a shave. How long

had he been listening to their conversation? At the sight of him, her heart knocked against her ribs.

She smoothed her palms over her hips. "There's more breakfast if you want some."

"Don't mind if I do." He caught a chair with his boot and sat down by Luckey. If he had any news about the stalker, he wasn't ready to share it with her.

"I didn't know your wife was such a great cook, Cy. Try the biscuits. They're sensational with strawberry jam."

"Yeah?" The two men glanced at each other. Kellie could tell streams of unspoken messages were passing between them.

She poured a cup of coffee for Cy and placed a plate of food in front of him along with utensils. "There's more where this came from."

"Bless you," he murmured, eyeing her with a look that sent coils of heat through her body.

"I'm sure you two have a lot to talk about, so I'm going upstairs. Thank you for watching over me, Ranger Davis."

"It was my pleasure."

Kellie darted out of the kitchen and hurried upstairs. When she reached her room, she fell onto the bed, so relieved Cy was all right she cried tears of happiness into her pillow. Taking a deep breath, she reached for her phone. No call from the stalker. There was only one message. It came from her parents. She should have phoned them last night before she'd gone to sleep.

Without wasting more time, she called them and brought them up-to-date on what was going on. Later

in the day she and Cy would drive out to the ranch to exercise the horses. At least that was her plan, but it all depended on him.

"How did the search go?"

Cy looked at Luckey while he ate. "I don't even know where to begin. It curdled my blood when we entered the town house opposite this one on the other side of the fence. According to the landlord, a married couple named Michael and Julie Sanders signed a year's lease in February. When the landlord was shown a picture, he identified Dan as the husband."

"Good grief!"

"No one was home. When we searched the upstairs, we found that the bedroom overlooking Kellie's garage had been made into a shrine. Her pictures were plastered all over the walls and ceiling. Hundreds of them." It had been a nightmarish experience for Cy.

"We found camera equipment and half a dozen guns along with a ton of ammo. One of the rifles has a high-powered scope and was set by the screened window he'd left open. All the weapons are loaded. There's duct tape, pepper spray, handcuffs, ether, everything used in their other murders.

"In the master bedroom Vic found that a part of the closet contained men's clothes. The other half held women's suits and jackets. The upstairs bathroom was filled with makeup and wigs.

"Just yesterday Vic had questioned the owner of a local theater costume shop in town. He remembered selling a lot of women's makeup, including a brown and

blond wig, to a man who said he needed them for a play he was producing. When Vic showed him the picture, the owner identified him immediately. The date of the purchase was the first of February."

Luckey shook his head. "That was right before they signed the lease."

"Yup. Those perverts have been holed up there all this time, eying Kellie's every move." Cy hissed the words. "While Denny held down the fort, Dan followed Kellie around the circuit. We found a motorcycle in the garage, so he's out somewhere either on foot or in another vehicle, maybe even a motorcycle."

"No doubt they're responsible for a slug of unsolved armed robberies here in Austin to finance their operation."

Cy's jaw hardened. "We fully expected Dan to walk in on us. When he didn't show up, we left and ordered the other condo renters on both sides of the alley to vacate the premises until further notice. We've organized the crew to stake out his place. After his last phone message to Kellie, my gut tells me he's going to make his move when he gets back from wherever he's been. I'll be his first target. I know how his mind works. He's planning to take me out with the rifle, then he'll break in here for Kellie."

"What do you want me to do?"

"Get some sleep on the hide-a-bed because I'm going to need you later." He got up from the table. "I'll be upstairs catching some sleep myself while I wait for a signal from Kit, who's heading the crew."

"Kit's outside?"

"Yup. TJ wanted the best fresh body to head the stakeout. I told him I wanted Kit. Vic has gone home to get some sleep. After I explain to Kellie what's happening, I'll be in the guest bedroom. She's free to roam around the house, but I don't want her leaving for her parents' ranch today. That will have to wait."

He reached for another tasty biscuit and popped the whole thing into his mouth before taking the stairs two at a time. "Kellie?" Cy knocked on her door.

Before long she opened it. He could see her laptop open, lying on the bed she'd made. She was so beautiful to him, he swallowed hard. When he thought of all the pictures smeared over the walls and ceiling in the other condo, rage for the maniacs who'd been lying in wait for her for almost a year threatened to take over.

"Luckey's asleep downstairs, but we need to talk. Shall we do it in here or in the guest bedroom?"

"Here is fine. Go ahead and use that chair." She walked over to the bed and sat on the side. He brought the chair around so they were facing each other. A quick glance around the room with its piles of soft, colorful pillows on the bed and comfortable accents around the room proved to him a very feminine woman lived inside the cowgirl.

Cy leaned forward with his hands clasped between his legs. "We've tracked down your stalker to his lair. He's not there at the moment. As we speak, a crew from the department has his place surrounded. I don't know how long it will be before he returns. If it extends into days, we'll deal with it. What you need to know is that you're safe as long as you stay in this condo."

She nodded. "I'll phone Dad and ask him to work the horses."

"Good. You're free to move around the condo. I'm going to catch some sleep in the guest bedroom, but I'll be leaving the door open. If there's any activity at all, someone will phone me and Luckey, so you're not to worry about anything. Keep your phone right with you. If the stalker calls, I want you to come and wake me before you answer it. Turn on the speaker and keep him on as long as you can."

"Okay." She stirred restlessly. "I-is he close by?" Her voice was full of fear.

What to say that wouldn't alarm her...? "Yes, but we have everything under control."

"I know that," she whispered and got off the bed to walk around. "What if he has a gun?"

"It won't matter. He'll be surrounded."

Her hands formed fists. "But it *does* matter. Even Texas Rangers with all the protection available have been known to get injured, or worse..."

"That's not going to happen."

Her eyes blazed a hot blue. "He's out to kill you for arresting his brother."

He got to his feet. "I won't give him the chance."

"But if you get shot, it'll be my fault. I couldn't bear it if anything happened to you."

Cy could have sworn that was her heart talking. When he'd agreed to take her case, he'd felt an attraction that had been growing so deep and fast, he didn't recognize himself anymore. TJ had warned him about walking that thin line. Unfortunately he'd already crossed it

after meeting her in Bandera and would have pursued her, case or no case.

Get out of her room, Ranger Vance. Now.

"I assure you everything's going to be fine." He put the chair back by the window and left for the other bedroom.

After putting his gun under the pillow, he took off his cowboy boots and lay down, desperately needing a couple hours of sleep. It seemed as if no sooner had his head touched the pillow than he heard a phone ringing. He glimpsed Kellie's face through his eyelids and bolted upright.

She answered the phone and turned on the speaker. "Why do you keep calling me?"

"I like to hear the fear in your voice."

"You like to make people afraid?"

"Why not?"

"That's sick. You're sick, sick, sick!" she yelled into the phone. That brought Luckey from downstairs. Both men listened while she got him going. *Keep it up, Kellie. Stick it to him where it hurts.*

"Does your mother know what kind of person you've turned into?"

Bingo.

"What mother? She didn't want us. We were orphans, but you wouldn't know anything about it with your rich daddy and mommy. You're going to pay for not going out with me. But first I'm going to finish off that husband of yours."

"You don't know who you're dealing with!" Kellie's

lethal tone lifted the hairs off Cy's neck. "Try to hurt him and you'll wish you'd never been born!"

Luckey flashed Cy a secret smile before a maniacal laugh came through the phone. He muttered several obscenities and clicked off.

Kellie looked at Cy. "Did I keep him on long enough?"

"It was perfect. He's ready to explode. That's what I've been waiting for. Let's all go downstairs." He glanced at his watch. To his shock he'd slept seven hours. It was already five thirty in the evening. After putting on his boots, he reached for his gun and followed them out of the room.

"Would you gentlemen like some iced tea?" She'd already gone into the kitchen.

"We'd love it," Luckey answered for them because Cy had made a detour to the living room to phone Kit.

"Any sign of him yet?"

"No."

"He just made another harassing call to Kellie. She pressed his buttons. I think he's going to make something happen as soon as he returns to the town house."

"I'll let you know the minute he shows up. Anything you need and we're ready."

"I owe you for this, Kit."

Cy hung up and walked back in the kitchen. Trust Luckey to get Kellie laughing about something. His friend had a way. "What's so funny?" He'd trained his eyes on her, unable to look anywhere else.

Before she could answer, Cy's phone rang. It was Kit. He turned his back to her. "What's up?"

"The second we got off the phone, a woman with

neck-length brown hair pulled into a stall driving a used blue Sentra sedan. She got out wearing a business suit and heels and has just let herself in the condo."

"We've got him!" Cy blurted with elation. It felt as if he'd been waiting forever for this moment. "He'll be watching from the upstairs window with the rifle. I'll give him ten minutes before I back out of the garage."

"We're on it."

He clicked off and turned to Luckey, who was drinking a glass of iced tea. Kellie was in the background cooking tacos for dinner. "This is it," he muttered. "You know what to do."

"Yup."

Cy hurried upstairs and put on his bulletproof vest. Over it he wore a gray hoodie, and he went back down to the kitchen. "Be sure and save me some dinner."

Kellie's eyes look haunted. "You're leaving now?" He heard the wobble in her voice. "You haven't even drunk your iced tea."

"Sorry. I've got some business to do, but Luckey will enjoy it. Remember he's here to protect you. See you soon."

He opened the kitchen door to the garage and closed it behind him. Once he was in the Subaru SUV, he sat there to synchronize his time to the second with Kit and the crew. He hoped that once he used the remote to open the garage door, the sound would alert the stalker that he was leaving. That was the signal for the crew to move in.

The plan was to back out slowly, giving Dan time to make his best shot.

Five, four, three, two, one.

Up went the garage door. Cy started the engine and let it idle for a minute to draw out the stalker. Then he started backing into the alley. At the point where he turned the car, he braked and shut off the motor. In the split second it took to open the door and roll to the ground, he heard three loud shots fired in succession, shattering the side windows.

Some of the glass grazed his neck and cheek. Moments passed as he stayed down and let the other Rangers do their jobs. Sirens blared as police cars and an ambulance converged in the alley. He got out of the car and saw the street now looked like a war zone. The paramedics ran over to him while he got to his feet and brushed off the bits of glass, but he was waiting for the call from Kit.

When it came, they were the sweetest words he'd ever heard. "Your plan worked perfectly. This stalker was caught in the act. He twisted and screamed while we cuffed him. Now he's on his way to join his twin."

Cy drank in gulps of air. "Thank God."

He couldn't wait to tell Kellie, but he had to ride in the ambulance first while they tended to his wounds, which were superficial. After he'd been taken to the ER, TJ was there to greet him. While Cy sat on the end of the examining table as the doctor put some small bandages over the cuts on his neck and cheek, the captain's eyes played over him with grave concern.

"That was a hell of a thing you did out there tonight, offering yourself up as the sacrifice."

"I was wearing my vest."

"He could have shot your head off."

"I ducked. It was all planned out."

"If you ever try a stunt like that again…"

"You told me this was a high-profile case and you needed it solved ASAP. I just wanted to make sure those two lunatics are put away forever. Trying to take me out added another lifetime sentence to their list of heinous crimes."

After the doctor left the cubicle, the captain said, "I phoned Ms. Parrish and her parents and told them the siege was over. They're probably at her condo right now celebrating."

Cy would have liked to tell her the news himself, but he'd had to follow protocol and get checked over first. "Their relief must be making new people out of them."

His boss nodded. "Thanks to you she's free to live her life fully and win that championship in December. Vic got on the phone to the agents back east. Once again the fame of the Four is going out over the networks for catching two of the vilest criminals wanted by the FBI from coast to coast."

"I'm thinking there may be other murders they've committed. With them both in custody, who knows what information we can get out of them. Hopefully, this will lead to solving some cold cases, too."

TJ flashed him a rare smile. "That's for the detectives to follow up on. What matters is that it took the Texas Rangers to solve this case. Something tells me we'll be hearing from the governor soon. *Again.*" He patted Cy's shoulder. "You've done great work," he said in a quiet voice. "I'm glad you didn't become an attorney."

"Amen," Cy whispered. Otherwise he would never have met Kellie. "Don't forget it took the whole team, TJ. But thanks for going along with my unorthodox plan. I believe that was the word you used."

"You flushed them out with your clever sting in record time. According to your buddies, this marriage seems to have agreed with you. What do *you* say?"

"The jury is out where that's concerned."

He nodded. "Vic's waiting in the lounge. When you're ready, he's going to drive you home. Take the day off tomorrow to recover before you write up all the details of the case. That's an order."

"Yes, sir."

After the captain left, Cy got off the table and reached for his hoodie and vest. He found Vic and they walked out to his friend's car. "I appreciate the lift home."

En route to Cy's house, Vic glanced at him several times. "The captain was right. You're damn lucky to have walked away from that shooting."

"If you're going to tell me you wouldn't have done the same thing, I wouldn't believe you. After Dan made his last harassing call to Kellie earlier today, I knew I was his next target. Which means the best move was to play it out on my own terms. While he was concentrated on me, the crew closed in, taking him by surprise."

They grabbed some burgers at a local drive-through, then headed for Vic's house in South Austin. Cy had chosen to live in a secluded neighborhood hidden away in a wooded area. His rustic lodge-style home with exposed wood appealed to him for several reasons. Besides a loft where he had his office, the open floor plan

was dominated by a cathedral ceiling with tons of natural light.

When they reached the entrance, it dawned on him he hadn't stepped foot in his three-bedroom house for over a week. Normally after being away on a case, home sounded good to him while he relaxed. But tonight he knew something was missing even before he got out of the car. He knew what it was. Kellie wouldn't be here when he walked inside.

Over the past seven days, they'd spent hours together. When they had to be apart, she'd been constantly on his mind. If it weren't so late, he'd drive over to her town house right now with the excuse that he wanted to collect anything he'd left while working the case.

But before that, he needed a shower and a shave.

Vic turned to him. "You look like death. Go to bed and we'll talk in the morning."

Cy opened the door. "I couldn't have done this without you. I owe you big-time."

"I'll remember that when the captain gives me my next case."

"Good night, Vic." He shut the door and went in the house carrying his vest and pullover. Without turning on lights, he climbed the stairs to his bedroom in the loft located across from his office. He plunked his things in the chair and moved over to the bed to pull off his boots.

The moonlight coming through the window caused the gold band on his ring finger to gleam. He needed to remove it before he went into headquarters in the morning. The boss had told him to take the day off. For the

first time since joining the Rangers, the thought of nothing to do all day long sounded like a death sentence.

A whole day without Kellie? He wouldn't know what to do with himself. The captain's question went round in his head.

According to your buddies, this marriage seems to have agreed with you. What do you say?

Cy threw back his head, afraid to answer it out loud. If he did that, it would be tantamount to a confession that could change his whole life. Especially if Kellie didn't answer it the same way.

Chapter Eight

Ten after midnight. No phone call from Cy. No door-bell ringing.

Kellie's parents had left her town house at ten thirty. They'd begged her to go home with them, but she'd told them she was exhausted. After the exciting phone call from the captain of the Rangers, who praised Cy's hero-ism for leading the team that caught both stalkers, she preferred to go straight to bed. She would drive out to the ranch in the morning.

Luckey had stayed with her until her parents arrived. He'd received a call from one of the other Rangers let-ting him know Cy had been taken to the hospital but his injuries were minimal.

She didn't believe that for a minute, and the fact that he hadn't tried to make contact convinced her some-thing was seriously wrong. She'd heard the shots and learned what had happened from Cy's superior. But he was trained to gloss over information he didn't want her to know. Luckey had prevented her from going out in back while it was still a crime scene. She recognized

he was only doing his job, but it killed her that she had to wait for information that came in bits and pieces.

That was the part of the exclusive Ranger brotherhood that bothered her. Surely Cy had to know she was anxious to hear his voice and make sure he was all right, even if she couldn't see him.

Restless and worried, Kellie paced the floor and then sank down on the couch. Cy's hide-a-bed was still in the living room. He would have to come back to get it, but obviously not tonight.

She glanced down at the rings. He'd be taking those back, too. But she felt as if they'd become a part of her. She would sleep wearing them one last time.

At one in the morning, she took some ibuprofen for a headache and went upstairs to bed. The painkiller helped her to fall asleep, but when she awakened Saturday morning, she realized she'd been crying. She'd had nightmares.

Because of her ordeal, her parents had worried she wouldn't sleep well and might have bad dreams. But oddly enough, it wasn't the stalkers who had filled her mind. Throughout the night she'd wandered endlessly in her search for Cy, unable to find him anywhere.

Thankful to be awake, she got out of bed to shower and wash her hair. If Cy came over this morning, she wanted to be ready for him. After putting on a clean pair of jeans and a plaid Western shirt, she applied some makeup and pulled on her cowboy boots before going downstairs.

While she was in the kitchen pouring herself a glass

of orange juice, her phone rang. Fighting her disappointment that it wasn't Cy, she reached for it. "Mom?"

"Honey? Turn on the news. We'll talk after it's over."

Taking her juice with her, she hurried into the living room and turned on the TV to one of the local stations. Between swallows she watched the breaking news.

"For those of you who've just joined us, last evening our own Texas Rangers finished up a sting that ended in the arrest of two killers on the FBI's most wanted list. Three brutal unsolved murders stretching from Illinois to Tennessee and South Carolina might have turned into four if it hadn't been for our state's bravest. We're standing by for a message from the governor."

Kellie sank down on the couch to listen.

"Today is one of the finest days for the Rangers, who prevented the murder of one of our celebrated Austin citizens, Kellie Parrish. She's the twenty-five-year-old barrel racer who will be competing in the National Finals in Las Vegas in December. She has been stalked by identical twin brothers whose killing spree started four years ago.

"The same rangers who brought down the drug cartel here six months ago took the lead in the capture of these predators. The criminals' names are being withheld as FBI agents in Illinois, Tennessee and South Carolina are putting all the facts together and notifying family members of the women they'd targeted."

A shiver ran through Kellie. The thought of the poor parents and families of the three women who'd been terrorized and killed brought stabbing pain to her heart. Because of Cy, they could now be provided with an-

swers. But those poor women hadn't been blessed to have Cy protecting them.

Without wasting a breath, she phoned her mother. The minute she heard her voice, she broke down sobbing. "Oh, Mom. Cy is so wonderful." She tried to hold back the sobs, but it was pointless. "I don't want to think what would have happened if he hadn't taken my case."

"Then don't, darling. Have you talked to him since last night?"

"No. He had to go to the hospital last night. Maybe he's still there. I have no idea how serious his injuries were. Even if he's been released, I'm sure he has so much to do."

"I don't wonder. How soon are you coming?"

She wiped her eyes with her other arm and took a fortifying breath. "I—I don't know yet."

"Sitting around waiting to hear from him isn't the answer."

Kellie jumped to her feet, hurt by her comment. "What do you mean?"

"The two of you have been living in close quarters throughout your ordeal, pretending to be married. Now that the threat has gone, I'm not at all surprised you miss having him at your side on a constant basis. He's the stuff heroes are made of. Heavens, I'm a little in love with him myself. Please don't tell your father."

"Oh, Mom." She let out a half laugh because her mother knew her so well.

"I'm not surprised you've lost your head, but you've got a championship to win, remember? Ranger Vance isn't going anywhere. Give it time."

Kellie hated it when her mother was right.

"Thanks for the talk. I should be at the ranch within the hour."

After she got off the phone, her mood was completely different. She rushed upstairs for her purse and came back down to write a note at the kitchen table.

Dear Cy,
Words can't express what I'm feeling, so I'm not going to try. I forgive you if you let yourself in to get the rest of your things while I'm not here. The governor gave you a ringing endorsement today. Congratulations. Just know that you will always have my undying gratitude. You saved my life. What greater service can one human do for another?
Kellie

She read it over several times, wondering if she needed to change anything. But no, it said what she wanted to say. Unlike the piece she'd written on the blog about their marriage, this one wasn't over-the-top. Viewing it objectively, she felt she'd hit just the right tone.

Without giving herself a chance to change her mind, she removed the rings and left them on top of the note. After grabbing the extra garage-door opener from the drawer, she hurried out to the garage and climbed in her car.

When she backed out, she saw no sign of the crime scene from last night. But it was out here that the stalker

had fired on Cy. Another shudder left her weak before she pulled herself together and started for the ranch.

During the drive, half a dozen messages were left on her phone. She knew she would be inundated by good wishes and concern from her friends for a while, but she wasn't ready to talk to anyone about this except her parents. Then she would take separate rides on Trixie and Starburst, exactly what she needed to sort out her head.

Her left hand gripped the steering wheel. It looked bare without the rings. *How do they feel, Mrs. Vance?* he'd asked, staring at her with his gorgeous dark blue eyes.

They'd felt natural.

Without them, without him, nothing felt natural.

Another two miles and she pulled up in front of the ranch house. Her phone rang again. She glanced at the caller ID and rushed to answer it. "Cy?"

If he hadn't known how she really felt about him, he did now.

"Good morning, Kellie."

He sounded wonderfully alive. She gripped the phone tighter. "Are you still in the hospital?"

"I'm at headquarters. Last night I was only there for a few minutes to have a couple of tiny cuts treated before going home."

"I'm so thankful you weren't seriously injured." Her voice shook. "I heard three shots."

"It's over now." It was obvious he didn't want to talk about it. "If you're still at your town house, I'd like to come over and get my stuff. Vic's coming with me.

We'll take out the hide-a-bed so you can have your house back."

Kellie moaned. If she hadn't left so soon…

"I'm sorry, Cy. I'm out at my parents' house. You still have a door key, right?"

"Yes."

"I can imagine how busy you must be, so feel free to drive over and let yourself in."

After a slight pause, he said, "Sounds good. I'll leave the key and your garage-door opener on the table."

Her eyes closed tightly. She'd purposely left the rings and the note in case something like this happened. "Cy? I want to see you again to thank you. Is there a night you could come over and I'll cook dinner for you?"

"You don't need to do that."

"There's every need. You saved my life."

"Tell you what. The captain has a new case for me. I need to take a look at it. When I know my schedule, I'll call to let you know what night would be good."

So now that he didn't have to guard her, he wasn't planning on taking her to his sister's engagement party on Sunday evening. Already he'd been put to work on another dangerous assignment. That was his job.

For one week out of her life, the two of them had been inseparable. But it was over. He'd never again be exclusively hers. How was she going to bear it?

"I hope you can make it Monday or Tuesday. Cody and I will be leaving for South Dakota on Wednesday."

Another silence before he said, "How long will you be gone?"

The breath froze in her lungs. "Seven weeks."

"Seven?" He sounded surprised. "Without a break?"

"After I leave Oklahoma I'm doing three rodeos throughout Texas with Sally and Manny. It'll be November before I return home." She stared blindly into space waiting for a response.

"If I can't make it either of those nights, will you give me a rain check?"

Kellie had to brace herself to handle the hurt. "Do you even have to ask? Ranger Vance will always have a standing invitation to my home."

"That's nice to hear."

She could hardly swallow. "I'm so glad you're all right. Take care of yourself, Cy. The Famous Four wouldn't be the same without you."

Enveloped in pain, Kellie clicked off before she said too much. Then she turned off her cell. She was glad he hadn't learned she was still at the condo earlier waiting around for him.

The remark her mother had made during their phone call had gotten her out of the house in time to save her from making the biggest mistake of her life!

CY PULLED THE van in front of Kellie's town house with a grimace. "Let's get this done fast." He didn't wait for Vic. After he got out and opened the side door to accommodate the hide-a-bed, he headed for her front door. The key was on his ring.

Vic followed him inside. They made quick work of getting the couch out to the van. In a few minutes he'd restored the living room to its former order. "I'll run upstairs to grab my laptop and any clothes I left."

"While you do that, I'll take down the camera from the garage."

"Good. Be back in a second."

When he came down with his bag, he went into the bathroom to pack the toiletries he'd left. All was done except to leave the key and garage-door opener.

Cy walked into the kitchen and put both items on the table. That was when his eyes were drawn to the diamond and wedding band he'd given her. They were sitting on a note she'd penned. A vise seemed to close around his chest.

He pocketed the rings before reading it. The last lines stood out. *Just know that you will always have my undying gratitude. You saved my life. What greater service can one human do for another?*

Kellie had written this before he'd phoned her. Now that the threat to her life was over, she hadn't been able to remove the rings fast enough. She hadn't mentioned tomorrow night's party, not even a hint that she still wanted to go with him.

So what in the hell did those kisses mean the other night when they'd both come close to losing control? Gratitude had nothing to do with the way she'd melted in his arms, kissing him until he felt immortal. She'd been on fire for him. That wasn't something you could hide.

Vic joined him. "What's going on, Cy? You haven't been the same since you walked into headquarters this morning. If I didn't know better I'd say you've seen a ghost."

Cy lifted his head. "TJ was right. He warned me

that pretending to be married meant I'd be walking a very thin line. At the time I didn't realize how much truth he spoke." *Or how much I wanted it to be real.* He turned to his friend. "That's why *he's* the captain. Let's get out of here."

He walked out of the house, making sure the front door was locked before he closed it. When they got in the van, Vic turned to him. "Come on, Cy. It's me you're talking to. Something's eating you alive. What is it?"

Cy tossed his head back. "I think I've been played."

"By whom?"

"Who do you think?"

"You couldn't mean Kellie."

"Until I read her note, I didn't think it was possible, either. Gratitude is the last thing I want from her."

Vic cocked his head. "I take it you two crossed the line."

"Only one time. After Dan threatened to kill her horse, she fell apart and I comforted her. Things got out of control for a few minutes. That's all."

"Apparently it was enough to turn you inside out."

"Never again," he vowed through gritted teeth.

"Listen to me, Cy. You're too close to the situation and not thinking straight. Try looking at this from her point of view. Before my wife died, I learned a lot from living with her. Not everything is what it seems to be. Kellie had to have feelings for you or she wouldn't have kissed you. But don't be upset because she's grateful to you for saving her life. Both emotions can coexist in the same universe."

He took a sharp intake of breath. "You saw the wedding rings on the table."

"Now that I think about it, I see you're not wearing your wedding band, either. How come?"

"You know damn well why."

"Can't you believe she took her rings off for the same reason?"

"But did she?"

"Only you can answer that question. Has she left you with no hope?"

Cy rubbed his eyes. "It's not like that. She said she wanted to cook dinner for me. I knew it was just her gratitude talking. But the other night I told her my sister's engagement party is on Sunday night. Since I didn't dare leave Kellie alone, I asked her if she'd be willing to go with me and she said yes. But now that the case has been solved, she didn't—"

"Didn't what?" Vic challenged. "Tell you she still wanted to go with you?"

"No," Cy muttered.

"Did you ask her if she still wanted to go? Maybe she was waiting for you to bring it up. You've been joined at the hip for a week in the most dangerous kind of situation, but now that you no longer have to pretend you're married, I'd say she's feeling a damn sight vulnerable... and probably nervous."

He flung his head around. "Nervous—of me?"

"You've been in charge all this time, dictating every move. Maybe she fears *she's* been played."

"*Hell—*"

"Yup. And hell is where you're going to stay till you get this thing straightened out."

Stirred up by Vic's perceptive comments, he started the engine and they took off for the warehouse at head-quarters. Once they'd dropped things off, Vic left for home while Cy walked through to his office.

Hell wasn't the place he wanted to be. He sat down at his desk and phoned Kellie. No doubt she was out riding and it would probably go through to her voice mail. If so, he'd wait until he got a live response, even if it took until he went to bed.

In the meantime he opened the file folder on the new case TJ had given him.

Fidel Ravelo is wanted in connection with the armed robbery of approximately $7 million from a security company in North Austin, Texas, that took place two years ago. He allegedly took three security employees hostage at gunpoint and handcuffed, bound and injected them with an unknown, nonlethal substance to disable them further. The FBI is offering a reward of up to $1,000,000 for information leading to Ravelo's capture. He's believed to be in Venezuela, but re-cent rumors say he's been seen in Brownsville, where he has ties to family.

After studying the specifics, he'd start by talking to the security employees. Maybe one of them could recall a detail that hadn't been included in the report. But he couldn't do any more work today. The captain had told

him to go home. Cy decided to take his advice because he could no longer concentrate.

KELLIE FINISHED SHAMPOOING Trixie and rinsed her off. After putting a little conditioner on her tail and mane, she brushed them to make them silky. Her last action was to use a damp cloth to rub her palomino's face. Then she gave her a kiss and some Uncle Jimmy's Squeezy Buns for a treat. She and Starburst chomped them down.

"There! Now you two look beautiful and I'm sure you feel much better." Both horses stood in the late-afternoon sun while she towel-dried them so they wouldn't catch cold. On Monday the vet would come out to look them over and check their hooves before the trip to South Dakota.

"All right, girls. It's time for dinner." She grasped their lead ropes and walked them to their stalls inside the barn. After removing their bath halters, they could eat from the hay nets and drink water.

The exercise had been good for her, reminding her these horses were her children and her passport to a championship. "See you tomorrow."

She could hear nickering and walked to Paladin's stall. Only two days ago Cy had ridden him. The memory of that heavenly afternoon made her ache for him. "You want a treat, too?" Kellie fed him the last of her horsey treats and walked out to clean up the grooming equipment. Once she'd coiled the hose, she headed back to the ranch house.

Today she'd wondered if she would make it through

to evening without Cy, but here she was still walking around. And thanks to him, still alive. Somehow she had to get beyond all this. Earlier in the day her father had told her this was a time for debriefing. By working with her horses, it would help put the horror of her experience behind her. The passage of time would do the rest, but she couldn't hurry the process.

Her mind thought about Cy. Every time he solved a case for the agency, how did he put the horror behind *him*?

She let out an anguished sigh. When she looked to the sun getting ready to set, she noticed the sky was shot through with pinks and yellows. The same sky Cy might be looking at tonight. How long would it take her to stop missing him? Was he missing her right now? Had the magic between them been a figment of her imagination? Those moments in his arms were real enough.

If he were her husband, how would she deal with their separations, knowing that every time he left the house it was possible he might not come back? Under those conditions, how long could the magic last?

"Not very long," she whispered to the air. Kellie didn't have the right stuff to live with a hero like Cy. That was what he was. It took a special type of woman who could compartmentalize her feelings in order to deal with that kind of stress on a day-to-day basis.

Once she reached the ranch house, she went upstairs to her old bedroom to shower. Since she had no appetite, she got ready for bed and reached for her laptop. It was time to draft a disclaimer to put on her blog. She'd

known this day would have to come. Who knew Cy would solve her case this fast?

Kellie got to work on it. When she'd finished, she read it over half a dozen times, but she needed another opinion before posting it. Since it was only eight thirty, she reached for her cell phone to call her friend Kathie. Seven messages were waiting for her, including one from Kathie. It wasn't until now she remembered that she'd turned off her phone. The last one was from Cy. He'd called hours ago. She couldn't believe it.

Her hand trembled as she pressed the button and listened. "Kellie? Call me ASAP."

The urgency in his deep voice gave her heart the greatest workout of its life. He'd solved her case and was already working on another one. Why was he calling her now? Had he left something at the town house he'd forgotten and didn't want to be accused of breaking in to get it?

If she didn't phone him back, she'd never know the answer to that question. His call gave her the excuse to talk to him again. Feeling light-headed from emotions bombarding her body, she pressed the digit for his number.

He picked up on the second ring. "Kellie?"

"Hi." She was trying to catch her breath.

"Thanks for calling me back."

"I didn't know you'd phoned until a minute ago. I've been out shampooing my horses and just finished."

"How lucky for them."

She chuckled in spite of her angst. "They love it and they were so good for me. They didn't move."

"That doesn't surprise me. They love you. Horses aren't that different from humans. Rosco P. likes to do tricks for me."

"Rosco P.?" Kellie was charmed down to her toenails by the revelation. "Was he the horse you rode in the Bandera parade?"

"That's right."

"I didn't know that was his name. Sounds like the bumbling character from the old *Dukes of Hazzard* television show with Boss Hogg."

"The very one."

"I adored that series. The way those brothers drove that car around, driving the Boss crazy, was hilarious."

"I got a kick out of it, too."

"What kind of tricks can you get your horse to do?"

"He can bow and do the Spanish walk."

"You're kidding!"

"Nope. Most of the time I use a ball to play with him. For incentive I feed him Rounders Molasses treats."

"Starburst likes those, too." Kellie almost said that they'd have to get their horses together, but she stopped herself in time. "Cy—I'm probably keeping you from your work. Did you forget something at the town house? Is that why you called me?"

"No. I phoned to ask if you want to go to my sister's engagement party tomorrow night. We'd talked about it before, but that was when I was protecting you. Now that the threat is over, we can go without worrying about our undercover lie."

She pressed a hand to her mouth to stifle a cry of joy. He still wanted her to go with him.

"I'd like that very much."

"If it works for you, I'll pick you up at your town house at six thirty. It's a semidressy affair."

"Thanks for telling me. I live in cowboy boots and forget they're not suitable for every occasion."

"Understood. I know you have questions about how everything went down last night. I'll do my best to answer them. See you tomorrow night. I look forward to being with you again, Kellie."

Her pulse raced. "Me, too. And you're right. I'd like a little closure. Good night." *I want to see how serious your injuries are.* She hung up in a daze, suddenly motivated because she knew she'd be with Cy tomorrow night.

In the morning she'd clean her one-stall horse trailer and living quarters to get it ready for her trip around the circuit. Kellie had to put fresh feed and hay on board, plus all her gear and plastic barrels.

She had nine or ten different bits and took them with her along with several pairs of reins and halters. In her dressage training routine she felt snaffles were the best, plus the square mouthpiece O-ring, so her horse's mouth would stay soft and undamaged.

Once the vet came out to check her horses, she and Cody would be ready to go. He and his fiancée would be over on Wednesday to load Starburst and they'd all drive in tandem. What she'd give if Cy were in a different line of work and could travel to the various rodeos with her.

You're crazy, Kellie.

One phone call from him and her head was in the

clouds again. She couldn't afford to forget what he did for a living. He'd dodged a bullet while protecting her, but what about his next case, and the one after that?

By the time she'd given herself another talking-to, a great deal of her excitement had dissipated. A night out with Cy would be wonderful, but she'd pay a price. She just knew it! But it was too late to cancel on him, and she didn't want to.

After turning out the light, she crawled under the covers with her mind made up that it would be their final goodbye.

Before she left for South Dakota she'd post her blog piece. But Kathie deserved an explanation over the phone first. She'd been hurt that Kellie hadn't told her about her marriage. That was something she could fix right now.

Kellie hadn't really been in touch with anyone since the stalker first approached her in Oregon. Cy had made up her whole world and still did.

Knowing she wouldn't fall asleep for a long time, she reached for her cell. While they were on the phone, she could run the blog piece by her friend and see if she had any other suggestions before it went out. When Kellie thought about telling everyone she really hadn't gotten married, she felt so hollow inside, she could hardly stand it.

BY SIX ON Sunday evening, Kellie had showered and shampooed her hair. There was enough natural curl that she blow-dried it into a wavy bob with a side part.

Once she'd applied her lipstick in a tangerine frost color she loved, it was time to get dressed.

She had several outfits, but in the end she chose her sleeveless black flared jersey dress with the high rounded neck. Her tiny black-and-gold puffed teardrop earrings went perfectly with it. On her feet she wore black sling-back high heels. Before she left the bedroom, she reached for her black clutch with the gold fastener.

One last look in the mirror and she realized she didn't need any blusher. The temperature she was running did it for her. Kellie would be meeting Cy's family tonight. She needed to look her best for him.

At twenty after six the doorbell rang. Her heart leaped because he was early. She hurried downstairs to let him in. How ironic that only two days ago, Cy had permission to come and go as if he lived here while he carried out his plans to protect her.

When she opened the door, the tall, spectacular-looking male in the midnight-blue suit and lighter blue shirt almost caused her legs to buckle. Kellie had to hang on to the door handle or she would have fallen. She noticed a small bandage on the side of his neck above the collar, but nothing else, thank heaven. He was here—and he was okay.

Chapter Nine

Cy took in the vision before him. Mounted on her palomino, Kellie Parrish in Western attire was a complete knockout. But tonight the champion barrel racer had taken on a different persona. To say she was dazzling in black was an understatement.

She had a glow about her he hadn't seen before now. The stalker brothers had stolen that radiance from her, but now that they'd been caught, she'd been restored to her former self. Her heart was in those blue eyes, and she was looking at him the way she'd done when they'd kissed each other senseless the other night.

"Hi" was all he could say until his breathing returned to normal.

"Hi," she answered in a soft voice. "I'm ready."

"Make sure both doors are locked."

It brought a smile to her face. "I did."

"Sorry. Old habits die hard."

"I forgive you," she murmured as he walked her to his Audi sports car parked in front of the town house. Once he'd started the engine and they were off, she

turned to him. "How long will it take us to get to Dripping Springs?"

"That depends."

"On what?"

"Maybe we'll just drive into the sunset. What would you say to that?"

The blood pounded in her ears. *I'd go anywhere with you.* "I'm not sure your sister would forgive you."

"What if I told you I'm tired of doing my duty?"

He felt her glance. "Your sister isn't a duty."

"True. But the way you're looking tonight, I'm not sure I want to share you with my family. You look stunning, Kellie."

"Thank you," she whispered. "You look better than I feared you would after being sent to the hospital."

He thought he heard a compliment in there somewhere. "I had no choice but to go in the ambulance. Those were the captain's orders. Otherwise I would have come back in the town house to talk to you."

She nodded. "Luckey told me as much."

"Well, Ms. Parrish—we have a half hour of privacy before we reach my parents' home, where you'll be bombarded with questions. Ask me anything you want."

"I want to know how you knew the stalker would come after you in the alley."

"When I realized the stalker had a clear look at your garage in order to take that picture, and to see his brother hauled out to the van in the very same place, I decided he could be hiding out in one of the town houses on either side of the alley. So Vic and I went door to door. We hit the jackpot when we entered the

town house opposite yours through the fence. Those two criminals had been renting it since February."

He heard her gasp. "I don't believe it. All this time?"

"We found enough evidence inside to help the agents in winding up the other murder cases back east." Cy didn't tell her about the shrine. It would horrify her, and she didn't need the added trauma now that they'd been incarcerated. "Dan kept a loaded rifle with a scope by the side of the bedroom window overlooking your garage.

"After he sent you that last phone message about getting rid of your husband, I decided to draw him out. When the team saw Dan return to the town house dressed like a woman, I figured he would make his move against me soon. So I set it up and hoped he'd hear the garage door open. If he hadn't done it when he did, then he would have tried again and again. It was my luck that he was so angry, he took the first chance he got.

"I backed the car out. As soon as I turned the wheels, I knew he'd take a shot if he was going to, so I stopped the car and rolled out to the ground. Those three shots shattered the glass. That was it. The team closed in on Dan, who had no idea they were staking him out, and took him away."

She lowered her head. "You could have been killed so easily."

"No. The setup was on my terms. I knew what I was doing. Those evil twins are going to be sent to prison for life without parole."

"The governor praised you on TV."

"It was all in a day's work."

"Don't be absurd, Cy. What you did was as great as what the Original Forty did when they saved Texas."

"That comparison is way over-the-top. Just remember that saving you was greater, and I couldn't have done it alone."

"But it was all your brainchild. Sometimes you seem bigger than life. I'm in awe of you."

Cy smiled to himself. He'd take that for a start. "It helped that the target of those killers happened to be a woman who's the pride of Texas. You showed courage under fire and stayed in control while they terrorized you. Kind of like the way you handle Trixie when you race into the arena. Thousands of rodeo fans across the country are in awe of you."

"You're never going to let me thank you properly, are you?"

They were driving into Dripping Springs. Cy took the first turnoff and drove to a neighborhood park with a small lake. After pulling to a stop in an area away from other people, he stopped the engine. He undid his seat belt and turned to her, sliding his arm along the back of her seat. "What is your definition of *proper*?"

He waited while she digested his question, then she undid her seat belt. His heart thudded as she launched herself at him, throwing her arms around his neck. She started kissing his face. Every feature. *"This and this and this!"*

Suddenly her mouth reached his and he forgot everything except the thrill of holding her in his arms once more. She was no longer the woman he had to protect. For the first time, he was free to kiss her and show her

what she meant to him without having to hold back his passion. He'd been aching for her since they'd kissed a few days ago.

"I've missed you for the last two nights," he whispered into her shimmering hair. Her fragrance enveloped him.

"It's been hard since you moved out," she admitted. "I know we were only together for a week, but I got used to being with you. To be honest, I feel lost."

"I know the feeling." Cy crushed her mouth again, never wanting this ecstasy to stop. They couldn't get close enough. He would never be able to get enough of her.

"We're going to be late for the party," she struggled to say after he lifted his mouth so she could breathe.

He groaned. "What party?"

"The one I got dressed up for."

"I guess we have to go so I can show you off."

"Does your family know you're coming?"

"I texted them I'd be there."

"Do they know you're bringing someone?"

He cupped her beautiful face in his hands and kissed her thoroughly. "No. It will be fun to surprise them. That is if we make it there."

They gave in to their desires once more before Kellie pulled away from him. "You *have* to go." She moved to her side of the car and fastened her seat belt.

Resigned for the moment that this would have to wait until later, he got the car going and they drove the rest of the way to his parents' home in silence. Before they pulled in the driveway, he saw a dozen cars parked on

both sides of the street. Hurricane lanterns with lighted candles lined the walkway to the front door of the spacious rambler.

"Since the wedding and reception will be held at the church, my folks have gone all out for this party." He turned off the car.

"I'm not surprised. Your sister is their only daughter."

"Beth has been doted on. She came along when my parents didn't think they could have another child."

"My parents had to wait a long time before they got me. How old is she?"

"Twenty-three. She has her degree in English. After New Year's, she'll be teaching at a middle school." He got out of the car and went around to help her out. "I'll tell you a secret. She's afraid of horses. Always has been."

Kellie looked up at him in surprise. "Was she hurt by one?"

"No. But she fell off her mount during a ride when she was little. My dad tried to help her overcome her fear, but she wouldn't do it. After that experience the only time she'd try it was if Dad or I took her on rides on our horses."

"Oh… What a shame. Does her fiancé ride?"

"He tolerates it if he has to."

She smiled. "Can you imagine having to tolerate Rosco P.?"

"No." Kellie was so lovely he lowered his head to kiss her mouth once more. "She and Tom are a good

match," he whispered against her lips before he walked her to the front door and let them into the foyer.

"Well, look who's here—"

Cy might have known his father's older brother would spot them first. "Your mom said you were coming. We've all been waiting for the man whose name has been in the news for the second time this year. Well done, Cy." He gave him a pat on the shoulder before his glance fell on Kellie.

"Uncle Bruce? Allow me to introduce Kellie Parrish. She's—"

"All of Texas knows who she is." His uncle shook her hand, eyeing her in admiration. "It's an honor to meet our state's leading rodeo champion." He looked back at Cy. "And *your* wife, I understand. You always were a dark horse."

"No—" Kellie blurted, darting Cy an anxious glance. *Hell.* "How many people know about that?"

"Everyone at the party." His uncle smiled at Kellie. "My son's wife, Terrie, reads your blog religiously, and the word spread. Come with me. We're all waiting to meet the two celebrities of the evening."

"I'll handle this," Cy whispered to her and put a hand on her back as they walked into the living room. All the chatting ceased, then everyone started clapping. "Sorry about this, Kellie," he said out of the side of his mouth.

"It was inevitable," she whispered back.

The din died down. "Hi, everyone. I didn't expect a greeting like this when it's my sister's engagement party. We don't want to intrude on yours or Tom's happiness, Beth, so let me just explain a few things so you

can all enjoy the rest of the party. I understand you're under the impression that Kellie and I are married. It's not true."

At that remark, expressions sobered. "We had to pretend to be married to smoke out the killer."

"Well, I'll be," one of his aunts exclaimed.

"It turned out there were two of them. Identical twin brothers who'd murdered three other women back east before they targeted Kellie."

Murmurs of horror came from the group. "Those two criminals have been arrested. Kellie is now free to continue traveling the rodeo circuit before she competes in the Finals in Las Vegas in December. Her next rodeo will be in South Dakota this coming weekend."

She tugged on his arm and whispered, "Do you mind if I say something?"

"Go ahead."

"We're together tonight because we're working on a statement to put out on my blog and the newspaper about the lie I told people. It was necessary to my case that the stalkers believe I had a husband. His captain and my parents agreed.

"Ranger Vance's brilliant idea frustrated those killers, who lost focus long enough for him and the other Texas Rangers to close in on them faster than anyone expected. But let me assure you he wouldn't have missed his sister's party for the world. Under the very real circumstances of life and death, I learned for a fact he loves his sister and family more than anything." A few *ohs* of sentiment followed her comment. "That's why I agreed to come with him. We'll finish up police

business after the party. Since I'm the only girl in my family, too, I know how important this night is to Beth and her future husband. Please forget we're here now and go on with your celebration."

Cy already knew he was in love with Kellie, but her ability to think on her feet under difficult circumstances added to her stature in his eyes. She was a living miracle.

AFTER CY SAID he wanted to leave the party, his mother walked Kellie to the door. He and his father were behind them. "You've been through an experience I wouldn't wish on my worst enemy." Her son looked a lot like his attractive mother. She had those dark blue eyes, too.

"Cy was heroic in his treatment of me. If my choice of words sounds strange to you, let me assure you chivalry isn't dead. Because of how he handled everything, it took away a lot of the horror." Kellie felt her eyes smarting. "He made me believe in him, that he could do anything if I went along with his plan. He affected my parents the same way."

His mother's eyes misted over. "He always did have the quality that instills confidence. Cy's father wanted him to go into law, but he had another dream. A dangerous one. To think he saved your life makes me ashamed that I ever wished he'd find another career."

"Then you can imagine how grateful I am to him."

It was obvious Cy's mother had found a way to live with it, but Kellie was afraid she would never be able to get over her fear for his safety. She knew herself too

well. To live in constant agony because of a man's occupation wasn't for her. A wave of deep sorrow washed over her, knowing that after tonight she wouldn't be seeing him again.

"Our family will be rooting for you in December."

"Thank you, Mrs. Vance."

"Call me Annette."

She smiled. "Your daughter is darling and Tom seems like a wonderful man. You must be so happy for her."

"I am. She's never given me grief. Cy has been a different story, but that's because he's definitely his own person."

"I found that out."

The older woman reached out to hug her. Then Cy's father gave her a hug.

"I understand you were the model of bravery during your ordeal. My son grew up esteeming that quality once he found out we had real Texas Ranger blood running in our veins."

"I've heard the story, and the more I learn about Cy and his colleagues, the more I know all the legends about the Rangers are true."

Cy reached her side. "What are you two talking about?"

"You and the Lone Ranger riding your trusty steed Rosco P.," she teased.

His dad laughed and winked at Kellie. "Drive home safe."

"We will. It was a lovely party."

She hurried ahead of Cy to reach his car. But he

overtook her and helped her into the passenger side. After they backed out of the driveway and headed toward Austin, he reached for her hand and wouldn't let go. "You were fabulous tonight."

"Your family is wonderful."

"Everyone thought *you* were wonderful." He squeezed her hand tighter before letting it go to make a turn.

"Beth looked the way every bride-to-be should look. Radiant with no cloud in her sky."

She felt his glance. "You said that with a degree of sadness." Cy was already picking up on her dark thoughts.

"I didn't realize it was that obvious." She changed the subject and they talked about the different relatives and friends she'd met at the party. They kept the tone light, but once they'd reached her town house and had gone inside, he shut the door and put his hands on her shoulders from behind.

"Tell me what was eating at you during the ride home," he murmured against the side of her neck.

This was going to be the hard part. She moved away, forcing him to drop his hands. "Before we talk, I want you to read the draft I've written for the blog. And after that I'd like your opinion on what we should give to the newspaper. The *Statesman* and the *Chronicle* have been asking for an article. My laptop is upstairs. I'll bring it down and we can work at the table."

She tossed her clutch on the couch and rushed away, praying he wouldn't try to stop her. When she'd told herself she could quit Cy cold turkey, that was before

she realized she was madly in love with him. This was the kind of love that would never go away, not in a millennium.

CY REMOVED HIS suit jacket and tie. He hung them over the back of one of the kitchen chairs before sitting down in another one. This place had been like home to him for a week. Now he was a guest.

While he waited for her, he pulled out his phone. There were messages from the guys, but those could wait. He listened to the one from the captain. "Call me on my private line ASAP. I have some news on the Ravelo case."

Since Kellie hadn't come down yet, he phoned his boss. "TJ?"

"I'm glad you called, Cy. There was a homicide over in East Austin tonight around ten. It turns out someone shot one of the hostages taken by Ravelo during the robbery two years ago. His name is listed in the file as Jorge Montoya. Go over to the morgue and see what the autopsy revealed before you come into work in the morning."

Kellie walked in the kitchen while they were talking and put her laptop on the table. He stood up and turned his back to her while he finished the conversation.

"I've been studying the case. Maybe Montoya was in on the robbery with Ravelo. But when he didn't get his cut of the take, he gunned for Ravelo and got liquidated by a hit man or Ravelo himself. I'll find out when I'm down in Brownsville."

"Trust you to come up with a better possibility than anything the police have been able to figure out."

"It's a guess."

"Nine times out of ten your guesses beat the hell out of everyone else's."

"Don't I wish. Good night, TJ."

When he hung up and turned around, Kellie had taken a seat at the table. "I'm sorry if I intruded on a private conversation."

He bristled. "You could never intrude. The captain and I were going over a new case."

"So I gathered." She averted her eyes and opened her laptop. "Take a look at what I wrote the other night. Tell me what needs to be added or deleted." She was all business.

Cy moved it around so he could read it. The sooner they got this out of the way, the sooner he could find out what was causing her to pull away from him. At the park before the party, she hadn't hidden anything from him. The old saying that he thought he'd died and gone to heaven had summed it up best. After that, how could she change so fast from the warm, loving woman he was crazy about to someone he didn't recognize?

To all my fans—If you haven't watched the news, then you may not know that I've been the target of two stalker brothers who have made my life a living hell for the past month. The Texas Rangers were called in to help me.

In order to draw these criminals out, I had to pretend to be married in order to trap them. Now that they've

been arrested in a cunning sting, I can announce that my marriage was a brilliant piece of fiction that kept me alive until they were caught. Besides my wonderful parents, I owe the Texas Rangers my life.

But I'll have you know that the husband I made up truly is the man of my dreams. Maybe one day... In the meantime, I'll be working hard riding the circuit until December, when I'll be participating in the National Finals Rodeo in Las Vegas. See you there! Long live the rodeo!

He sucked in his breath. "I can find no fault with it."

"Good. I thought I could send the first two paragraphs to the newspapers. But I'll put the entire article on my blog."

"Again I think what you've written is just right. One question, though." He shot her a glance. "Why did you use the word *cunning*?"

"Because you had to fight fire with fire. It's what you do. No one else comes close to your genius. *Cunning* means deceitful, crafty and full of guile. Those words describe the two stalkers who would have murdered me if it hadn't been for you. That's why you're such a brilliant Ranger."

He rubbed the side of his jaw, trying to figure her out. "Why are you suddenly distancing yourself from me?"

She sat back in the chair and stared at him through veiled eyes. "Because you became my hero throughout this reign of terror. My prince, if you like. But when you brought it to an end, I realized you do this every day

for a living. You move on from one ghastly, gory case to another, and then another and another. On the phone just now I heard you discussing a hit man and a robbery.

"Those aren't just words to me anymore. A hit man is someone who actually goes out and kills people. Those brothers were planning to kill me. They became real. The whole situation became agonizingly frightening when Dan started stalking me. Then he tried to kill *you*. I've lived through a nightmare and will never be the same again."

"Kellie—"

"Let me finish. The other day Dad brought up the possibility of my getting therapy. I didn't want to hear it, but I think he's right. Forgive me for throwing myself at you in the car. I didn't know any other way to express my feelings. It shows how off-kilter I am. You're a man and you responded like any red-blooded man. But I'm a wreck, Cy."

His stomach roiled. "So what are you saying? That you take it all back? That you don't want to see me again?"

"Yes— No— I'm not explaining myself right. I would love to be with you again and again, but I can't bring myself to do it because—"

"Because what?"

"I'm afraid I'll lose you while you're in the line of duty. The other night you made yourself a target for Dan to shoot you. I was there, and I was dying inside. I went through that experience with you. Don't you see?" She got to her feet.

"I know that when you go to work, you're going to

put yourself in jeopardy laying your life on the line every day, or night, depending on the circumstances." She clung to the back of her chair. "You asked me why I sounded sad tonight. I'll tell you why.

"I saw your sister and her fiancé so happy, and I was so envious. She never has to worry when he goes to work at your dad's law firm that he'll be shot or blown to bits by a bomb or stabbed to death. I know there aren't any guarantees in this life for any of us, but he'll probably live a long full life and raise a family with her.

"I don't see that in your stars, Cy. I'm being honest. I couldn't handle it if anything happened to you. Though I'll never forget you, if I don't see you again, hopefully in time I'll fall in love and get married to someone who's—"

"Safe?" He cut her off.

"Yes!"

"Where's the barrel racer who stares down danger every time she enters the arena?"

"For heaven's sake, Cy. You can't compare that to what you do. I don't care about me. It's you who matters! Just hearing about this new case you're going to work on makes me sick to my stomach. I don't want to think about it. I know someone has to protect us from the evil out there, but I don't want the man I love to be the one who does it."

He grabbed hold of the table, hoping he'd heard her right. "You *love* me?"

She swallowed hard. "What do you think I've been saying all this time? Yes, I love you. I'm madly in love

with you. Isn't that crazy? We only met nine days ago, yet I know to the marrow of my bones it's true.

"But I don't want to be in love with you. Your poor parents didn't have a choice when you made up your mind what career to go into, but I *do*. So I'm going to ride away from you while I still can."

"That's not going to solve anything," he said in a grating voice.

"Maybe not, but when I'm off on my rodeo circuit, I'll be spared knowing that you were shot and killed by some lawless felon while I was gone. I don't want to be anywhere around when that happens. Now, I think you'd better go. The vet is going to be out early in the morning to give my horses a checkup."

The fact that she loved him would help him get through all the other things she'd said that he hadn't wanted to hear. She needed more time.

"Will you let me hold you for a little while before I leave?"

She shook her head. "No. I don't dare. Kissing you in the car was a big mistake."

Like hell it was…

"Kellie? Look at me."

"Please don't ask me. I enjoyed the evening with your family. Let's let it rest there with that memory."

"Would it help if I told you I'm head over heels in love with you?"

"For the second time, you mean?" she asked in a sharp tone. "If I recall, you told me you barely escaped marriage the first time around."

"That's because I wasn't ready for a commitment."

"Even so, someone will come into your future who will be the right fit for you. Maybe a woman in law enforcement who can deal with the risks to her own life and yours. They say the third time's the charm."

"You're being intentionally cruel, but it's not working. You and I were on a collision course from the moment we bumped into each other in Bandera."

"That's what they said about the last meteor coming toward Earth. But before it got caught into our gravity, its orbital path suddenly missed us and flew in another direction."

"Your metaphor doesn't apply to us. We got caught in the gravity you and I created together. There's no greater force. You can take off for South Dakota, but we'll never be able to escape each other's pull."

"I pray you're wrong," she said with tears in her voice. "Goodbye, Cy. As I heard Vic say to you, watch your back. Might I add, keep Sylvia close. She gets to go with you wherever you go because she has no issues. She even gets to sleep under your pillow and will be with you to the end. What a lucky woman."

Kellie... Kellie...

He reached for his jacket and tie. "Will you walk me to the door?"

"I'd rather not." She clung to the chair back. "Is this new case going to take you to Brownsville?"

"Maybe, but it's nothing for you to be concerned about."

"You see what I mean? Already I'm sick with worry because there are so many killings down there and you haven't even left my house."

"I'm sorry you heard me on the phone."

"So am I. Forgive me for being so awful to you, Cy. I wouldn't be alive today if you hadn't come to my rescue. Please go before I make everything worse."

She was in so much turmoil, he realized there was nothing he could do right now. "I'm leaving." He crossed through the living room to the door. After opening it, he waited to see if she would call him back, but it didn't happen. The evening had turned into a nightmare of new proportions.

Cy pushed in the night lock and shut the door. After reaching the car, he sat there behind the wheel for a few minutes. Kellie loved him. But after what she'd lived through, if he asked her to marry him, then he needed to get into a different line of work.

The thought of leaving the Rangers tore him up inside.

The thought of losing Kellie ripped his heart out.

Chapter Ten

"This is Lydia Olson from Rider Rodeo Connection in Rapid City, South Dakota, for the Black Hills Pro Rodeo. The reigning champion barrel racer for tonight's win is Kellie Parrish with a 13.90 score. You're just racking up the wins, girl. Congratulations!"

"Thank you so much."

"I had to pull out my cheat sheet to list all your stats. You're a Wrangler NFR Qualifier ten times, a College National Finals Qualifier two times, the National High School Rodeo Finals Qualifier four times, and the Pro Wrangler Finals winner in Oklahoma City, Oklahoma, three times. And this year has been the best for you so far."

Kellie nodded. "It's been a good year for me." A year that had changed her life in ways she would never have imagined, but she didn't want to think about Cy right now. "My horses have been terrific and I'm hoping to do well at Finals in December. There's a lot of money to be won and the competition is tough. You're only as good as your last win, so you can't let down. I've got six more rodeos to go before I head to Las Vegas."

"You've thrilled the folks tonight and I wouldn't be surprised if you come out number one in Las Vegas."

"I'm excited to try."

"Where are you headed next?"

"Cheyenne, Wyoming."

"Well, we wish you luck. Thank you for talking to us for a few minutes. What plans do you have to celebrate tonight?"

"I'm going to go pet my horse before I do anything else. She was perfect tonight."

"There it is, folks! Kellie Parrish, who stunned the crowd on her champion horse, Trixie."

"Thank you."

Kellie left the arena and hurried to the rear of the pavilion to see Trixie. Cody had already taken care of Starburst.

Trixie neighed when she saw Kellie, who rushed up to her and threw an arm around her neck. "You were wonderful, Trixie. Here." She pulled a horsey treat out of her jeans pocket. The palomino gobbled it noisily. Kellie chuckled as she led her by a lead rope out the back of the facility to the trailer.

For the next half hour she went through her routine of removing the saddle and bridle, followed by a brush-down before loading her inside the trailer for the night. Earlier in the day Kellie had mucked out her stall, where she'd provided water and had put fresh hay in the net.

"Good night, Trixie. Dream of grassy meadows and sunshine."

Her horse neighed in response before Kellie shut the door.

"That horse is half human."

"Hey, Cody." Her dark-haired buddy had parked next to her. "How's Starburst?"

"I rode her for a while. She's in good shape. Great job out there tonight. I've never seen you ride better. Frankly, after knowing what you've just been through, I don't see how you stayed so focused."

The determination to erase Cy from her mind had played a big factor.

She smiled at Cody. "I couldn't do any of it without you, but I guess you know that. We've made some good money. Depending on what happens at Finals, we should both have enough to get started on our careers after the New Year."

"That's what Jenny and I are counting on. Want to celebrate with us tonight? We're going to grab a bite and take in a movie."

"Thanks, but I'm exhausted. I'll follow you back to the RV campground and call it a night."

They both started up their trucks and drove the short distance to the outskirts of Rapid City. After checking on her horse once more, she visited Starburst and gave her some horsey treats. Then she went into her trailer and took a shower. Once ready for bed, she phoned her parents. They celebrated her win by informing her they would fly to Greeley, Colorado, in two weeks to watch her performance. What would she do without her loving, supportive parents?

After she got off the phone, she posted a message on her blog to keep her fans informed of tonight's performance. Once that was accomplished, she returned phone

calls from Olivia and Sally, who told her Manny was competing at the rodeo in Greeley. Kellie would look forward to seeing them there and introducing Sally's bull-rider-champion husband to her folks.

At last ready for bed, she got under the covers and turned on the radio. But the country-and-western station played the kind of music that talked of breakups and unhappiness. She turned to KBHB broadcasting from Sturgis, South Dakota. Lots of farm news and world news interspersed, but she wasn't able to concentrate and finally shut it off.

In the dark of the night she couldn't kid herself. She'd been hoping she'd hear from Cy all week. It hadn't happened. Kellie hadn't seen him since last Sunday night. They'd parted on such an ugly note, it had left her shaken. Was he deep into his new case?

When she couldn't stand it any longer, she looked up Luckey's number on her contacts list. The temptation to find out what he knew about Cy had been driving her crazy. Tonight she gave in to it and phoned him. The call went directly to his voice mail, but she held off from leaving a message and hung up. She was a fool. Luckey would know she'd called and would probably tell Cy. So much for going cold turkey. She eventually fell asleep, furious at herself for succumbing to the impulse.

The next morning Kellie got up and dressed. After eating a bowl of cereal, she planned to walk both her horses before they all started the drive to Wyoming. On her way out of the trailer, her cell rang. She checked the caller ID and felt a swift surge of adrenaline. It was Luckey. She answered on the third ring.

"Hi, Luckey."

"Hi, yourself. I saw you called last night, but I didn't get a chance to return it until now."

"I shouldn't have bothered you."

"Surely you didn't think I'd mind."

Like Cy, he had those special qualities and charm that made him stand out. "No. I'll be honest. Ranger Vance and I said goodbye last Sunday night. Since then I've been out on the circuit. But I couldn't help overhearing part of a conversation he had with the captain. It had something to do with a case that could take him to Brownsville." She moistened her lips nervously. "I've been a little worried because of all the tension on the border."

"I'm on another assignment and can't discuss any cases, but as far as I know all is well with him."

"I guess I'm having a hard time letting this go. After he saved my life, naturally I don't want to see him injured or worse."

"It's understandable considering he went undercover to protect you. You wouldn't be human if you didn't come out of your experience unchanged. I'll tell you a secret. When I applied to join the Rangers, there was a saying printed at the top. 'Decide that you want it more than you are afraid of it.' I thought about it long and hard before I submitted it."

Kellie had to stifle a moan. "That explains the spirit of the Sons of the Forty."

"It explains why you're a rodeo star," he replied. "Not everyone is driven by the same passion. Since the guys

and I saw you at the Bandera Rodeo, we're all planning on you winning the World Championship."

"Thank you for those kind words. For everything," she half whispered. "You've given me a lot to think about. Watch your back, Ranger." She hung up to prevent further conversation.

Decide that you want it more than you are afraid of it. Such a simple statement, yet such profound wisdom.

AFTER HIS FLIGHT from Brownsville to Austin on Saturday evening, Cy went straight to his house to get some much-needed sleep. So far the Ravelo case wasn't opening up for him. If there were any family members still living there, Cy hadn't found evidence of one. He'd been concentrating in the wrong place and would pursue his angle on Montoya's tie-in to the robbery now that he was back.

Sunday morning he got up late and checked his laptop for emails. Nothing from Kellie, no phone calls. She had his cell-phone number, but it seemed she'd meant what she'd said two weeks ago. She didn't want to love him. *Damn* if she wasn't proving it by her silence.

He glanced at her rodeo schedule on the website, then read her latest entry on her blog. Last night she'd had another winning performance in Cheyenne, Wyoming. Two wins in two weeks. Without the specter of the stalkers, she was going ahead full steam on her road to a dazzling championship in Las Vegas.

In a dark mood and feeling empty, he left for the office. On Sundays it was fairly quiet around there and he'd be able to get through the paperwork that had been

piling up while he'd been gone. Halfway through it, his cell rang. The caller ID said Bronco Parrish.

His heartbeat quickened and he clicked on immediately. "Mr. Parrish?"

"No. It's Nadine Parrish."

"Hello, Nadine. How are you?"

"I've been fine until just now."

"What's wrong?"

"I'm sorry to bother you, Ranger Vance. Maybe it's nothing, but I found something in Kellie's mailbox. I went over to her town house this morning to check on things and water her plants. Maybe this isn't important, but I thought you should know."

He frowned. "What is it?"

"Besides her usual mail, there was another typewritten envelope with her address, but no return address. It's postmarked two days ago. I brought the mail inside, but I haven't opened it."

"Are you still at her condo?"

"Yes."

"Don't touch it. I'll be right over and park in front."

Cy's mind raced with possibilities as he left headquarters and drove to Kellie's town house. Maybe it was simply a note from a friend, but something in his gut told him that wasn't the case. He reached into the glove compartment and pulled out a pair of latex gloves from a box he kept there.

Nadine had opened the front door and was waiting for him. Judging by the lines on her face, she was worried. They'd all assumed this case was over. He hoped

to heaven he was wrong about a third party being involved with the stalkers.

She gave him a hug he reciprocated. By tacit agreement they went into the kitchen and sat down at the table, where she'd left the mail. The white envelope stood out from the rest of the bills and ads.

"Let's see what's in here." He put on the gloves and opened it.

You're a little *fresa* who should have been eliminated a long time ago. No one wants a badass like you around in your skinny designer jeans.

This wasn't the language that came from either stalker. The type was different. If he didn't miss his guess, it was sent by a jealous female. Dan could have been using her, possibly her car. He lifted the typewritten note to his nose. There was a faint smell. Not perfume. Because it had been posted only two days ago, maybe residue lotion had clung to the paper. Kellie's mom eyed him nervously.

"What do you think?"

He didn't show her what was typed. "I'm not sure, but you were wise to call me. I'll take this to headquarters. If you're through here, I'd rather you didn't come back until I've done an investigation. I'll let you know when I deem it safe. Whatever you do, don't tell Kellie. I understand she's come in first at both rodeos so far. Let's not throw her off track unless we have to. If I think she needs to know, I'll get in contact with her."

"I agree. Thank you so much for coming right over."

After Nadine locked the front door, he walked her to her car then got into his own. On the way to the office, he phoned Vic, who'd put on his voice mail. Cy left him a message and asked if he'd meet him at headquarters if at all possible.

The second he got in his office, he opened the paper file on Kellie and searched through the evidence, but he didn't see the report on the Sentra sedan. While he was studying the notepaper already in the file, Vic walked in.

"Hey, Vic—I'm sorry to bother you on a family day."

"It's all right. Jeremy is at his aunt's house playing with his cousin Randy right now. For you to be here on Sunday meant your message was urgent. Have you gotten a break on the Ravelo case?"

"No. That's why I'm back in Austin, but something else has come up and I'm afraid it could be serious. Here's a pair of gloves." Cy pulled them out of the box in his bottom drawer. "Take a look at this. Kellie's mother found it with the mail when she went over to her town house this morning."

Vic put the gloves on and checked the note, then looked at the envelope. "This was mailed two days ago from the Del Valle post office."

"That's only seven miles southeast of here. Where's the paperwork on the Sentra sedan impounded the night of the takedown?"

"Maybe forensics didn't send it up yet, but it should be on the computer. What are you thinking?"

"I'm wondering if Dan had a girlfriend who lives around there and was using her car."

"I took a look at it. A 1999 model that looked like it's been through a war."

"Maybe she found out about Kellie and couldn't stand the competition. This note has a scent. The other notes don't. They're not made of the same kind of paper and the language isn't like Dan's."

His friend picked it up to test. "You're right, but news of the arrests has been all over the internet and TV. If such a person exists, why would she send Kellie a note now?"

"I don't know, Vic. It's just a hunch, nothing more, but I don't like it. I want to find the person who mailed this. For a start I need the name of the owner of that car."

"I'll phone Stan at home. Maybe he can tell us where the report is backed up in the system. I have his home phone number on a list in my office." He pulled off the gloves and tossed them into the wastebasket. "Give me a second and I'll get it."

Vic had been gone only a minute when he came right back and handed Cy a file. "The report was on my desk. I guess they thought you'd be in Brownsville longer, so they gave it to me. It must have been put there after I went home yesterday."

He sat down next to Cy and they pored over it. "The present owner is Martina Martinez with an address in Garfield, Texas. That explains the postmark when they moved the Garfield post office to Del Valle."

"She has a rap sheet for petty crimes starting at the age of fifteen. At the present age of twenty-one, her last known address is 16 Spring Street, and her last known

employment is a manicurist job at the Travis County Hair Salon."

"Maybe he hit on her when he went in to get a mani-cure or another wig or some such thing."

"That's what I'm thinking," Cy murmured. "Her car went missing the night we arrested Dan. I think we both know why she didn't call the police to report it stolen."

"No doubt she stole it off someone else."

"Let's find out right now. I'll drive us."

They left the building and took off. The GPS guided them to a small bungalow in a run-down neighborhood on Spring Street in Garfield. Cy parked two houses away from the actual address and turned off the engine.

"While you knock on the front door, I'll move around the back so any escape is covered."

"Right."

They'd worked together for a long time and could read each other's minds. Cy walked to the rear and planted himself next to the back door. It didn't take long before it opened and the woman they'd hoped to find came flying out as he suspected she would. Cy caught her tattooed arm and forced her hands behind her back to cuff her. She let go with a stream of Spanish curse words, trying to kick him. By this time Vic had joined him. "I've called for backup."

"Good. Martina Martinez, you're under arrest for evading police during an official investigation. You have the right to remain silent until an attorney is pres-ent. If you don't have one, the court will appoint one for you."

An older Hispanic woman of maybe fifty hid herself

behind the partially opened door. "What do you want with my Martina? She's done nothing wrong."

Vic's hands were on his hips. "She shouldn't have run when I asked if I could talk to her."

"What do you want with me?" the suspect cried. "I haven't done nothing."

"Where's the blue Sentra car belonging to you?" Cy questioned.

"I don't know what you're talking about."

"Your rap sheet says you're the owner, but it showed up at a town house in Austin. The man driving it has been arrested for murder. The police already have your fingerprints on file from your former arrests. When they match them to the ones found in the car along with his prints, then you'll be going to prison along with the guy for being an accomplice."

"There's no guy!"

"Sure there is. Is he your boyfriend? How about that threatening letter you mailed to Kellie Parrish from the Del Valle post office?"

She tried to spit at him. "You can't prove I sent anything to that spoiled *fresa*."

Convicted by her own mouth. *Fresa* meant "strawberry," a derogatory term she'd written in her note.

"Your fingerprints will be all over that letter when it's examined. What happened? Did he take off in your car to see Kellie and didn't come back? Did that make you so angry you lashed out at her?" Cy heard sirens getting closer by the second.

"Shut your mouth, *chota*!"

Cy had hit a nerve. Nothing could have pleased him

more than to be called a crooked cop. "We'll let you tell that to the judge."

Vic took her other side. They dragged her around to the front of the house while the older woman screamed at them. Neighbors in the area came out of their houses to see what was going on. Two police cars had converged on the scene. The officers took over and put her in the back of one of the patrol cars. After giving information for the incident report, Cy walked back to the car with Vic.

"I'll ask TJ to get a warrant so the crew can search the house for signs that Dan might have stayed there from time to time. Someone needs to take down a statement from the mother."

When they got back to headquarters, Vic left to go pick up his son. He invited Cy to come over to his house later and they'd kick back with a beer. That sounded good since Cy dreaded going home to his empty house.

He went into his office to leave a message on the captain's phone about the arrest of the Martinez woman. Then he phoned Nadine Parrish to give her the news. She wasn't the only one greatly relieved. For a second when he'd first seen that letter postmarked only two days ago, his heart sank at imagining there was still another stalker out there.

The two of them decided Kellie didn't need to know anything about this until her tour of the circuit was over. Before they hung up, Nadine informed him she and her husband were flying to Greeley the next Saturday to watch her compete in the rodeo.

Kellie's mother could have no conception of the kind

of pain he'd been in for the past two weeks. All he could say was he hoped she'd make the best time and he wished her well.

"I'll tell her."

With that phone call over, he was emotionally drained and left for his car. Before he turned on the engine, he received a call from Luckey and clicked on.

"I'm glad to catch you, Cy. Are you still in Brownsville?"

"Nope. I came home when my lead there went dry. It's a good thing I did." For the next few minutes he told his friend about the letter and the arrest of the Martinez woman.

"That must have knocked you for a loop when you saw another note."

"I have to admit it did."

"Does Kellie know about it?"

"Not yet. Her mother will probably tell her when she and her husband meet up with her in Greeley to watch her performance."

"Why not you?"

"Because we parted company two weeks ago."

"As in…"

"I won't be seeing her again."

"Cy… there's something you ought to know."

He inhaled sharply. "What's that?"

"She phoned me last weekend."

"Kellie *what*?"

"Yeah. I was on a case and couldn't answer it. She didn't leave a message. The next morning when I saw that she had called, I phoned her to find out what she

wanted. At first she was apologetic for bothering me. Then she asked if you were down in Brownsville.

"I told her I couldn't discuss a case, but assured her all was well with you. She thanked me and then just before hanging up she said, 'I guess I'm having a hard time letting this go. After he saved my life, naturally I don't want to see him injured or worse.'"

Cy bowed his head. In one week she'd broken down to Luckey. To Cy's joy, the ice was cracking. He'd warned her they could never escape each other's pull. After hearing this bit of telling news, the longing for her was so great he knew he had to do something about it. Knowing her folks were flying to Colorado next week gave him an idea, but he'd have to clear it with his boss.

"Thanks for being my friend, Luckey. I owe you."

Chapter Eleven

14.00. Second place for the night at the Oklahoma rodeo. Not good enough.

Cynthia Lyman had taken first with a 13.95.

"It wasn't your fault, Starburst." Kellie threw an arm around her neck and fed her a treat. She'd been losing concentration and there was only one reason why. Instead of getting over Cy, her love for him was stronger than ever. She was dying to talk to him, to be held and kissed. But she needed to nail some first places at the three upcoming rodeos in Texas in order to maintain the highest average. That wouldn't happen if she didn't snap out of it.

The most despondent she'd been since leaving Austin, she walked Starburst back to the trailer and loaded her inside. Once she'd taken care of her, she drove to the RV campground where she and Cody were staying.

There were headlights behind her she could see through the side-view mirror on her truck. Someone else was coming into the RV park. She wound her way through to their reserved area. The lights stayed with her. Maybe it was Cody.

Soon she turned into their spot and could see Cody's truck and trailer ahead in the distance. Her cell rang. She knew it was Cody. He always phoned her when he saw she was back. After stopping the truck, she clicked on without looking at the caller ID.

"I know…you don't have to say anything, Cody. I didn't have a good night."

"14.00 nabbed you a second place. From where I was sitting, you wowed the audience."

At the sound of the familiar male voice, she almost went into cardiac arrest. *"Cy?"* Kellie was trying to comprehend it. "You were in the audience tonight?"

"Yup. I flew into Oklahoma City and rented a car at the airport so I could drive to the arena and watch your performance. I wanted to join you while you were walking Starburst to the trailer, but I didn't want to frighten you. I've probably made things worse by following you. Thus the phone call."

Kellie was speechless.

He'd come all this way to see her.

She forgot everything and scrambled out of the truck. He was moving toward her. She couldn't get to him fast enough and started running. He caught her up in his arms and swung her around like a bride.

"Cy—" But anything else she would have said was stifled by the hunger of his kiss. Delirious with love and wanting, she kissed him back without thinking about anything else. All she could do was show him what he meant to her. They melted together, trying to become one.

"I love you, Cy. You were right about everything. I miss you too horribly to let you go."

"That's all I need to hear. I'm in the middle of a big case and have to be back at the airport in a half hour to catch the red-eye from New York to Austin. It makes one stop here. We don't have much time. Come and get in the car with me. We have to talk fast."

She wanted to scream that it wasn't fair to experience this much rapture, only to have it snatched away in so short a time. But this was Cy's life. Even working a dangerous case, he'd come for her. She had to find a way to deal with it, because he really was her whole world.

After they got into the car, he pulled her to him. She needed his kiss as she needed air to breathe. What they were doing was devouring each other, but there wasn't enough time to pack in all their feelings in a matter of minutes.

"I love *you*, Kellie. You're so much a part of me at this point, I can't live without you."

"I can't either, darling. I've been so afraid of loving you for fear I'd lose you. But Luckey told me something that straightened out my dilemma in a hurry."

"He said you called him."

"Obviously I couldn't bear even a week apart from you. He told me about what was written on the application when he wanted to become a Texas Ranger. It said, 'Decide you want it more than you're afraid of it.'" She looked into those dark blue eyes. "I want you more... so much more you can't even imagine."

"Good old Luckey," he whispered against her lips before driving his kiss deeper. After he lifted his head, he

reached into his Western shirt pocket. "Will you marry me for real this time?" He held up a diamond ring.

She let out a cry. "It's the same one you gave me before. I thought it was property from the agency's warehouse."

The smile she loved broke out on his face. "It's not the same one, exactly. But it's the same style, yes. I wanted the ring to look like the one you wore when we pretended to be man and wife. I think I wanted our marriage to be real from the beginning." He slid it home on her ring finger.

Tears filled her eyes to feel it back where it belonged. "So did I. The blog piece I put on about our fake marriage wasn't fake to me. I meant every one of those words you said were over-the-top."

He pressed his cheek to hers. "I said them because I wanted to think you meant them, but I was afraid that dream could never become a reality." He found her mouth and kissed her passionately, over and over again. "Have you put your disclaimer in the paper and on your blog site yet? I've been too busy to look."

"No. I've been holding off. It's because I haven't been able to take back the words I wrote. I'm afraid they're written in my heart forever. I could feel myself falling for you after your captain first brought me into your office at the agency. There you were again, the Ranger I'd bumped into in Bandera. You were the most glorious sight this cowgirl had ever seen, standing there in the sun in your Stetson."

"Someday I'll tell you all the things I thought about you that day, but we don't have much more time. How

would you feel about getting married secretly in Fort Worth three weeks from now? I'll arrange to take the weekend off."

"Only the weekend?"

"I can't take more while I'm still on this case. We could be married by a justice of the peace in the afternoon, then I'll watch you win your last rodeo. We'll honeymoon for a day on our way back to Austin. After Finals we'll have a family wedding at the church and a reception."

She burrowed her face in his neck. "I think it's perfect, but I don't know how I'm going to last until Forth Worth without you."

"I'll phone you every opportunity I get."

"If you're undercover, I don't want to know about it."

"That's good. We'll both be happier that way. Tomorrow I'll tell my folks we're engaged."

"I'll do the same and inform the parents we want to be married right after Finals. I'll tell Mom to call your mom. The two of them will get together to plan the wedding."

"My folks have been waiting for this day forever. I have a three-week vacation coming up whenever I want to take it. The last night of Finals will be Saturday, December 12. We could get married on New Year's Day and take off for that long honeymoon you announced on your blog."

She crushed him to her. "I can't believe this is really happening."

"You will." After another kiss, "I have to leave for

the airport now, sweetheart. Come on. I'll walk you to your trailer."

"You don't need to do that. I know you're in a hurry." On a groan, she gave him one more kiss to last until they saw each other again in Fort Worth. "Never forget how much I love you, Ranger Vance."

Somehow she forced herself to get out of his car. She ran to the trailer and opened the back to check on Starburst. The headlights of his rental car shone on her and her horse. When she couldn't see them any longer, she turned to Starburst and half sobbed for joy against her neck.

"He loves me, Starburst. See my engagement ring?"

Her horse nickered in response as if to say she already knew.

KELLIE HAD A hard time keeping her secret from Cody, even though he knew she was engaged for real. On Friday they reached Fort Worth. After getting settled at the RV campground, she told him she had some shopping to do in town and would work out with the horses later in the day.

After several stores she found a lovely oyster-colored two-piece lined wedding suit with long sleeves and pearl buttons. The jacket had lace trim on the collar and around the hem. She wanted to look bridal yet smart and sophisticated for this fabulous man she was marrying. This outfit was for him alone. She bought matching high heels and a beaded clutch bag. A new pair of pearl earrings caught her eye plus new underwear and a nightgown,

the kind she'd never worn in her life. All soft lace and tiny straps.

Once she was back in Austin, she'd hunt for a gorgeous wedding dress with her mom. Her parents were thrilled Cy had proposed and were already planning a New Year's Day wedding with his parents.

Excited out of her mind because she was marrying Cy in the morning, she hurried back to the RV park and exercised both her horses. She told Cody she'd be going into town in the morning, but would be back by noon to prepare the horses for the drive to the arena.

That evening she put her children to bed and she got started working on herself. First to wash her hair, then do her nails and toenails.

Cy would fly into Forth Worth in the morning. Everyone would presume he was out of town on a case. They planned to meet in the lobby of the Fort Worth Police Administration Building on West Belnap at 9:30 a.m. He'd arranged everything and Justice of the Peace Wilford Hayes would marry them.

Trust her fiancé to want their marriage to take place at the police bureau. As for Kellie, she didn't care where it happened, as long as it did!

At a quarter to nine the next morning of November 7, she left for the police administration building, not wanting to be late. The parking was in a lot adjacent to the building. She drove in and parked her truck. As she walked out and across the street, she received so many wolf whistles and horn honks, it was embarrassing.

"That's some lucky dude!" a guy called out from his cement truck.

She was almost to the doors of the building when she caught sight of the most handsome man she'd ever seen. He stood in front of the doors holding a small florist box. He was wearing a light gray suit and dazzling white shirt. *Cy.*

"I'm the lucky dude all right."

Those piercing dark blue eyes were alive with desire as they swept over her. "Good heavens you're gorgeous." He pulled her into his arms and kissed her right on the street where everyone could see them. "These are for you. Let me pin them on."

While she stood there in a daze, he undid the lid and fastened a gardenia corsage on her shoulder. People waited to go in until he'd finished and had opened the door for her. He ushered her inside and kept his arm around her waist all the way to the elevator. "If it was your plan to take my breath, you've succeeded."

"I'm out of breath myself. I didn't know three weeks without seeing you could be so long. It's embarrassing how much I love you."

They got out on the next floor and walked down the hall to Judge Hayes's office. The secretary smiled and told them to be seated while she let the judge know they had arrived. Cy put the corsage box on the next seat over and clasped her hand in his.

"If you only knew how long I've been waiting for this moment." The throb in his deep voice resonated throughout her trembling body.

"I *do* know," she whispered back. Kellie would have said more, but the judge came into the outer office. The older man studied them for a moment.

"I believe I'm about to marry two of our state's most famous celebrities this morning. Come into my chambers." In an aside, he asked his secretary to find the other witness and join them. Cy squeezed Kellie's hand a little harder before walking her into the judge's office. He put the necessary papers on the desk. Two women came into the room after them and shut the door.

After the judge made the introductions, he asked Kellie and Cy to stand in front of him and join hands. They reached for each other automatically.

"It's my privilege to marry a fine Texas Ranger and our state's champion barrel racer. If you're ready, we'll begin the ceremony."

"We've been ready for a long time." Cy spoke boldly.

A smile broke out in the judge's eyes. "Is that true?" he asked Kellie.

"Yes."

"I can tell your husband-to-be is impatient."

"Not as impatient as I am, Your Honor."

"All right, then. Let's get to it. Kellie Parrish, do you promise to love him and cherish him and all that other stuff?"

Kellie couldn't help but laugh. "I do."

"Cyril Vance, do you promise to love her and cherish her and all that other stuff?"

Cy looked at her. "I do."

"We both do," Kellie said emotionally. "Forever."

The judge nodded. "Forever it is. I now pronounce you man and wife. Have you got a ring?"

Kellie stared at Cy in concern. He pulled the gold

band out of his pocket and handed it to her. She pushed it onto the ring finger of his left hand.

"Now you may kiss your bride, but make it a short one."

"I'm afraid I can't do that," her new husband said.

"I get your point. Well, don't just stand there—and don't forget you've got a rodeo tonight, Mrs. Vance. After the favor I've granted this superhero here in cutting this ceremony short, I expect a star performance."

"I'll try."

"I do believe you've got him hog-tied, and that's a real feat. According to his captain, who happens to be a good friend of mine, no female has been able to succeed until now. But I can see why she's brought you to your knees, Ranger Vance. If I were forty years younger, you'd have some tough competition. Now, get out of here and live a happy life!"

"Thank you, Judge," she said to him as Cy rushed her into the other room. No bride had ever had such a unique wedding ceremony.

Before she could take a breath, he drew her into his arms and gave her a kiss to die for. "Let's get back to your trailer. I'll drive. If an officer pulls us over, I'll flash my star."

This was a side of Cy she hadn't seen before. He was like a different person. Funny, playful. Life with him was going to be filled with surprises. She almost had to run to keep up with him. They flew down the hall. He didn't want to wait for the elevator. Instead he opted for the stairwell. Before she knew it, they were outside and headed across the street to the parking lot.

"The truck's down there on the right."

"I know where it is. I watched you drive in and park."

That was her Texas Ranger. Always ten steps ahead of everyone else, and he was her *husband*!

"The keys."

She rummaged in her beaded bag and handed them to him. After he helped her into the passenger side, he ran a hand over her thigh and leg before shutting the door. His touch, so unexpected and convulsive, had set her on fire.

On their way out he paid the fee and they took off for the RV park with her directing him. "How soon do we need to leave for the arena?"

She checked her watch. "An hour."

"No matter how high I go over the speed limit, that won't leave us time for a wedding night until after your win tonight."

What?

He shot her a glance. "You couldn't be as disappointed as I am, but I need a whole night to make love to my wife for the first time. Since I'm counting on you clocking the lowest time in your event, I'm going to have to be patient a little longer. While you get ready, I'll hitch the trailer to the truck and do any odd jobs you need doing."

Kellie loved him so terribly, her heart hurt.

Cy spoke the truth. Their wedding night wouldn't be perfect if she couldn't hold him all night long. But they'd wanted to be married today. Even though a price had to be paid, nothing in life had made her this happy.

When they drove up to her trailer, Cody was outside

it checking one of the tires. When he turned and saw the two of them in their wedding finery, a huge smile broke out on his face.

"Well, what do you know? You got hitched and beat me and my fiancée to the punch." He walked over to give her a hug and shake Cy's hand.

Cy wrapped his arm around Kellie. "We didn't want to wait any longer. Would you mind taking a couple of pictures of us with my cell phone? We need to record this day for posterity. One day we hope to have children who will deserve to see the way their gorgeous mother looked the day we got married."

"And their father," she added with tears in her eyes. They hadn't talked about children. There were still so many things they didn't know about each other. Every revelation made her love him more.

He fixed the phone so all Cody had to do was keep pressing the button.

Trust Cody, who behaved like a photographer at a photo shoot. He had them pose this way and that, and of course lined up a few shots of them kissing.

"Yeah, yeah. That's what we want," Cody teased them until she was red in the face.

"No one knows we got married except you, Cody," she informed him. "Where's Jenny?"

"Out shopping. I'll pick her up on the way to the arena."

"You can tell her, of course. Cy and I will be having a big church wedding after Finals. This wedding was just for us."

"You two have been through hell. I'm happy for you."

He handed Cy the phone. "I'm just going to put a little more air in this tire."

Cy reached for her hand and they walked to her trailer. "It's the painted blue key," she said as he looked at the key chain. He unlocked the door and they went inside. For a few minutes the world was shut out.

She heard the sigh that came out of him. He turned to her and removed the gardenias from her jacket. "I wouldn't want to smash these." He put them on a chair, then took off his suit jacket and tie. "How long will it take you to change into your riding clothes?" He'd started undoing the top buttons of his shirt.

"Five minutes."

"Do it now while I hitch up the trailer. That will give us ten minutes to say hello to each other as man and wife before we have to get out of here."

The romantic side to Cy sent ripples of delight through her nervous system. He was excitingly methodical. As soon as he left the trailer, she rushed to change clothes. Tonight she'd wear a new Western shirt with fringe and a new pair of jeans. She had to remember to remove the pearls and put in her gold cowboy-boot earrings.

Once she'd hung up her wedding suit and put on her Western outfit, she pulled on her cowboy boots. Then she put on her cowboy hat so she wouldn't forget it.

"Leave the hat off for a few minutes."

Her heart leaped when she realized Cy had already come back inside.

The burning in his eyes made her legs tremble.

"Come here to me, darling. I need to hold you for a few minutes so I can believe that you're really mine."

Like being underwater, she moved slowly toward him and slid her hands up his chest and around his neck. He lowered his head to kiss her mouth, and the world stood still. She couldn't get close enough. No kiss was long enough. They'd gone beyond words to a place where hearts and desires had taken over.

It seemed as if they'd barely had a moment together when she heard a rap on the trailer door. "Sorry to bother you, Kellie. I'm heading over to the arena. See you soon."

A sound of protest broke from Cy before he put her away from him. But he had to hold on to her so she wouldn't fall. "I shouldn't have started kissing you, Mrs. Vance."

"I'd have died if you hadn't, Mr. Vance."

December 1

"I've been nauseated for the last couple of days, Dr. Shay. I'm supposed to leave for the Finals championship in Las Vegas tomorrow, but I need something to help me get over this flu fast."

"You don't have the flu, Mrs. Vance. You're pregnant."

Kellie came close to fainting. "Are you positive?"

"Your blood test didn't lie."

"But I've been on birth control pills for over a year to regularize my periods."

"Even so, there are reasons why you weren't pro-

tected. Women who become pregnant while taking an oral contraceptive either miss one or more doses, or you take a dose at a different time from the normal interval. If you took one in the evening instead of the morning, that can throw things off."

She tried to think back. Had she done either of the things he'd just mentioned? Wait—the day of their marriage she might have taken the pill that night instead of that morning because she was so excited about meeting Cy. Maybe she did miss a dose or two. She simply couldn't remember.

But one thing was certain. Her obstetrician couldn't be wrong. She was going to have Cy's baby. The news filled her with a joy beyond comprehension. But her nausea was so severe, she couldn't possibly compete.

"I'll give you some sample packets of nausea pills. You can take something before bed and see how it affects you. For some women it works after a few days. With others, you just have to wait until the nausea passes with time."

"Thank you."

When she got into her car, she had to sit there for a few minutes before she felt she could drive home to the condo. Once she got there, she lay down on the couch and phoned Cy. She had to leave a message on his voice mail.

"Darling? Please call me ASAP. It's an emergency."

Half an hour later he came bounding through the back door of the kitchen. "Kellie?"

"I'm here on the couch."

He hurried into the living and knelt down by her. "You're pale. What's wrong?"

"I went to the doctor this afternoon. I thought I had the flu. Cy? We're going to have a baby. It had to have happened on our wedding night."

His eyes flared with a light she'd never seen before. "You're pregnant?"

"I know it doesn't seem possible, but the blood test didn't lie. Even though I'm so nauseated I want to die, I'm so happy to be carrying your baby, you just can't imagine."

He looked anxious and vulnerable. She'd never seen him like this before. "I'm so sorry you're feeling ill. What can I get you?"

"Some ice chips? I've taken one of the pills he gave me."

"Anything."

He was gone in a flash and brought some ice back in a cup. She put several chips on her tongue. "Will you phone the parents? We may need to postpone the wedding. Thank heaven the invitations haven't gone out yet."

Cy kissed her lips. "We'll send wedding announcements instead and wait until you're over your morning sickness before we have a reception."

"Will you call Olivia in Colorado Springs tonight? Tell her I have to withdraw from Finals because we're expecting. She'll take care of everything."

"Oh, Kellie—" He made a tortured sound in his throat. "To think my marrying you has caused you to miss the thing you've wanted most in life."

She shook her head. "You're wrong, my love. The first time we bumped into each other in Bandera, I knew I wanted you more than anything else in life. I've won lots of events over the years and have had my thrills. But knowing I'm going to have your baby is a gift beyond price."

"Darling!" Cy put his arms around her.

"I hope our parents will forgive us for getting married without telling them—" she spoke into his hair "—but to be honest, I feel so sick right now, I can't think about that."

"I'll take care of everything. You just lie here. Do you need a blanket?"

"No. The thought of heat makes me sicker. Oh—" she moaned. "You need to call Cody. Tell him he'll get his share of the money even though I didn't compete. I'll send him a check in a few days. They're getting married soon and will need it."

"I'll do it. What else?"

"Call TJ and ask him if he can spare you for twenty-four hours. I need you with me."

She could see his throat working. "As if I'd be anywhere else."

"Those psycho twins you took down changed the very structure of our lives. There should have been a happier, safer way to have met. But I wouldn't trade that week we spent together playing man and wife for anything on earth."

He smoothed the hair off her damp forehead. "I've said this before, but I'll say it again. I thought I'd died and gone to heaven."

"What a story we have to tell our baby one day." She closed her eyes, starting to feel sleepy. "I was the undercover bride of a Texas Ranger. Promise me something?"

"Anything, darling."

"If it's a girl, we're not naming her Sylvia."

While joyous laughter poured out of her husband, she reached for some more ice chips.

Men had it so easy. It wasn't fair. But she wouldn't have it any other way, and she wouldn't have any other man.

* * * * *

FROM BEST FRIEND
TO BRIDE

JULES BENNETT

There's nothing like spending all of your days with your best friend. This book is dedicated to not only my best friend, but my real-life hero. Love you, Michael, And I love our very own happily ever after.

Chapter One

"You know how to please a man."

Megan Richards desperately wished those words coming from her best friend's kissable lips had been said in a different context. Alas, Cameron St. John was only referring to the medium-well steak she had grilled, and not a bedroom romp.

One day she would shock them both when she declared her desire, her need for the man she'd known since kindergarten, when he'd pulled her pigtails and she'd retaliated by taking her safety scissors to his mullet. A mutual respect was instantly born, and they'd been friends since—sans pigtails and mullet.

"I figured you'd been eating enough take-out junk and needed some real food," she told him, watching in admiration as he picked up their dinner plates and started loading her dishwasher.

Oh, yeah. His mama had raised him right, and Megan didn't think there was a sexier sight than a domestic man…especially one with muscles that flexed so beautifully with each movement.

Since his back was turned, she soaked up the view. The man came by his rippled beauty honestly, with hours dedicated to rigorous workouts. She worked out, too—just last night she'd exercised with a box of cookies—which would be the main reason his body was so perfectly toned while hers was so perfectly dimpled and shapely.

Cameron closed the dishwasher door and gave the countertop a swift swipe with the cloth before turning to face her. With his hands resting on either side of his narrow hips, he might have looked all laid-back and casual, but the man positively reeked of alpha sexiness. His impressive height and broad shoulders never failed to send a sucker punch straight to her active hormones.

Too bad he was married to his job as chief of police in Stonerock, Tennessee. Besides, she was too afraid to lose him as a friend to really open up and let years of emotions come pouring out. Well, that and Cameron and his family had been the only true stability she'd known since her parents were killed in a car accident during a snowstorm when they'd been traveling up north to visit friends. Megan couldn't risk damaging the bond she had with Cam.

Oh, and he'd made it perfectly clear on more than one occasion that he wouldn't get into a committed relationship. Not as long as he was in law enforcement,

thanks to an incident involving his partner when they'd been rookies.

Yup, he didn't do relationships; just like he didn't do healthy food.

"I don't eat junk," he defended himself.

Megan tipped her head, quirking a brow.

"I'll have you know that Burger-rama is real food, and they know my order without me even repeating it." Cameron crossed his arms over his wide chest and offered her that lady-killer smile.

Laughing, Megan came to her feet. "I rest my case."

With a quick glance at his watch, Cameron pushed off the counter and sighed. "I better get going. I need to rest before heading out tonight."

She had no clue what he was working on; she rarely did. He was pretty adamant about keeping his work absent from their conversations. He'd tell the occasional funny drunken-fight story, but when it came to a serious investigative case, he was pretty tight-lipped.

Whatever he was working on must be major, seeing as how he'd been heading out to work at midnight several nights a week—not something a chief normally did. The new lines between his brows and the dark circles beneath his eyes spoke volumes about his new schedule.

"You're working yourself to death. You know that, right? Between all the crazy hours and the junk food. You can't be getting enough sleep."

One corner of his mouth tipped up in a smile. That cocky, charming grin always had the same heart-

gripping impact. How many women had been mesmerized by that beautiful, sexy smile?

"I'll be fine," he assured her, pulling her into a friendly hug. "This case should wrap up soon, and I'll be back to somewhat normal hours, complete with sleep. The junk food remains, though."

Two out of three wasn't too bad. Besides, normal for him meant ten-hour days instead of twelve or fourteen. Reminding him of his father's bypass surgery last year would do no good. The St. John men were a stubborn bunch. She should know; she'd been the family sidekick since grade school.

Megan kept her mouth shut and wrapped her arms around his waist as she slowly inhaled his familiar scent. Closing her eyes, she wished for so much. She wished Cam would wake up and see how deeply she cared for him, she wished her brother would straighten his life out and she wished she knew what to do about the out-of-town job offer she'd just received.

None of those things were going to happen right now, so she held on tight and enjoyed the moment of being enveloped by the man she'd loved for years. If friendship was all they were destined for, then she'd treasure what she had and not dwell on the unattainable.

Cameron eased back, resting his firm hands on her shoulders. "You okay? You seem tense."

Really? Because she'd pretty much melted into his embrace. The cop in him always managed to pick up every little detail around him, yet the man in him was totally oblivious to the vibes she sent out. It would be

so much easier if he just magically knew how she felt and took that giant first step so she didn't have to. The passive-aggressive thing was never her style, but in this instance she really wished he'd just read her mind.

"I'm fine," she assured him, offering a grin. "Just a lot on my mind lately."

Wasn't that an understatement?

His dark brows drew together as those signature bright blue St. John eyes studied her. "What can I do to help?"

Oh, if he only knew. One day.

"Nothing." She reached up, patted his stubbled jaw and stepped back to avoid further temptation. "Go rest so you can head out and save Stonerock from all the bad guys."

The muscle in his jaw jumped. "I'm working on it."

"I hope you're careful," she added, always worried she'd get a phone call from one of his brothers or his parents telling her the worst. Because Cameron would put his life on the line for anybody. He just wouldn't put his heart on the line.

He laughed. "Yes, Mom, I'm careful."

Swatting him on his hard pec, Megan narrowed her eyes. "I have to ask. You make me worry."

"Nothing to worry about," he assured her, with a friendly kiss on her forehead. "I'm good at my job."

"You're so humble, too."

With a shrug, he pulled his keys from his pocket. "Eli and Nora's baby is being christened tomorrow. You're still planning on coming, right?"

"Are you going to make it?"

Cameron nodded and headed toward the back door. He always came and went via her back door. He never knocked, just used a key when it was locked and made himself at home.

"I'll make it," he told her, his hand resting on the antique knob. "I may even have time to run home and nap and shower for the occasion."

"How about I pick you up?" she offered.

He lived in her neighborhood, and they tended to ride together when they went anywhere. They were pretty much like an old married couple, you know, just without the sex and shared living quarters.

"Be there at nine." His finger tapped on the door-knob. "Lock up behind me."

Rolling her eyes, she gave him a mock salute as he left. The worry was definitely a two-way street.

Now that she was alone with her thoughts, she had to face the unknowns that circled around in her mind. This job offer had come out of nowhere.

Was it a sign that she needed to move on? She'd been in Stonerock nearly her entire life; she was still single and had nothing holding her back.

Except Cameron.

After scrubbing her sink and table, Megan was still no closer to making a decision. She loved being a therapist at the local counseling center; she loved her patients and truly felt as if she was making an impact in their lives.

The new job would be in Memphis, nearly two hours away. The new facility would offer her a chance at helping more people, even taking charity cases, which

would allow her to comfort and guide people she never could've reached otherwise.

How could she say no?

As she sank onto the chair at her kitchen table, she thought of her brother. He was an adult, but he'd never been able to take care of himself. The questionable decisions he made kept snowballing into more bad decisions—each one seemingly worse than the last. He always counted on her as a crutch to fall back on. What would happen to him if she left? Would he finally man up and take control of his life? See just how dependent he'd become and actually want to change?

More to the point: What would happen with Cameron? Before she made the decision, she would have to seriously consider gathering up the courage to tell him the secret she kept in the pit of her soul.

This job was a catalyst for pushing her in that direction. She needed to move on one way or another… though she'd rather move on with him. Either way, she'd know if years of wanting and dreaming had been for naught.

She'd wanted a relationship with him since they'd graduated high school, but the timing to reveal her feelings had never been right. Between her parents' deaths, his deployment and Megan always putting her life on hold to help her brother, she just had never found an opening.

Cameron was the only solid foundation in her life. What happened if she told him how much she loved him and it ruined their friendship? Could she take that risk?

He'd told her he'd never consider being in a com-

mitted relationship. He'd shared the story of the night his partner had died and how he'd had to witness the widow's complete breakdown. Cam had told her he'd never put anyone through that.

Still, she had to let him know how she felt. She couldn't go through life playing the what-if game forever, and he deserved to know. By not giving him a chance to make a decision, she could be missing out on the best thing that had ever happened to her.

Megan folded her arms across the table and rested her head on them. She really had no choice…not if she wanted to live her life without regrets.

Some risks were worth taking. She knew without a doubt if Cameron wanted to take things beyond friendship, the joy would be totally worth the bundle of nerves that had taken up residence in her stomach.

Cameron had managed about a three-hour nap before the christening. He'd also showered and shaved for the occasion. His mother would be so proud.

He'd just finished adjusting his navy tie when his front door opened and closed. Heels clicked on the hardwood floor, growing louder as Megan approached the hallway. He assumed the visitor was Megan, unless one of his brothers had opted to don stilettos today.

He knew of Megan's love for breakneck shoes when she wasn't wearing her cowgirl boots. Didn't matter to him if she was barefoot. Cameron had fought his attraction to Megan for a few years now. At first he'd thought the temptation would go away. No such luck. Being a cop's wife, even in a small town, wasn't some-

thing he'd put on anyone he cared about. He couldn't handle knowing he'd put the worry and stress of being a cop's wife on Megan, so he pulled up every bit of his self-control to block his true feelings.

Unfortunately, Cameron had never wanted to avoid his best friend as much as he did right this moment. Dread filled his stomach as he recalled the things he'd witnessed last night while monitoring the drugstore parking lot. The events that had unfolded on his watch put a whole new spin on this case…and quite possibly his relationship with Megan. No, not quite possibly. Without a doubt the new developments would shatter their perfect bond.

Her brother had gotten involved with the wrong crowd—a crowd Cameron was about to take down.

She deserved to be happy, deserved to live free from her brother's illegal activities, and Cameron would do anything and everything to keep Megan safe.

Although he was torn about whether or not she should find out, he was obligated to his job first, which meant he had to keep every bit of this operation to himself. She would be hurt and angry when she discovered what her brother was doing, and even more so when she realized Cameron had hidden the truth from her.

"You wearing pants?" she called out.

With a chuckle, Cameron shoved his wallet and phone into his back pocket. "Pants are a requirement?"

When he stepped into the hall, he stopped short. *Damn.* Megan had always been beautiful, and she always presented herself as classy and polished for work, but this morning she looked even more amazing than

usual. There went that twist to his heart, the one that confirmed she was the most perfect woman for him. But he couldn't let her in, wouldn't subject her to his chaotic schedule, his stress from the job. Because if he was stressed, he knew she'd want to take some on herself to relieve him of any burden. He'd signed up for this career…Megan hadn't.

With her fitted red dress, a slim black belt accentuating her small waist and rounded hips and her dark hair down around her shoulders, she stole his breath—something that rarely happened with any woman. Always Megan. Everything was always centered around Megan. She was special.

Which was why he shouldn't be looking at her as if she were a woman he'd met at a bar and wanted to bring home for the night. Not that he remembered what that was like. He hadn't been in a bar for personal recreation in so long, never mind bringing a woman back to his bed.

Megan deserved to be treasured, to be loved and come first in any man's life. Unfortunately he could only offer two of the three.

Cameron had always figured one of his brothers would scoop Megan up, and the thought had crippled him each time the image crept through his mind. Thankfully, both Eli and Drake had found the loves of their lives. Cameron was thrilled for them, but love wasn't for all the St. John boys. Cameron barely had time to catch any sleep, let alone devote to a relationship.

"Should I go back home and change?" she asked,

raising a brow with a smirk on her face. "You're staring at me."

"No, no." He adjusted his jacket, hating the confining garment and feeling somewhat naked without his shoulder holster. "You're just looking exceptionally beautiful this morning."

"You mean my old paint-stained tank and tattered shorts I had on yesterday didn't make me look beautiful?" She fluttered her eyelids in a mocking manner he found ridiculously attractive.

He loved that no matter what life threw at her, she always found a way to be a bit snarky. Why hadn't some guy come along and swept her off her feet? Any man would be lucky to have her. She grilled an amazing steak, she was always there for him no matter what, she joked and she even drank beer with him.

If she married someone who loved her and treated her the way she deserved to be treated, Cameron might be able to get this notion that he was worthy of her out of his head. Because he sure as hell knew that was false. He wanted to see her happy with that family she'd always wanted. But she wasn't even dating anybody. Still, he couldn't tell her his feelings because there wasn't a happy ending if he chose that path. Telling Megan would only cause an awkward, uncomfortable wedge between them, and hurting her in any way would destroy him.

As she stood in his hallway, looking like a classy pinup model with all her curves, Cameron cursed himself for allowing his thoughts to travel where they had

no business going. Her curves weren't new, but when the two of them got together she never dressed like this.

It was the dress. That perfectly molded dress. He was used to seeing her in professional work clothes or old tees and shorts. If he was looking at her in a way that stirred him, how would other men be looking at her today? They were attending a church service, for crying out loud, and he was standing here fighting off an ever-growing attraction to his best friend. There was so much wrong with this situation he didn't even know where to start.

"I'm ready." He moved into the foyer, careful not to touch her as he passed, and retrieved his keys from the side table.

After he'd locked up behind them, Cameron followed her down the stone path toward her black SUV parked in his drive. They'd barely gotten their seat belts fastened before her cell chimed. Casting a quick glance down to where it rested on the console, Cameron spotted Evan's name on the screen. More anxiety filled his stomach, but he kept his mouth shut. Now was not the time to expose him. He'd actually made a point to not come between Megan and her brother. Their issues went way beyond those of regular siblings. He might not be able to tell Megan what had happened last night, but Cameron would throw himself in front of her to protect her from anyone...including Evan. Family loyalty meant everything to him; unfortunately, her brother was only loyal to himself.

Megan's bright green eyes darted up to his as she sighed. "I'm sorry."

Wasn't that the story of her life? Always apologizing for her brother, always coming to his defense? Megan was never fully able to live her own life the way she wanted because she'd had to play mom, dad, sister and therapist to the ungrateful punk for years.

She snatched her cell on the second ring. "Hello."

Cameron couldn't make out what Evan was saying, only the rumble of a male voice filtered through the SUV. Not that Cameron needed to know what Evan was saying. The man only called his sister to ask for money, use her car or some other random favor.

Megan's head fell against the back of her seat as she gripped the phone with one hand and her steering wheel with the other. "I can't, Evan—I'm busy right now."

Cameron resisted the urge to pull the phone from her hand and tell Evan to grow a set and quit using his sister as plan A. The man, and he used the term loosely, had never held a job that Cameron was aware of...or at least not a legal one. Evan had been a troublemaker in school, getting kicked out of two before he even started junior high. Megan's parents had moved the family to the next town as a result of Evan's troubles, causing Cameron and Megan to lose touch for a year. Thankfully Megan had transferred back and their relationship had picked up right where they'd left off—with them goofing off and her hanging at his house with him and his brothers.

Unfortunately, switching schools had only made Evan angrier, resulting in his behavior growing more reckless. Now, as an adult, he had made no strides to

clean himself up. Actually, after what Cameron had witnessed last night, he knew Evan was even worse than he'd thought. The man was straight up running drugs. And there was no way in hell Megan knew the trouble her brother was in.

No wonder Megan adored Cameron's family so much. They were all she had in the form of a loving, solid foundation.

"I'm sorry, Evan," she went on, her tone exhausted. "That's not something I can do right now. If you can wait until this afternoon, then I can help. Otherwise, I don't know what to tell you."

The more Megan argued, defending herself, the more Cameron felt his blood pressure soar. He was thankful that even though he and his brothers had been hellions in school, they'd never crossed the line into illegal activity. They'd been standard cocky teens. There just happened to be three of them with that arrogant attitude, and when one had done something, the others had jumped on board.

"No, Evan, I—"

Cameron refused to let this go on another second. He pried the phone from her hand and ended the call without a word. Megan jerked toward him, but Cameron clutched the device in his hand, holding it by his shoulder as a silent sign he wasn't giving in.

Her deep red lips parted in protest before her shoulders sank and her hands fell to her lap. Megan's head drooped. With all her hair tucked back, he could see every emotion that slid over her face, even though he could only see her profile. Her eyes closed, she bit her

lip and her chin trembled. She looked positively defeated.

That right there was why Cameron loathed Evan Richards. The man constantly deflated the life out of fun-loving, bubbly Megan. Moments ago, when she'd stood in Cameron's hallway, she'd been sassy, confident and vibrant…everything he loved. What he didn't love was how quickly one person could bring her down. Evan was nothing but a bully, always seeking his own selfish desires and not giving a damn who he hurt along the way.

"Don't you dare feel bad," he scolded, maybe harsher than he should have. "That's exactly what he wants, Meg. He plays that guilt card with you because he knows you'll give him anything he wants."

"I know," she mumbled. Smoothing her hands down her fitted skirt, she let out a sigh and turned to face him. "I'm trying, really. It's way past time he stood on his own two feet. It's just so hard…"

She shook her head and reached for the keys in the ignition. After sliding his hand over her slender arm, Cameron gripped her hand.

"That's what he's counting on." Cameron gave her a gentle squeeze as he softened his tone. She wasn't a perp; she was his friend. "He continually plays the poor sibling, expecting you to ride to his rescue. He's the one who made this mess of his life."

Cameron seriously doubted she knew just how much of a mess Evan was in. There was no way he could protect her from the end result. The helpless feeling in the pit of Cameron's stomach nearly made him sick.

Tears brimming in her eyes, she held his gaze. "You think I don't know how much Evan has screwed up? That he doesn't use me on a daily basis? You don't know what I go through, Cameron. You have the picture-perfect family. I have no parents and a brother who'd just as soon wipe out my bank account as spend five minutes talking with me on how to straighten his life out, how to help him. I'm praying maybe one of these times he comes to me, he'll be there for more. I'm praying he'll let me help him, that he'll be ready to turn his life around. So if I have to get stepped on along the way, it's worth it."

The last sentence came out on a choked sob. Well, hell. Now he was the one feeling guilty. He never wanted to make her cry, make her feel as if his life was better than hers.

After placing her phone back on the console, Cameron reached across and wrapped his arms around her the best he could, considering their positions.

"I'm sorry." Her silky hair tickled his cheek, and her familiar floral scent reminded him she was nearly everything to him and he'd die before he'd hurt her. "I don't mean to be hard on you. I just hate seeing what he does to you."

Megan's hands slid up his torso between his jacket and his shirt, coming to rest against his chest. "What I deserve and what I'll have are two different things."

Easing back, Cameron studied her face. "You deserve everything you've ever wanted."

A sad smile spread across her face as she reached a

hand up and cupped his freshly shaven jaw. "All I've ever wanted may not want me back."

What?

Before he could question her further, her hand fell away and she started the vehicle. Whatever secret longing she kept locked deep inside was obviously something she'd all but given up on. Cameron refused to let Megan give up on any dream or goal she had.

He vowed that once this major case was over, he'd find a way to make her happy, living the life she desired and deserved. It would be worth everything to him. For years he'd seen her always put her needs behind everyone else's. And while he may not be the man to settle into her life intimately, he would do everything in his power to make sure her dreams were fulfilled.

Chapter Two

"I'm so glad you could make it."

Bev St. John hugged Cameron after the christening service, then looped her arm through his as they walked back up the wide aisle of Santa Monica Church.

"You don't know how much this means to me to have all my boys here for my first grandbaby's milestone," Bev said, her wide smile spreading across her face.

Straight ahead, near the tall double doors, Nora and Eli stood with Megan. Megan held his infant niece, who was just over a year old. Cameron's heart filled. The glow on Megan's face as she placed a kiss on top of Amber's curly blond head solidified the fact he couldn't be the man for her. She would be an amazing, loving, selfless mother. Just not to his kids.

Cameron's dad, Mac, approached and looked over Megan's shoulder, smiling down at his granddaughter. Cameron didn't know where Megan would be if it weren't for his family. She'd taken to them even before her parents had died suddenly, but she'd really leaned on them during that difficult time. Even as strong as Megan was, she'd been so blindsided by the shock of losing both parents, and then taking over the care of her younger brother when she'd barely gotten out of high school herself. "I'm so glad Megan could make it." His mother's soft tone pulled him back. "I just love that girl."

Over the years his mother had made it no secret she wouldn't mind Megan being part of the family— in the legal, choosing-china-patterns type of way. Of course now that Eli and Drake were taken, his mom would just have to settle for Megan being a friend and the daughter she'd never had.

Cameron steered them toward the little grouping, and Megan glanced up, caught his eye and smiled. Yeah, there was that invisible pull once again that threatened to wrap around his neck and strangle him.

He wanted her. Wanted her so much sometimes he physically hurt. But she deserved more.

The memory of the darkest time in his life took over. His partner had taken a bullet meant for Cameron. On his last breath, his partner had made Cameron promise to make sure his wife knew he loved her.

That moment changed everything. Letting a woman into his life, letting her get close enough to be devastated like his partner's wife had been, was not some-

thing he'd ever take a chance with. If he entered into a deeper relationship with Megan and something happened to him, it would kill her. Besides, worrying about her while he was trying to do his job was a sure way for him to get hurt. He needed to concentrate, needed to keep Megan out of his mind.

If he could only figure out how the hell to do that.

"Megan, you look beautiful, as always." His mom leaned forward and kissed Megan's cheek. "Thanks for being here today."

"I wouldn't miss it."

"Are you and Megan coming to eat with us after?" Eli asked Cameron. "We're heading to that new Italian place just outside of town."

Cameron started to agree, but Megan chimed in. "I have to get home, but if you want to go, go ahead."

Oh, no. If she was going home to wait on her freeloading brother to show, Cameron would be right there with her. No way would Evan try to pull her into this latest mess. Hell no.

"I need to head out, too," Cameron stated. Work was always beckoning, so he knew everyone would just assume that's why he needed to go. "And she's my ride."

Cameron and Megan said their goodbyes and stepped out of the church. The bright sun hit them as they descended the concrete steps. Cameron pulled his glasses from his jacket pocket and slid them on to block the brightness. A headache from lack of sleep and plenty of worry had settled in, and the fiery glare was making it worse.

"Skipping out?"

Cameron turned to see his other brother, Drake. Right at his side was his fiancée, Marly, and Marly's daughter, Willow.

"Megan and I need to head out," he told Drake.

"You look pretty," Willow said, standing beside Megan and looking up at her as if she were looking at a movie star. "I like your hair."

The free-spirited little six-year-old had on her beloved cowgirl boots, as usual, and was sporting a new grin, sans two teeth.

Megan bent down and slid her hand through Willow's long ponytail. "I love yours, too. I used to wear my hair just like this when I was your age. You have good taste."

"I was going to call you," Marly told Megan. "Nora and I were hoping for a girls' night sometime soon. You interested?"

Megan smiled and nodded. "Sounds good. Just let me know when."

More goodbyes were said, and finally Megan and Cameron were settled back in her SUV and headed toward their neighborhood.

"That was a beautiful service," she commented after a bit. "Thanks for inviting me."

"You're family." Cameron tried to hold back the yawn but couldn't. Damn, he was getting too old to pull all-nighters. "You belong here, too."

"You know, one day you may actually replace me with a girlfriend or a wife. I doubt she'll understand if I'm still hanging around your family."

Cameron snorted, shifted in his seat and rested his

elbow on the console. "For one thing, you could never be replaced. For another, I think you know my stance on committed relationships and marriage."

"Your reasons may be valid, but they can't be your crutch for life."

"It's not a crutch," he muttered in defense.

Megan threw him a glance and a smile as she pulled onto their road. "You never know when the right woman will come along and claim you."

The only woman he'd ever allow to "claim" him was sitting right next to him, but he'd never do that to her. He'd seen firsthand what being a cop could do to even the strongest of marriages. Even though he and Megan had a bond that rivaled the toughest relationships, he wouldn't put that kind of strain on something, or someone, so important.

She was part of his life in the deepest way he could allow and he'd just have to be satisfied with that. The fact she would likely marry one day was something he couldn't even think about right now. If he thought of Megan with another man, Cameron would likely lose that wall of control he'd built up.

Megan put on her signal to turn into his drive.

"I'm going to your house," he told her.

Totally ignoring him, she pulled up to his garage. After throwing her SUV in Park, she turned to face him, her green eyes studying his face. "You need to go in and get more sleep."

She was preaching to the choir. Unfortunately, even if he went in, he wouldn't be able to just close down and relax. Besides, he wanted to make sure Evan didn't

show up and try to pour on more guilt or ask for any favors.

"I'll be fine," she assured him, patting his leg as if he were some toddler. "I know what you're doing, but don't worry. I've handled Evan long enough."

Cameron slid his hand over hers and squeezed. "And that's the problem. You shouldn't have to deal with a grown man whose behavior is that of an out-of-control teen."

Megan tilted her head, and her hair spilled over her shoulder; the strands tickled his arm on the console. "I deal with you, don't I?"

He couldn't help but smile. "You only keep me around to set your mousetraps in the winter."

"True." With a smile, she turned her hand over in his and squeezed. "Seriously. Go sleep."

Stroking his thumb along the backs of her smooth fingers, Cameron stared into those eyes that were too often full of worry—eyes that had captivated him on more occasions than he could count.

"I'm a guy and a cop. I can't help but want to take care of you."

Drawing in a shaky breath, she offered a sweet smile, one he'd witnessed for years and never grew tired of seeing. Megan's genuine, contagious smile that came from within, that lit up a room…that's what kept him going.

"I love you for that," she told him. "But really, you need to take care of yourself, and I'm going to make sure you do. Now go."

Stubborn woman. She wouldn't pull out of this

driveway until his butt was out of her car. *Fine.* He was just as stubborn, but he knew how to play the game. He knew his Megan better than anyone else did. She would always put herself out to make others comfortable, to keep those around her happy. But Cameron wasn't about to let her fall down his priority list. She was, and always had been, at the top. Just like family.

"All right," he conceded. "You will call me if you need anything."

It wasn't a question, but she nodded anyway as she leaned over to kiss his cheek. "Go on, Chief. You can't protect the town if you're dead on your feet."

"Yes, Mommy."

Cameron tugged on the handle and stepped from the SUV. Turning to rest his arm on the open door, he peered back inside. "You know, tough love is a good thing."

"Yeah." Megan sighed, and her shoulders fell slightly. "It's just easy to say and harder to do."

Cameron hated how torn she was between loyalty and forgiveness. He, too, was torn between loyalties right now. Megan had been his everything for so long. Yet he couldn't protect her, couldn't even warn her of the evils hovering so close to her life.

Tapping the top of her car, he stepped back. "I'll call you later."

As he made his way up to his porch, Cameron knew he wouldn't be sleeping. Too much was on his mind, and it all involved work and Megan. She always seemed to be the center of his thoughts. Unfortunately, this scenario had nothing to do with his desires.

Yet Megan's odd declaration earlier alluding to something or someone she wanted still weighed heavily on his mind, too. They shared everything…at least all the personal stuff. What was she keeping from him?

Granted, he'd been holding back his own feelings for so long, but he didn't think she reciprocated those emotions. Or did she? That would put a whole new spin on things and add another layer of worry to his already stressful life. Damn it, why couldn't he just have those friend feelings or that brotherly bond? When had he taken that turn into wanting more?

Cameron waited until Megan headed down the narrow road toward her own house before he turned in the opposite direction and took off for a much-needed walk around their neighborhood. He needed to clear his head and figure out how best to approach this delicate situation with Evan.

Cameron also needed to figure out how to get the image of Megan in that classy yet sexy-as-hell red dress out of his mind. No other woman could shoot for polished and timeless and come off as a siren. Megan's beauty had always been special, but today she'd taken it to a whole new level. The more time passed, the deeper his feelings went. There was nothing he could do; he'd tried denying it, tried ignoring it. Unfortunately, Megan had embedded herself so deeply into his life that he had no clue how to function with all of these lies.

Yeah, a walk was definitely what he needed to get his head on straight because losing himself in his thoughts where Megan was concerned was only throwing fuel on the proverbial fire. Too often when they

were close together in a car, on her sofa watching a movie, he'd fought not to kiss her, not to touch her. The struggle he battled with himself was a daily occurrence, but he'd sacrifice anything, even his desires and his sanity, to keep her happy and safe.

Lust, love or anything other than a simple friendship had no room in the well-secured bond they'd honed and perfected since childhood.

So focusing on this case from hell that had just taken a turn for the worse was the only thing he had time to dwell on. Because in the end, no matter his feelings for Megan, she would hate him for standing by and watching her brother make mistake after mistake, for waiting to take down him and his criminal friends. But Cameron didn't have a choice. His job had to come before his feelings for Megan.

Clothes were strewn around her room, hanging over the treadmill, draped across her bed, adorning the floor mirror in the corner. Pretty much every stationary object had taken a hit from the purging of her closet.

Megan tugged on the black tank-style dress that used to be her favorite. When she gave a pull to cover her rear end, it pulled the scoop neck down. When she tried to pull the material up over her breasts, her butt nearly popped out.

Damn that new Ben & Jerry's flavor. Ice cream was her weakness, and now she'd discovered something else to feed her addiction…and her thighs.

So here she was, going through her closet because she needed to de-clutter. Nobody needed this many

clothes, and she'd gained a few pounds, so why keep all this stuff? If she ended up losing the extra weight, she deserved a shopping spree, anyway. And if she opted to take that new job in Memphis, she would want to start fresh. That meant getting rid of this too-tight, hoochie-mama-looking dress.

Besides, reorganizing her overflowing closet was a great stress reliever and a good way to keep her mind off Cameron.

With a laugh, she fingered through the pile of too-small clothes on her bed. Like Cameron was ever off her mind. She'd nearly slipped up and bared her soul to him earlier when he'd declared he wanted her to have all she'd ever desired. Could the man be so blind that he couldn't see she desired him? Did he pay no attention to the fact she rarely dated and when she did it was only one date because nobody could ever compare with Cam?

She knew why he didn't go out with women. He was married to his job. But he'd never questioned her on why her social life was nonexistent.

Or perhaps she was the blind one. Maybe she wasn't ready to face the fact that he truly didn't want anyone in his life, and even if he did, she would only be a friend to him.

Though he had given her a visual sampling when he'd first seen her before the christening. That was a good sign…right? Or maybe he'd just had indigestion from all the garbage he ate the night before. Who knew?

Groaning, she started to attempt to get out of the

body-hugging dress when she heard her back door open and close. Jerking around, she tried to listen to the footsteps.

Evan? Cameron? Either way she was clearly not dressed for company.

"You wearing pants?"

A slight sigh of relief swept through her as she laughed at Cameron echoing her earlier question to him. Her body was half hanging out, but extra pounds or not, men usually just saw skin and got excited. Could this work to her advantage? Maybe being a bit more out there, literally, would get Cameron to wake up.

"Actually, no," she called back, then stepped into the hall to tell him she'd be right out.

As soon as she left her room, she ran into Cameron's solid chest. Firm, strong hands immediately came up and gripped her shoulders. Her breasts, already spilling out of her dress, pressed against his hard pecs. Megan sucked in a breath, unable to think of anything but how nicely they molded together in all the perfectly delicious ways.

The way his eyes widened, his nostrils flared and his fingertips bit into her bare skin told her he wasn't so unaffected by her femininity.

Game on.

Chapter Three

Holy—

Cameron couldn't breathe, couldn't think, couldn't form a damn thought with Megan's curvy body pressed against his. This was his best friend, yet with the way her breasts were all but spilling out of her barely-there black dress, his thoughts weren't very friend-like at the moment.

Hadn't he just pep-talked himself into trying to keep his thoughts out of the gutter?

"Wh-what are you doing here?" she asked.

Why was her voice all breathy and sultry?

Cameron dropped his hands and took a step back, but that didn't help his hormones settle down. Now he was able to see just how hot she looked wearing that second-skin dress that hit her upper thigh at a very

indecent level and scooped low enough to show off her breasts.

Jealousy ripped through him. "Where the hell are you going like that?"

She flinched. Maybe he'd sounded a tad gruff, but seriously? Every visual that came to mind involved a bedroom.

Megan lifted her chin defiantly as she crossed her arms, doing nothing to help her cause of breast spill-age. "For your information, I'm cleaning my closet and trying things on. Now, why are you here and not home asleep?"

He was starting to question that himself. "I couldn't sleep."

Not that he'd tried, but she didn't need to know that. He glanced into her room and laughed. Megan always had everything in its place, but something tragic had transpired with her clothes. He wasn't dumb enough to make a comment because he was pretty sure that some rage had been unleashed in that room.

"Not a word," she growled, as if daring him to com-ment on the chaos. "Let me change real quick."

Before she turned away, the back door opened and closed. Cameron nearly groaned. Nobody else would just walk in other than him or Evan.

Megan let out a sigh. "Be nice," she whispered. "I'll go change."

Cameron turned away just as Evan rounded the hall corner. His disheveled hair and black eye were so pre-dictable. He looked like a deadbeat who'd obviously been on the wrong end of one of his "friends'" fists.

Cameron wouldn't allow him to come in here and make Megan feel like crap.

"Am I interrupting something?" Evan asked, his narrowed eyes darting between Cameron and Megan.

Cameron wanted to tell the guy yes, but he didn't figure Evan would leave and the lie would only make Megan upset. No matter what, he was treading a fine line because if this weren't Megan's only living relative, Cameron wouldn't think twice about hauling his butt in if for nothing else than to shake him up a bit.

Megan stepped into her room and came out seconds later tying a robe around her waist. At least she was covered now. Cameron didn't like that judgmental glance that Evan had thrown at them. Even if Cameron and Megan had been doing something intimate, that wouldn't have been Evan's business…or anyone else's for that matter.

"What happened?" Megan asked, stepping toward her brother.

Evan waved a hand, his eyes still moving between Cameron and Megan. "Nothing for you to worry about."

Cameron knew those blow-off comments hurt Megan. The woman obviously cared for her brother, and Evan didn't even acknowledge the fact.

"I do worry," she told him with a softer tone.

Cameron maintained his place between the two siblings. No way was he budging. When it became clear that Evan wasn't going to offer any more feedback over his recent fight, Megan sighed.

"What do you need, Evan?" Megan asked as she took a step back, landing her next to Cameron.

Good. Cameron wanted her to feel safer with him there. The silent gesture clearly showed who she trusted, who she felt more comfortable with. The primal part of Cameron liked to think her easing closer to him showed whose side she was on, as well.

"I need to talk to you," Evan told her, then shifted his eyes to Cameron.

"Go ahead," Cameron replied, resting his hands on his hips and in absolutely no hurry to budge.

"Alone."

Megan moved down the hall, squaring her shoulders. "I'm not giving you money," she informed him as she got closer. "If you want to visit with me, that's fine."

Evan raked a hand through his hair, then threw another glance at Cameron and back to Megan. Cameron didn't move, didn't even consider giving them privacy because he wanted Megan to know he was here for support. He wouldn't chime in, wouldn't say a word unless he saw she couldn't be strong. But he had faith in her. He knew she was getting tired of her brother only coming around for money.

Evan leaned down, whispered something to Megan and gripped her arm. Cameron went on full alert.

"No, Evan," Megan said softly, shaking her head. "I don't have it to give. I'm sorry."

"You're not sorry," he spat as he released her with a forced shove. "I don't need that much."

Megan stumbled back a step, but caught herself as she crossed her arms and tipped her chin. "I have ob-

ligations, too, Evan. I can't always give you money because you get into trouble."

Evan's focus darted over Megan's shoulder, and Cameron merely narrowed his eyes, silently daring Evan to cross the line. The arm incident was more than enough to have Cameron ready to smash his face, but Megan wouldn't like Cameron interfering. Plus as an officer of the law, Cameron couldn't just go around punching all the people who pissed him off. Such a shame.

Cameron would like nothing more than to show Evan some tough love, but Megan was right. That was easier said than done. And as much as Cameron loathed the man, he *was* Megan's brother and she loved him.

"I'll come back when we can talk in private," Evan said, looking back to Megan.

"My answer won't change," she informed him. "But you're always welcome in my house."

Evan merely grunted and started to turn.

"I love you," Megan said, her voice shaky.

Evan froze, didn't look back, didn't comment, just paused before he disappeared around the corner. Moments later, the back door opened and closed again.

Megan turned, a fake smile pasted across her face, and started down the hall toward her room, skirting around him. "Well, let me change and then maybe we can do dinner. You want to go out? I'm not sure I have a lot here—"

Cameron followed her into the bedroom and watched as she jerked off her robe and tossed it onto the mound of clothes on her bed. As she glanced into

the mirror and sighed, Cameron came up behind her, resting his hands on her shoulders and meeting her gaze in the reflection.

"You don't have to pretend with me."

Her bright green eyes held his. "I'm not pretending," she assured him. "I'm ignoring the fact that for years I've been an enabler to someone who really doesn't care about me, and I'm done. I'm also starving, so while I change, figure out what you want to eat."

Cameron knew there was so much more in her, but he wasn't pressing the matter...not when she was staring back at him with such vulnerability and was half-naked. They were back to that damn body-hugging dress again, and Cameron didn't know if he wanted to keep looking or if he wanted her to cover up.

Megan's entire body relaxed against his. Her bottom nestled against his groin, and Cameron tried to ignore the innocent gesture as he wrapped his arms around her shoulders and held her securely. She needed comfort, needed to lean on someone even though it was against everything she stood for. She'd never admit she needed to draw from his strength, but Cameron was freely giving it.

Unfortunately, his fingertips barely brushed across the tops of her breasts before he could complete his hold. A shiver racked her body and vibrated through his.

"I'm glad you're here," she whispered, her eyes still locked on his in the mirror.

Looking at her reflection was quite different from being face-to-face. He didn't know why, but in the

mirror he saw so much, too much. Her vulnerability stared back at him at the same time that her killer body mocked him. He was her friend, damn it. He shouldn't be having these thoughts of how perfect she felt against him, how sexy she was.

"I wouldn't be anywhere else." Even though his libido was taking a hard hit, it was the truth.

With a deep breath, Megan straightened and turned, all but brushing those breasts against his chest. Okay, really. He was a guy already on the brink of snapping the stretched line of control, and there was only so much more of this he could take.

"Are you working tonight?" she asked, oblivious to his inner turmoil.

"No." He dropped his arms to his side and took a slight step back, away from that chest, the killer body that was slowly unraveling him. "Why don't I run to the store and grab something while you change?"

"A night in?" She beamed. "Only if I get to pick the movie."

Cameron groaned. "If I have to watch *The Godfather* again…"

With an evil laugh and a shrug, Megan stepped around him and started digging through clothes. "You choose the meal—I choose the movie. You know that's how we work."

Yeah, that's how they worked. They'd been working like this for years, before his deployment and since. But in all the years they'd had this routine of spontaneous date nights with each other, never once had the urge to peel her out of her clothes been this strong.

Of course now that he'd seen her, held her and visually enjoyed her in this dress, he could think of little else. So in a moot attempt at holding on to his sanity, and their friendship, Cameron conceded.

"You win," he told her. "I'll be back."

Even if he removed himself from the situation, Cameron knew he was screwed. Now that he'd seen her lush, curvy body, and felt it so intimately against his, he couldn't *not* see it. The image, the feel of her, was permanently ingrained into him.

Penance for his sins of lying to her.

Every single time they settled in for a movie, Megan fell asleep within the first hour without fail. Tonight was no exception.

She'd curled her feet beneath her, rested her head on his shoulder and before the mobsters could leave the gun and take the cannoli, Megan was out.

Cameron propped his feet up on her coffee table and slid farther down on the sofa. Carefully, he adjusted Megan so she lay down, her head on his lap. Resting his own head against the back cushion, Cameron shut his eyes and attempted to relax. Her delicate hand settled right over his thigh as she let out a soft sigh.

With his hand curled over her shoulder, feeling the steady rise and fall, Cameron realized he actually preferred resting just like this to his bed at home. At least here he had company. At home he had thoughts that kept him awake and staring at the ceiling fan. Work never fully left him—occupational hazard.

But here, with Megan, he could let work shuffle to

the back of his mind. He didn't want to burden her with his stress, so he purposely tried to be a friend first and a cop second whenever he was with her. Added to that, he reveled in the fact she was comfortable and sleeping soundly. He wanted to be her protector, her stable force. Somehow knowing he was all of that allowed him to let down his guard just a bit.

Crossing his ankles, Cameron rested an elbow on the arm of the couch. He'd muted the movie once Megan had fallen asleep, but the flicker of the screen lit up the room. As always, when they had movie night, all lights were off.

A shrill ring pierced the silence, and Cameron jerked awake. The TV had gone black, indicating he'd dozed off for a good bit, but he didn't really recall how long ago that had been. The ring sounded again. He grabbed his side, but Megan's phone on the table was the one lit up. Normally his phone was the one that rang at all hours.

She was still out with her head on his lap. He didn't recognize the number on the screen. Shocked the caller wasn't her brother, Cameron nudged Megan's shoulder.

"Meg."

She groaned and rolled to her back, blinking as she looked up at him. The sight of her utterly exhausted and rumpled from sleeping on his lap shouldn't have his body stirring. Damn that red dress from the christening and the skimpy number she'd had on earlier.

The third ring ripped through the silence, and Megan was on instant alert. She jerked up, grabbed the phone and answered.

Cameron shifted his legs to the floor, immediately getting some blood flow back. They'd obviously been asleep for a while, which was what they had both needed.

Megan came to her feet and spoke in hushed tones as she walked into the other room. He assumed it was a client. Megan often counseled long after regular office hours were over. She was so good at her job because of how caring she was, how much she sacrificed to make sure her clients' needs came first.

Cameron got to his feet, then twisted at the waist until his back popped in all the right places. He was getting too old to sleep on a couch, a car, his office. Unfortunately, he didn't see an end to his bad habits anytime soon.

He turned off the TV, sending the living room into utter darkness. Megan rounded the corner from the kitchen just as he started to reach over and click on the lamp, but his hand bumped the stand and sent the light to the hardwood floor. He cringed at the racket.

"Don't move." Megan turned on the kitchen light, sending an instant glow shining into the living room. "Let me grab my broom."

"You're barefoot," he told her. "Let me clean it up."

"You don't have shoes on, either." She disappeared down the hall and came back with broom and dustpan in hand. "Sit on the couch, and I'll get this."

Like hell. Ignoring her, he reached down to pick up the cockeyed lampshade and the remains of the lamp. The bulb and base had completely shattered.

"I'll bring you a new one later." He set the awkward

shade and lamp guts on the coffee table and reached to take the broom.

Stepping around him, she handed him the dustpan and started sweeping. *Stubborn woman.* No wonder they were best friends. Nobody else would put up with how hardheaded they both were.

He squatted down and held the pan while she scooped in the shards. "At least this wasn't a family heirloom," he joked.

Shoving her hair from her eyes, she threw him a glance. "Funny."

Cameron headed into the kitchen to toss the debris. As he was tying the bag, the vacuum kicked on in the living room, the occasional cracking noise indicating she was removing the rest of the slivers from the floor.

He tugged the liner from the trash can and tied it, wanting to get it out so she didn't cut herself later. As Cameron jerked the knot in place, a hunk of glass he hadn't seen poking from the small hole sliced through the edge of his hand.

Damn. That hurt.

He opened her back door, tossed the bag into the larger can on her patio and closed and locked the door. The vacuum shut off in the other room as Cameron headed to the sink. Running his hand beneath the cool water eased the burning sensation and washed away the mess, allowing him to see just how deep the cut was. Megan didn't need to know he'd hurt himself. She'd make a bigger deal of it than need be.

After rinsing his hand, he examined the area fur-

ther. Instantly he started bleeding again. Apparently it was deeper than he thought.

"Hiding something?"

Cringing, Cameron ripped off a paper towel, pressed it against the side of his hand and turned toward his accuser. Megan rested one shoulder against the door frame, arms crossed over her chest, and merely lifted a brow.

"Just a scratch." That hurt like hell. Apparently he was old and wimpy. Great combo for the police chief.

Cameron's eyes locked on to her shapely legs as she crossed the room. *Damn it.*

Carefully, she took his hand and pulled the paper towel away. "Oh, Cam. This needs stitches."

She examined his hand, then brought her gaze up to meet his. In the middle of the night, with everything so quiet and intimate, Cameron knew for a fact he was starting to delve into a territory he had no business being in.

Her eyes held his, dropped to his mouth, then traveled back up. That gesture said more than any words could. But this was Megan, his best friend, the girl who'd been his senior prom date and the girl who'd sneaked out with him and his brothers that same night and got absolutely plastered near the lake.

She was pretty much family. So why was she looking at him beneath those heavy lids? Why was he enjoying this rush of new sensations, wondering if she had deeper feelings? He shouldn't want her to have stronger emotions for him. That added complication was the last thing either of them needed.

"Come with me."

Cameron blinked. "Excuse me?"

Megan smiled. "To the bathroom. You're too stubborn to go get stitches, so I'll fix you up with my first-aid kit."

When she turned and headed back down the hall, Cameron released a breath he hadn't been aware he'd bottled up. Had he been the only one thinking about what would happen if they kissed? The way she'd looked at him, his mouth, as though she wanted more, wasn't something he'd made up. But the desire flashing in her eyes was gone in a second.

What was going on in that head of hers? More to the point, what the hell was he going to do if her feelings did match his?

"Cam?"

Pushing off the edge of the counter, Cameron moved through the kitchen. They were both sleep deprived; that was all. He'd been without a woman for so long, was so wrapped up in work, and Megan had quite a bit on her plate, as well.

Once daylight came, once reality settled back in and the ambience was gone, this intense moment would be forgotten. Wouldn't it?

Chapter Four

Megan squeezed her eyes shut and willed her hands to stop shaking. That was a close call. She'd nearly ignored every single red flag waving around in her mind and kissed Cameron.

She'd been examining his hand one second and the next she'd found herself lost in those St. John signature blue eyes. After just coming off a phone call with one of her teen clients, Megan had wanted to lose herself in Cameron, even if only for a moment. Bad idea, bad timing.

Heavy footsteps sounded down the hall. Megan stepped aside to give Cameron room. Her guest bath was the smallest in her house, but it was where she kept her first-aid kit.

Without a word he came in and sat down on the

edge of the garden tub. If she thought the bathroom was tiny before, having a man of Cameron's size there only solidified the fact.

"I can take care of this at home," he informed her. "It's the middle of the night."

Ignoring him, Megan cleaned the area, concentrating on her task and not the enclosed space or the warmth radiating from Cameron's body...or the fact she stood directly between his spread legs and only had on a tank and a pair of old boxers.

You'd think she'd at least take a bit more pride in her appearance when he came over, but this was Cameron. He knew her better than anybody so if she donned something halfway dressy, he'd wonder what was wrong.

Megan feared she'd doomed herself into the friend category for life where Cameron was concerned. She'd had feelings for him for years, yet the man was utterly oblivious.

Once the area was clean and dry, Megan quickly placed butterfly bandages over the cut. The strips weren't nearly as effective as stitches, but she wasn't fighting with the stubborn man. Men were like children—you had to pick your battles.

Megan turned to throw away the used supplies and wrappers, only her body and her mind weren't in sync and she swayed slightly. Strong arms circled her waist, holding her steady in an instant.

"You okay?"

Nodding, Megan closed her eyes as his caring words

and warm breath washed over her. "Yeah. The room started spinning for a second. I'm just tired, I guess."

With a gentle power she'd come to appreciate, he eased her down onto his leg. Megan twisted to face him, wondering if this would turn awkward. She didn't want awkward anywhere near their perfectly built relationship. They'd been friends too long to allow anything negative or evil to slip in.

When Cameron's uninjured hand covered her bare thigh, Megan's first thought was how she was glad she'd shaved that day…or the day before, considering it was after midnight.

Her second thought was that she hoped he didn't feel her body trembling beneath his touch. Unfortunately, keeping her body controlled around Cameron was impossible.

"Was that call earlier from a client?" he asked, his thumb tracing an invisible pattern over her thigh.

Staring into those eyes, Megan could only nod.

"You're working yourself too hard, Meg." His bandaged hand slid up, pushing her hair off her shoulder and down her back. "I know you want to be there for your patients, be there for your brother, but when will you do something for yourself?"

Actually, being on his lap right now fell nicely into the "doing something for yourself" category.

"Are you the pot or the kettle?" she asked with a smile.

A corner of his mouth tipped up into a tired grin, causing the corners of his eyes to crease. "Whichever one you aren't."

Megan yawned. "Sorry. You want to crash in the guest room tonight?"

"I'll just walk home."

As Megan came to her feet, Cameron stood with her and kept a hand on her waist.

"Dizzy?" he asked.

Shaking her head, Megan started putting the first-aid kit back. "I'm fine. I've just not been sleeping lately and with the call and then your injury, I think my body was trying to crash before I was ready."

Without even looking at the man, she knew his eyes were on her. She could feel them, feel him.

"Is your client all right?"

Megan thought back to the call. No matter how many years she'd been counseling, certain topics never got easier to deal with, and there were those special cases that truly touched her heart. Megan wished more than anything she could wave a magic wand and heal all the hurt she dealt with on a daily basis.

"Honestly, no." Megan put the kit back under the vanity. She leaned back against the counter and crossed her arms over her chest. "She's unstable, scared and can't live a normal teenage life. It's not fair and I want to go get her and bring her here. She needs love and guidance and to be able to sleep without worrying about her family."

After taking one step, Cameron stood in front of her. His good hand came down and rested on the edge of the sink beside her hip.

"You can't make up for the past, Megan."

How easily this man could see through her. He

knew how she equated every teen to her brother when he'd been an out-of-control hellion after their parents' deaths. Still, the day Megan quit caring about her clients would be the day she quit her job.

"I can't," she agreed, trying not to think about how close he was, how his breath tickled her face or how his body was nearly covering hers. "But I can help one person. I can help steer them toward a better future."

Cameron wrapped his other arm around her shoulders and pulled her against his hard chest. Tilting her head to rest her cheek against him, Megan inhaled the familiar masculine scent. What she wouldn't give to be able to wrap her arms around him and have the embrace mean so much more than friendship. An embrace that led to something intimate, something that would take them to the next level.

"Why don't you concentrate on getting sleep for what's left of the night?"

Megan eased back and smiled. "You sure you don't want the spare room?"

Cameron shook his head and took a step back. "I need to be back at the station early. I'll just head home."

A sliver of disappointment slid through her, but Megan kept smiling. Seriously, if he stayed it wasn't like she'd make a move, even though she'd thought she was ready to admit her feelings. Why couldn't she be more forward about what she wanted? She admired women who targeted a man and went after him.

Megan walked him to the door, rubbing her tired, burning eyes. "If that hand still looks bad by after-

noon I want you to think about getting stitches. I'm not a nurse, you know."

Cameron glanced down to the bandage and shrugged. "It's not my shooting hand. I'll be fine."

Rolling her eyes, Megan reached around him and opened the front door. The living room and foyer were still only illuminated by the light spilling in from the kitchen.

"I have a crazy schedule the next couple of days, but I swear I'll get that lamp replaced."

"Don't worry about it." Megan covered her mouth as another yawn slipped out. "I'll just take one from the spare room until I get to a store. No big deal."

The screen door creaked open as Cameron stepped onto her porch. A cool breeze drifted through as he turned and studied her once more. He opened his mouth as if to say something, but he ended up tightening his lips. Megan wanted to know what he was thinking after they'd shared those intense moments.

Finally he swallowed and nodded. "Lock up behind me."

Megan reached for the screen door to prevent it from slamming. "Always."

"You've got to be kidding me."

Cameron crossed his arms over his chest and stood back, admiring the gaudy gold dragon lamp he'd found on his lunch break at one of the antiques stores in town.

"What?" he asked, pretending to be offended. "It puts out more light than the one you had—plus it was only eight bucks."

Megan laughed. "You got screwed if you paid more than a dime for that hideous thing."

"So you'd rather pay more for something that does the exact same thing?"

Megan stepped closer, bending down to inspect the new piece. She wrinkled her nose, squinted her eyes and her mouth contorted into an expression that looked as if she'd just inhaled the sickening aroma of a sewer plant.

This was the exact reaction he'd expected…which was why he'd bought the ugly thing.

"You did this on purpose," she accused, turning her scrunched face to him. "You know how I am about gifts, and you know I'll keep it just because you got it for me."

Cameron shrugged. "Maybe. Do you still have that unicorn salt-and-pepper-shaker set?"

Her eyes narrowed as she crossed her arms and mirrored his stance. "You know I do. I just don't get it out of the cabinet."

For years he'd randomly bought her tacky things from time to time just for a laugh. He knew how she treasured every present because she hadn't had much growing up and gifts were few and far between. Megan had a loving heart, and she'd never give away something someone bought her.

And now this tacky dragon lamp, with the light shooting out of the open mouth directed toward the ceiling, adorned her neutral-toned living room. A dragon that projectile vomited light? This was a new

level of tacky. Cameron had to really bite the inside of his cheek to keep from bursting out laughing.

"I thought you were too busy to see me today."

The list of things Cameron needed to do flooded his mind. Tonight he'd be staking out another parking lot, waiting for the familiar crew of drug runners to pass through. Cameron only hoped Evan wasn't with them this time. He truly hoped Megan's brother would get away from that crowd. This case would not have a positive ending, and Cameron didn't want to arrest Evan and help convict him of a felony. That crushing blow would kill Megan.

"I'm on my way back in," he told her. "But when I saw this, I just knew you had to have it. I couldn't wait to see your face."

"There will be retaliation," she promised with a gleam in her eyes.

"I can't wait," he retorted, laughing.

Rain started splattering the windows as the gray clouds moved over the sun, blocking out the natural light.

"Got this lamp in just in time," he said, not even trying to hold back his grin. "It's supposed to storm all night. It'll be good for you to sit in here and read."

"I'd hate for the power to go out and my lamp to have some malfunction due to the storm."

Cameron patted the top of the beastly thing. "This is an antique. I'd say she's been around through many storms. Don't worry."

"She? You're giving that thing a gender?"

Cameron may have initially been drawn to the lamp

because of the shock factor and the entertainment value of presenting it to Megan, but there was more. After he'd gotten over the amusement, he realized in some weird way, this dragon reminded him of Megan. Sturdy and fierce. Of course, if he mentioned any of that to her she'd probably launch the heavy atrocity right at his head.

"You can give her a name," he added, just wanting to get under her skin. The unladylike growl was perfect. "Think about it. No need to call her anything right now. You'll want to acquaint yourself."

"I'm thinking of a few names," Megan said through gritted teeth. "None of them are for her, though."

Cameron swatted her arm. "See? You're already thinking of the lamp as her. You'll have her named by the end of the day."

Another unladylike growl escaped Megan as her eyes narrowed to slits. "Don't you have a city to protect?"

More so now than ever, yet he found himself not wanting to leave. This was the first time in a while he actually smiled for good reason. Added to that, he felt they needed this ridiculous moment after way too many close calls. His control was about to snap.

Even if he had wanted to risk their friendship and delve into a more intimate relationship, he couldn't ignore the flashes of his old partner that ripped through him. The man had been married to his job and he'd had a beautiful young wife at home. Now she was a widow. Cameron tried to check in on her from time to time, and he would never forget her face when she'd learned

her husband had been killed in the line of duty. Killed by a bullet meant for Cameron. The guilt used to eat at him, but now he realized he would've done the same thing. Jumping into the line of fire wasn't something you thought about, you just did it.

"Cam?"

Megan's hand on his arm and her soft tone pulled him from his thoughts. "Yeah. Sorry."

"You left me for a minute." Her arched brows drew in. "You can talk to me. I know you can't discuss open cases, but you can at least get out some frustration."

No, he couldn't because the second those words left her lips, he found himself studying her mouth. The very thought of kissing her should have made awkwardness rise to the surface, but he found himself curious how she would taste, how she would respond. There was only one way to get her out of his system.

"I'm fine," he assured her. Well, as fine as he could be considering he was now fantasizing about kissing his best friend and keeping the fact that her brother was in way over his head with drug runners a secret. "I need to get going."

Megan reached out, wrapping her arms around him. She held on tighter than usual and damn if that didn't send a shot of arousal straight through him. Cameron slid his arms around her waist, loving how she just knew when he needed a connection most.

"Be careful," she whispered just before she stepped back. "I know you're working on a big case, but promise me you're cautious."

Cameron swallowed, hating the worry that settled

in her bright eyes. This was the reason he wouldn't subject her or any other woman to his line of work.

"I promise," he told her. "Text me and tell me what you name her."

Megan's eyes darted to the dragon lamp and back to him. "Distracting me from worry won't work."

Cameron gave her shoulder a squeeze and headed to the door. "No need to worry. Call me if you need anything."

"You know I won't call you." She smiled and tipped that adorable defiant chin up a notch. "I'm perfectly capable of taking care of myself."

Yes, but she didn't know what she was up against if her loser brother opted to somehow use her in his latest dealings. Cameron had to be on full alert because the likelihood of Evan trying to get something from Megan or bringing the rest of the cronies into her life was viable. Cameron might be watching the entire city, but his focus was zeroed in on keeping Megan safe and oblivious to the activity hitting way too close to home.

Granted, this was a small town, but that didn't mean evils wouldn't try to reach their arms in and infiltrate anyone who proved to be an easy target. Cameron wouldn't allow his town to be overrun by corrupt, illegal activities as long as he was chief.

Cameron headed back to the station, where he would be meeting up with an FBI agent to discuss the case. Too often cops developed inflated egos and didn't want outside assistance. Cameron wasn't that stupid. When the FBI had come in, he had welcomed the extra help. He'd do anything to keep his town safe, to keep drugs

from filtering into the schools and homes of innocent, unsuspecting kids.

He wasn't naive enough to believe he could stop all drug trafficking, but he was damn sure going to stop this group from bringing shipments into Stonerock. Every bust, every seller taken off the streets, could possibly be saving someone's life.

Cameron couldn't wait for this case to wrap up. They had a good amount of evidence so far, but they needed a bit more. An undercover FBI agent had been placed deep in the runners' inner circle months ago. Another reason Cameron was elated to have them all on board.

All they had to do was wait on his signal, and then the group would be taken down.

Glancing back at Megan's one-story cottage, complete with cheery colorful flowers and a yellow front door, Cameron only hoped he could save her from the pain of seeing her own brother in prison. Unfortunately, Cameron didn't think that was possible.

Chapter Five

The storm had ripped through the night, putting off the surveillance. Cameron and a few other officers and FBI agents had waited around the station, hoping the storm would pass. Unfortunately, with lightning bolting across the sky and claps of thunder raging at the same time, even the dealers weren't stupid enough to be outdoors.

At around three in the morning, Cameron headed home, ready to get a few hours of sleep before coming back. Their informant had told them another meet was scheduled to happen in three days. Cameron honestly thought of taking a day off to do absolutely nothing. He was running on fumes. All he wanted to do was fall face-first into his bed and sleep for a good solid eight hours. Was that too much to ask?

He and the other agents and officers were convinced

it would only take one or two more meets before they could bring the group down. The day wouldn't come soon enough.

His headlights cut through the darkness as he pulled into his drive. He needed a shower and a bed. He actually needed food, but that would have to wait. He was too exhausted to even pry open a package of toaster pastries at this point.

After letting himself in the back door, he removed his shoulder holster and gun. After carrying it through the darkened hall, he stepped into his bedroom and placed the gun on the dresser just inside the door. Turning around, he went into the bathroom directly across the hall from his room.

The shower was quick, hot and enough to loosen his sore muscles and have him one step closer to falling into oblivion as soon as he slid between his sheets.

Wrapping the towel around his waist and tucking the edge in to secure it in place, Cameron padded back across the hall. He kept his blackout shades pulled at all times, seeing as how he never knew when he'd get shut-eye and he wanted to keep the room nice and dark. Of course tonight, with the storm, the moon wasn't even out to offer a glow.

Cameron jerked off the towel and hung it on the closet doorknob. Shuffling toward the king-size bed, Cameron nearly wept at the thought of falling asleep. Now, if he could stay asleep that would be a miracle.

Jerking back the covers quickly revealed two things: there was a woman in his bed, and there would be no sleep tonight.

* * *

His hands glided over her bare skin, sending ripples of satisfaction coursing through her. Finally, after all these years, she would finally know what making love to her best friend was like.

A soft groan escaped her lips; her body arched in eager anticipation.

"Megan."

Even his voice aroused her. That low, throaty tone. She'd imagined him growling her name while looking into her eyes as his body leaned over hers.

"Meg."

The firm grip on her shoulder had her lifting her lids, blinking. Darkness surrounded her, but the shape before her was so familiar, so close. She reached up, slid her hands over his stubbled jaw and pulled him down. Her mouth covered his and for a second she wondered why he wasn't responding.

The thought was fleeting as Cameron's hesitant state snapped; his hold on her shoulders tightened. His mouth opened, his tongue plunging in to tangle with hers. Yes, this is what she needed, what she craved.

The weight of his body pressing hers back into the bed, the sheer strength of this man, consumed her in every single way and made all her fantasies seem so minor in comparison.

The euphoria of coming from a dream into reality—

Megan froze. Dream into reality? *Oh, no.* She had been dreaming earlier…now she wasn't.

As if sensing her detachment, Cameron stilled and lifted his head. She lay on the bed, the top half of his

body covering hers, the tingling sensations still rippling through her as she focused back on the cold, harsh reality.

"Cam?"

"Yeah." His husky voice did nothing to rid her body's ache. "Um…sorry. That was…I don't…why did you kiss me?"

With her palms plastered to his bare chest—his bare, damp chest—Megan closed her eyes and battled with telling the truth or saving her pride.

"I was dreaming."

Pride won out. How could she tell her best friend she'd been dreaming of seducing him and fully succeeding? How could she tell him that for years she'd dreamed of taking control and making him see just how amazing they'd be together?

"That was one hell of a dream." He eased himself off her, and as her eyes fully adjusted to the darkened room, she realized he wore… *Oh, mercy.* He wore absolutely nothing.

Embarrassed, yet incredibly still aroused, Megan shoved her hair away from her face. "I didn't want to bother you at work and I thought I'd be gone by morning since I figured you'd be out all night." She realized she was rambling, but nerves had taken over and she'd lost all control. As she rambled, though, it gave him time to retrieve a towel from the closet knob and secure it around his waist. "I couldn't sleep at my house and had you been home I would've taken the couch, but since you were out…"

Cameron smiled as she trailed off, and she figured

she sounded as nervous as she felt. Silence settled between them, and he crossed his arms over his chest, as if wearing only a towel was the most comfortable thing in the world.

Was he not affected at all by that kiss? She knew for a fact he'd been somewhat aroused when he'd been on top of her, but now he merely looked at her with that lopsided grin she'd come to love.

"I don't mind a bit that you came here," he informed her. "But what was wrong with your house?"

Restless on so many levels, Megan came to her feet and started smoothing out the covers. "My back door had been tampered with and the lock was broken. I wasn't comfortable sleeping there. I didn't figure you'd mind."

"What the hell, Meg?" Reaching around her, he clicked on the bedside lamp. "Someone broke in and you were afraid to call my cell?"

"I wasn't afraid," she defended herself, testing every bit of her self-control as she kept her eyes on his and not on the stark white towel riding low on his hips or the sprinkling of dark hair across his bare torso. "I knew you were busy and...can you put some pants on? I can't talk like this."

A corner of his mouth kicked up into a grin. "You've seen me in swim trunks, Meg."

Yes, but in those instances he hadn't just been lying on top of her, kissing her back as if she were his next breath of air. Would her lips ever stop tingling from all that heat? His body's imprint was permanently ingrained onto hers.

Her eyes darted to the bed, re-creating an image of how close she'd been to attaining her greatest fantasy. When she glanced back up, Cameron's jaw was clenched, his eyes holding hers as if he knew exactly where her thoughts had traveled and he was having a hard time keeping his own from going there.

"It's not the same," she whispered.

With a nod, he turned, pulled a pair of shorts from his drawer and slid them on beneath the towel. With a flick of his wrist, the towel came off and he hung it back on the doorknob before he crossed the intimate room to stand within a breath of her.

"Now, tell me what the hell is going on. What happened at your house?"

Megan pulled in a deep breath, giving herself an extra minute to figure out how to control her emotions and get back on track to where their conversation needed to be.

"My back door had been kicked in or something. It was open and the lock was busted."

Cameron raked a hand over his still-damp hair and muttered a curse. "You'll call me next time anything happens. Me, not the department, not another officer. You'll call my cell."

A little surprised at his demanding tone, Megan propped her hands on her hips. "What would you have done? Left whatever you've been working undercover on for months?"

His narrowed eyes held hers as he eased forward just enough for his bare chest to brush against her. "Yes."

He'd put work second? That was a first. Work never

came after anything for Cameron. He took pride in keeping his town's reputation favorable and the crime rate low. To know he would've dropped everything for her caused a new warmth to spread through her, overlaying the previous heat from their intimate encounter moments ago.

"I didn't need to call you for a busted door," she said. "I knew you'd look at it sometime in the morning. I just wanted to sleep. Like I said, had I known you'd be home, I'd have taken the couch."

While his small cottage had two bedrooms, the second bedroom was full of workout equipment that aided in bulking up his already magnificent physic.

"I'll take the couch," he told her. "Go on back to sleep."

Oh, sure. As if she could crawl back into that bed after what had just happened. She'd had a hard enough time getting to sleep in the first place because she'd nearly suffocated herself by burying her face into his pillow and inhaling that familiar masculine scent. She really needed to get a grip before she made a complete fool of herself.

"I'll take the couch." She smiled up at him, hoping the friendly gesture would ease the tension. Granted, the tension was most likely all one-sided. "You've been up long enough and there's no way you'll fit."

"What kind of gentleman and friend would I be if I booted my best friend to the couch?"

Best friend. Had he thrown those two words at her to remind her of their status? Had she completely freaked him out when she'd attacked him, rubbed her-

self all over him and claimed his mouth? Part of her was mortified; the other part of her was a bit relieved she'd finally kissed him. She'd not only kissed him, she'd full-out devoured him. But now she knew how he tasted, how he felt. That knowledge was both a blessing and a curse.

"I either take the couch or I head home where it may not be safe."

True, she wasn't fighting fair because no way would he let her go if he thought for a second she wasn't well protected. He studied her for a moment, and Megan tried not to look away or fidget beneath that hypnotic gaze. Would she ever stop tingling? Would she ever forget how perfectly his body felt pressed against hers? She hoped not. Those were memories she'd want to re-live over and over for as long as possible.

"You're stubborn."

Megan shrugged. "One of my many talents," she told him, patting his bare shoulder because she was having a hard time resisting all that glorious skin mere inches away. "Sleep tight."

Inching around him, inhaling that fresh-from-the-shower scent, Megan made her way out of his room and headed to the couch. She may as well just head on home because there was no way she could sleep now, not after that kiss. But she would stay. If Cameron knew she was home, he wouldn't rest, either, and he desperately needed to before he worked himself to death.

Megan pulled a blanket from the back of the couch, fluffed the throw pillow and lay on her side, facing the

hallway. The darkened space offered nothing of comfort or peace. The silence was equally as empty.

Was Cameron already lying in bed? Had he already slid between the sheets she'd just come from? Had that kiss even made an impact on him, or was he completely repulsed at the fact his best friend had tried to consume him?

More than likely the man's head had barely hit the pillow before he was out. At least one of them would get some sleep tonight.

Chapter Six

How the hell could a man rest after finding a woman in his bed, being kissed in such an arousing way by said woman and now smelling her fruity scent on his sheets?

Cameron laced his fingers over his abdomen and stared up at the ceiling fan. Whoever Megan had been dreaming about was one lucky man. The way she'd all but plastered her curvy body against his had him instantly responding. Hence the problem with sleeping. How the hell did he react to this? For a few brief moments, he'd found something with Megan he'd never experienced with any other woman. Ever.

What was the protocol for discovering your best friend kissed like every man's fantasy? He knew he'd wanted her on a primal level, but to actually have evidence of the fact only added to his confusion.

This was Megan, the woman who knew all his secrets, all his annoying quirks. They'd been through everything together from riding their first rollercoaster to her brother's ups and downs.

She was like family, only he was feeling close to her in a way that had nothing to do with family. He'd secretly hoped if he ever got his hands or lips on her, he'd get her out of his system because he'd feel nothing. Unfortunately, that was completely the opposite of what had just happened. He felt too much, too fast.

Cameron's body still hadn't settled back down, and it wouldn't anytime soon. Who the hell had Megan been dreaming about? She wasn't dating anyone, unless she was keeping it a secret.

Damn it. Jealousy was an ugly, unwelcome trait.

Swiping a hand down his face, Cameron cursed himself. Here he was, dead on his feet, unable to sleep for fantasizing about his best friend dreaming about a mysterious man. How messed up had his life become in the past hour?

Licking his lips, he still tasted her. He couldn't want more. Wanting anything more from Megan was out of the question. Their friendship was solid—why mess that up just because she kissed like every dream he'd ever had?

Movement in the house made him focus on the darkness instead of his wayward thoughts. Bare feet slid over the hardwood. The refrigerator door opened, closed, followed by the sound of a cabinet being shut softly. She was trying to be so quiet, but he wasn't

sleeping and he was trained to hear even the slightest disturbances.

This new tension that had settled between them wasn't going anywhere. She may have tried to act calm after what they'd shared, but he knew her well enough to know she was anything but. Her nerves and emotions were just as jumbled, just as buzzing, as his were.

With a sigh, he sat up and swung his legs over the side of the bed. Might as well face this head-on. He didn't want uneasiness to become an uninvited third party in their relationship. Maybe she really was just dreaming, but the way his body responded, the way she'd been jittery afterward, told him there was more.

He padded his way down the hall, his eyes adjusting to the darkness in his familiar surroundings. The living room was empty, so he turned toward the kitchen, where he saw her. Leaning against the counter, looking out onto the backyard, Megan held a glass in her hand. Cameron studied her in a new light. He couldn't deny her beauty, with her perfectly shaped curves and hair that tumbled down her back. Those green eyes could pierce you in an instant, and now he knew that mouth could render a man speechless.

Still clutching the glass and staring, Megan hadn't moved one bit since he'd stood here. Something, or someone, consumed her mind.

"Who is he?"

Megan jumped, turned and the glass she'd been clutching dropped to the floor with a crackling shatter.

"Damn it." He started to move forward but stopped. He reached around the doorjamb and flicked on the

light, blinking against the bright glare. "Don't move. Neither of us have shoes on."

First the lamp at her house and now this. They hadn't even delved into relationship territory, and already things were breaking all around them. A metaphor for things to come?

He ran back to his room and shoved his feet into a pair of tennis shoes at the foot of the bed. When he got back to the kitchen, Megan was bending over, picking up pieces of glass.

"I told you not to move," he growled, not knowing which situation he was angrier at.

"I didn't take a step. I'm just picking up the large pieces."

He jerked open the small built-in utility closet and grabbed the broom and dustpan. After sweeping up the majority of the glass, Megan set the shards she'd held into the dustpan, too.

After dumping the mess into the trash, he went back and scooped her up into his arms without a word.

With a squeak of surprise, Megan landed against his chest and he had no idea how to react to the fact his body warmed and responded with her against him once again.

"This is overkill—don't you think?" she asked, sliding one arm around his neck.

"I need you out of the way so I can get the rest and you're not wearing shoes. So no, I don't think it's overkill."

He deposited her on the couch in the living room and made his way back to clean up the water and make

sure all the fragments were swept up. Several minutes later, he headed back into the living room to find Megan gone.

Heading down the hall, he heard water running from the bathroom. She'd left the door open, allowing the light to spill into the hallway. When he peeked into the room, Megan was at the sink, holding one hand under the water. Blood seeped to the surface of her palm as soon as water could wash it away.

"Why didn't you tell me you'd cut yourself?" he asked.

"Like you told me the other day?" Throwing him a glance over her shoulder, Megan shrugged. "You were cleaning up the mess. Seriously, it's very minor. I could use a bandage, though."

Stepping forward, Cameron reached around, shut the water off and held on to her wrist to examine her hand. Her hair tickled the side of his face, and the pulse beneath his fingertips sped up. Gritting his teeth to shove aside any emotions outside the friend zone, Cameron inspected the injury.

"It is small," he agreed, still inspecting the area.

She glanced up, catching his eyes in the mirror. "It just needs to be cleaned up and a bandage. I wasn't lying."

When he continued to stare at her, she merely quirked a brow. Damn woman would make a nun curse like a sailor.

"Sit," he said, pointing to the toilet lid. "It's my turn to take care of you."

Grabbing the first-aid kit from beneath the sink, he

shuffled the supplies around and found what he needed to fix her up.

He took a seat on the edge of the tub and balanced the supplies on his thigh. With careful movements, he uncurled her fingers and examined the cut again. It was bleeding pretty good, but it wasn't deep at all.

"I'm thinking you and I need only plastic, child-safe things in our homes," she joked.

"At the very least, we should stop handling glass in the middle of the night."

Cameron appreciated her attempt to lighten the mood, but he'd come out of his room for a reason and he needed to get this off his chest.

"Why couldn't you sleep?" he asked, keeping his eyes locked on his task as he swiped her palm with gauze.

"Insomnia has become a close friend of mine lately."

That was something he definitely understood. Still, she'd been sleeping just fine earlier in his bed.

"I'll make sure your door is fixed so you can sleep in your bed." Confident the bleeding had slowed enough not to come through the bandage, Cameron held a fresh gauze pad over the cut and applied pressure. "I'm sorry I startled you earlier."

Her hand tensed beneath his touch. "What were you asking me when you came into the kitchen, anyway?"

Keeping his thumb over the pad, he lifted his gaze to hers. Those bright green eyes outlined by dark lashes held him captivated and speechless for a second. "Nothing. Forget it."

"You asked who he was," she went on. "What *he* are you referring to?"

Knowing she wouldn't back down, Cameron opted to face this head-on as he'd originally intended. He was chief of police, for crying out loud, yet the thought of discussing another man with Megan had him trembling and nearly breaking out into a sweat…not to mention ready to punch someone in the face.

"I wanted to know who you were dreaming about."

Megan lowered her lids, took a deep breath and let it out. "I'm not sure you're ready for that answer."

Not ready for the answer? What was she about to tell him? Was she fantasizing about someone he didn't care for? Cameron got along with nearly everybody on the right side of the law.

"It's none of my business," he repeated, not sure he was ready for the answer, either. "The way you kissed me…"

Megan stared at him as his words died in the crackling air between them. "I was dreaming of you."

Nerves and fear settled deep in her stomach as if weighted by an anchor. She kept her gaze on his, refusing to back down or show weakness. He wanted the truth—he got it. Now they would both have to deal with the consequences because she'd just opened a door and shoved him right on through into the black abyss. Neither of them had a clue what waited for them.

Cameron's warm hand continued to hold hers, protecting her injury. He clenched the muscle in his jaw

as if he was holding back his response. Not knowing what was going on in his head was only adding to her worry.

"Say something." She tried for a smile but swallowed instead, blinking as her eyes began to burn with the threat of tears. *Oh, no.* She wouldn't break down. Not here, not now. "It was a kiss, Cam. No big deal."

Okay, so she'd tried to be strong and not back down, but right now, in the wake of his silence, she figured backpedaling was the only approach.

"Don't lie to me," he commanded. "I was on the receiving end of that kiss, and it was definitely a big deal."

Megan pulled her hand away and got to her feet, causing him to scoot back and try to catch all the supplies from his lap before they scattered to the floor.

"I was still asleep, Cameron. I was in your bed, surrounded by your scent. I can't help what I was dreaming."

Lifting the pad from her hand, she studied her palm. The cut only stung a little, not enough to keep her focus off the fact she was in this minuscule bathroom with Cameron and she'd just told him she'd been fantasizing about him. There wasn't enough air or space because he came up right behind her, practically caging her in between his hard, broad body and the vanity.

"So you're saying if I kissed you now that you're fully awake, you wouldn't respond like earlier?"

His bold, challenging question had her jerking her gaze up to meet his in the mirror. Slowly turning to face him, brushing against every plane of his torso in

the process, Megan clutched her injured hand against her chest. Though the cut was insignificant in the grand scheme of things, holding on to it gave her a prop she needed to calm her shaky hands.

"It's late…or early," she told him. "Let's forget any of this happened and try to salvage what's left of the night. We both need sleep."

He braced his hands on the sink, officially trapping her in between his arms. "You're not a coward."

"No, I'm not. But this little exercise is ridiculous."

Lowering his lids, he stared at her mouth. "Then this won't be a problem."

His mouth slid over hers, and Megan pulled up every ounce of self-control to keep from moaning. Earlier she'd been half dreaming when she'd kissed him, but now she was fully awake and able to truly enjoy how amazing her best friend was in the kissing department.

Even though he was demanding and controlling, Cameron somehow managed to also be gentle with his touch. One strong hand splayed across her back, urging her closer. Her injured hand remained trapped between their bodies, and she fisted the other at her side because she didn't want to show emotion, not now. As much as she yearned to wrap herself around him and give in to anything he was willing to offer, she wasn't ready.

Cameron nipped at her lips, easing his way out of the kiss. But he didn't stop. No, the man merely angled his head the other way and dived back in for more.

The way he had her partially bent back over the van-

ity, Megan had to bring up her good hand to clutch his bare shoulder. She couldn't recall the last time she'd been so thoroughly kissed. No matter the time, she'd certainly never been kissed as passionately, as intensely, as now. Even those kisses that led straight to the bedroom had never gotten her this hot, this turned on.

Cameron fisted her T-shirt in his hand, pulling it tighter against her back as he lifted his head slightly. His forehead rested against hers.

"You're awake now," he muttered. "Feeling anything?"

Because she needed to think, and she knew *he* needed to think, Megan patted his shoulder and smiled. "You're a good kisser, Cam. No denying that. But I'm not dreaming anymore."

Cameron stepped back, hands on his narrowed hips where his shorts were riding low. "Tell me that didn't make your body respond."

She knew for a fact his body had responded, but she wouldn't be so tacky as to drop her gaze to the front of his shorts. They both knew she was fully aware.

Cameron had never even hinted he wanted to kiss her before. And even though she knew she should take this chance to tell him how she felt, she found herself lying to his face to save hers.

"Like I said, you're a great kisser," she told him. "But I've had better."

With that bold-faced lie, she marched from the bathroom and straight to the sofa, where she lay down facing the back cushions and covered up with the throw.

Megan wasn't quite sure if she'd put this experiment to rest or if she'd awakened the beast inside Cameron.

She had a feeling she'd find out soon enough. Thrills of anticipation coursed through her at the prospect.

Chapter Seven

Cameron needed this break. Between work and keeping track of Evan at various late-night meetings and that semierotic evening spent with Megan, he was about to lose it.

Drinking a beer on Eli's new patio with his brothers while their wives sat in the house discussing babies or shoes or some other frightening topic was exactly what he needed to relax.

Of course the incident with Megan had happened only two days ago and he still hadn't been able to get a grasp on how much that kiss, both kisses, had affected him.

"We've lost him again," Eli mocked, pulling Cameron from his daze.

"He's still working in his head." Drake took a pull of

his beer, then let the bottle dangle between his knees. "You're off the clock right now. Enjoy it."

Cameron rested his forearms on the edge of the deck railing and glanced out into the wooded backyard. Eli had built an addition on his home and then added the deck. He and his wife of nearly a year, and their baby, lived in their own little corner on the edge of town.

Drake, with his new bride and adorable stepdaughter, was embracing family life, as well. Drake had even mentioned how he and Marly wanted to try for a baby of their own.

Cameron couldn't be happier for his brothers, but they could keep their minivans, grocery lists and scheduled bedtimes. That wasn't a lifestyle he saw himself settling into anytime soon…if ever.

"I'm not working in my head," he defended himself. "I'm just enjoying listening to you two go on about recipes and paint swatches like a bunch of old ladies at a hair salon."

"Someone's grouchy," Eli muttered.

"Maybe he doesn't have a recipe worth sharing and he's embarrassed," Drake added with a low chuckle.

Cameron turned, flipping his brothers the one-finger salute. He missed getting together with them. They used to try to have a cookout or something once a week, especially since Eli's deployments were over and he was officially a civilian now, but Cameron's schedule was anything but regular. He hated putting work ahead of his family, but sometimes he couldn't help the matter. The criminals didn't seem to keep nine-to-five hours.

"Oh, hell," Drake whispered as he sat straight up in his deck chair. "You've finally got woman issues."

Eli's head whipped around, his gaze narrowing on Cameron. "Seriously? Because if you have woman issues, that means you have a woman, which is a damn miracle."

Finishing off his beer, knowing full well he needed something stronger to get into this discussion, Cameron tossed his empty bottle into the bin.

"I don't have a woman," he ground out, dropping onto the settee. "I have a headache over one."

Why did he have to go and issue Megan that challenge? Why did he have to push her into proving she was lying? Because all he'd gotten out of the deal was a hell of a great kiss, sleepless nights full of fantasies fueled by his best friend and a whole lot of anger with himself for crossing the line.

His own issues aside, how could he actually move to another level with Megan knowing her brother was well on his way to prison? Hell, Cameron was having a hard time keeping that bottled up now, and they were just friends. How could he keep secrets if he allowed intimacy to slip into the picture?

"Who is she?" Eli asked. "Oh, is it the new lady in town that lives out behind the grocery store? I hear she's single and if those tight-fitting clothes and spike heels aren't an invitation—"

"An invitation to what?" Nora asked from the patio door with her arms crossed over her chest, a quirked brow and a knowing grin on her face.

Eli cleared his throat. "Hey, babe," he said, cross-

ing the wide area to wrap an arm around her waist. "I was just thinking about you."

She swatted him in the stomach. "If you think I'll ever dress like I work a pole every night, you're insane."

Eli groaned. "Please, don't mention a pole."

Cameron and Drake exchanged a conspiratorial look before they busted out laughing. "Still scarred from the image of Maddie Mays?"

Squeezing his eyes shut, Eli shook his head. "I'm trying to forget, but she was in again yesterday. Why does she always bring up her workout regime with me?"

"Because you're her doctor," Cameron smirked, enjoying the idea of his brother in such an awkward position. "Aren't you sworn to secrecy? I don't think you should share such things with us."

Eli blinked, narrowing his gaze. "If I have to suffer at the image, then so do you two."

"Mad" Maddie Mays had seemed to be a hundred years old when they were kids. At this point she may have been the same age as Noah and survived by hiding out on the ark. She'd never been a fan of the St. John boys and found their shenanigans less than amusing. More often than not, she'd chased them out of her yard wielding a rolling pin, baseball bat or sometimes both to really get her point across.

Now with Eli taking over their father's clinic, Maddie had no choice but to associate with at least one of the St. John boys, unless she wanted to find a doctor in a neighboring town. Apparently she'd warmed up

to Eli. Perhaps sharing her unorthodox exercise routine was just her way of getting back at him for being a menace as a kid.

"If you guys are done discussing that poor woman, I wanted to know if you all had mentioned date night to Cameron." Nora took the bottle from Eli's hands and took a drink.

"What date night?" Cameron eyed his brothers. "You two aren't my type."

Nora smiled. "Actually we were wondering if you'd like to play the cool uncle while we went out. I was hesitant to ask you, but Eli and Drake assured me you wouldn't mind if you weren't busy."

Stunned, Cameron considered the idea, then shrugged. "Sure, I can do it." He'd just schedule the diaper changing and mac-and-cheese dinner around watching for drug smugglers. "How hard can watching a baby and a six-year-old be?"

His brothers exchanged a look and nearly turned red trying to hold back a comment or laughter. *Oh, they think I'm not capable? Challenge accepted.*

"Seriously?" Cameron went on. "You're already thinking I'm going to blow this? I run a town, for pity's sake. Surely I can handle two kids."

Nora stepped forward, patted his arm and offered a smile that was a bit on the patronizing side. Did nobody have faith in him?

"Just tell us when you're free," she told him.

Running his crazy schedule through his mind, Cameron knew there wouldn't be a great night, but he could

surely spare a few hours. "I could do it Sunday evening."

"I work until four, but we could go after that," Drake chimed in.

"Great." Nora beamed. She leaned down, kissed Cameron on the cheek and patted his shoulder. "I'll go tell Marly."

She raced back into the house and Cameron leaned his head back against the cushion on the settee. Both brothers stared down at him.

"What?"

"You're not getting off the hook about this woman that has you tied in knots just because you're babysitting," Eli insisted. "We'll get the truth out of you one way or another."

Cameron didn't even know what there was to tell. Megan had kissed him, he'd kissed her and since then they hadn't spoken. What a mess, and most of it was his fault. If he hadn't insisted on challenging her, if he'd let her lie her way out of the first kiss, they would've moved on and ignored that pivotal turn they'd taken.

No way would he reveal Megan's name to his brothers. She was like a sister to them, and he wasn't sure they'd be on board with how Cameron had treated her.

But damn it, she'd tied him up in knots the second she'd slid her body against his.

"Come on—you can't sit there brooding and not fill us in." Drake leaned an elbow against the railing. "It has to be someone you know since you work every waking second. You don't have time to meet women

unless it's someone you're arresting. Please, tell me you don't have some prisoner-guard romance going because if you do we're staging an intervention."

"Do you ever shut up?" Cameron asked, without heat. "Can't a guy keep some things to himself?"

"No," Eli and Drake replied in unison.

Raking a hand down his face, Cameron came to his feet. He couldn't stay any longer. If he did, they'd figure out who had him in knots and he couldn't afford to let that out right now, not when he was so confused. And he had no clue what was going through Megan's head, either.

"Now he's leaving." Eli laughed. "This must be bad if you're running from your own brothers."

"It's a small town," Drake added with a smile that stated he'd get to the bottom of it. "Secrets don't stay hidden long. The truth will come out eventually."

Cameron glared at his brothers before heading into the house to say goodbye to his sisters-in-law and his nieces.

The truth coming out was precisely what he couldn't have happen. But he knew he wasn't telling anybody about the incident and he doubted Megan would tell anyone, so that left the secret bottled up good and tight.

The question now was: When would it explode?

Megan hadn't even made it home from work when her cell rang. She'd just pulled onto her road when she answered without looking.

"Hello."

"I'm sorry to bother you."

Instantly Megan recognized the voice of one of her clients…a girl who'd just been in earlier that afternoon and the same one who'd called in the middle of the night days ago. Farrah wasn't the most stable person, and Megan made a point to really work with her. Megan cared for all her clients' well-being, but Farrah was extremely unstable and truly had no one else to turn to.

"Don't apologize," Megan insisted as she neared her driveway. "I'm here for you anytime."

"Earlier you told me that moving forward was the only way to start over."

Megan eased her car into the detached garage. "That's right."

Farrah sniffed. "I'm going to look for a job tomorrow. It's time I move out and try to make my life my own."

Megan had been waiting for Farrah to see that she needed to stand on her own two feet, to get away from the controlling man who held so much power over her. Megan had tried to stress how control can often quickly turn to abuse.

"I just wanted to thank you for today, and maybe… Could I put you down as a reference?"

Megan smiled as she killed the engine. "That would be fine. I'm really proud of you, Farrah."

Farrah thanked her, then ended the call. By the time Megan gathered her things and headed across the stone walkway to her back door, her phone was ringing again. She glanced at the screen and saw Evan's number. She hated how her first instinct was to groan.

How was it she could counsel total strangers, yet her own flesh and blood refused to take her advice or even consider for a moment that she wasn't trying to control him?

With a sigh, she answered as she shoved her key in her new doorknob. "Hi, Evan."

"Can I stay with you for a few nights?"

Stunned, Megan froze with her hand on the knob. She wasn't shocked at his abrupt question without so much as a greeting, but at the request. It was unusual for him not to ask for money first.

"Are you all right?"

"Yeah, yeah. I just…I need a place to crash. You going to help me or not?"

Closing her eyes, Megan leaned her head against the glass on the door. Even though his tone was put out and angry, he was at least coming to her for support.

"I'll always help you, Evan. But are you asking because you're ready to make changes in your life or because you're hiding?"

"Forget it," he grunted. "You're always judging me."

"No, Evan. I'm not judging—I'm worried."

Silence filled the line. Megan straightened and strained to hear.

"Evan?"

"If I wanted to change, could you help me?"

Now his voice came out in a near whisper, reminding her of the young boy he'd once been. At one time he'd looked up to her. When did all of that change?

"I'd do anything for you," she assured him. "Do you need help? I can come get you right now."

Again silence filled the line. She waited, not wanting to push further. This was the first time he actually sounded as if he may want to let her in. Megan prayed he would take the olive branch she'd been holding out for so long.

Commotion from the other end of the line, muffled voices and Evan's swearing told her the conversation was dead.

"I'll, uh, I'll call you later," he whispered as if he didn't want to be heard.

Gripping her phone, Megan pushed her way into the house. She didn't know why she'd let herself get her hopes up for those few seconds. She didn't know why she was constantly beating herself up over a man who might just continue to use her for the rest of their lives. But he was her brother and she would never give up. She may be frustrated and oftentimes deflated, but she wasn't a quitter and she would make damn sure he wasn't, either.

He'd called; that was a major step.

After hanging her purse on the peg by the back door, Megan slid her keys and phone inside. Her stomach growled, reminding her that she'd skipped lunch again in order to squeeze in one more client. Her supervisor kept telling her she needed to take breaks, but how could Megan justify them when someone's life could very well be in her hands? What if it was the patient who was contemplating suicide or leaving a spouse and they needed to talk right then? Megan couldn't turn them away.

Her eyes landed on the letter she'd tacked to the side

of her refrigerator. The letter outlining every detail for the new position she'd been offered in Memphis. The job was almost too good to be true, but it meant leaving Cameron, leaving the chance for something she'd wanted her whole life.

The directors had certainly pulled out all the stops to get her to take the position. The opportunity to help launch a free clinic in an area of town where people had been forgotten, left to their own devices. Megan wasn't married, didn't have kids and had been recommended for this job by her boss. How could she say no?

Two very valid reasons kept her from jumping at this chance of a lifetime: Evan and Cameron. Both men were fixtures in her life, and both men needed her whether either of them admitted it or not.

She hadn't spoken to Cameron in a few days, and emptiness had long since settled into that pit in her stomach, joining the fear and worry there. This was precisely why she hadn't made a move before, why she'd kept her feelings to herself. If a few kisses had already wedged an awkward wall between them, what would've happened had she told him she wanted to try a real relationship with him?

Megan glanced at the letter again and sighed. Maybe she should go. Maybe she needed to get away from the man who was a constant in her life but would never fill the slot she needed him to. And perhaps her new start would be the perfect opportunity for Evan to make a clean break, as well.

Chapter Eight

"I need you." Cameron surveyed the chaos around him and cringed. "How soon can you be at my house?"

Shrill cries pierced his eardrums for at least the fifteenth time in as many minutes. Every single parent in the world officially had his respect and deserved some type of recognized award for their patience.

"Where are you?" Megan asked. "What's all that noise?"

Cameron raked a hand over his hair and realized he needed to get a cut. He'd add that to the many things he'd slacked on lately. Right now, though, he was groveling to his best friend to come save him even though he'd been a jerk and hadn't spoken to her since.

His house was a complete war zone thanks to a spunky six-year-old and an infant.

Willow was dancing her stuffed horse in front of Amber's reddened, angry, tear-soaked face in an attempt to calm the baby, but Cameron figured that was only making it worse. Not to mention the fact that Willow had a slight goose egg on her head after tripping over the baby and falling into the corner of the coffee table.

Why had he insisted on watching the kids at his house? A house that was as far from baby proof as possible. He was a bachelor. Unfortunately, his bachelor pad had now tragically converted into a failing day-care center.

"Please," he begged. He never begged. "I'm home, and you can't get here fast enough. I'm…babysitting."

Okay, so he muttered that last word because he knew Megan well enough to know she'd burst out laughing and he wasn't in the mood.

"I'm sorry. Did you say *babysitting*?"

Cameron bent over and pulled Amber into his arms. "Front door's unlocked," he said right before disconnecting the call and sliding his cell back into his pocket. He had no time for mockery; this was crisis mode. Code red.

Megan would most likely dash down here within minutes, if nothing else to see firsthand how out of his comfort zone he was. The humiliation he was about to suffer would be long lasting, but at this point he didn't care. He needed reinforcements in the worst possible way.

This was not how he'd intended to apologize to Megan or how he'd planned on contacting her for the

first time since he'd all but consumed her in his bathroom. Cameron hadn't mapped out a plan, exactly, but he knew he needed to be the one to take the next step. But the step he wanted to take and the step he needed to take were on opposite ends of the spectrum.

Cameron patted Amber on her back and tried to console her. How could someone so tiny be so filled with rage? Fatherhood was not his area of expertise. He wished there was some how-to manual he could read. Did Eli have this much trouble with his little girl? Cameron had never seen this side of his infant niece.

"Maybe you should sing her a song," Willow said, smiling up at him with a grin that lacked the front two teeth. "Do you know any songs?"

AC/DC's "Back in Black" sprang to mind, but he didn't figure an infant would find that particular tune as appealing as a nearly forty-year-old man did.

"I bet you know some," he countered. "What songs have you learned in school so far?"

Brows drawn, Willow looked lost in thought. Apparently, something brilliant came to her because she jumped up and down, her lopsided ponytails bouncing off her shoulders.

"'Wheels on the Bus'! That's my favorite."

After taking a seat on the sofa, Cameron adjusted Amber on his lap so the infant could see Willow and hopefully hear the song.

What else could he do? He'd fed her. Then she'd played on the floor with her toys, and now she was angrier than any woman he'd ever encountered on either side of the law.

Willow started singing, extremely off-key and loud, but hey, the extra noise caught Amber's attention and for a blessed moment she stopped screaming.

Then she started again, burying her face against his chest. Unfazed, Willow continued to sing.

The front door flew open, and Megan stepped in, instantly surveying the room. A smirk threatened to take over, but Cameron narrowed his gaze across the room, silently daring her to laugh.

He'd never been so happy to see another person in his entire life.

Willow stopped singing the second the door closed. "Hey, Megan. I didn't know you were coming over."

Megan smiled and crossed the room. "I didn't, either, but here I am."

Cameron tried to focus on the reason he'd called her here, but his eyes drank in the sight of Megan wearing a pair of body-hugging jeans and a plain white T-shirt with her signature off-duty cowgirl boots. With her hair pulled back in a ponytail, she looked about twenty years old.

Megan reached for Amber and held the infant against her body. Without giving Cameron another glance, she turned and started walking around the room, patting Amber's back and singing softly.

Well, what did he expect? He'd called her to help with the situation he obviously had lost control over, not to take up where they'd left off the other night.

Still, the fact she didn't say a word to him made him wonder if he'd hurt her more than he realized. He

was botching up their relationship in every way, and he didn't blame her for being upset or angry.

Almost instantly the crying ceased. "Seriously? You hold her and she stops?"

Megan laughed, easing back to look Amber in the face. "I don't think it was me at all," she corrected him. "I think her stomach was upset. I just felt rumbling on my hand."

Cameron glanced to Megan's hand resting on Amber's bottom. Realization hit him hard. "Oh, no."

Willow giggled. "She feels better now."

Megan lifted Amber around to face Cameron. "She doesn't smell better," Megan said, scrunching up her nose.

Oh, please, please, please. There were few things that truly left him crippled, but the top of that list was changing a diaper...a dirty, smelly diaper.

Slowly rising to his feet, Cameron locked eyes with Megan. "I'll give you a hundred bucks to change that diaper."

Megan quirked a brow, her eyes glazed over with something much more devious than humor. "Keep your hundred bucks. I'll decide payment later."

Oh, mercy. Was she flirting with him? No, she was upset...wasn't she? Chalk this up to reason number 947 as to why he didn't do relationships. He'd never understand women. Ever.

"Where's the diapers and wipes?" she asked.

"Oh, I know," Willow raised her hand as if she were in school. "Follow me."

Megan trailed after Drake's stepdaughter and went down the hall to his bedroom. His bedroom.

"Don't change that diaper on my bed," he yelled. Laughter answered him, and he knew he was in for it. This was all part of his punishment.

The reeking smell in his bedroom was the least of his worries, because in just over an hour his brothers would be back to retrieve their kids—leaving him and Megan alone once again.

She should've left when everyone else did, but she'd put her pride and her emotions aside because she and Cameron needed to talk. He also needed help picking up his living room. Between the fort with couch cushions and blankets and the towels Willow had used as capes, making sure Cameron and Megan were superheroes, too, the place was anything but organized. The furniture had been pushed aside to allow room for "flying," and Megan hadn't even walked into the kitchen yet. She'd started making marshmallow treats with Willow just before she left and the mess was epic. She had to get in there before Cameron, with all his straight, orderly ways, had a heart attack.

Another thing she and Cameron saw eye to eye on. They both had a knack for cleanliness and keeping everything in its place…except for these emotions. They were all over, and nothing was orderly about them.

Best to start in the kitchen. Not only could she get that back in order, she could think of how best to approach being back in his house and all alone together…

Especially after that giant gauntlet she'd thrown down when he'd offered her a hundred bucks.

What had she been thinking? The flirty comment had literally slid out of her mouth. Clearly she needed a filter.

She'd been so amused by him babysitting, at the chaos his normally perfectly polished house was in. Then she'd seen him holding Amber and something very female, very biological-clock-ticking, snapped in her. She'd always known Cameron was a strong man who could handle anything. Yet the sight of those big tanned hands cradling an infant, of Cameron trying to console her with fear and vulnerability in his eyes, had sent her attraction to a whole new level. As if she needed yet another reason to be drawn to every facet of her best friend.

Surveying the cereal on the floor, Megan tiptoed carefully through to the other side of the kitchen to get the broom from the utility closet. In the midst of sweeping, a tingle slid up her spine and she knew she wasn't alone.

"Sorry." She went back to her chore, keeping her back to him. "Willow wanted to do everything on her own, so I let her. She's too cute to deny. I'll get this cleaned up and be gone."

When a warm, firm hand gripped her arm, Megan froze. Her heart kicked up, and she hated how she'd become this weak woman around her best friend. A part of her regretted sneaking into his bed. She'd cursed herself over and over for dreaming of him. The timing of the all-too-real dream at the same time he'd

tried to wake her had thrown her control completely out the window.

But she couldn't wish away those kisses. No matter how she wanted things to be different between them right now, she would cherish those moments when his mouth had been on hers, his body flush against her own.

"Stop avoiding me." His low tone washed over her, and Megan closed her eyes, comforted in that familiar richness of his voice. "We haven't talked in days, and when the kids were here you barely said a word to me."

So she'd been using two innocent children as a buffer. What was a girl to do when she was so far out of her comfort zone she couldn't even see the zone anymore?

"You called me to help, so I helped." She started sweeping the dry cereal again, her swift movements causing Cameron's hand to fall away. "Let me get this cleaned up before you step on it and make it worse."

"Damn it, would you turn around and look at me? Stop being a coward."

That commanding tone had her gripping the broom, straightening her shoulders and pivoting, cereal crunching beneath her boots.

"Coward?" she repeated, ready to use her broom to knock some sense into him. "You could've contacted me, too, you know. How dare you call me a coward after that stunt you pulled? Did you think I'd wither at your feet or declare my undying love? What did you want me to say or do when you all but challenged me?"

She hated how anger was her instant reaction, but damn it, the man was dead-on. She had been a cow-

ard. She'd purposely not contacted him. Still, in her defense, he could've texted her or something.

"I'm not trying to start a fight." That calm, controlled cop tone remained in place, grating on her nerves even more because now she was fired up and he wasn't proving to be a worthy opponent. "I just wanted to talk."

"Fine," she spat. "You talk while I clean."

Angrier at herself for letting her emotions take control, Megan went back to focusing on the floor. With jerky movements, she had a rather large pile in no time. When she glanced out the corner of her eye and saw Cameron with his arms crossed over his chest, she had to grit her teeth to keep from saying something even more childish. The last thing she wanted was to be the reason this relationship plummeted, and if she didn't rein in her irritability about the fact he'd called her out, that's exactly what would happen.

Once she'd scooped up the mess and dumped everything into the trash, she put the broom and dustpan back in the closet. The counters weren't as bad, but the big brute was blocking them.

Propping her hands on her hips, Megan stared across the room. "You're going to have to move."

He moved—leaning back against the counter, crossing one ankle over the other. "You can't seriously be mad at me. Let's put the kissing aside, which I know for a fact you enjoyed. An hour ago you flirted with me and now you're ready to fight. What has gotten into you?"

The way he studied her, as if she were a stranger,

made her want that proverbial hole to open and swallow her. To be honest, she didn't know what had gotten into her, either. One minute she was ready to tell him her true feelings; the next minute she was angry at him for not reading her mind and at herself for being afraid to risk dignity.

Yeah, she was all woman when it came to moods and indecisiveness.

"We've already established the kisses were good," she agreed. "I didn't want your hundred bucks, and now I have leverage over you when I actually need something."

"I think you know I'd do anything for you," he told her. "You don't need to hold anything over me."

With a shrug, Megan went to the sink to wet the rag. "Fine, then get out of my way so I can clean and get home. I've had a long day, and I'm pretty tired."

She wrung out the water and turned, colliding with a hard, wide chest. Megan tipped her head slightly to look into Cameron's blue eyes. Those signature St. John baby blues could mesmerize any woman… She was no exception.

"Thank you for coming." He slid his hand up her arm, pushing a wayward strand of hair behind her ear and resting his hand on her shoulder. "I'm sorry for how I treated you the other night. Sorry I made you uncomfortable. But I'm not sorry I kissed you."

Megan heard the words, even processed what he was saying; she just couldn't believe Cameron was confessing this to her.

"Cam—"

The way his eyes locked on to hers cut off whatever she was about to say. The always-controlled cop she'd known most of her life looked as if he was barely hanging on. The level of hunger staring back at her was new. Had she misread him? Had he responded to that kiss in a way that mirrored her own need? Physically he'd responded, but what about emotionally?

"I won't lie and say I haven't thought of you as more than a friend before," he started. "I can't deny you're stunning, and you know more about me than anyone outside of my family."

Why did this sound like a stepping-stone to a gentle letdown?

"You don't have to defend your feelings," she told him, offering a smile. "I'm not asking for anything. I feel the same way."

Those strong hands came up to frame her face. "I liked kissing you, loved it, if I'm being honest."

Between that firm hold he had on her and his raw words, Megan wanted to let that hope blossom, but she wasn't ready to start celebrating just yet. The worry lines between Cameron's brows, the thin lips and the way he gritted his teeth between sentences were all red flags that he was in a battle with himself. Nothing spoke volumes like that raw passion staring back at her.

"Then why do you look so angry?" she asked.

His hands dropped to her shoulders, his fingertips curling into her skin. "Because this is such a bad idea on so many levels, Meg."

Heart beating fast, nerves swirling around in her

stomach, Megan forced all the courage she could muster to rise and take center stage.

"Why is that?" she countered with a defiant tip of her chin. "You're afraid of what it would do to our relationship? You think this is just some random emotion and it will pass?"

"Yes to both of those." His clutch on her shoulders lessened as he leaned in so close, his warm breath tickled her face. "And because if I start kissing you again, I won't stop."

Every nerve ending in her entire body instantly went on alert at his declaration. How could he drop a bomb like that and not expect her to react? Did he think he was helping matters? Did he truly believe with this knowledge she now possessed that she would give up?

"What if I don't want you to stop?"

By his swift intake of breath, she knew she'd shocked him with her bold question.

"You don't mean that," Cameron muttered.

Megan flattened her palms against his chest, slid them up to his shoulders and on up to frame his face. Touching him intimately like this was just the first step of many she hoped they'd take together. She wanted him to see she wasn't blowing this off anymore, wasn't pretending whatever was happening between them wasn't real.

"I mean every word. If you want something, why not take it?"

The way he continued to stare at her, as if listening to both the devil and the angel on his shoulders, made her take action into her own hands.

Rising to her toes, she pulled his head down and captured his lips with her own. She knew she'd made a good judgment call when Cameron instantly melted against her.

Chapter Nine

Every single valid reason for keeping his distance from Megan flew out the window with her lips on his. He'd always admired her take-charge attitude, but she'd never fully executed that power with him before.

He didn't know if he should be terrified or turned on.

Wrapping his arms around her, pulling her flush against his body, just seemed to happen without him even thinking. One second he was talking himself out of kissing her ever again. Then he'd touched her, and the next thing he knew she was on him...which wasn't a bad thing.

Cameron held one arm against her lower back, forcing her hips against his, and slid one hand up to the nape of her neck to hold her right where he wanted her.

Soft moans escaped Megan, and he couldn't stop the dam of need from bursting.

Bending her back, Cameron eased his fingertips beneath the hem of her shirt. Smooth, silky skin slid beneath his touch. The ache he had burning inside completely blindsided him. He'd known he'd wanted her, but the all-consuming passion that completely took hold of him was new.

Megan's hands traveled down to the edge of his shirt and the second her petite hands roamed up his abdomen, Cameron nearly lost it. It wasn't as if he hadn't been touched by a woman before, but never by the one woman he'd craved for years. Her touch was so much more hypnotizing than he'd ever imagined…and he'd imagined plenty.

Megan tore her mouth from his, tipping her head back and arching against him. "Cam," she panted.

Hearing his name on her lips in such an intimate way was the equivalent of throwing cold water on him. This was Megan. Evan's sister. A guy he was within days of arresting.

Cameron jerked back, his hands falling from beneath her shirt. Megan got tangled in his until he lifted the hem and took another step back.

Her moist, swollen lips seemed to mock him, showcasing what he'd just had and what he was turning down. He clenched his fists at his side, trying to grasp on to some form of control. Lately, where Megan was concerned, he was losing every bit of it.

"This can't happen."

Why did it sound as if his vocal chords were rubbing

against sandpaper? He couldn't put up a strong front if he didn't have control over his own voice.

Her eyes searched his, and Cameron hated the confusion laced with arousal staring back at him. Of course she was confused. He'd all but taken over the second she'd touched him and nearly devoured her; then he told her no and backed away as if she had some contagious disease.

Megan pushed off the counter. "What is the problem?"

Swallowing the truth, Cameron gave her another reason that was just as valid. "Sex would take us into a whole new territory. Who's to say that once we give in to this lust, that we won't resent each other or regret what happened?"

She crossed her arms over her breasts and shrugged. "Judging from that kiss, I can't imagine either of us would have regrets. So maybe we would actually enjoy ourselves and find that we may want to keep moving and building on our relationship."

That right there was the biggest worry of all. No way would he go through with this knowing he would have to tear her and her brother apart. Megan would hate Cameron when that time came, and if he slept with her now, she would hate him even more. He couldn't handle it. He only hoped their friendship would carry them over this hurdle once Evan went to jail and Megan understood that Cameron had no choice but to do his job.

Besides, if they went beyond the lust, beyond the sex, Cameron refused to let Megan lead a life married to a cop.

Married? Yes, he loved Megan more than any other woman, but marriage was not in his future.

"There's a reason I don't have relationships, Megan. You know that."

After staring at him for another minute, she laughed and threw her arms out. "So, what, you're just giving up before anything can get started? You're denying yourself, denying me what we both want because you already know the outcome?"

Pretty much.

"We can't come back to this after we have sex," he retorted.

"Come back to what?" she asked, taking a step closer, fire blazing in her eyes. "Friendship? We already crossed that threshold when your mouth was on mine and your hand was up my shirt."

Her angry, frustrated tone matched the turmoil raging inside him. What could he counter with when she was absolutely right? The second they'd crossed that line, an invisible wall had been erected, preventing them from turning back.

Why had he allowed this to happen? Why hadn't he let it go after she'd kissed him when she'd been dreaming? Even though she'd been dreaming of him, he could've moved on to save their friendship. But Megan's kiss had turned something inside him; something had clicked into place…something he couldn't identify because he was too scared to even try.

Megan threw her arms in the air and let out a low groan. "Forget it. Clearly you don't even know what

you want. Or, if you do, you're afraid to face it. I don't have time for games."

"Games?" Cameron all but yelled, and he never yelled at anyone, let alone his best friend. "You think I'm playing a game here?"

When she started to walk by him, he reached out and snagged her arm until their shoulders were touching, her face tipping up toward his. The fury in her eyes wasn't something he'd seen too often and never before directed at him. Her chest rose and fell as her heavy breathing filled the silence. He didn't release his grip on her arm, apparently because he wanted to torture himself further by feeling that silky skin beneath his fingertips once more.

"Let me go," she whispered, her chin quivering.

Even with her eyes starting to fill, the anger penetrated through the hurt. As he watched her struggle with holding her emotions together, Cameron's heart jumped as he reluctantly slid his hand down her arm, stopping at her wrist and finally releasing her.

"I'm not trying to hurt you." That pitiful statement sounded flat and cold even to his own ears. "You're the last person I want to make cry."

A watery laugh escaped her. "You think I'm crying over you? These tears are over my own foolishness."

One lone tear slid down her cheek. Just as she reached up to swat it away, he caught her hand in his and used the pad of his thumb to swipe at the moisture.

He turned toward her and tugged her until she fell against him. Wrapping his arms around her, ignoring

her protest, Cameron waited until she stopped struggling before he spoke.

"I don't want this between us, Meg. I can't lose you."

Her head dropped to his chest as she sniffed, her
palms flattened against his shoulders. "This is just a
really bad time, and my emotions are getting the best
of me. Don't worry."

Cameron stroked her back, trying to ease all the
tension, knowing he'd never fully get her relaxed and
calm. But that wouldn't stop him from trying.

"You don't have to defend yourself," he muttered
against her ear. "We've both had pressure on us lately.
Finding you in my bed the other night and then kissing
you, it was all unexpected and it takes a lot to catch
me off guard."

Megan eased back, lifted her eyes to his and
blinked. Wet lashes framed her green eyes as a wide
smile spread across her face. "The fact that I manage
to keep you on your toes after all these years makes
me happier than it should."

The way she worded that, *after all these years*,
sounded so personal. More personal than friendship.
Married couples said such things to each other.

"I'm not blaming those kisses on pressure or the
chaos in my life," she told him. "I realized soon after
your lips touched mine that I wasn't dreaming anymore. I could've stopped, but it just felt so good and
you were responding."

Hell yeah, he'd responded. He hadn't been with a
woman for so long, but even he couldn't make that his
excuse. Cameron had to at least be honest with him-

self. The second her lips had touched his, her arms encircled his neck, he'd been pulled under. All control had slid from him to her in the span of a second, and he hadn't minded one bit.

Then reality had come crashing back and he'd known what a mistake he'd made. Unfortunately, he'd gotten her in his system and now he was paying the price.

Damn it.

"I need to get going." She pulled completely away, eased around him and headed toward the living room. "The kitchen is done. Can you handle the living room?"

Why did his eyes have to zero in on the sway of her hips? Why was his body still humming from the way she'd been leaning against him?

Years ago he'd wondered, but he'd never made a move because either she or he had been dating someone. Then they got to a point where they were just perfectly happy being friends and not expecting anything more. He'd been deployed and hoped when he'd returned the feelings would've lessened. They hadn't. And then he'd become a cop, lost a partner and hardened his heart toward anything permanent.

So here they were, still best friends who each knew just how well the other one kissed. Cameron was also extremely aware of exactly how Megan liked to be touched and how hard and demanding she wanted those kisses. Her sighs, her moans, the way she arched her body against his were all images he'd live with forever.

He had to endure his own personal hell because he couldn't have her, wouldn't put her through com-

ing in second to his job. And he damn well wouldn't expect her to want more once she learned he'd spent months bringing down a drug ring that now involved her brother.

Megan grabbed her keys off the small table just inside the entryway. "I'll be out of town Thursday and Friday," she told him without turning to look at him as she pulled open the door. "I should be home late Friday night."

"Where are you going?"

With her hand on the knob, she tossed her hair over her shoulder and stared back at him. "Just something for work."

Cameron curled his fingers around the edge of the wood door. "Is it a conference?"

"You might say that."

She was lying. Whatever she was doing, she didn't want to tell him.

"I don't expect you to share every aspect of your life," he told her. "But don't lie to my face."

Megan reached up, patted his cheek. "Kind of like you lying about not wanting more with me? That goes both ways, Cam."

Before he could respond, the cell in his pocket vibrated. *Damn it.* Now was not the time to deal with work unless it was to bring this ring down once and for all.

He pulled the phone out, saw his brother's number and didn't know if he was disappointed or relieved that work wasn't calling him in.

"Hang on," he told Megan. "It's just Eli. I'm not done with you."

Her eyes flared, and he realized how that sounded considering all that had transpired between them within the past week.

"What?" he growled into the phone.

"Mom fell." Eli didn't bother with any pleasantries. "I'm pretty sure her ankle is broken."

"Oh, hell." Cameron ran a hand down his face and sighed, meeting the concerned look in Megan's eyes. "Want me to meet you at the hospital?"

"I've already got her here," Eli answered. "You don't have to come, but I wanted to let you know what was up. Dad is home, and he's watching Amber for me. Nora came with me to sit with mom. Drake got called into work when one of his guys reported in sick."

"I'll be right there."

Cameron shoved the phone back in his pocket and yanked his keys from the peg by the door.

"Mom fell," he said, answering Megan's worried look. "Eli thinks her ankle is broken. I'm heading to the ER now. Dad is babysitting for Eli."

Megan stepped out onto the porch, holding the screen door open for him. "I'll go by your parents' house and sit with Mac and Amber. I'm sure he's worried. Keep me posted."

Before she walked away, Cameron reached out, wrapped his hand around the nape of her neck and looked her straight in the eyes. "I meant what I said. We're not done talking."

Megan's eyes locked on to his, her shoulders

straightened and that defiant chin lifted. "I'm pretty sure we're done discussing just how much you're denying both of us something that could be amazing. Until you're ready to face the fact you enjoyed kissing me, rubbing your hands on me, and admit you're just running scared, don't bring it up again."

She pulled away and bounded down the porch steps. "Just text with an update on your mom. No need to call."

And with that she headed toward her house, leaving Cameron to stare at those mocking hips.

Yes, he'd liked kissing her, thoroughly appreciated the feel of her curves beneath his hands. He was a man and she was a sensual woman whom he'd wanted for years. So what if he was running scared? Better to stop the disaster before it completely ruined their friendship.

As Cameron headed to his truck, he had a sinking feeling their friendship had already rounded a curve and was speeding out of control, and there wasn't a damn thing he could do about it.

Chapter Ten

"This fuss isn't necessary." Bev tried to maneuver her new crutches as Eli and Cameron flanked her sides, assisting her into the house. "I'll be fine. There's no need for everyone to hover."

"You will be fine," Eli agreed. "But for now we're going to hover. Just be glad Drake had to go in or you'd have all of us."

Megan held the door open with one hand and propped Amber on her hip with the other. "You know it's useless to argue with these guys, Bev," Megan said, catching the woman's grin. "Just let them think what they want to boost their egos."

Cameron's gaze swung to hers, and Megan merely lifted a brow. If he wanted to apply those words to the turmoil they had going on, so be it. Wasn't her fault if he had a guilty conscience.

Megan closed the door and pulled Amber around to settle against her chest as the baby continued chewing on her cloth rattle.

"I've already brought your pillows and pajamas down to the guest room," Mac stated, moving forward to take the place of his sons. "We'll be sleeping down here until you're healed and can do the stairs."

"And I'll be stopping by in the mornings," Nora stated, coming in through the door, holding Bev's purse. "I can do your grocery shopping after work so Mac doesn't have to worry about anything."

"One of my patients has volunteered to babysit Amber until you're feeling better," Eli added.

"Oh, for pity's sake." Bev stopped in the foyer and sighed, shooting glares at all those around her. "I can get through these next six weeks without rearranging everyone's lives."

Mac placed a hand over her shoulder. "Complain all you want, but when I had bypass surgery, you all steamrolled me and took care of me. Now it's our turn to cater to you."

A lump formed in Megan's throat at the sincere, loving way Mac looked to Bev. They'd always been such a dynamic couple, always strong even when dealing with hellion teen boys and all their shenanigans.

Megan knew that Mac's bypass surgery last year had rocked them all because the pillar of the family wasn't as indestructible as they'd all thought him to be.

Megan's eyes traveled to Cameron. Her breath caught in her throat when she found herself under the

scrutiny of his bright blue eyes. Amber started fussing, pulling Megan's focus back to the infant in her arms.

"It's okay, sweetheart." Megan patted her back. "You're just getting sleepy, aren't you?"

Nora smiled, set the purse down on the accent table and reached out. "I can take her. She's not used to being awake this late."

"I'll run Eli home," Cameron chimed in. "Go on ahead and take her."

Nora said her goodbyes in a frantic attempt to get her unhappy child out the door. Once she was gone, Mac assisted Bev down the hall and into the spare room.

"I'll get her meds from the car," Eli volunteered. "She won't need any more tonight, but I'll put them in the kitchen where Dad can see them."

Eli headed out the front door, leaving Cameron and Megan alone. Why did they always somehow gravitate toward these situations? Before last week she wouldn't think twice about being alone with Cameron, but with all this tension crackling between them, she truly didn't know what step to take next. And she'd made it clear that the ball was in his court.

"I'm heading out," she told him. "Let your mom know I'm here if she needs anything. I'm free all weekend once I get back."

Cameron nodded. "Thanks for your help."

She waited for him to say something else, but he continued to stare in silence. Eli came back inside, carrying a small white pharmacy bag. He glanced between Megan and Cameron.

"Everything okay?" he asked, his brows drawn together.

"Fine," Megan and Cameron replied in unison, still eyeing each other.

"O-kay," Eli whispered as he moved on through to the kitchen.

Shoving her hair away from her face, Megan gritted her teeth as she reached into her pocket and pulled out her keys. Without another word, she headed out the front door and into the cool evening. She'd just hit the bottom step when she heard the screen door slam.

"Is this how it's going to be?" Cameron yelled. "This awkward, sometimes-polite chitchat like we're virtual strangers?"

Megan took in a deep breath before turning to face the man on the porch illuminated by the soft glow of outdoor lights. With his hands on his narrow hips, black T-shirt stretched tightly over toned shoulders and that perfectly cropped hair, Cameron gave off the impression of someone in control and pulled together.

Megan knew better. She'd experienced just how much he relinquished that power when she'd touched him, kissed him, pressed her body to his. And that interesting tidbit of information was something worth hanging on to.

The chill in the air slid through her. A shiver racked her body as she wrapped her arms around her midsection.

"If you feel awkward around me, then it sounds like you have some issues to work out," she threw back. She wasn't going to make this easy on him, not when he

was being so infuriating. "I've always heard intimacy helps people relax."

Maybe she shouldn't poke the bear, but they'd already gone past the point of no return. She may as well toss it all out there.

Cameron took a step forward, his eyes still locked on hers. "Why are you acting like this?"

Megan shrugged. "Maybe that kiss was a wake-up for both of us, and I'm willing to face it instead of run from it."

Cameron bounded down the steps, coming to stand right in front of her. So close, she could feel his warm breath, but he didn't touch her.

"You keep coming to me," she added, looking up into those eyes filled with torment. "You keep provoking me, too, but then you back off. You can't have it both ways, Cam."

He gripped her arms in an almost bruising manner as he leaned over her, giving her no choice but to lean back to keep her gaze locked on to his.

Without a word, his mouth crushed hers. The instant demand had her clutching his shoulders and cursing herself for giving in to his impulses so easily. But damn it, she was human. She'd wanted this man for as long as she could remember, and she was going to take what she could get…for now. She wasn't settling for seconds; she was biding her time until Cameron realized this was right. Everything about them coming together was perfectly, wonderfully right.

Reluctant, Megan tore her mouth away. "If you're

only kissing me because you're angry with yourself or you're trying to prove a point, then stop."

His forehead rested against her temple, those lips barely touching her jawline. "I don't know, Meg. You make me crazy. I can't do relationships, and I won't do a fling—not with you. But part of me can't seem to stop now that we've started."

Not quite the victory she'd hoped for, but one she would definitely take. She had him torn, had him thinking. Still, she wanted, *deserved*, more.

"I won't be someone you figure things out with along the way," she told him, sliding her hands away from his taut shoulders. "If you want more, you say so."

She stepped back, waited until he looked at her before she continued. "Be damn sure if you come to me that you want what I've offered because there's no going back."

Megan waited, giving him an opportunity to respond. When silence greeted her and the muscle in Cameron's jaw moved, Megan swallowed, turned on her heel and headed to her car.

Maybe her going out of town would give them the space they both needed to regroup. Maybe the time away would give her the insight she needed on whether to stay or go.

That reminded her—she still needed to inform Evan that she'd be gone. Hopefully he wouldn't tell his questionable friends that her house sat empty. She wanted to be honest with him, wanted him to know that she trusted him, but in all honesty, she didn't. She knew the group he was with was only making his attitude worse,

hence his phone call. She had no clue what he truly did with his free time, but she had a feeling it wasn't legal.

Evan had obviously felt himself sinking deeper into a place he didn't want to be when he'd reached out to her. Megan could only pray while she was gone for these two days that the most important men in her life came to some decisions…and she hoped the outcomes would be what she wanted.

"Care to explain what I just saw?"

Cameron winced as he stepped back into his parents' house. Eli stood in the foyer near the sidelight like some Peeping Tom.

"Yeah, I care," Cameron mumbled. The last thing he wanted was to discuss what had just happened because each time he lost his damn mind and kissed Megan, he always felt worse afterward. He was using her to feed his desires, knowing he couldn't go any further.

"Then would you like to tell me why you and Megan look like you're ready to fight one minute and the next thing I know I look out and see you all but devouring her?"

Cameron clenched his fists at his side. Eli's arms crossed over his chest as his eyes narrowed. Eli had married his high school sweetheart, but Megan had been around for so long. And they'd all been friends. *Damn it*. Cameron hadn't even thought of how his brothers would react if they knew…

Hell. Cameron couldn't even put a label on the debacle he'd made of his life in the past month.

"Leave it," Cameron warned as he started down the hall to check on his mom.

"She's resting and Dad's in there." Eli moved quickly, coming to block the entrance to the hall. "I told them we'd lock up and turn off all the lights."

"Fine. You get the lights. I'll check the back door."

Eli made no attempt to move. Raising his gaze to the ceiling, Cameron sighed. He should've known this wasn't going to be easy.

"I have no idea what's going on," he conceded, looking back to his brother. "We've kissed. I know on every level it's a bad idea, but I can't stop myself."

A little of the anger in Eli's eyes dimmed as his shoulders relaxed. "How does she feel?"

Cameron couldn't help but laugh. "Oh, she's made it clear she's ready to step from the friend zone to something more."

Eli tipped his head and shrugged. "And you're angry about this?"

"You know I've made it clear for years I don't want a commitment. Megan's heard me say it over and over." Damn her for making him so confused. "I won't use her, Eli. She's the type of woman who deserves stability and a family. I can't give her either."

"Can't or won't?"

No, he wasn't getting into this. Cameron maneuvered around Eli and went to make sure the back door was locked. When he came back to the front, Eli had turned off the lights except the small lamp on the accent table.

Eli opened the door and gestured for Cameron to

go on ahead. Once they were on the porch, Cameron started to head down the steps, but Eli had to open his mouth again. Ridiculous to think he'd be able to make a break for it.

"You can't be married to your job forever," Eli called out. "At some point you're going to be lonely. Megan's a great girl. You two would be good together."

Cameron spun around. "I'm not looking for advice on my love life. There are complications that you don't know about and I can't get into. So just drop it, and don't mention what you saw to anybody."

Eli stared back, not saying a word.

"Promise me," Cameron demanded. "Not Drake, not Mom or Dad."

After a minute, Eli nodded. "Fine. But you better not mess around and hurt Megan. She's the only woman in your life other than your mother who puts up with your moodiness and your unruly schedule."

Cameron turned back, heading toward his truck parked last in the driveway. He wasn't even entertaining thoughts of how much Megan had put up with. Because then he'd have to admit how much she truly did care for him.

Cameron knew he wasn't going to get any sleep at all tonight, so he headed to the station. Might as well check in with his guys and see if there were any new developments. Of course, if there had been anything, he would've been called. Still, he couldn't go home because Megan's presence was in every single room... especially his bedroom.

His office was practically Megan-free, and he al-

ways had work he could do. But Eli was right. Cameron was afraid to go deeper with Megan. How could he be anything else? Too much rested on his shoulders, and no matter what weight he relieved himself of, he'd have more taking its place.

Everything in his life, both personal and professional, all pointed back to Megan somehow. There wasn't a damn thing he could do to save her from his choices, regardless of the path he took.

Chapter Eleven

Megan thought for sure that after visiting the new facility and meeting the staff she'd potentially be working with, she'd have a clearer insight on a decision.

As she maneuvered her car onto the exit ramp that would take her back into Stonerock, she was more confused than ever.

Yes, the facility was beautiful. But the nicest computer equipment or fancy waiting areas, complete with a waterfall wall for a calming atmosphere, weren't going to sway her into making a life-altering decision.

What Megan cared about was the people she'd be able to reach, to help, the difference she could make in their lives. Megan's potential supervisor had gone into great detail about the areas the clinic planned to target. Topping the list were poverty-stricken neigh-

borhoods where alcoholism and drug abuse had spiked in the past few years.

Just the mention of that area had pulled Megan's mind back home with Evan. She knew he had a problem, and she'd give anything to fix him. That's what she did; she had a degree to fix people. But if he didn't want to change completely, she could use all the fancy words and textbook cures in the world and he'd still remain in the pit he'd dug for himself. Though she didn't think he was using drugs—she hadn't seen the telltale signs—she did believe he was mixed up with a group who wasn't immune to the industry. Why else did he always need money? Why else would he always be worried about his safety?

So did she truly want to leave, risking Evan choosing to stay behind? Or did she want to stay in Stonerock where she'd already developed relationships with clients? Those clients trusted her, counted on her. Would they feel as if they were being abandoned if she accepted the new position?

Megan's cell rang, cutting off the radio. Pressing the button on her steering wheel, Megan answered.

"Hello?"

"Hey, Megan." Marly's chipper voice came through the car speakers. "Are you busy?"

"Just driving. What's up?"

"Nora and I were wondering if you were free tonight. I know it's last minute, but Eli said he didn't mind keeping the girls for us."

As exhausted as she was from her whirlwind trip, a girls' night out sounded like the reward she needed.

Megan couldn't remember the last time she'd been out with a group of friends. Going out with Cameron didn't count, not that they went out. They tended to grill at his house or watch movies, and then she'd go back to her house.

"Count me in," Megan said, turning onto her road. "I'm almost home. I need to change, but I can meet you all somewhere."

"We're heading to Dolly's Bar and Grill."

They arranged the time and Megan suddenly found herself getting another burst of energy. She wouldn't think about Evan, Cameron or her work situation. She'd have a beer, chat with the girls and have a good time. A simple, relaxing evening.

With the days losing light earlier and earlier, she too often found herself in pajamas by six o'clock. When had she gotten to that stage in life that the best part of her day was spent in pj's? Mercy, she was getting old.

As soon as Megan examined her closet, she knew she wanted to dress a little sassier than usual tonight. Even if she was just going out with Nora and Marly, Megan had that female urge to step up her game a notch.

When had she let herself get so dowdy and boring? Lately she'd only donned the barest of makeup for work, and she couldn't remember the last time she'd pulled out her curling iron or straightener. If she looked under her bathroom sink, she'd probably find them overtaken by dust.

Glancing at the clock, Megan decided she had time to put some effort into her appearance tonight. After a

quick shower, she opted for the big iron and put large, bouncy waves into her hair. A little more shadow than usual made her green eyes pop. Why didn't she do this more often? Just what she'd done so far had boosted both her energy level and confidence.

After pulling on a simple yellow tank-style dress, Megan wrapped a thick belt around her waist, threw on a fitted navy cardigan and pulled on her favorite cowgirl boots. Surely she had earrings that went with this outfit. Digging through her meager stash of jewelry, she managed to find some dangly hoops and a chunky silver bracelet.

Megan grabbed her purse and headed out the door. She hadn't heard from Evan in a couple of days, and, surprisingly, her house hadn't been bothered while she'd been gone.

The guilt of expecting him or his friends to steal something weighed heavily in her gut.

Megan shook off all negative thoughts as she pulled into Dolly's. It being a Friday night, the place was bustling with cars filling the parking lot and people piling in through the front doors.

Music blasted out of the bar as a group of guys held the door open and gestured for her to enter. Smiling her thanks, Megan stepped inside, quickly scanned the room and found Nora and Marly in a booth along the wall.

With a wave, Megan wove her way through the crowd as a slow country song filled the room. Hand in hand, couples made their way to the scarred wooden dance floor. Megan refused to allow the image of her

and Cameron dancing to occupy her mind. She was here for fun and for a girls' night. Nothing more.

Nora slid over, giving Megan room to ease onto the leather seat.

"You look beautiful," Nora said with a huge smile. "I was just happy to shower and actually attempt to fix my hair."

Marly laughed. "You're always gorgeous, Nora. But, seriously, Megan, you look great."

"Thanks." Megan sat her purse between her and Nora and thanked God she'd taken some extra time to get ready. "I was going for the fun Megan instead of therapist Megan."

"Well, honey, you nailed it." Nora waved her hand at a waitress. "First round's on me."

"I need a drink," Marly stated. "I've been sewing on Willow's Halloween costume for a week and it still looks like a hot mess. Why the hell did I think I could be supermom instead of just buying one?"

Nora patted Marly's arm. "Because you're an awesome mom and Willow doesn't care what it looks like. She's just excited her mom is making the Darth Vader-cowgirl-princess getup."

Marly moaned. "I suppose. I think letting her pick her favorite themes was a bad idea. I meant one character, not three combined."

Once they ordered their drinks plus a basket of chips and salsa, Megan turned to Nora.

"How's Bev? She getting used to those crutches?" Megan asked.

"Eli said she's still complaining about using them,

but he told her she'd get used to it." Nora rested an elbow on the dull wooden tabletop and smiled. "As long as Mac is there, though, she doesn't have to get up for anything except to use the bathroom. He's right at her side making sure she doesn't even have to ask."

Marly laughed, pushing back a wayward curl from her forehead. "The St. John males have a tendency to go overboard with protecting and assisting their ladies."

Megan thought about how Cameron had wanted her to show Evan some tough love. Cameron was ready to step in and be her human shield, but she had held him back. She remembered a time in high school when a guy was insistent she leave a party with him and all but dragged her toward his car. Cameron had stepped in then, as well, and punched the guy in the face.

The waitress came back with the drinks and each woman took a long, sigh-worthy sip. Megan licked the frothy, fruity foam off her top lip and glanced up to see the other two staring at her.

"What?"

"You were daydreaming." Nora quirked a brow while sliding her fingertip over the condensation on her tall, slender glass. "I know this is absolutely none of my business, but we've known each other a really long time."

Megan braced herself for whatever Nora was about to ask.

"Any chance you and Cameron…" Nora let the silent question settle between them as she pulled the tooth-

pick full of pineapple out of her drink and plucked a piece off.

Marly eased her forearms onto the table and leaned forward, obviously eager to hear the answer, as well.

Megan shrugged. "We're best friends." That was the truth. "I'm not sure we would know how to be anything else."

"Have you tried?" Marly asked.

The waitress returned, setting a giant basket of tortilla chips and three small bowls of salsa on the table.

Megan pretended to look for the perfect chip while she contemplated the answer she should give over the answer she wanted to give.

"I believe the silence speaks for itself," Nora proudly stated as she dipped her chip. "There's no way a man like Cameron can ignore you for years."

Yeah, well, he had. At least in any form beyond friendship. But when his mouth had been on hers, his hands up her shirt, he'd certainly given off the vibe he was staking a claim.

"How long have you guys been a secret?" Nora asked, leaning in just a bit more, a wide, knowing smile spread across her face.

Megan sighed. "There's no secret. To be honest, we only kissed for the first time last week and that was because I was sleeping, he startled me from a dream and I…"

"Please, please don't stop there." Marly reached across and squeezed her arm. "I may not have known you that long, but I'm wrapped up in this and I know

it's not my business. So, tell Nora and just let me listen in."

Megan laughed and took a drink, welcoming the chill of the strawberry-flavored, alcohol-enriched slush. "I yanked him down and kissed him," she muttered.

Both women's eyes widened as their grins spread even wider. Megan couldn't help but smile back because she so had to get this off her chest. And there wasn't a doubt in her mind these two ladies would offer her some much-needed advice.

"Then he cornered me in his kitchen the other night after we watched your kids during your date." Megan found herself moving forward with the story without being prompted. She wanted to blame the alcohol, but after only two sips, that defense fell flat. "He was angry at the kiss we'd shared."

"If he cornered you and was angry, sounds to me like he's turned on and is mad at himself," Nora supplied. "Probably for just now taking notice, if you ask me."

"Yeah, well, we argued. That led to another kiss and his hand up my shirt."

Nora and Marly high-fived each other across the table, and Megan felt her face flush. "This is silly." She laughed. "I feel like I'm in high school."

"Better than high school," Marly chimed in. "Way better. So what happened next? This is the best girls' night ever."

Megan reached for another chip. "Sorry to disap-

point, but he pulled back and we argued again. I just don't know what to do."

Nora shifted in her seat and all smiling vanished as she looked Megan straight in the eyes. "Take my advice. Don't wait to tell him how you feel, what you truly want. I did that with Eli the first time. We let a lot of years and hurt build between us, and then we had to overcome so much to be together. You're not guaranteed a tomorrow."

Megan felt the quick sting in her nose as her eyes started to fill. Nora had been in love with Eli in school, and then he had gone into the military. After a few years, Nora married Eli's friend, who had ultimately died while deployed. Nora had taken the long, hard road to find love, and Megan could only nod as the lump formed in her throat.

"Damn it." Marly yanked her napkin from under her drink and dabbed beneath her eyes. "I had my makeup so nice, too, thanks to that pin I saw on Pinterest."

"I didn't mean to cause tears," Nora defended herself, passing another napkin over to Marly. "I'm just trying to help."

Megan blinked back her own unshed tears and gripped her icy-cold glass. "You did help. I know I need to tell him how I feel, but I guess I just needed encouragement. I'm a bit of a coward. What if we mess up? He's the most stable person in my life, and I can't lose him as a best friend."

Nora nodded. "I understand the fear, but if he loves you beyond friends, isn't that worth the risk? Is he worth it?"

Without a doubt. Cameron was worth risking everything for.

Her phone chimed from her purse. She thought it was rude to be on the phone when out with a group of people, but it could be a patient in need.

"Sorry," she said, digging out the phone. "Give me one second."

The caller ID flashed her brother's name. Megan swiped the screen and answered.

"Evan?"

"I'm ready."

Those two words held so much meaning. "You want me to come and get you?"

"Yeah, um, I was dropped off at the parking lot beside the old gas station that closed. You know where that's at?"

Megan nodded, even though he couldn't see her. "Yes. I'll be there in five minutes."

She hung up, quickly pulled money from her purse and tossed it on the table before explaining to the girls that she had to get her brother. There was no time to go into further details because Evan changed his mind so often, she wanted to jump through this window of opportunity.

Besides, he might be in danger if he was in a parking lot at night all alone.

Megan raced for her SUV. As she pulled into the lot, at first she didn't see anybody. As soon as she got out, she felt the presence of someone behind her. Spinning around, her heart leaped into her throat. The hulking figure wasn't Evan.

Pulling all her experience and courage to the surface, Megan lifted her chin and squared her shoulders. "Where's my brother?" she asked.

The sneer on the stranger's face sent a cold chill down her spine. He stepped closer, all the while raking his eyes over her. Curse this dress she'd felt beautiful in earlier. Why was she now feeling as if she was being punished for wanting to look nice?

"I'm right here."

Megan jerked around to see Evan, hands in his pockets, staring across the open space. She could barely see him for the glow from the streetlight that was at the other end of the block. But the tone of his voice worried her. He sounded sad, nervous, almost desperate.

"What's going on?" she asked Evan as she started to take a step forward.

The man behind her gripped her arm. Megan had taken a self-defense course, a requirement for her job. Instantly the lessons came flooding to her mind. She whirled around and shoved the palm of her free hand straight up into the man's nose.

With a howl, he dropped her arm and covered his face. She shook out her wrist and glanced over her shoulder to Evan.

"Get in my car," she ordered, her gaze volleying back and forth between her brother and the man who would no doubt be angry. She didn't want to be there when he decided to retaliate. "Now, Evan."

"I can't."

Another man seemed to materialize behind Evan. This man held a gun...pointed at her. The hulk behind

her gripped her arm once again, this time tighter as he yanked her back against his chest.

"They'll kill us if we don't do what they want," Evan told her. "I had no clue they were setting me up, Meg. I'm sorry."

Apologies could wait. Right now she needed to figure out how to get them out of here without getting shot. "What do you want?" she asked, still trying to keep her voice calm though she was anything but.

"Your brother here owes us twenty thousand dollars," the man behind her stated, his hot breath against her cheek making her gag. "And after that stunt you just pulled on me, I'm adding another five K."

Why hadn't she paid more attention to her brother? Whatever mess he'd gotten wrapped up in had apparently been going on awhile if he owed that kind of money. Still, all that could be dealt with later. Right now she needed to figure out a way to survive the night. She wanted Cameron. He wouldn't be afraid; he would arrest these guys and save her and Evan. But Cameron wasn't here, and she'd have to fend for herself.

"I'm sure you know I don't have that much money on me," she told them, her eyes darting to the gun still aimed at her.

Sirens filled the night, and Megan nearly wept with relief. She forced herself to keep in mind her surroundings and the men who were threatening her. She may not be a cop like Cameron, but she'd counseled enough addicts to know that if they were high, they didn't care who they hurt. They had nothing to lose. Which meant she was expendable.

Before she knew it, the man behind her let go, causing her to stumble back from the force of his departure. The man with the gun patted Evan on the shoulder as if they were the best of friends.

"Come on, man." The guy shoved his gun in his waistband. "You ain't waiting to talk to no cops. You're with us till you pay up."

Evan threw her one last pained look and mouthed "sorry" before turning and running off into the night with the men who'd just threatened their lives. With shaky knees and tremors overtaking her body, Megan sank to the cool concrete. Moments later, a cruiser pulled in, too late to save her brother.

Chapter Twelve

Never in his life had fear crippled him to the point of losing control and being ready to throw it all away.

But the sight of Megan in the clutches of notorious gang leader "The Shark" was an image that would haunt him forever.

Then the gun had appeared, and Cameron had to get a patrol car sounding that second. He knew those guys. He knew they wouldn't shoot Megan unless provoked. The siren did its job and the criminals fled—including her lowlife brother. Cameron wanted to get ahold of that man and punch him in the face for not protecting his sister.

What the hell had Megan been doing there, anyway? His heart had nearly exploded in his chest when he saw her black SUV pull into the lot. He'd gotten a

good look at her sexy little dress and cowgirl boots, showcasing those shapely legs. But even that punch of lust had vanished the second those dangerous thugs had surrounded her.

Now, an hour later, Cameron stood on her porch. He knew she was inside because his officer had told him he'd driven Megan's car home while another officer drove her in his cruiser. She was too shaken up, too scared to drive.

Cameron slid his key into her lock and let himself in. The second he stepped over the threshold, he called her name, not wanting to alarm her because he'd come in the front door and not the back as he normally did.

He heard the sound of her boots clicking over the wooden floor from the rear of the house. Megan came down the hallway, her arms wrapped around her midsection, her face pale.

For her fear alone he vowed to get enough evidence on these guys to put them away for a long, long time. Right now, though, he wished he wasn't on the right side of the law. He wished more than anything he could track them down and beat them within an inch of their lives, forgetting about the justice system altogether and saving the taxpayers' dollars.

"I knew they'd call you." She pasted on a smile that fell short of convincing. "Did they find Evan? I've texted and called him, but…"

Fury threatened to take over. She was worried about Evan? After a man had held her at gunpoint while another practically held her captive?

"My officers were more concerned with you." Only

because the FBI was still out there right now keeping an eye on the traffickers…and because Cameron had told his two officers to make sure Megan was watched until he arrived. "Evan is a big boy."

Anything else he said would be out of anger, and the last thing he wanted to do was fight. Between the way her vulnerability had settled between them like a third party and the way that dress hugged her body, Cameron was having a really difficult time prioritizing his emotions.

"Are you okay?" he asked, taking a step forward, then another, until he was within reaching distance. But he fisted his hands at his side. "My officers told me you weren't hurt, but I needed to hear it from you. I needed to see you."

Those bright green eyes seemed even more vibrant than usual. Cameron didn't know if he was just now noticing or if she'd done something tricky with her makeup. Regardless, the way she watched him, the way she seemed to be holding herself back, had him nearing the breaking point. He'd been holding on by the proverbial thread for so long now; it was only a matter of time before he fell.

Megan reached up, shoved her hair back from her face. "I'm fine."

Her action drew his gaze to her arm, to the fingerprint-size bruises dotting her perfect skin. Cameron clenched his teeth, reining in his anger because none of this was her fault and he wouldn't make her the target simply because she was the only one here once the rage fully surfaced. The only thing he could

fault Megan with was having a kind heart and wanting to help people who would continue to stomp on her and use her.

Cameron gripped her wrist in one hand and slid a fingertip from his other over around the marred skin. "You're not fine. This never should've happened."

He'd cursed himself for standing by and watching as events unfolded, but had he gone charging for her as he'd wanted to, as his heart told him to, his cover would've been blown and she would have known the cops were watching Evan. *Cameron* was watching Evan.

That heavy ball of guilt was something he'd have to live with. If there had ever been any doubt before, tonight just proved that he would choose his job first every single time. He hated himself for it, but that's how he was made up.

"They're just bruises," she whispered, her eyes still on his.

Goose bumps raised beneath his fingertips as he continued to stroke her skin. "I don't like them."

Megan placed a hand over his, halting his movement. Her lids closed as she whispered, "Please, Cam. I just…"

Bowing her head, Megan sighed.

"You what, baby?"

"I wanted you to come," she muttered beneath the curtain of her hair that had cascaded around her face. "I wanted you here because I knew I'd feel safe. But now that you're here, I can't let you touch me." Slowly

lifting her head, she brought her eyes up to lock on to his. "It makes me want things. Want you."

Damn it. There went that last thread he'd been holding on to.

Cameron stepped into her, trapping their hands between their bodies. The tip of his nose brushed against hers, leaving their mouths barely a whisper apart.

"You are always safe with me," he told her, slowly moving his lips across hers with the lightest of touches. "And tonight you're mine."

"Just tonight," she agreed. "We don't need to put a label on it, and I don't want to think beyond now."

Cameron captured her mouth, completely ignoring all the warnings pounding through his head. Totally shoving aside all the reasons this was a terrible idea: the investigation, the risk of losing his best friend and the fact he'd just admitted to himself that his job would always come first. All that mattered was Megan and this ache he'd had for her for years. It wasn't going away no matter how noble he tried to be. His hormones didn't give a damn about his morals or standards.

Megan's mouth opened beneath his as she tried to pull her hands free. Cameron was quicker, holding them firm as he broke from the kiss.

"You're mine," he repeated, nipping her lips, her chin, trailing a line down to her collarbone. "I don't know why you have on this dress with these boots, but it's driving me crazy. Tell me you weren't on a date earlier."

Tipping her head back, arching into him, Megan let out one of those sweet moans he was starting to

love. "No, no date," she panted. "I was out with Nora and Marly."

The fact she was out with his sisters-in-law thrilled him because if she'd been out with a guy, Cameron would've had to admit jealousy.

Cameron released her hands and slid his palms over her curvy hips. He gripped her and pulled her pelvis flush with his as he continued to rain kisses along her exposed skin just above the dip in her dress. Just above the perfect swell of her breasts.

Megan wrapped her delicate fingers around his biceps and squeezed as he yanked down the top of her dress. Material tore, but he didn't care. He'd buy her a new one.

"Cam."

He froze at her plea. "Meg, I'm sorry. After what you went through tonight, I wasn't thinking."

Her lips curved into a smile. "I wasn't complaining. I know you'd never hurt me."

Seeing her lips swollen from his kisses, her neck and the tops of her breasts pink from arousal, an instant flood of possessiveness filled him. The only mark he ever wanted on her was from him, from passion.

"If you keep this up, I don't know how much longer I can stand." Her arms slid around his neck as she rubbed her body against his. "You make my knees weak and we're still fully clothed."

"I'm about to fix that problem."

He unbuckled her belt and let it drop with a clatter to the wood floor. He gripped the hem of her dress,

yanked it up and over her head, then tossed the unwanted garment aside.

The sight of her standing before him wearing a pale
pink bra and matching panties along with those cowgirl boots was enough to make his own knees weak.

Megan reached for his shirt, but he pulled it off before she could touch him. In record time their clothes
were mere puddles on the floor. From the way her eyes
kept sampling him, Cameron knew if he didn't try to
keep some sort of control, this night would be over before he could truly enjoy it.

"I've waited to see you look at me like that," Megan
told him, rising up on her toes to kiss his jawline. "Like
you really want me."

She was killing him. With the way the lace from
her bra pressed against his bare skin, her raw, honest
words and the delicate way her mouth cruised over him,
Megan was gradually overpowering him.

Gliding his hands around her curves, Cameron lifted
her until her legs went around his waist. The leather
from her cowgirl boots rubbed his back, but the fact
he finally had this woman wrapped all over him over-
rode his discomfort.

"I'm too heavy for you," she argued, nipping at his
ear.

Palming her backside, his thumb teased the edge of
her lacy panty line. "Baby, you're the perfect weight for
me," he growled as he headed toward the living room
and the L-shaped sofa. "Absolutely perfect."

Without easing his hold, Cameron settled her onto

the corner of the couch as his lips took hold of hers once again. He could kiss her forever.

Too bad he couldn't do forever. Selfishly, he was doing now, tonight, and he'd hate himself later for taking advantage even if she had given him the green light.

Megan's legs fell away from his waist, her boots landing on either side of his feet. Cameron eased back, picked up one leg at a time and pried off her cowgirl boots. She watched him beneath heavy lids, her chest rising and falling as she licked her lips in anticipation.

Coming to his full height, Cameron stared down at this magnificent woman practically laid out for him. His throat grew tight with emotions…emotions he could certainly identify but he couldn't allow to take over.

"You're stunning," he told her, completely taking in the display.

Without a word, Megan sat up, reached behind and unfastened her bra. After sliding it down her arms and tossing it to the side, she hooked her thumbs beneath her panties and slid them down, never once taking her eyes off his. The minor striptease was the most erotic moment of his life, and it had lasted all of ten seconds. Megan had a power over him that no other woman could match.

"Tell me you have protection," she whispered as she reached for him. Flat palms slid up over his chest and around his neck.

Cameron allowed her to pull him down, and he loved the feel of her beneath him. He had to remind

himself not to get used to this, not to want this ever again.

"I don't have anything." One fingertip slid up and over her breast. "But I'm clean. I have regular physicals for work and I've always used protection. It's your call."

"I'm clean, too, and I've always been protected." Megan smiled, wrapping her legs around Cameron's narrow waist once again. "So what are we waiting for?"

The darkness that had settled into Cameron's blue eyes revealed so much. Who knew her best friend had a possessive streak when it came to intimacy? The way he held her, spoke to her, dominated her, thrilled Megan in a way she'd never before experienced and she knew without a doubt that this was it for her... *He* was it for her. No other man would compare with Cameron St. John.

She wanted to lose herself in him, wanted to forget all the ugliness and worries in her life. She wanted him to show her how beautiful they could be together because her fantasy had already paled in comparison.

"Tell me what you want," he murmured against her lips.

She trembled beneath his touch. No, that wasn't her. Cameron's hands were shaking as he slid them over her breasts.

Framing his face with her hands, she held his gaze. "You're nervous." She didn't ask and she wasn't making fun of him.

Cameron closed his eyes, resting his forehead against hers. "Nobody else has ever mattered this much."

Megan didn't know what to say to that revealing piece of information, so she tucked it in the back of her mind. Stroking his bottom lip with her thumb, she kept her eyes on his.

"I want anything you're willing to give," she said, answering his earlier question. "Anything you want to do."

A low groan escaped him. Then, as if some invisible barrier broke, Cameron consumed her. His hands took journeys all over her body, leaving goose bumps in their wake. That talented mouth demanded kisses, demanded passion.

Cameron settled himself between her legs, gliding one hand down her quivering abdomen to cup her most aching area. Megan tilted her hips, ready to burst for just one simple touch. She was officially at his mercy.

Easing his hand away, he held on to her waist. "Look at me," he demanded. "Only me."

"Only you."

As he slid into her, Megan gasped. Every dream, every waking fantasy she'd ever had about her best friend, didn't prepare her for the onslaught of emotions, waves of pleasure and such an awakening. They moved together as if they'd been made for each other, as if their bodies automatically knew how to respond to each other.

Cameron's arms wrapped around her as he lifted her off the couch. Still connected, he turned and sat, leaving her to straddle him...surrendering all power and control to Megan.

In that moment, she knew he loved her. He may not say it, he may not want to face the fact, but there was no

way this man could look at her, make love to her, as if she were the only woman in the world and not love her.

Ripples of pleasure began to build, each one stronger than the last. Megan wanted to be fully fused with him when her body flew apart. Gripping his shoulders, she leaned down and claimed his mouth. Seconds later spasms took hold. With one hand firmly against the small of her back and the other cupping the nape of her neck, Cameron held her tight against his body as he stilled and trembled right along with her.

Moments after they fell over the edge together, Cameron still held on to her, still commanded her lips. The man wasn't done just because his body had hit the finish line.

His tongue slid along her bottom lip, his kisses softer, shorter…as if he didn't want this moment to end. At least, that's how she hoped he felt.

"Stay with me," she muttered around his kisses. "In my bed. Just for tonight."

His darkened, heavy-lidded gaze met hers. She thought for sure he'd deny her—they'd only agreed on this one time—but she had to ask. She wasn't ready to let him go.

Circling his arms tighter around her waist, Cameron came to his feet. Megan's legs instinctively wrapped around him.

"You seem to like my legs here," she joked, hoping to break the tension because he still hadn't answered her.

He headed out into the hall and toward her bedroom. "I intend to keep them here."

Chapter Thirteen

He'd guaranteed nothing beyond that night. Hadn't promised pretty words or a happily-ever-after. Megan had known exactly what she was getting into with him. He'd made his intentions perfectly clear before he'd peeled her out of her clothes.

So why did he feel like a jerk for leaving her before she woke?

Because he was.

Cameron sat on his deck, looking out over the pond as the morning sun reflected off the water. He didn't take time out here anymore, didn't just relax and enjoy life.

Last night he'd enjoyed life to the absolute fullest, which only made him want more. But his career didn't mesh well with a personal life. He couldn't compart-

mentalize and keep things separated, neat and orderly anymore. But he wanted Megan in one area, the friend area. He wanted her far away from anything that could harm her, like her useless brother who hadn't been able to protect her last night.

Cameron cursed, propping his bare feet up on the rail. He hadn't been able to protect her, either. Apparently he was no better than Evan at this point.

Opting to beat himself up over how everything went down last night was better than rehashing all that could have gone wrong in those few seconds. It also kept his mind off what had happened afterward.

Okay, so that was a lie. Even Cameron couldn't pretend to be unfazed by what had happened at Megan's house. How could he forget how perfectly they'd come together? How she'd clung to him? He could practically still feel her breath on his cheek, feel her curvy body beneath his hands. Those sighs of pleasure tickling his ear and the way she called his name on a groan were locked so deep in to his soul, he knew forgetting the intimacy they'd shared was impossible.

Closing his eyes, Cameron clenched his fists on the arms of his Adirondack chair. He hadn't given a thought to what would happen after he'd made love to Megan. Hadn't cared about feelings or excuses after the fact. All Cameron had wanted was to feel her, consume her. The fantasy come to life had been his only focus, and now here he sat with a sated body and a guilty conscience.

Between his ever-evolving feelings and the worry he'd seen in her eyes when he'd arrived at her house,

Cameron had told himself he was there to console her. That was a flat-out lie. He'd needed to comfort himself because he'd been a trembling mess.

Now his priority was to check in with the station, where some of the FBI agents had set up temporary headquarters until this case was over. He knew if something major had happened, he would have been notified. Still, as the chief, he needed to check in and get an update.

His cell vibrated in his pocket. Dropping his feet to the deck floor, he slid the phone out and read the screen.

I didn't take you for a coward

The harsh words hit right where Megan intended… his heart. Her text couldn't have been more accurate. He was a coward, and she'd called him out. One of the things he loved about her was her ability to never back down.

He honestly had no clue how to reply, and this wasn't a conversation to be had via text. He wouldn't be that guy and he sure as hell would treat Megan with more respect. The thought was laughable, considering he'd done the walk of shame out her back door, but he would make it up to her. Somehow.

Ignoring the text wasn't an option, either. Cameron quickly replied.

Be at my place at noon

That would give him time to check in with the station, figure out where the hell Evan was and grab a

quick shower. Cameron planned to have a little talk with Evan. Cameron had to play every scenario out in his head because he couldn't tip off the guy. But he had every intention of making it clear that dragging Megan into his illegal mess was unacceptable and intolerable.

The phone vibrated in his hand.

If I have time

Smiling, Cameron came to his feet. She'd be there. He was sure of it. If she wasn't, then he'd find her. They weren't done. Not by a long shot.

Now he just had to figure out what the hell to do with his feelings and how to eliminate the possibility of hurting hers. Because, damn it, he still wanted her. Wanted Megan with a passion that went beyond all they'd shared last night. How could he tell her that and still try to keep her at a distance? How could he even try to take a chance with her but keep her safe and away from his job?

Granted, he worked in a small town and the crime rate, for the most part, was low. But there were instances that crept up, and he was the man to take control. He couldn't have his life both ways, and the decision ate at him because he knew he'd have to give up something—or someone—he loved.

Cameron headed inside to make a few calls. First things first. Right now he needed to find Evan and have a man-to-man talk. Then he'd deal with Megan.

If Cameron St. John thought he could turn her world inside out with a few orgasms, leave without a word

and then have the nerve to summon her to his house, he truly didn't know her.

Megan took a deep breath, counted backward from ten and mounted the steps to Mac and Bev's house. She hadn't seen Cameron's truck in the drive or along the street, so she figured now would be a good time to stop and check on Bev. No doubt the woman was fed up with St. John testosterone ordering her to stay put while they did everything for her.

Megan didn't want to go in all angry and frustrated because then she'd have to explain. There was absolutely no way she'd be revealing to Cameron's parents why she was a bit irritable this morning.

After ringing the doorbell, Megan stepped back and waited. Mac pulled the door open, sending the fall floral wreath swaying against the glass.

"Megan." Mac extended his hand, taking hers and pulling her into the foyer. "I'm so glad to see you."

Laughing, Megan allowed herself to be ushered in. "Wow, I've never had such a lovely greeting before."

"I think Bev hates me," he whispered. "She just threatened to bash me with her crutch if I asked her one more time if she needed anything."

Megan patted Mac's arm and smiled. "I'm sure the threat was out of love."

Glancing toward the living room, Mac shook his head. "I doubt it," he said, turning back to her. "If you're going to be a few minutes, would you mind if I ran out to the hardware store? I hate to leave her even though she's told me to go."

Megan nodded. "You go on. We'll be just fine."

Mac seemed to breathe a sigh of relief as his shoulders relaxed. "Thanks, Megan. I'll only be twenty minutes, at the most."

"Take your time."

Mac eased around her, grabbed his keys from the table and headed out the door. Still amused at the fear in Mac's eyes, Megan headed to the living room, where Bev had her feet propped up on the footrest of the recliner. Some cooking channel was muted on the TV.

"Thank God he's gone," Bev said as soon as Megan stepped into the room. "That man needs to stop hovering."

Megan sank onto the edge of the old sofa, angling her body to face Bev. "He just loves you."

Bev dropped the remote into her lap. "I know. I keep telling myself that, but it's a broken ankle. I'm not dying."

Megan glanced around the walls at all the years of memories, family vacations and military medals adorning the space. This family was full of love, full of life and always so supportive.

She couldn't help but wonder what her life would've been like had her parents survived. What would her brother's life have been like? Would he still have felt that urge to rebel at every single thing? "You okay, honey?"

Glancing back to Bev, Megan nodded, swallowing the lump of emotions threatening to clog her throat. "I've been better," Megan answered honestly. "But I came to check on you, not discuss me."

Bev waved a hand. "Oh, please. Everyone has checked on me. I'm fine. What's got you so worried?"

There was no way Megan would get into all the issues that swirled around in her mind. Whatever she and Cameron had going on—or not going on—would remain between them. She had no label for it, had no way of knowing where the next step would take them.

Bev knew enough about Evan, though, that Megan found herself opening up about him. She explained what happened the night before, stopping at the point where Cameron ended up staying the night. Megan had been around this family for so long, Bev had seen Evan's downfall, witnessed Megan's frustration.

"As a woman who raised three hellions, let me tell you that you can only do so much." Bev shifted in her chair until she could reach out and take Megan's hand in hers. "You guide them the best way you can, but in the end they have to make their own decisions."

These were all facts Megan knew, but she still ached for a peace she may never find with her only living relative.

"Those were your kids. It's a bit different with Evan because he's always quick to throw in my face how I'm not his mother." Megan smiled and shrugged. "Besides, your boys all turned out perfect."

Bev's laughter filled the cozy living room. "Oh, honey. They're far from perfect. I had a full head of gray hair by the time I was thirty-five. I swore I wouldn't make it through their teen years without getting a call from the cops about one or all three. They seemed to travel in a pack."

Megan couldn't help but laugh herself. "Yeah, they got me drunk during my senior prom."

"Oh, mercy," Bev whispered, shaking her head. "I think I'm better off not knowing some of the things they did. I cringe just thinking of the stuff I know about."

Megan took comfort in Bev's gentle hand. So many times she'd wanted motherly advice and she'd always known she could turn to Bev at any time. Unfortunately, with the Cameron situation, Megan wasn't about to seek support. She'd have to figure out that one all on her own.

"Evan wouldn't keep in contact with you if he didn't love you," Bev went on. "He may take some time, but you're the only stable person in his life. He'll come back to you."

Megan squeezed Bev's hand. "I hope so."

Because even though she didn't have concrete evidence of his extracurricular activities, she wasn't stupid. If he didn't change his ways, the end result would be either jail or death. Megan didn't know if she had the strength to get through either of those.

Cameron kept his voice low, his back to the brick building, so he could keep an eye on the open end of the alley. He'd found out Evan was in the shady part of a neighboring town, just outside Cameron's jurisdiction.

After throwing on a ball cap and sunglasses, Cameron had gone into the pool hall and firmly told Evan to meet him out back.

Now the coward had the nerve to look worried.

"Maybe you should've been a little more concerned last night for your sister." It took every ounce of Cameron's self-control to keep him from pummeling Megan's brother. "Do you have any idea how scared she was? You may run with these guys, but she doesn't, and she has a heart of gold. You realize that afterward she was more worried about you than what could've happened to her?"

Evan glanced away, but Cameron wasn't having it. Cameron smacked his cheek. "Look at me. Megan said one of your so-called friends had a gun on her. Do you want to see your sister wrapped up in this mess you're in? Do you want to see her hurt or worse?"

Something flared in Evan's eyes. Anger, hatred, who knew what, but at least there was some sign that he actually cared about Megan.

"You have no idea what's going on in my life," Evan spat.

Cameron didn't react, didn't say a word. No sense in giving away that he in fact knew nearly everything that was going on. Knew so much that warrants were about to be processed for the arrest of two major players in the drug-running ring and for Evan, though Evan's charges weren't as harsh. Still, Cameron wanted the charges to stick. He wanted Evan to hit rock bottom so he'd get the help he needed and maybe eventually be the brother Megan deserved.

Disgusted that he was getting nowhere, Cameron started to turn away. "Keep her safe." Evan's low, pleading words froze Cameron in his tracks.

Glancing over his shoulder, Cameron met Evan's

eyes and for the first time he actually saw a man who showed genuine concern and fear for someone other than himself. "She doesn't have anybody else," Evan stated, still holding Cameron's gaze.

Cameron nodded. "Whose fault is that?"

When Evan continued to stare, as if waiting for affirmation, Cameron replied, "I won't let anything happen to her."

As he walked away and headed back toward his truck, he wondered if he'd just lied. Could he honestly keep Megan from getting hurt? Oh, he could prevent her from physical harm, but what about her heart?

The mental scars from this entire scenario would live with her forever. She'd blame herself; she'd question every decision she ever made where her brother was concerned. And she'd hate Cameron.

He slid behind the wheel and brought the engine to life. The clock on his dash showed only thirty minutes until she was due at his house. Knowing Megan, she'd keep him waiting out of spite—which was fine. He needed the extra time to calm down from seeing Evan, from realizing that so much was about to come to a head. All Cameron could do was sit back and proceed with his job…just like always.

Chapter Fourteen

So what if it was nearly two o'clock? Megan wished she could chalk up her tardiness to stubbornness or even the fact she'd been visiting with Bev and Mac. In reality, she'd stuck around with Bev out of nerves.

What would she and Cameron discuss? How did they jump from best friends to the most intimate experience of her life to her waking up alone? Did he really think they would just pal up, watch a movie, grill a steak and hang like they always did on their days off?

Only one way to find out.

Megan mounted the steps and raised her hand to knock. She'd never knocked before. Letting out a sigh, she opened the screen door and twisted the knob on the old oak door. She wouldn't put it past Cameron to lock it since she was late, but the knob turned beneath her palm.

She stepped over the threshold, nerves swirling in her stomach as the familiar scent of Cameron's masculine aroma surrounded her. She'd inhaled that woodsy scent when her face had been pressed into his neck as he'd lowered her into her bed. Never again could she breathe in Cameron's signature scent and not instantly be taken to the time when he'd fulfilled her every desire, her every wish.

Closing the door at her back, Megan sat her purse and keys on the built-in bookshelf to the left of the doorway. The same place she always sat her things when she came in, as if this were her home, too.

Silly thought, really. They'd slept together, not exchanged rings or vows.

A part of Megan wouldn't mind doing just that, but she wouldn't beg any man to love her. Either Cameron would want the same things she did or he wouldn't. No matter how this next phase played out, Megan was a big girl and she'd survive.

But even knowing they'd taken another step deeper into their relationship, Megan still didn't know what to do about the job in Memphis. Being with Cameron was more important than any position she could ever have. She'd give up her dream job in order to have a life with him, but was that something she could convince him of?

She didn't want to have to convince him, though. Megan wanted Cam to come to the realization they belonged together.

And if he didn't, Megan knew she'd have to make

the move because she couldn't live here, see him every day and act as if her heart wasn't shattered.

Heavy footsteps sounded from overhead. Megan glanced toward the stairs just as Cameron came down the first set, then stopped on the landing. His piercing blue eyes held hers as she remained by the door.

"Contemplating whether to stay or go?" he asked.

Shoving her hands in the pockets of her favorite pair of faded jeans, Megan tipped her head. "I don't run away."

Cameron rested his hand on the newel post as he continued to stare down at her. What was he thinking? And why did he look even sexier today now that they'd been intimate?

Keeping his eyes on hers, Cameron slid his hand down the banister as he descended the steps. Megan didn't move, didn't glance away even though her heart was pounding so hard. Cameron came to stand directly in front of her. The way he towered over her had Megan tipping her head back to hold his gaze. Nowhere did he touch her, yet his demanding presence commanded her body to react.

Cameron leaned forward, his lips by her ear. "Don't call me a coward again," he growled.

Pleased he was just as affected by their predicament as she was, Megan forced herself to remain still, to not reach for him and cling as she desperately wanted to. And that was the problem wrapped in the proverbial nutshell. She was desperate for this man's touch, his passion.

When Cameron eased back, just enough for a sliver

of sunlight from the windows to pass through, Megan smiled.

"Hit a nerve, did I?"

"You knew you would."

"Maybe."

Was he just going to stand within a breath of her and not touch her? Maybe he wasn't as affected by their connection as she'd thought. Or perhaps he was into torturing her.

"What's the protocol here, Cam?" she asked, unable to stand the tension for another second. Someone had to step up and start this conversation. "What happens now?"

"What do you want to happen?" he countered.

Megan pulled in a deep breath, knowing full well she walked on a tightrope. "I think I've made things pretty clear. It's you who seems to be torn about what you want."

The muscle in his jaw jumped. He gripped her wrists with one hand, tugging them over her head, causing her to lean back against the door. He trailed his other hand down her arm until she trembled, all the while keeping his eyes locked on hers. She held her breath, unable to fully comprehend the power he had over her and the helpless state she was currently in.

"I'm not torn," he corrected as he brought his palm up to cup her cheek, his thumb stroking her lips. "I know exactly what I want."

That low, sultry tone of his made her body hum with anticipation. Or maybe she was still shaking from the simple touch of his fingertips. Perhaps every single

thing about the man made her tingle now that she had let her guard down.

His eyes held hers. "What I want and what is possible are two different things."

It took a moment for the words to register. Megan made to pull his hands away, shaking her head. "That makes no sense," she all but shouted. "You're an adult. You pretty much decide what you want. Do you not want me? I can handle it if that's the case."

Okay, she might not handle it very well, but she would move on. She wasn't playing around anymore.

"I'd say after last night it's obvious I want you."

"Nothing is obvious," she hissed, hating how she still was held captive by him. "I have no clue what's going on with you, Cam. What are you fighting against?"

Cameron opened his mouth as if to say something, but then he shut it. Glancing toward the ground, he muttered a curse as he rubbed the back of his neck and released his hold on her.

He was battling some inner turmoil. Whatever it was, he wasn't opening up about it. The fact he was keeping something that obviously involved her locked inside had Megan hurting in a way she hadn't known possible.

"You know what, forget it." She sighed, throwing her hands in the air. "We'll go back to being friends. We'll chalk last night up to a—"

His eyes narrowed in on her. "Don't say mistake."

"An amazing experience," she finished slowly. "I

won't call it a mistake. What we shared can't be labeled as a mistake. But it won't happen again."

When he merely nodded, a portion of the hope she'd been clinging to died. He offered nothing but that simple gesture of agreement, as if his entire life hadn't changed after the intimacy they'd shared.

Seeing as how he was not much into conversation today, Megan turned toward the built-in and grabbed her keys and purse. In an instant, Cameron's hands covered hers, his body was plastered to her back, his arms stretched out with hers.

"Don't go," he whispered in her ear.

Closing her eyes, Megan dropped her head between her shoulders. "Why did you tell me to come?"

"I wanted to see you." He nuzzled his way through her hair, his lips barely brushing against the side of her neck. "I had no clue what I'd do once you got here. I told myself to keep the friendship above my desire for you. But I can't."

His fingers laced through hers as he placed open-mouthed kisses over the side of her neck and down onto her shoulder. Megan didn't want to respond, wanted to make him work for it, but her head tipped to the side before she could even think.

"I don't know what the hell to do here, Meg."

So much tension radiated from him. She wanted to turn, to hold him and comfort him. Whatever war he waged with himself was something he felt he needed to face alone.

"I've fought this for so long," he went on as his lips continued to travel over her heated skin. "I never

wanted to cross this line with you because I knew once I had you, it wouldn't be nearly enough."

Well, that certainly sounded promising.

"Then why do you sound so upset?" she asked, trying to focus on his unspoken problem and not the way he was setting her body on fire with each simple touch of those talented lips.

"I've always said I won't get involved." His fingers tightened around hers, balling their joined hands into fists. "I'm married to this job. The stress, the worry, I wouldn't put that on anybody, least of all you."

Everything always came down his job. She loved how noble he was, but, damn it, he was a man, too. A man with needs, desires. And he was ready to shove it all aside for the sake of his badge?

"I don't mind," she answered honestly. "Maybe you wouldn't feel so stressed if you had someone to share the burden with."

"I can't," he muttered, resting his forehead on her shoulder. "You don't understand."

She started to turn, but he held her away. "Damn it, let me look at you," she cried.

Finally he eased back, releasing her hands. When Megan fully turned to face him, angst and torment stared back at her. She'd never thought she'd see a day when Cameron St. John seemed anything but strong and resilient.

They needed to get off this emotional roller coaster. They needed to return to familiar territory where they weren't so wrapped up in what the next step should be. If that step happened to be in opposite directions,

then so be it. But they couldn't lose sight of what was important.

Megan slid a fingertip along the worry lines between Cameron's indrawn brows. "We need a break. *You* need a break." Smiling, she dropped her hand. "I have the perfect idea. Don't go anywhere. I'll be back in thirty minutes to pick you up."

His eyes narrowed. "What do you have in mind?"

"Oh, please." She laughed. "After the shenanigans you and your brothers got into, you're afraid of me?"

His gaze darted to her lips, then back up. "More than you know," he whispered.

How could her body continually respond to his words, his tone and those heated looks? How much did she have to endure before she was put out of her misery and he either moved forward or stepped away? In all honesty, she was done playing. So she was going after all she wanted…and she wanted him.

"I'll be back," she told him. "Just be ready."

"I'm not sure that's possible," he said.

So Cameron didn't miss the meaning in her final warning. *Good.*

Chapter Fifteen

How the hell did he go from telling himself he'd keep the intimacy and sexual tension out of his mind to sitting in Megan's SUV heading toward an unknown destination, fantasizing about peeling that dress up and over her head?

Cameron gritted his teeth and watched out the side window as his familiar town flew by. Megan may be teetering on the edge of speeding, but he wasn't about to say anything. In all honesty, he could use the distraction. He needed to focus on something other than the way she'd shown back up at his door with a wide smile, a little white dress that shifted against her thighs when she turned and those beat-up brown cowgirl boots. She'd done this on purpose. He wasn't a fool, and he knew Megan better than he knew any

other woman. When she set her mind to something, she got it. Which meant he was not only fighting himself; now he'd be battling her.

He didn't stand a chance.

"Where are we going?" he asked, still not turning to look back at those tanned thighs peeking beneath the lacy edge of her dress.

"You're like a little kid." Megan turned onto a dirt road just outside the city limits. "This property is for sale and there's a cute little pond. We're having a picnic. Nobody is around, and I doubt there's even cell service here because it's nestled in the woods. It's too nice of a day to waste inside. The temperature is perfect."

Private. Woods. No cell service. Yeah, she'd definitely be the end of him. They were officially going to be alone, and Cameron knew without a doubt he wouldn't be able to keep his hands off her no matter how good his intentions may be. He was human, and every part of him wanted Megan for himself.

She pulled her SUV under a canopy of trees and killed the engine. Before he could pull on his door handle, Megan reached over the console and gripped his hand.

"No pressure, Cam." Her eyes held his; her unpainted lips called to him. "I just wanted to get away and relax. You've been tense the whole way here."

"I wouldn't say tense," he defended himself.

Megan laughed, smacked a brief kiss on his lips and patted his arm. "You're right. Not tense. Terrified. Now help me get the stuff out of the back."

Cameron had no choice but to follow her around to

the back and pull out the basket she'd hidden beneath a large red blanket. Allowing her to lead the way, Cameron had a hard time keeping his eyes off the sway of the hem of her skirt as the lace edge shifted against her skin. He knew firsthand how silky she felt, how perfectly his fingertips slid over her.

Those damn cowgirl boots were only adding to his arousal. She was so modest, so small-town girl, yet everything about her called to him on a level so primal and carnal she'd probably be terrified if she discovered just how much he craved her.

Beyond the physical pull he had toward her, Megan was the only woman who made him want more for his personal life. She was the only woman who inspired him to want to make the impossible actually work.

"I can practically hear you thinking," she called without looking back. "You're not relaxing."

Megan stopped near the edge of the pond. After giving the folded blanket a jerk, she sent it floating down over the grass. Cameron set the basket down and took a seat. She was right. The weather was rather warm for this time of year and he doubted they'd have many days like this left. Taking advantage of the time was a great idea. Now he just had to figure out how to remain in control here.

"For your information, I'm more relaxed now than I have been in weeks," he told her as he flipped the lid on the basket.

Easing down onto the blanket, Megan shifted her legs to her side and smoothed her skirt around her knees. "Liar. You've barely said a word. That tells me

you're analyzing something." She pulled out two bottles of water. "Most likely you're overthinking us."

Us. They were an *us* at this point whether he wanted to admit it or not.

Megan continued to pull out items from the basket, as if discussing their confusing relationship with the surmounting tension was an everyday occurrence. Grapes, slices of bread, peanut butter, chips and cookies were all scattered around the blanket before he felt confident enough to speak.

Damn it. He was police chief, for pity's sake. He'd put up with quite a bit in his years on the force, dealt with even more before that when he'd been in the army. Yet here he was, trying to find the right words, the courage to talk to Megan as if nothing had changed.

Everything mattered where she was concerned. That's why he was so nervous about hurting her.

"Can I be honest?" he asked.

Her hand froze in the middle of smearing a generous amount of peanut butter onto a slice of bread. Her eyes lifted to his as a slow smile spread across her face.

"You must really be torn up about something. You've never asked permission to do anything and I've never known you to lie to me." She quirked an arched brow. "Have you lied to me?"

That smile held in place, and he knew she was joking. Little did she know how close she was to the truth. He had lied to her—by omission. He'd kept a secret that would most definitely crush her. And that was just the one about her brother, never mind the truth behind his feelings toward her.

"Okay," she muttered as she went back to making a sandwich. "Apparently your lack of smile or response tells me all I need to know. I never thought you'd actually lie to my face."

Cameron reached out, wrapping his hand around her slender wrist until she looked at him again. "There are things I can't tell you, Megan. You know that. Right now I wanted to talk about what's going on with us. I know you wanted me to relax, but I can't when there's so much between us that we're both trying to ignore."

"Oh, I'm not ignoring anything," she countered. "I'm giving you space to come to grips with the fact we slept together."

A soft breeze filtered through, picking up the curled ends of her hair and sending them dancing. Those silky strands had slid all over his body, he'd threaded his fingers through them, and right now he itched to touch her intimately once again.

"I handled that entire situation wrong," he told her, releasing her wrist.

She reached for another slice of bread and put it on top of the peanut butter. When she offered him the sandwich, he shook his head and started making his own.

"You were so vulnerable," he started, still recalling exactly how she'd trembled. "I was, too, for that matter. I'd hit a breaking point, though. I couldn't hold back anymore."

Megan swallowed a bite of her sandwich, reached for a bottle of water and took a drink before respond-

ing. "I don't understand why you denied either of us for so long when we wanted the same thing."

"Because in the end we *don't* want the same thing," he corrected her. "You know my stance on serious relationships, and I know you want a family. We're better off as friends, and I never meant to cross the line because now we're having a damn hard time finding our way back."

Megan plucked off a grape and popped it into her mouth. "There's no reason to turn back. Unless you think sleeping with me was a mistake."

The way her green eyes held his, the way so many questions stared back at him, Cameron found himself shaking his head. "No. That wasn't a mistake. I didn't plan on it, but no way could I call what happened a mistake."

"But you don't want it to happen again."

She couldn't be more wrong. "It can't happen again. Big difference."

With a cocky smile, she went back to her sandwich. He had no clue what that smile meant; more than likely he'd find out because he had no doubt she was plotting something. Cameron finished his sandwich and dived right into the BBQ chips, his favorite. She always kept them on hand for him at her house.

And it was all those little things that added up to make a giant impact on his life.

"So how did you know this property is for sale?" Cameron stretched his legs out in front of him, resting his hands behind his back.

Megan started putting the leftover food back into the

basket. "I have a coworker whose sister is the Realtor. She told me I could come anytime and fish or swim until the property sold. I guess the land was their parents' and now the sisters don't want it, so they're selling it and splitting the profit."

Cameron looked around at all the old oak trees, the perfectly shaped pond, complete with a small dock for fishing or jumping off. He could practically picture a large, two-story cabin-like home off in the distance on the flat stretch of land.

"Beautiful, isn't it?" she asked.

Cameron glanced back to her. "It is."

He watched as her eyes surveyed the land, saw a soft smile settle on her face. Such a look of happiness and contentment.

"You want this land, don't you?"

Blinking, she met his gaze and shrugged. "Who wouldn't? It's just another daydream, though."

He wanted her to have this, wanted her to achieve all those dreams because her entire life she'd put everyone ahead of her own needs. He knew she'd already fantasized about having a family here, kids running through the field and jumping off a dock into the pond. "Buy it," he told her. "Nothing is holding you back. Buy this land and it will be here when you're ready to build."

Megan lay on her back, her head on his thigh and her booted ankles crossed. She laced her fingers over her abdomen and stared up at the sky.

"There's so much holding me back." Her reply came on a soft sigh as she smiled. "I just want to lie here and pretend for a bit longer. I love the sound of abso-

lute nothing. There's something so peaceful, so perfect about it. Like the world is one big happy place."

Her eyes drifted closed, and Cameron's heart broke for her. All she'd ever wanted was for everyone around her to be happy and have a peaceful life. She wasn't naive by any means, but Cameron wondered if she truly believed she could make that happen. The woman was relentless; she'd try to help everyone she knew or she'd go down swinging.

Unable to keep his hands from her another moment, he smoothed her hair away from her face, trailing his fingertip down along her shoulder. "What's holding you back from buying?" he asked.

He knew she was extremely frugal with her finances and she rarely bought anything for herself. Her house and SUV were both paid off. She wasn't a shopper like some women he knew.

Those bright green eyes focused on his. Sometimes looking at her physically hurt him, because he knew one day she'd find the one. She'd settle down and marry, probably have children. And all that happiness was exactly what he wanted for her. He just couldn't be the one to supply her needs.

"I may be moving."

Cameron's hand stilled, and the fine strands of her hair slid right out of his fingers. "You're moving?"

"I haven't decided yet."

All Cameron could do was stare. The air seemed a bit thicker as the severity of her words hit him like a punch to the stomach. He hadn't seen this coming, and it took a lot to send his shock factor gauge soaring.

"Where would you be moving?" he asked.

"Memphis."

Almost two hours away. Not terribly far, but not down the street, either, as he'd grown used to. He'd already told himself he couldn't have his job and her. Something had to give. He just hadn't been prepared to let her go so far. Damn it, he didn't want this, but she had to make her own choices.

"I was offered a position at a new facility," she told him, her tone soft as if she was afraid to go into details. "That's where I was when I went out of town."

Nodding, Cameron rested his hand at his side. "Did you like the place?"

Why did the selfish part of him want her to say she hated it? Why did he hope she would turn this opportunity down? Hadn't he just told himself he wanted to see her happy, to see all her wishes and dreams come true for once?

Yet here he was, craving her, knowing he wouldn't give in to his own desires all because he wanted her to live the life she deserved and not be tied to the stress and obligations of being with a cop.

"I did." Megan focused back on the sky as the sun took cover behind a large white cloud. "There's just so many pros and cons no matter what decision I make."

"You need to do what's best for you, not what's best for everyone else."

There, that was the right thing to say. Still, the thought of her leaving was like a vise on his heart. He didn't want her to go, but he wouldn't sway her decision unless she asked his opinion. Even then, he

wouldn't tell her to stay because he selfishly couldn't stand the thought of going days or even weeks without seeing her.

She was obviously just as torn or she would've told him her decision sooner. "Have you talked to Evan about the move?"

Megan sighed. "No. On one hand, I think leaving and having him come with me would be the fresh start he needs. On the other hand, I don't know that he would come."

Cameron really wished he could tell her that most likely Evan would be in jail before long.

"Don't let Evan factor into this," he commanded, a little harsher than he'd meant to.

Megan's eyes snapped to his. "How can I not?" she asked, jerking up into a sitting position. The way she twisted to confront him had their faces within inches of each other. "He's my only family, and he needs me."

"He needs to help himself for once."

Anger flashed through her eyes. "I won't fight with you about this again. You love Eli and Drake no matter what they do, and I love Evan no matter how much he screws up. He's still my brother."

Cameron wasn't about to state the obvious, that Evan wasn't near the men Eli and Drake were. Megan knew exactly how those three men lived their lives.

Tamping down his worry and frustration, Cameron lifted his hand to her cheek. Stroking his thumb along her soft skin, he held her gaze.

"I want you to make a decision that is strictly selfish," he told her. "I want you to do whatever you want

without thinking of the consequences, without thinking of who will be hurt or angry. What does Megan want?"

Without a word, she shifted away and came to her feet. Toeing off her cowgirl boots, she kept her eyes locked on to his. In a move he hadn't seen coming, she lifted the hem of her skirt and pulled the dress over her head, tossing the garment to the side. Seeing her standing before him in a simple white cotton bra and panties shouldn't have turned him on as much as it did, but every single thing about Megan had his body responding.

"What are you doing?" he asked, cursing his raspy voice.

Reaching around to unfasten her bra, Megan let the straps slide down her arms. "I'm making a selfish decision. Right now, I want to go lay at the edge of the pond and get lost in a fantasy." She met his gaze as she hooked her thumbs in her panties and pulled them down. "With you."

He'd never been one to turn away from a challenge. No matter how many warnings blared through his head, there wasn't a man alive who would turn Megan Richards away.

Even with the high, full trees, sunlight filtered through and seemed to land right on the perfect body she'd placed on display for him.

"What if someone sees us?" he asked.

Megan laughed. "Well, we're pretty secluded and nobody is around. We'll hear a car if it comes up the road. Plus I'm the only one naked, so I guess I'm the

only one who should worry about being seen. Am I right?"

She quirked a brow and turned away, heading toward the deck. Cameron came to his feet and began to strip, all the while watching that soft sway of those rounded hips.

There would be no good outcome to this story. Not one. He figured he might as well enjoy every moment with her that he could, because once those warrants came through, Megan would not be throwing those sassy, sultry smiles his way any longer. She'd look at him with disdain, and the thought crushed him.

Right now, he wanted to feel her in his arms, wanted to show her he truly did love her…even if he could never say the words aloud and mean them the way she needed him to.

Chapter Sixteen

Out of all the spontaneous things she'd done in her life, not that there had been many, making love with Cameron out in the open without a care in the world had to top the list.

Come to think of it, making love with Cameron had topped any and all lists she'd ever made or ever would make.

As Megan pulled into her drive after dropping Cameron off, she realized they'd been out much later than she'd meant and she hadn't left a porch light on. The street lamp was enough for her to see, but she still hated coming home to a dark, empty house.

She didn't regret one moment of today, though. Spending the day with Cameron, not worrying about Evan or how this change in her and Cam's dynamic would affect their friendship was quite refreshing.

Speaking of refreshing, her body still tingled as she recalled how Cameron had lifted her naked body against his and walked into the water. The water had been surprisingly warm. When Cameron had knelt down, with her wrapped all around him, and made love to her as the water lapped at their waistlines, she'd fallen completely in love with him. The moment had been perfect, the man even more perfect. And she knew she'd loved him all along, but that moment, that beautiful, special moment, had opened her eyes to what was truly happening between them.

Megan pulled into the garage, grabbed the basket from the trunk and headed to the back door. Holding up her keys toward the glow from streetlights, Megan squealed when a shadow of a man stood on her back steps.

"It's just me."

Heart pounding nearly through her chest, Megan gripped her keys and the basket. "Evan, you scared me to death. Why are you out here in the dark?"

"Can I stay here? At least for tonight?"

Megan stepped forward, still unable to see him very well. "Of course you can. You're my brother."

He shrugged. "I just…I didn't know after the other night."

"Let's get inside and then we'll talk."

She opened the back door and ushered him in ahead of her. After flicking on the kitchen light and setting the basket on the dinette table, she turned to Evan.

"What happened?" she asked, examining his swollen eye and cut lip. This looked far worse than the in-

jury from the other day. And this was the other eye because the other one still sported a fading purple bruise.

Evan sank into a wooden chair at the table. "Wrong place, wrong time. Story of my life."

She wanted to tell him he'd written his own story and it was never too late to start a new chapter, but she figured all that psychoanalyzing would only irritate him even more. It would be the equivalent of teaching a drowning person to swim. Not the time.

So, for now, she'd tend to his wounds and listen. He was here because he felt safe, and she wasn't about to run him off with all the questions swirling around in her mind or by scolding him like a warden.

"Let me get my first-aid kit."

By the time she came back, Evan had flipped the lid off the basket and was making a sandwich.

"I can make you real food if you're hungry." She sat in the chair at the head of the table and checked the supplies in the kit. "I know I have some spaghetti and a quesadilla I could heat up."

Evan shook his head. "This will be fine."

After pulling out the things she needed to fix Evan up, she turned toward him. "I only have one question."

His eyes came up to meet hers. Eyes so like hers, but they'd dimmed somewhere along the way. Perhaps the process had been slow, and that's why she hadn't noticed. Most likely the light started fading when he'd been kicked out of two schools in two years, before junior high. They'd had to move, but eventually Megan

came back to her school in Stonerock because she'd missed Cameron and his brothers.

Evan's eyes definitely lost some shine on the night their parents died. Since then he'd been at a rapid decline and spiraling into a territory she feared she'd never rescue him from.

"Are you ready to get out?" she asked.

Evan reached across the space between them and gripped her hand. "Yes."

Relief flooded through her. "Are you on something now?"

She didn't need to go into details; he knew exactly what she was asking.

"No. I don't use. I only supply."

As if that made his position any better? Megan sandwiched his hand in her grip so he'd understand how much she wanted him here, how much she loved him and would support him on all levels.

"We'll get through this, Evan," she promised. "But first we need to go to the police."

"No." He jerked back, shaking his head. "I can't do that. You don't know what those guys are capable of."

Megan repressed a shudder as the memory of being held at gunpoint flashed through her mind. "I've got a pretty good idea," she told him. Easing forward, she pleaded, "Cameron can help, but you have to tell him everything."

Evan closed his eyes and sighed. "I can't right now."

Megan started to say something, but Evan opened his eyes and offered a weak smile. "Just let me get some rest tonight. Okay? Can we discuss this tomorrow?"

He was exhausted and broken. Megan's heart ached for him. But he was making progress, and she wasn't about to upset him further and risk driving him away.

The job opportunity in Memphis was weighing heavily on her mind, especially after being with Cameron again. He'd seemed stunned and speechless about her offer, but she desperately needed to know how he felt about her moving, how that would impact anything they had. At some point he was going to have to be honest with her about what he wanted.

Megan dabbed at the cut on Evan's swollen eye with a cotton ball. After applying some antibiotic ointment, she placed a small butterfly bandage on the wound and turned her attention toward his mouth.

"If we could move away, would you go?" she asked.

"Where would we go?"

Shrugging, Megan didn't want to give too much away about the job offer. "I've thought about Memphis, but I wouldn't do anything without discussing it with you."

"I like it here."

Megan nodded. "If you want to escape the mess you're in, you need to get away, and not just in theory."

A frustrated sigh escaped him. "I don't want to fight. I just want to rest."

"Fine." She wasn't going to get anywhere right now. She had to be patient. "You're more than welcome to stay. Will they come here looking for you?"

"I don't think so."

Megan finished up and started putting supplies

away. "If they come, I am calling Cameron. No arguments. Got it?"

Evan straightened in his seat. "Meg—"

She held up her hand. "No. Arguments." This was her turf, and no way in hell was it going to be penetrated by guys who were only out to cause harm.

"Fine."

He scooted away from the table, rising to his feet as he grabbed his side.

"What's wrong?" She started to reach for him, but he stepped back. "Are you hurt there, too?"

"It's nothing but some bruised ribs. I'm gonna go crash."

With that, Evan turned and headed toward the spare bedroom. Megan stared at the empty doorway, wondering how the conversation would go in the morning. Would Evan still be ready to talk about a new life or would his current fear disappear?

For now, he was safe and she wouldn't go to Cameron unless someone from Evan's circle showed up. She would do anything to keep her brother safe, and now that he was in her home, nobody would get through. She kept a gun for security in her closet. She'd never had to use it before, but she wouldn't hesitate to defend her family. No matter what.

Megan was thankful today was Sunday and she could relax. She tended to work a few hours on Saturday, so Sunday was her only full day off.

Halloween was tomorrow night. She enjoyed seeing the kids in her neighborhood all dressed up in adorable

costumes. She couldn't wait until the day she got to parade her own little gremlin or witch around.

Megan had finished making breakfast an hour ago, and when Evan continued to sleep, she covered his plate and set it in the microwave. She wanted him to have a nice home-cooked meal because she doubted anyone else truly cared for him.

Her phone vibrated on the kitchen table. Glancing at the screen, she read Cameron's message.

Still coming to the cookout at my parents'?

Megan hesitated. She'd forgotten all about the cookout and bonfire, complete with s'mores, at Mac and Bev's. But she couldn't leave her brother behind to go to the St. Johns' house, and she couldn't very well take him.

Until she knew how the day unfolded, she wasn't going to respond.

By the time Evan woke, Megan had already cleaned the entire kitchen and dusted her living room. Wearing only his jeans, Evan shuffled in and sank onto the couch. His dark hair stood on end, the bruises over his face and along his right side more prominent this morning. He hadn't let her look last night and she wasn't going to coddle him today. He was a grown man, and he was here for security, not lecturing.

"Morning," he mumbled, raking a hand over his face, the stubble along his jaw and chin bristling beneath his palm. "Thought you'd be at work."

Megan leaned a hip against the back of her oversize chair and crossed her arms. "I don't work on Sunday."

"It's Sunday? I've lost track of the days." He eyed her, drawing his dark brows in. "You have plans?"

"Not really," she replied with a shrug. "You have anything you want to do?"

Evan scratched his bare chest. "I need to get my stuff sometime."

"Where is it?"

"All over. My clothes are at Spider's place. He's cool, though, so I can go there alone. I have a few things at this girl Mary's house, but she's probably sold it all by now."

As Megan listened to her brother go through his list of minute belongings scattered all around, another layer of how different their lives were slid into place. He had no stability, while she thrived on a solid foundation. He had no real friends, and she'd had Cameron and his family since grade school. Evan worried about day-to-day life, whereas Megan worried about advancing in her already successful career.

Where had she gone wrong? At some point along the way she'd missed something.

"If you have plans, go on and do them," Evan told her. "I'm going to go get my clothes and just chill here. I don't expect you to put your life on hold for me."

"I'm not putting my life on hold," she corrected him, easing around the chair. Taking a seat on the edge, she angled her body to face him fully. "Do you have a plan beyond today?"

"Not really." Wincing and grabbing his side, he

started to sit up. "I know you like details and schedules, but that's not me, Meg. I'm not sure about moving, but I wouldn't mind staying here for a while if you don't mind."

Reaching out to pat his leg, she offered a smile. "You're always welcome here, Evan. I just can't have the group you hang around with. I've worked hard to get where I am and I'll do anything to help you. Consider this your home, but if anyone jeopardizes my little world, I won't back down. I'm not afraid of them."

Covering her hand with his, Evan's eyes held hers. "You should be afraid. They're ruthless, Megan. They don't care who they hurt, so long as they have money and drugs. Maybe I should stay somewhere else."

"No," she answered without thinking. "I worry when I don't see you or hear from you. You're staying here, where I can help you."

The muscle moved in his jaw, and his eyes darted down, then back up. "I don't even know if getting out is possible."

"We'll make it possible," she promised.

The back door opened at the same time Cameron's voice called out for her. "Megan?"

"Living room."

Evan's face went from worry for her to instant stone. "You didn't respond earlier so—"

Cameron's words died as he stepped around the corner and froze in the entryway. "Evan."

The tension between these two was so thick it was like a concrete block had been dropped into the room.

Still, she loved them both, and if they loved her, they'd just have to grow up.

"Evan needed a place to crash," she explained.

Cameron didn't take his eyes off Evan. "Looks like he was already in a crash."

"Something like that," Evan muttered.

They'd never made it a secret they weren't buddies, but still, couldn't they at least try to be civil while she was around?

Megan twisted in her seat, letting go of Evan's hand. "What's up?"

Cameron stared at Evan another few seconds before turning his attention to Megan. "I didn't hear from you earlier, so I thought I'd see if you were coming tonight."

"Actually, I probably won't."

"Megan, go," Evan told her. "Don't stay here because of me."

She glanced back to her brother, knowing he expected her to just leave him in pain. He'd just have to get used to the fact that not everyone abandoned him. Damn it, she wanted him to see that she was here no matter what and his needs came before her own.

"I really don't want to leave you alone."

"Because you don't trust me?" he asked, masking his hurt with a rough tone.

"No," she told him, purposely softening her voice. "Because I worry about you, especially after last night."

"You can come, too."

Both Evan and Megan turned to Cameron as his invitation settled in the air between them.

"You're inviting me to your family dinner?" Evan asked.

With a shrug, Cameron leaned a shoulder against the door frame. "Sure. It's no big deal, and you have to eat, too."

Megan held her breath, her eyes darting between the two men. She was beyond shocked that Cameron had invited Evan. That was the type of noble man he was. Cameron was reaching out all because he cared for her and—dare she hope—loved her.

"I don't think your family would want me there," Evan said as he came to his feet.

"They won't mind. Come with Megan if you want or don't come. No big deal. Just extending the offer."

Megan caught Cameron's gaze and mouthed "thank you" when Evan wasn't looking. Cameron's eyes held hers, a small smirk formed on his lips and Megan knew he was only doing this for her.

If she hadn't already loved him, this would've sealed the deal. He was trying. Did that mean he wanted to try more with her, as well?

"I was just heading out for a run and thought I'd swing in," Cameron stated, pushing off the frame. "Megan, I'll see you tonight."

So, he wanted to see her whether Evan came or not. When the front door closed again, Evan glanced down to where she remained seated.

"He's in love with you."

Jerking her eyes up to him, Megan laughed. "Don't be ridiculous, Evan. We've been best friends since grade school."

"The guy has always been territorial with you, but he was looking at you like… Oh, great." Evan shook his head and laughed. "Tell me you didn't fall in love with him. Come on, Meg. He's a cop."

Yeah, he was a cop. He was also perfect for her little world, amazing in bed and irreplaceable.

"Who I love or don't love is really none of your concern," she told him. "I'm not being rude, but you have your own issues to work out. Now, if you want to come with me later, that's fine. If you don't, that's fine, too. I'll be leaving at six."

Megan turned and left Evan alone. She didn't want to hear anything else about why she should or shouldn't fall in love with Cameron. The reasons were moot at this point because she'd already fallen so deep, she'd never find her way back out.

Chapter Seventeen

Keep your friends close and your enemies closer.

Cameron had always hated that saying. Having enemies so close made him twitchy and irritable.

As he glanced across the field toward Evan, who sat in a folding chair all by himself, Cameron figured if Evan was here, he wasn't getting into anything illegal. Megan could rest easy tonight.

Speaking of Megan, she'd gotten cold earlier when the sun had gone down and he'd grabbed a hoodie sweatshirt from the back of his truck. The fact she was wrapped in his shirt made him feel even more territorial. The way she all but disappeared inside the fleecy material made her seem even more adorable. How could a woman be so many things at once? Sexy, cute, intriguing, strong… Megan was all of that and much more.

She laughed at something Eli said before turning her gaze and meeting his. Instantly the air crackled. Nothing else mattered but Megan. The case should be wrapped up by tomorrow evening when the next "trade" took place. He knew all key players were supposed to be in attendance, according to their inside source.

Maybe once all of this was tied up, maybe once Evan was out of the picture and not weighing so heavily on Megan's mind and conscience, she would figure out how to seek that happiness she deserved.

Drake came to stand beside Megan, and she turned, breaking the moment. Only Eli knew of the tension between them, and Cameron doubted anyone else was picking up on the vibes he and Megan were sending out.

Cameron's gaze darted back to Evan…who was shooting death glares across the distance. Okay, maybe one more person knew something was happening between him and Megan, but Cameron didn't care what Evan's opinion was.

"You seem quiet tonight."

Cameron merely nodded as his father came up beside him. "Been a stressful time at work," Cameron replied.

"Looks to me like you have something else on your mind."

Cameron glanced to his father, who was looking straight at Megan. She excused herself, picked up a roasting stick and took it over to her brother. Cameron watched as they talked, and finally Evan came to his feet, took the stick, and he and Megan went over to the fire to roast marshmallows.

"I figured you two would figure this out eventually," his father went on.

Cameron groaned inwardly. "There's nothing to figure out, Dad. We're friends."

"Friends is a good start," Mac agreed. "Building on that only makes a stronger relationship."

Frustration slid through him. He really didn't want to get into this right now with his dad...or anybody else for that matter.

"Look, Dad—"

"Hear me out." Mac turned to face Cameron. The wrinkles around his father's eyes were more prominent as he drew his brows together. "You are overthinking things, son. Megan isn't going to wait around for you to come to your senses."

Clenching his fists at his side, Cameron nodded. "I don't expect her to. Things would be easier if she met someone and moved on."

"Easier for you?" he asked. "Because from where I'm standing, Megan only has eyes for one person. I figured you'd be smart enough to make your friendship more permanent."

"You don't get it," Cameron began, absently noting that Evan had taken a phone call.

"Get what?" Licking marshmallow off his thumb, Drake came up beside their dad.

"Nothing," Cameron stated.

"Your brother is having women problems."

Still focused on his gooey thumb, Drake laughed. "Megan giving you fits?"

What the hell? Is nothing sacred around here?

"I'm going to kill Eli," Cameron muttered.

Drake's smile widened. "He didn't tell me. Marly

did. Women just seem to be in tune with each other, but I think something happened when they all went out to Dolly's the other night."

Had Megan mentioned him to Marly and Nora? Surely she hadn't.

When he sought her out again, she was helping Willow roast a marshmallow. She fit in perfectly with his family. What would happen if he decided to take a chance? What would happen if he gave in to both of their needs and took this friendship beyond the bedroom?

"For what it's worth," Drake went on, "I think Megan is great. I always figured you guys would end up together."

Apparently every single person in his family had some creepy psychic ability because Cameron had fought the urge for years to ever make Megan more than a buddy or a pal. Unfortunately he knew firsthand just how sexy and feisty his "pal" was.

Evan rushed to Megan's side as he slid his phone back into his pocket. Just as Evan said something to her and hurried toward the front of the house, Cameron's cell vibrated in his pocket.

"Excuse me," he told his father and Drake.

Stepping away from the crowd, he pulled out the phone and read the text.

Moving day changed. 30 min.

Damn it. That's why Evan rushed out?

Cameron caught Drake's eye. "Something came up. Tell everyone—"

Drake waved him away. "Go—we know."

This family was more than used to Cameron getting called away. All three St. John brothers were in high demand in Stonerock, so it wasn't unusual for at least one of them to get called away from a family gathering.

Cameron rushed to his house to grab his work gun and Kevlar vest. Thankfully, the designated parking lot was less than ten minutes away. By the time he pulled in, he still had ten minutes to spare.

The outcome tonight was not going to be good, but right now all Cameron could focus on was doing his job. Just when he'd been about to open himself up to the possibility of a relationship with Megan, this call had come through. Was it a sign that keeping his distance was the right thing to do?

Cameron settled in with his fellow officers and FBI agents. Now all they had to do was watch and wait, and hopefully this entire ordeal would be wrapped up tonight.

He had no idea if he should be elated or terrified.

Megan had no clue where Evan had run off to and then Cameron had gotten called into work. She'd stayed behind and chatted with Nora and Marly, roasted more marshmallows than her stomach appreciated and now lay curled up in the corner of her sofa trying to read a book by the vomited light of the evil dragon.

Megan couldn't help but look at that tacky piece and laugh. Because if she didn't laugh, she'd surely cry. Some people had a beautiful art sculpture or painting as the focal point in their living rooms. Nope, Megan had this monstrosity.

Flipping through the pages of her book, Megan wanted to see when the good scenes were coming up because the current chapter was nearly putting her to sleep.

Before she could decide whether or not to give up, her cell rang. Dropping the book on the end table, she picked up her phone, not recognizing the number. Most likely a client.

"Hello?"

"Meg. I've been arrested."

Jumping to her feet, Megan started toward her bedroom to put clothes on. "What happened, Evan?"

Dread flooded her. Whatever he'd hightailed it out of the St. Johns' party for had obviously not been a good idea.

"Your boyfriend brought me in." Evan's tone was filled with disgust. "I wasn't doing anything, Meg. I need you to come get me."

Cameron arrested Evan? How the hell had the night gone from roasting marshmallows to her brother being thrown in jail?

"How much is bail?" she asked, shoving her feet into her cowgirl boots.

"I don't think they're allowing it to be set."

Megan froze. "What did you do?"

"Listen, I need you to fix this, Meg," he pleaded, near hysterics. "I don't want to be here. Call your attorney and get me out of this place."

Megan sank onto the edge of her bed. "If bail isn't an option, there's nothing I can do right now. I'll call

my lawyer, but I doubt he can do anything tonight, either."

"Maybe you should tell Cameron I'm innocent," he spat, seconds before hanging up.

Defeated, angry and cold, Megan stared at the cell in her hand. In her heart she'd known this day was coming. Evan had reached out to her for help only twenty-four hours ago…obviously too late to make a difference.

Before she could allow her mind to travel into what Cameron knew about this situation, she had to call her attorney. Evan's fear had been apparent through the line. She knew from a few of her clients just how terrifying being arrested for the first time could be. No matter what the attorney's fee would be, she'd pay it and do every single thing in her power to get him away from this city where he was only staying in trouble. If he wanted to truly get away, he needed a fresh start away from the thugs he'd been with.

Hours later, Megan was still wound tight. She'd discovered there was nothing to do for Evan right now. There would be a hearing on Monday morning to decide the next step.

Megan had hung up with her attorney thirty minutes ago and couldn't go in to bed if she tried. She glanced at the book on the end table and knew that wouldn't hold her interest, either.

Heading to the hall closet, she was just about to sink to a whole new level of desperate and pull out her vacuum when her back door opened and closed.

The late hour didn't stop Cameron from letting him-

self in. *Great.* She wasn't sure she was ready to deal with this, with him. She was still shaking from the fact that her brother was behind bars with criminals and her best friend had arrested him.

Moving down the hall, she met Cameron just as he stepped out of the kitchen. The dark bruise beneath his eye, the cut across his other brow and his disheveled clothes stopped her in her tracks.

"What the hell happened tonight?" she cried. "Evan's arrested and you've been in a fight."

Cameron's tired eyes closed as he shook his head. "I wanted to be the one to tell you about Evan, but I knew there was no way I could finish everything up and get here before he called you."

Anger coursed through her. "You knew my brother was in trouble. Enough trouble to get arrested, didn't you?"

Slowly, his lids opened, those signature baby blues locked on her. "Yes. I've been watching him for some time now. Him and several others."

Megan felt as if someone had taken a pointy-toed shoe and kicked her straight in the stomach.

"Evan wasn't a key player," Cameron went on. "He just fell in with the wrong crowd and ended up deeper than I think he intended."

Bursts of cold shot through her system. Megan wrapped her arms around her waist and pushed past Cameron.

"So you just arrest him anyway?" she asked, moving to the living room to sink onto the sofa. "You know

he's trying to break away and you still arrest him like some hardened criminal?"

Cameron rested his hands on his hips, remaining across the room. "He is a criminal, Meg. He was with the group we've been tracking for months. Evan has been running drugs."

No. This was her brother, her baby brother. She didn't want this to be his life even though he'd admitted as much to her just yesterday. He'd said he wanted to get out. She'd give anything if he would have come to her sooner; maybe they wouldn't be in this position now.

Bending forward, her arms still tight around her midsection, she wanted to just curl up and cry or scream. "You should go," she whispered, already feeling the burn of tears in her throat.

"I'm not leaving until we talk."

Of course he wasn't.

"I know you aren't happy with me right now," he started. "But you have to know I was doing my job. I can't let our relationship prevent me from keeping Stonerock safe."

A laugh erupted from her before she could prevent it. Megan sat back up and rested her elbows on her knees.

"I don't expect you to not do your job, Chief. But I never thought you'd be spying on my brother one minute and sleeping with me the next."

Okay, he deserved that. Megan needed to get all her anger out because he'd had months to deal with the fact

that Evan was into illegal activities. While Megan had suspected her brother's involvement, tonight she'd been dealt some cold, hard facts—and then learned her best friend was the arresting officer.

"How could you do this to me?" she asked, her voice husky from emotion. "How could you use me like that? We've been friends so long, Cam. I trusted you with everything in my life and you just…"

Her words died in the air as she covered her face with her hands. Sobs tore through her, filling the room and slicing his heart. Cameron knew full well that right at this moment she felt she hated him, but that didn't stop him from stepping forward and squatting down in front of her.

"I didn't use you," he said, realizing how pathetic he sounded. "I couldn't tell you, Meg. I wanted to. I wanted you to know what you were in the midst of. I wanted to somehow soften the blow, but my hands were tied."

Her hands dropped to her lap as she focused her watery stare on him. Tear tracks marred her creamy skin, and Cameron knew if he attempted to reach out to wipe away the physical evidence of her pain, she would push him away.

"You mean you chose your job again over every-thing else. Over me."

Cameron eased up enough to sit on the edge of the coffee table, his elbows on his knees, as he fought the urge to take her hands in his. She had to get all this anger out, and he had to absorb it. There was no other

way to move beyond this mess…if they even could move on.

"Wait." Megan sat up straighter, her gaze darting to the floor, then back up to his. "You were there, weren't you? The night I was with Evan and those guys showed up?"

Regret filled him, cutting off any pathetic defense he could've come up with. As if the entire lying-by-omission thing weren't enough, now he had to face the ugly truth that he'd not done a damn thing to help her.

She continued to stare at him, continued to study him as if she didn't even recognize him anymore. "Tell me you weren't there," she whispered.

Swallowing a lump of rage and remorse all rolled into one, he replied, "I can't."

He expected her to slap him, to stand up and charge from the room or start yelling and throwing things. He expected pure anger. Anger he could've dealt with.

But when she closed her eyes, unleashing a fresh set of tears as she fell back against the couch, defeated, Cameron knew he'd broken something between them. He'd broken something in her, and he had no idea how to fix it or even if their relationship was repairable.

"I want to hate you right now."

Those harsh words from such a tiny voice was the equivalent of salt to the wound…a self-inflicted wound. He had absolutely nobody to blame but himself.

Megan eased up, just enough to look him in the eye. "I want to hate you so you'll be out of my life, so I never have to see you again," she told him through tears. "But I can't because no matter how deeply you

hurt me, I still love you. Damn it, Cameron, I love you more than I've ever loved anybody. I was prepared to turn down this job in Memphis for you. I was ready to fight for you, for us."

Her voice shook as she went on, swiping at the tears streaking down her cheeks. "I was ready to live with your dedication to your job. I foolishly thought you could love me just as much, but now I know I'll never be equal, never be enough."

Cameron had no clue he'd shed his own tears until he felt the trickle down his cheek. He'd never cried over a woman. Hell, he couldn't recall the last time he'd cried at all. But Megan was worth the emotion; she was worth absolutely everything.

"Stay," he pleaded. "Don't take the job. We can get through this."

"Can we?" she tossed back. "And how would we do that? You spied on my brother for who knows how long. You watched me from a distance during one of my scariest moments. I think that is enough to prove you'd never put me first, so don't preach to me about staying to make this work. I've been here for years, Cam. Years. I can't help it if you're just now ready."

Megan came to her feet, anger fueling her now if the way she swatted at the tears on her face was any indication. Cameron eased back on the table but didn't rise. He knew she needed the control, the upper hand here.

"You always said you wouldn't ever make a woman compete with your job," she went on. "But what do you think I've been doing all this time? I was with you during deployments, during the police academy and your

entire law-enforcement career. You think I worried less because we were friends and not married? You think I didn't play the 'what-if' game while you were overseas or if a day or two went by that I didn't hear from you?"

Reality hit him square in the gut.

"You're right." Slowly, he got to his feet. Considering she didn't back away, he reached for her hands. "You were there for me every step of the way. I didn't see your angle until now, or maybe I was afraid to."

Megan fisted her hands beneath his. "You need to go. I'm exhausted. I've got to figure out what I can do for Evan, and I need to make arrangements for Memphis."

The last bit of hope he'd had died as he released her fists. "You're leaving."

Megan's gaze slid to the floor as she nodded, not saying a word. Conversation over.

There had never been such an emptiness, such a hollow feeling in his soul. The bond they'd honed and strengthened for years had just been severed in the span of minutes. He'd known how this would hurt her, but he hadn't expected her to erect this steel wall between them, completely shutting him out.

Cameron turned, headed toward the back door.

"Did you ever love me?" Megan's question tore through the thick tension.

Stopping, Cameron leaned a hand on the door frame to steady himself. Not only was he starting to tear up again but his knees were shaking.

"I've always loved you," he told her. "More than you could ever know."

When she said nothing in reply, Cameron headed straight out the back door. He had to keep going or he'd drop to his knees and beg her forgiveness. But Megan wasn't in the frame of mind to forgive.

He had a feeling after all he'd done to destroy their friendship and the intimacy they'd discovered, she never would be.

Chapter Eighteen

Two weeks later, Evan was still in jail. She'd been able to see him several times and each time she went her heart broke even more. He'd hinted that maybe he'd be getting out soon, but she couldn't get details from him.

After taking another picture from the wall, Megan wrapped it in bubble wrap and placed it in the box with the other fragile items. Her new job was to start in two weeks and she was moving in to her new rental within days.

The thought of leaving this house that she'd loved for so long had her reminiscing with each room she walked through, each item she boxed up. She'd yet to pack the dragon lamp because each time she passed by the hideous thing, she started tearing up once again.

In the two weeks since she'd last seen Cameron, her

emotions had been all over the place. She'd gone from angry to depressed, from crying to yelling at the empty space. Other than during his deployments, she'd never gone this long without seeing or talking to him. How could her best friend since childhood be out of her life so fast? How did she move on without the stability and support he'd always offered?

By sticking to her plans. She would move towns, make new friends and start a new life. And if Evan somehow miraculously got out, he could join her.

Of course, all of that would be in a perfect world, and she knew she lived in anything but.

Tomorrow she'd have the difficult task of telling her clients that she was leaving. She'd really formed some wonderful friendships during her time at the counseling center. Her supervisor was sorry to see her go, but understood, considering she'd been the one to recommend Megan for the position.

Before she could pull another piece of artwork from the wall, the doorbell rang. Glancing around the boxes, bubble wrap and her own state of haphazardness, Megan shrugged. She wasn't expecting company, though she'd been surprised Cameron hadn't attempted to contact her again. A piece of her was disappointed and a little more than hurt at the fact, but she'd told him to go and he was honoring her wishes. Noble until the end, that man was.

Adjusting her ratty old T-shirt and smoothing back the wayward strands that had escaped her ponytail, Megan flicked the lock and tugged on the door.

Speak of the devil.

Only he didn't look like the devil at all. He didn't even look worn and haggard as she did. Damn the man for standing on her porch looking all polished and tempting. The fall breeze kicked up, bringing his familiar scent straight to her and teasing her further.

His eyes darted behind her, no doubt taking in the chaos.

"When do you leave?" he asked, returning those baby blues to her.

Gripping the door frame, she prayed for strength, prayed to be able to hold it together while she figured out the reason for his visit.

"Next week."

He glanced down, then back up and sighed. "Can I come in? Just for a minute?"

Said the lion to its prey.

Megan stepped back, opening the old oak door even more to accommodate his broad frame. As soon as he entered, she closed the door, leaned back against it and waited while he continued to survey the room.

"I came to fill you in on Evan."

He turned to face her, and now that he was closer, she could see the worry lines etched between his brows, more prominent than ever. The dark circles beneath his eyes were evidence he'd been sleeping about as much as she had.

"What about him?" she asked, crossing her arms over her chest, resisting the urge to touch Cameron just one more time.

"I'm not supposed to tell you this, so please don't say anything. This could cost me my badge."

Megan stood up straighter. He was here as her friend, putting her above his job for once. A piece of the hard shell around her heart crumbled.

"Is he in more trouble?" she asked, fearful for the unknown.

"No." Cameron toyed with the open flap of a box on the coffee table. "He's actually going to take a plea bargain. He was offered immunity in exchange for every bit of information he knows."

Elation filled her. Megan clutched the scoop neck of her T-shirt and sucked in a deep breath. "Thank you," she whispered, unable to say anything else.

"There's more."

She tensed up at Cameron's hard stare. Whatever the "more" was apparently wasn't good news.

"He's going to go into Witness Protection first thing in the morning."

Witness Protection. The words registered but not fully at first. Then she realized what Cameron was truly telling her.

"I won't see him again?"

Shaking his head, Cameron held her gaze for a moment, then looked away as if he couldn't bear to see her. "I tried to get you in, but that power is above me. I had to fight to get the immunity. He had some stiff charges against him, but since he was a latecomer to the group, we needed the big names he could provide."

Megan nodded, hating what he was saying but knowing this was for the best. This was the only option for her brother to make a fresh start and stay safe.

"Could I write him a letter or something?" she asked. "Maybe you could get it to him?"

The muscle in Cameron's jaw jumped. "I can't."

Megan pulled in a shaky breath and pushed away from the door. Heading back to her task, something she had control over and something she could concentrate on, she pulled a picture off the wall and tore off more bubble wrap.

Methodically, she wrapped the frame, all the while coming to grips with the new level of pain that had settled deep into her chest.

"If you happen to have something that needs to be said, I could perhaps stop by and tell him before they take him away."

Cameron's generous offer hovered between them. After placing the package in the box, she closed the flaps and held her hand over the opening as she focused on Cameron.

"Tell him…just tell him I'm proud of him and I love him." Megan couldn't believe she'd never be able to tell him in person again, but if this was all she had, she was going to take it. Cameron nodded and turned to go. Megan stared at his back. Had he only come to deliver the message? Weren't they going to talk about anything or even pretend to be…what? What could they discuss at this point? She'd thrown him out weeks ago, and she hadn't extended a branch to him since.

"Cam," she called just as his hand fell to her door-knob. "Wait."

Glancing over his shoulder, he raised a brow as his eyes locked on to hers.

Gathering her strength and courage, she stepped around the coffee table and crossed the room to stand in front of him. He turned to face her, but the minuscule space between them may as well have been an ocean for all the tension that settled in the slot.

"Thank you."

Megan looked up at him, at the man she'd fallen so deeply in love with, and seriously had no clue how she would go on without Evan or Cameron in her life.

"I know Evan and I had our issues," Cameron started. "But we have one thing in common. We both love you."

Megan swallowed the tears that threatened. The last time Cameron had been here she'd cried enough to last a lifetime.

"We both want to see you happy," he went on. "Unfortunately we both had a terrible way of showing it."

Cameron started to reach out, then stopped. She glanced at his hand, hovering so close, and slid her fingers through his.

"They always say the ones you love the most can hurt you the most." The feel of his hand in hers sent a warmth spreading through her—a warmth she'd missed for two weeks. "I didn't know that to be true until recently."

Cameron's free hand slid along the side of her face. Megan tilted her head just enough to take the comfort he was offering.

"To know that you did this for Evan means every-

thing to me," she added. "The thought of not seeing him again hurts, but it's far better than seeing him through glass. He'll have freedom and he'll be able to start over. That's all I've ever wanted for him."

"What about you?" Cameron's thumb stroked her cheek, the simple touch sending chills all over her body. "Are you going to start over?"

"That's my plan," she muttered. "It's my only option at this point."

Cameron's mouth covered hers without warning. The hungry kiss started so demandingly, Megan had no choice but to clutch at his wide shoulders. Just as she was getting used to being overtaken, Cam lightened his touch, turning the kiss into something less forceful but every bit as potent and primal.

By the time he eased away and rested his head against hers, they were both panting.

"I'm begging you, Meg. Don't leave." Both his hands framed her face; the strength of his body covered hers, and the raw words hit her straight in her heart. "I don't care if I look weak or pathetic. I'll beg you to stay. I need you so much more than you need me. You're so strong, and I know you would be just fine in Memphis. But I would not be okay here without you."

Wrapping her arms around his waist, Megan couldn't hold back any longer. The dam completely burst and tears she'd sworn never to shed in front of him again came flooding out. Cameron enveloped her, pulling her tighter against his chest as she let out all her fear, worry and uncertainty.

"I know I broke something in you with the choices I made." His hand smoothed up and down her back, comforting her. "I'll spend the rest of my life making all of that up to you. Please, please give me a chance."

"I'm scared, Cam," she murmured into his chest. "What happens when another big case comes along? What happens the next time you shut me out? What will I do when you decide the job is more important than I am or we are?"

Pulling back, Cameron looked her in the eye. "Nothing is more important than you are. Nothing. I came here expecting nothing from you, Megan. I came here to tell you about Evan, knowing full well that I could lose my job if anyone found out. I don't care. You are worth every risk, every chance I'll ever take."

Megan hiccuped as the next onslaught of tears took over. "I'm a mess," she told him, wiping the backs of her hands over her cheeks. "Look what you do to me."

His eyes focused on her. "I'm looking, and I've never seen a more beautiful woman in my life. You're it for me, Megan. I want to marry you and start a family with you. I know that's a lot to absorb right now, but just stay so we can work this out."

Megan couldn't believe what he was saying. He wanted to marry her?

"If you can't stay, if you're already committed and cannot get out of the Memphis job, or if that's really where your heart is, we can buy a place between here and there and we'll commute." Cameron kissed her lightly once more. "Just say you'll give us a chance."

"How could I refuse you?" she told him, raining kisses over his face. "How could I ever let you go?"

Cameron picked her up and started toward the hallway. "You'll never have to find out."

By the time they hit the bedroom, Megan knew she wasn't going anywhere for a long, long time.

Epilogue

"How much farther?"

Cameron squeezed Megan's hand and laughed. "Just don't move that blindfold. We're almost there."

"I think you're just driving in circles," she mumbled. "If you keep going too much farther, I'm going to get carsick. We're supposed to be on our way to our honeymoon."

They'd been married for three hours. He'd promised her a memorable wedding night, and he intended to deliver, but they weren't going far. He'd requested she keep her wedding dress on, told her it was important to him.

He glanced over, still a little choked up at the vision in white lace beside him. Her strapless gown fitted her body beautifully from her breasts to her waist

with such a delicate fabric, he was afraid to touch her. In just a few short minutes she'd see why he wanted to keep her in her wedding gown. The airport could wait until tomorrow.

Tonight, he had a special surprise.

Cameron turned onto the dirt road and brought his truck to a stop just in front of the clearing. "Don't move. I'll come around to get you."

By the time he'd gotten Megan out of the truck and stood her beside him, she was looking a bit pale.

"You feeling okay?" he asked. "I thought you were joking about the carsick thing."

Megan whipped off her blindfold. "I'm not carsick—I'm pregnant," she cried.

Shock slid over him at the same time she gasped as she took in her surroundings. "What are we doing back here?" she asked.

Cameron couldn't think, couldn't speak. His gaze darted to her flat stomach beneath her vintage gown and all he could think was he was going to be a father. He and Megan were going to be parents.

With a shout, he wrapped his arms around her, picked her up and spun her in a circle, the train of her dress wrapping around his feet.

"Sickness, remember?" she yelled.

Easing her down, Cameron kissed her thoroughly. "How long have you known?" he asked when he pulled back.

"I just took a test at home this morning. I wanted to wait until after the reception to tell you, when we

were alone, but then you said you had a surprise for me so I waited."

The flash of her coming down the aisle, smiling with tears in her eyes took on a whole new meaning now. She'd been radiant, beaming, a bright light coming toward him to make his life complete. She'd been there all along, and he was so thankful she hadn't given up on them.

Their ceremony had been perfect, planned by his sisters-in-law, his mother and Megan. The church had been covered in a variety of flowers, vibrant colors splashed all around. No doubt all of it was gorgeous, but he'd only had eyes for Megan. There was nothing more beautiful than seeing your best friend walk toward you, knowing you were going to start down a path that would forever bind you in love. And when she'd kissed him, he'd felt every bit of her love. And he wanted to spend the rest of his life showing her how precious she was to him.

Cameron choked back his own tears because this was the happiest day of his life. He didn't deserve all of this, but he was going to embrace every bit of it and build a family with the only woman he'd ever wanted.

"You've picked the perfect time to tell me." Laughing, Cameron held out his arms and eased the train aside with his foot. "This is it. I bought this for us to build our house on."

A wide smile spread across her face. "You're serious? You mean it?"

Seeing how happy she was made draining his entire savings completely worth it. A baby on the way,

a new house and a wedding just around the holidays was a whole lot to be thankful for.

"I wanted to see you here, on our land in that dress." He reached out and stroked her cheek. "I wanted to capture this moment, this memory with you because I know it's only going to get better."

"I'm so glad I decided not to take that job in Memphis," she told him, still smiling. "How did you keep this a secret from me?"

Cameron shrugged. "It wasn't easy and I know I promised not to lie to you ever again, but I really wanted this to be a surprise."

"Oh, Cameron." Megan plastered herself against his side, wrapping her arms around his waist. "This is going to be perfect for our family. And maybe by this time next year we'll have our house done, and we can have all of your family over for the holidays. We'll have our little baby for everyone to fuss over."

Kissing the top of her head, Cameron smiled as he surveyed the land. "I think that sounds like a plan. First thing we'll move into the house will be—"

"Don't say it," she warned.

"Come on," he joked. "The lamp has to come with us."

Megan tipped her face up to his. "The only place that lamp needs to go is the Dumpster."

Squeezing her tight, Cameron rubbed her back. "Well, we can negotiate that later, but I think it would be a great piece for the nursery."

Smacking his abdomen, Megan groaned. "I will not give our child nightmares."

"You're right. It should stay in the living room. It has made quite a conversation starter."

Megan laughed, easing up on her toes to kiss his cheek. "You know I love you, but it's either me or the dragon lamp."

Turning to fully engulf her in his arms, Cameron smiled and slid his lips across hers. "You. It's always been you."

* * * * *

ONCE UPON
A BRIDE

HELEN LACEY

For Robert
Because you get me...

Chapter One

"**Y**ou made a *what?*"

Lauren Jakowski shrugged her shoulders and bit down on her lower lip, musing whether she should repeat her words. But her two best friends' imploring looks won over.

"I made a vow," she said, and glanced at both Cassie and Mary-Jayne. "Of celibacy."

The other women snorted through the drinks they were sipping, sending liquid flying across the small poolside table. It was her brother's wedding, and once the bride and groom had cut the cake and shared their first dance, her bridesmaid's duties were officially over for the night. So she'd left the hotel ballroom and met her friends by the pool.

"Yeah, sure you did," Cassie said with a laugh, wiping her face.

"I did," Lauren insisted. "When my marriage ended."

"So you, like—" Mary-Jayne mused slowly as her dark hair swayed in the breeze "—made a commitment to never have sex again?"

"Exactly," she replied. "Not until I'm certain he's the right one."

"*He* being this dull and passionless individual you think you'll find so you can have your mediocre happily ever after?" Cassie asked, watching Lauren over the rim of her glass of soda.

She ignored how absurd it sounded. "Yes."

Cassie's brows came up. "And where are you going to find this Mr. Average?" she asked. "ReliableBores.com?"

"Maybe," Lauren said, and pretended to drink some champagne.

"So no sex?" Mary-Jayne asked again. "Even though you caught the bouquet, look sensational in that dress and there are at least half a dozen single men at this wedding who would happily throw you over their shoulder, carry you off and give you the night of your life?"

"I'm not interested in anything casual," she reiterated.

Mary-Jayne's eyes widened. "Not even with—"

"Not with *anyone*," she said firmly.

"But he's—"

The original tall, dark and handsome...

"I know what he is. And he's not on my radar."

Which was a great big lie. However, she wasn't about to admit that to her friends. Lauren stared at the flowers sitting in the center of the small table. She *had* caught the bouquet. But she didn't want some meaningless romp at her brother's wedding.

And she certainly didn't want it with Gabe Vitali.

In the past six months, she'd been within touching distance of the ridiculously good-looking American several times. *And avoided him on every single occasion.* He was exactly what she didn't want. But since he was her brother's friend—and Crystal Point was a small town—Lauren accepted that she would be forced to see him every now and then.

"I like Gabe," Mary-Jayne said, and grinned. "He's kind of mysterious and…sexy."

Lauren wrinkled her nose. "Trouble."

"But still sexy?" Cassie laughed gently. "Come on, admit it."

Lauren let out an exasperated sigh. "Okay, he's sexy. He's weak-at-the-knees sexy.… He's handsome and hot and every time I see him I wonder what he looks like out of his clothes. I said I was celibate…not comatose."

The two women laughed, and Lauren pushed aside the idea of Gabe Vitali naked.

"Still, you haven't had sex in over two years," Mary-Jayne, the more candid of the two women, reminded her. "That's a long time. Just because you got divorced doesn't mean you can't have sex."

Lauren shrugged. "Isn't there an old saying about not missing what you don't have?"

Mary-Jayne shook her head. "Please tell me you've at least *kissed* a guy since then?"

"No," she replied. "Nor do I intend to until I know he's exactly what I've been looking for."

"You mean, *planning* for," Cassie said, ever gentle. "You know, there's no neat order to falling in love."

"Who said anything about love?" Lauren pushed back her blond bangs.

Cassie's calm expression was unwavering. "Is that really what you want? A loveless relationship without passion and heat?"

Lauren shrugged. "Marriage doesn't have to be about sexual attraction. Or love."

She saw her friends' expressions, knew that even though they were both fiercely loyal and supported her unconditionally, they still thought her thinking madness. But she wasn't swayed. How could they really appreciate her feelings? Or understand what she wanted?

They couldn't.

But she knew what she wanted. No lust, no crazy chemistry. No fairy-tale love.

No risk.

"That's just grief talking," Cassie said quietly. "When a marriage breaks down, it's natural to—"

"I'm not *mourning* my divorce," she insisted. No, definitely not. Because she knew exactly what mourning felt like. "I'm glad it's over. I shouldn't have married a man I hardly knew. I've tried being in love, I've tried being in lust…and neither worked out. Believe it or not, for the first time in a long time, I actually know what I want."

"Which is?" Mary-Jayne prompted, still grinning.

Lauren smiled at her friend. "Which is an honest, uncomplicated relationship with someone I can talk to…. Someone I can laugh with…have children with…grow old with. You know, the usual things. Someone who's a friend. A companion. And not with a man who looks as though he was made to pose for an underwear ad on one of those highway billboards."

"Like Gabe?" Mary-Jayne suggested playfully, and drank some champagne. "Okay, I get it. You want short, chubby and bald…not tall, dark and handsome. But in the meantime, how about we all get back to the ballroom and find some totally *complicated* man to dance with?"

"Not me," Cassie said, and touched her four-month-pregnant belly. Her boyfriend was a soldier currently on tour in the Middle East. "But I'll happily watch from the sidelines."

Lauren shook her head. "I think I'll stay out here for a while. You two go on ahead."

Her friends took another couple of minutes to leave, and when she was alone, Lauren snatched up the colorful bouquet, stood and walked the ten feet toward the edge of the pool. Solitude crept over her skin, and she sighed. Wed-

dings always made her melancholy. Which was unfortunate, since she owned the most successful bridal store in Bellandale. Weddings were her life. Some days, though, she thought that to be the most absurd irony.

Of course, she was pleased for her brother. Cameron deserved every bit of happiness with his new bride, Grace Preston. And the ceremony had been beautiful and romantic. But she had a hollow spot in her chest that ached with a heavy kind of sadness. Many of the guests now inside the big hotel ballroom had witnessed her union to James Wallace in similar style three years earlier. And most knew how it had ended. Tonight, more than ever before, Lauren's sadness was amplified by her embarrassment at being on the receiving end of countless pitying looks and sympathetic greetings.

She took a deep breath and exhaled with a shudder. Somehow, her dreams for the future had been lost. But two years on, and with so many tears shed, she was stronger. And ready to start again. Only this time, Lauren would do it right. She wouldn't rush into marriage after a three-month whirlwind romance. And she definitely wouldn't be swept off her feet. This time, her feet were staying firmly on the ground.

Lauren swallowed hard, smoothed the mint-green chiffon gown over her hips and turned on her heels.

And was unexpectedly confronted with Gabe Vitali.

Stretched out on a sun lounger, tie askew and with his black hair ruffled as if he'd been running his hand through it, he looked so gorgeous, she literally gasped for breath. He was extraordinarily handsome, like one of those old-time movie stars. His glittering, blue-eyed gaze swept over her, and a tiny smile creased the corners of his mouth.

And she knew immediately...

He'd heard.

Everything.

Every humiliating word. Heat raced up and smacked her cheeks. *Great.*

Of course, she had no logical reason to dislike him… other than the fact he was good-looking and sexy and made her insides flip-flop. But it was enough to keep her from allowing her fantasies to take over. She gripped the bouquet tighter and planted her free hand on her hip in a faux impression of control, and spoke. "Whatever you might have thought you heard, I assure you I wasn't—"

"How are the knees?" he asked as he sprang up.

He was tall, around six-two, with broad shoulders and a long-legged frame. And he looked way too good in a suit. Resentment burned through her when she realized he was referring to her earlier confession.

"Fine," she replied, dying of embarrassment inside. "Rock solid."

He came around the lounger, hands thrust into his pockets. "You're sure about that?"

Lauren glared at him. "Positive," she snapped, mortified. She wanted to flee, but quickly realized she'd have to squeeze herself in between him and the sun lounger if she wanted to make a getaway. "I think I'll return to the ballroom now, if you don't mind."

His mouth curled at the edges. "You know, just because someone knows your vulnerabilities, it doesn't necessarily make him your enemy."

Lauren's skin heated. *"Vulnerabilities?"* She sucked in a sharp breath. "I don't quite know what you mean by that, but if you're insinuating that I'm *vulnerable* because I haven't… Because I… Well, because it's been a while since I was…you know…" Her words trailed off as mortification clung to every pore. Then she got annoyed as a quick cover-up. "Let's get this straight. I'm not the least bit vulnerable. Not to you or to anyone *like* you."

He grinned. "Whoa. Are you always so prickly?"

Prickly? She wasn't *prickly.* She was even tempered and friendly and downright *nice.*

She glared at him. "Do you always eavesdrop on private conversations?"

"I was simply relaxing on a pool lounger," he replied smoothly, his accent so delicious, it wound up her spine like liquid silk. "And I was here before you, remember? The fact you spoke about your sex life so openly is really no one's fault but your own." One brow rose. "And although it was entertaining, there's no need to take your frustration out on—"

"I am not *frustrated,*" she snapped, figuring he was probably referring to her being sexually starved in some misguided, macho way. Broad shoulders, blue eyes and nice voice aside, he was a jerk. "I just don't want to talk about it anymore. What I'd like is to forget this conversation ever happened."

"I'm sure you would."

Lauren wanted a big hole to open up and suck her in. When one didn't appear, she took a deep breath. "So we have a deal. I'll ignore you, and you can ignore me. That way we never have to speak to each other again."

"Since this is the first time we have actually spoken," he said, his gaze deep enough to get lost in. "I don't think it will be a hardship."

He was right. They'd never spoken. She'd made sure of it. Whenever he was close, she'd always managed to make a quick getaway. Lauren sniffed her dislike, determined to ignore the fact that the most gorgeous man she'd ever met probably thought she was stark raving mad. And she would have done exactly that. Except she turned her heel too quickly, got caught between the tiles, and seconds later, she was tumbling in a cartwheel of arms and legs and landed into the pool, bouquet flying, humiliation complete.

The shock of hitting the water was quickly interrupted

when a pair of strong hands grasped one arm, then another. In seconds, she was lifted up and over the edge of the pool and set right on her feet.

He still held her, and had his hands intimately positioned on her shoulders.

She should have been cold through to her bones. But she wasn't. She was hot. All over. Her saturated dress clung to every dip and curve, her once carefully styled hair was now draping down her neck and her blood burned through her veins like a grass fire.

"Steady," he said softly, holding her so close she could see the tiny pulse in his jaw.

Lauren tried to speak, tried to move, tried to do something, *anything,* other than shake in his arms and stare up into his handsome face. But she failed. Spectacularly. It was he who eventually stepped back. When he finally released her, Lauren's knees wobbled and she sucked in a long breath to regain her composure. Of which she suddenly had none. He looked at her, *over her,* slowly and provocatively and with just enough male admiration to make her cheeks flame. She glanced down and shuddered. The sheer, wet fabric hugged her body like a second skin and left *nothing* to the imagination.

She moved her lips. "I should…I think I should…"

"Yes," he said quietly when her words trailed. "You probably should."

Lauren shifted her feet and managed one step backward, then another. Water dripped down her arms and legs, and she glanced around for a towel or something else to cover herself. When she couldn't find anything suitable, she looked back at him and noticed he still watched her. Something passed between them, a kind of heady, intense awareness that rang off warning bells in her head and should have galvanized her wobbly knees into action. But she couldn't move.

Seconds later, he shrugged out of his jacket and quickly draped it around her shoulders. The warmth from the coat and his nearness enveloped her like a protective cloak, and Lauren expelled a long sigh. She didn't want to feel that. Didn't want to *think* that. She only wanted to escape.

"Thank you," she whispered. "I appreciate—"

"Forget it," he said, cutting her off. "You should get out of those wet clothes before you catch a cold," he said, and then stepped back.

Lauren nodded, turned carefully and rushed from the pool area, water and humiliation snapping at her heels.

One week later Gabe pulled the for-sale peg from the ground, stuck the sign in the crook of his arm and headed across the front yard. The low-set, open-plan brick-and-tile home was big and required a much-needed renovation. But he'd bought the house for a reasonable price, and it seemed as good a place as any to settle down.

And he was happy in Crystal Point. The oceanfront town was small and friendly, and the beaches and surf reminded him of home. He missed California, but he enjoyed the peacefulness of the small Australian town he now called home instead. He'd rented a place in the nearby city of Bellandale for the past few months, but he liked the seaside town much better. Bellandale, with its sixty thousand residents, was not as populated as Huntington Beach, Orange County, where he'd lived most of his life. But it was busy enough to make him crave the solitude and quiet of Crystal Point. Plus, he was close to the beach and his new job.

He liked the job, too. Managing the Crystal Point Surf Club & Community Center kept him occupied, and on the weekends, he volunteered as a lifeguard. The beach was busy and well maintained, and so far he'd only had to administer first aid for dehydration and a couple of jelly-

fish stings. Nothing life threatening. Nothing he couldn't handle. Nothing that made him dwell on all he'd given up.

Gabe fished the keys from his pocket, dropped the sign into the overgrown garden bed and climbed the four steps to the porch. His household items had arrived that morning, and he'd spent most of the day emptying boxes and wishing he'd culled more crap when he'd put the stuff into storage six months ago. His cousin, Scott, had offered to come and give him a hand unpacking, but Gabe wasn't in the mood for a lecture about his career, his personal life or anything else.

All his energy would go into his job and renovating the house, which he figured would keep him busy for six months, at least. After that, he'd tackle the yard, get the place in shape and put the house on the market again. How hard could it be? His brother Aaron did the same thing regularly. True, he wasn't much of a carpenter, and Aaron was a successful builder in Los Angeles, but he'd give it a shot.

He headed inside and flicked on some lights. Some of the walls were painted black, no doubt a legacy from the previous tenants—a group of twenty-something heavy-metal enthusiasts who were evicted for cultivating some suspicious indoor plants—so painting was one of the first things on the agenda. The kitchen was neat and the bathrooms bearable. And although the furniture he'd bought a few months ago looked a little out of place in the shabby rooms, once the walls and floors were done, he was confident it would all look okay.

Gabe tossed the keys in a bowl on the kitchen table and pulled his cell from his pocket. He noticed there were a couple of missed calls. One from Aaron and another from his mother. It would be around midnight in California, and he made a mental note to call them back in the morning. Most days he was glad the time difference let him off the hook when it came to dealing with his family. At least his

younger brother, Luca, and baby sister, Bianca, didn't stick their nose into his life or moan about his decision to move to Crystal Point. As the eldest, Aaron always thought he knew best, and his mom was just…Mom. He knew she worried, knew his mom and Aaron were waiting for him to relapse and go running back to California.

He'd come to Crystal Point to start over, and the house and job were a part of that new life. Gabe liked that his family wasn't constantly around to dish out advice. Bad enough he got lectures on tap from Scott. Hell, he understood their motives…he might even have done the same thing had the situation been reversed. But things had changed. *He'd* changed. And Gabe was determined to live his life, even if it wasn't the one he'd planned on.

The private cul-de-sac in Crystal Point was an ideal place to start. It was peaceful, quiet and uncomplicated. Just what he wanted. A native bird squawked from somewhere overhead and he stared out the kitchen window and across the hedge to the next house along just as his cell rang. He looked at the screen. It was an overseas number and not one he recognized.

Uncomplicated?

Gabe glanced briefly out the window again as he answered the call. It was Cameron Jakowski, and the conversation lasted a couple of minutes. *Sure, uncomplicated.* Except for his beautiful, blonde, brown-eyed neighbor.

The thing about being a *go-to,* agreeable kind of person…sometimes it turned around to bite you on the behind. And this, Lauren thought as she drove up the driveway and then pulled up under the carport, was probably going to turn out to be one of those occasions.

Of course, she *could* have refused. But that wasn't really her style. She knew her brother wouldn't have called if

there was any other option. He'd asked for her help, and she would always rally her resolve when it came to her family.

What she didn't want to do—what she was *determined* to avoid doing—was start up any kind of conversation with her new next-door neighbor. Bad enough he'd bought the house and moved in just days after the never-to-be-spoken-about and humiliating event at the wedding. The last thing she wanted to do was knock on his door.

Ever.

Lauren had hoped to never see him again. But it seemed fate had other ideas.

She took a breath, grabbed her bag and jacket and stepped out of the car. She struggled to open the timber gate that she'd been meaning to get repaired for the past three months and winced when the jagged edge caught her palm. Once inside her house, she dumped her handbag and laptop in the hall and took a few well-needed breaths.

I don't want to do this....

But she'd promised Cameron.

And a promise is a promise....

Then she headed next door.

Once she'd rounded the tall hedge, Lauren walked up the gravel path toward the house. There was a brand-new Jeep Cherokee parked in the driveway. The small porch illuminated with a sensor light once she took the three steps. The light flickered and then faded. She tapped on the door and waited. She heard footsteps before the door swung back on its hinges, and she came face-to-face with him.

And then butterflies bombarded her stomach in spectacular fashion.

Faded jeans fitted lean hips, and the white T-shirt he wore accentuated a solid wall of bronzed and very fine-looking muscle. His short black hair, clean-shaven jaw and body to die for added up to a purely lethal combination.

He really is gorgeous.

Memories of what had happened by the pool came rushing back. His hands on her skin, his glittering gaze moving over her, his chest so close she could almost hear his heartbeat. Mesmerized, Lauren sucked in a breath. He knew all about her. He knew things she'd told only her closest friends. He knew she'd thought about him…and imagined things.

But if he dares say anything about my knees being weak, I'll…

She finally found her voice. "I'm here…"

One brow cocked. "So I see."

"Did Cameron—"

"He called," he said, and smiled as he interrupted her. "Is he…"

"He is." He jerked his thumb over his shoulder and toward the door behind him. "Safe and sound and flaked out in front of the television."

She ignored the smile that tried to make its way to her lips and nodded. "Okay, thank you."

When she didn't move, he looked her over. "Are you coming inside or do you plan on camping on my doorstep all night?"

"All night?" she echoed, mortified that color was creeping up her neck. The idea of doing *anything* all night with Gabe Vitali took the temperature of her skin, her blood and pretty much every other part of her anatomy up a few notches. "Of course not."

He dropped his arms to his sides and stepped back.

Lauren crossed the threshold and walked into the hall. He was close, and everything about him affected her on a kind of sensory level. As much as she didn't want to admit anything, she was attracted to him. And worse luck, he knew it.

Her vow of celibacy suddenly seemed to be dissolving into thin air.

She walked down the short hallway and into the huge, open-plan living area. The furniture looked new and somehow out of place in the room. And sure enough, on the rug in front of the sofa, was her brother's one hundred and fifty pound French Mastiff, Jed. Fast asleep and snoring loudly.

"Thanks for picking him up from my brother's place," she said as politely as she could. "When Cameron called this morning, he said the house sitter had left quickly."

He nodded. "Her daughter is having a baby. She took a flight out from Bellandale after lunch and said she'd be back in a week."

Lauren bit down on her lip. "A week?"

"That's what she said."

A week of dog-sitting. Great. As much as she liked Jed, he was big, needy, had awful juicy jowls and a reputation for not obeying anyone other than Cameron. Too bad her parents had a cat that ruled the roost, or she would have dropped him off there. She had to admit the dog seemed comfortable draped across Gabe's rug.

She looked around some more. "So…you've moved in?"

"That was the general idea when I bought the house," he replied.

Lauren's teeth ground together. "Of course. I hope you'll be very happy here."

She watched his mouth twist with a grin. "You do? Really?"

"Really," she said, and raised a disinterested brow. "Be happy, or don't be happy. It's nothing to do with me."

His blue eyes looked her up and down with way too much leisure. The mood quickly shifted on a whisper of awareness that fluttered through the air and filled up the space between them. A change that was impossible to ignore, and there was rapidly enough heat in the room to combust a fire.

Warmth spread up her neck. He had a way of doing that to her. A way of heating her skin. "I need to…I need…"

"I think we both know what you need."

Sex…

That was what he was thinking. Suddenly, that was what *she* was thinking, even though turning up on his doorstep had nothing to do with her *lacking* love life or her vow to stay celibate. Lauren's cheeks burned, and her knees trembled. "I don't know what—"

"You don't like me much, do you?" he asked, cutting her off with such calm self-assurance, she wanted to slug him.

"I'm not—"

"Or is it because you *do* like me much?" he asked, cutting her off yet again. "And that's why you're so rattled at being in my living room."

Conceited jerk! Lauren sucked in some air, pushed back her shoulders and called Jed to heel. By the time the dog got up and ambled toward her, she was so worked up she could have screamed. She grasped Jed's collar and painted on a smile. "Thank you for collecting him from Cameron's."

"My pleasure."

Pleasure? Right. Not a word she wanted to hear from him. Not a word she wanted to think about in regard to him. And when she was safely back in her own home, Lauren kept reminding herself of one thing…Mr. Right was *not* Mr. Right-Next-Door.

Chapter Two

It was the dress.

That was why he'd had Lauren Jakowski on his mind for the past week.

When Gabe pulled her from the pool, the wet fabric had stuck to her curves so erotically, it had taken his breath away. She was as pretty as hell. A couple of years back he wouldn't have hesitated in coming on to her. He would have lingered by the pool, made small talk, flirted a little, asked her out and gotten her between the sheets by the third date. But he wasn't that man anymore.

Not so long ago, there had been no short supply of women in his life and in his bed. He'd mostly managed to keep things casual until he met Mona. She was the daughter of a colleague, and after dating for six months, they'd moved in together. At thirty years of age, he'd convinced himself it was time he got around to settling down. Gabe had a girlfriend, a career he loved, a nice apartment and

good friends. Life was sweet. Until everything had blown up in his face.

Eighteen months later, he was in Crystal Point, working at the surf club and trying to live a normal life. A life that didn't include a woman like Lauren Jakowski.

Because she was too…wholesome.

Too…perfect.

A beautiful blonde with caramel eyes and porcelain skin. *Exactly my type.*

But by the pool, she'd made it clear to her friends what she was looking for—stability, reliability, longevity. And since he couldn't offer her any of those things, she was everything he needed to avoid. He didn't want her turning up on his doorstep. He didn't want to inhale the scent of the flowery fragrance that clung to her skin. And he certainly didn't want to remember how it felt to have her lovely curves pressed against him.

The best thing would be to ignore her…just as she'd suggested.

Damned inconvenient, then, that he'd bought the house right next door. If he'd known that before he'd signed on the dotted line, he might have changed his mind. But it was too late to think about that now. All he had to do was get through the renovation and the resale without remembering that she was merely over the hedge.

Lauren was not one-night-stand material…and he couldn't offer anything more.

Gabe dropped into the sofa and flicked channels on the television for half an hour before he thought about eating something. He headed to the kitchen and stopped in his tracks when he spotted the pile of canine accessories by the back door. Damn. He'd forgotten about that. When Cameron had called and asked him to make an emergency stop at his home to collect the dog, the vacating house sitter had thrust the bed, bowls, food and lead into his arms

along with a note listing feeding instructions. Things that Lauren would need.

Realizing there was little point in avoiding the inevitable, Gabe shoved his feet into sneakers, swung the bag of dog food over one shoulder, grabbed the rest of the gear and his house keys and headed next door.

Lauren's home and gardens were neat and tidy, and the only thing that seemed out of place was the rickety gate. He pushed it open and headed up the steps. The porch light was on and the front door open, so he tapped on the security screen. From somewhere in the house, he could hear her talking to the dog, and the obvious frustration in her voice made him smile. Maybe she was more a cat person? He tapped again and then waited until he heard her footsteps coming down the hall.

"Oh…hi," she said breathlessly when she reached the door.

Her hair was mussed and her shirt was pulled out from the front of her skirt, and Gabe bit back a grin. She looked as if she'd been crash tackled on the thirty-yard line. "Everything all right?"

She glanced over her shoulder. "Fine."

Gabe didn't quite believe her. "I forgot to give you this."

Her mouth set in a serious line. "Just leave it out there and I'll grab it later."

"It's heavy," he said, and jangled the bag of kibble resting on his shoulder. "I should probably set it down inside."

She looked at him for a second and then unlocked the screen. "Okay. Take it to the kitchen, at the end of the hall."

Gabe pushed the screen back and crossed the threshold. When he passed the living room doorway he immediately figured out the reason for her distress. Stretched out with legs in the air and jowls drooping, the dog was rolling around on her flowery chintz sofa.

"Jed looks as though he's made himself comfortable," he said, and kept walking.

"Yes, very comfortable."

When they reached the kitchen, Gabe swiveled on his heels and stared at her. She had her arms folded, her chin up and her lips pressed together, and even though she looked like she'd rather eat arsenic than spend a moment in his company, Gabe couldn't stop thinking about how beautiful she was.

I haven't gotten laid in a while...that's all it is.

He wasn't conceited, but he'd heard enough by the pool that night to know the attraction was mutual. He also knew she clearly thought it was as impossible as he did. Which suited him just fine. He didn't want to be stirred by her. He didn't want to spend restless nights thinking about having her in his bed.

"Where do you want it?" he asked.

"By the door will do."

He placed the gear on the floor and turned around to face her. "Would you like me to remove him from your sofa?"

"How did you know I couldn't...?"

"He's got about thirty pounds on you," Gabe said when her words trailed. "I just figured."

She shrugged. "I tried dragging him off, but he's as heavy as lead."

Gabe smiled and withdrew the note from his pocket. "Feeding instructions," he said, and dropped the paper onto the countertop. "If you want to get his food sorted, I'll get him off the sofa."

"Thank you," she said, then laid her hands on the back of a dining chair and grimaced. "Ouch."

He saw her shake her hand. "What's wrong?"

"Nothing," she replied and shook her hand again. "Just a splinter I got earlier from my gate."

"Let me see."

She curled her hand. "It's nothing."

Gabe moved around the kitchen counter. "It might become infected," he said, suddenly serious. "Do you have a first-aid kit?"

"It's nothing, really."

"It won't take a minute," he insisted. "So your first-aid kit?"

She shook her head. "I don't like needles."

"Don't be a baby."

Her eyes flashed, and she pushed her shoulders back as she marched into the kitchen and opened the pantry. "Here," she said, and tossed something through the air.

Gabe caught it one-handed and placed the kit on the table. "I'll be gentle. Sit," he said, and pulled out a chair.

She glared again, and he marveled that she still managed to look stunning with a scowl on her face. She sat down and waited while he dropped into a chair opposite.

"Hand?"

She pushed her hand into the center of the table and turned it over. "Gentle, remember?"

He smiled, opened the kit and took out an alcohol swab and an individually wrapped needle. When he took hold of her fingertips, his entire body crackled with a kind of heady electricity. Being so close wasn't helping his determination to steer clear of her.

"So what kind of work do you do?" he asked to try to get his mind off her soft skin and flowery perfume.

"I own a bridal shop in Bellandale."

He stretched out her palm. "That sounds interesting."

"Does it?"

Gabe looked up. She really did have the most amazing brown eyes. Warm and deep and intoxicating. She was remarkably beautiful, and he doubted she even knew it.

"Just making conversation," he said.

Her brows shot up. "To what end?"

"Are you always so suspicious?" he asked.

"Of what?"

"People," he replied. "Men."

She tensed, and Gabe held her hand a little firmer. "Not usually," she said quietly.

So it was just him? "I don't have any sinister intentions. So relax," he said as he extracted the splinter without her noticing at first and then gently rolled her fingers into her palm. "I'm not making a pass."

She swallowed hard. "I didn't think—"

"I would," he said quietly. "If you were looking for a no-strings, no-commitment kind of thing. But you're not. You're a commitment kind of girl, right? Abstaining from anything casual and with a clear plan for your future. Isn't that why you made your vow of celibacy?"

It felt right to get it out in the open. Maybe it would help diffuse the heat between them. Maybe it would stop him from thinking about kissing her.

She jerked her hand back and stood. "I... What I said at the wedding... It was private and personal and not up for discussion."

"I'm not mocking you," he said, and rested his elbows on the table. "On the contrary, I think I admire you for knowing what you want. And knowing what you don't."

Lauren's skin burned. He admired her? He'd pretty much admitted he wanted her, too. The awareness between them intensified, and she wished she could deny it. She wanted to dislike him. She wanted to resent him. She wanted to get away and never speak to him again.

"Thank you for the first aid," she said, and managed a tight smile. "I didn't feel a thing."

"Then we should keep it that way."

There was no mistaking his meaning. He thought it was a bad idea, too. She was happy about that. Very happy.

"So...about the dog?"

He stood up and pushed the chair back. "Get his feed ready and I'll drag him off your sofa."

Once he'd left the kitchen and disappeared down the hall, Lauren got to her feet and quickly sorted the dog's bedding and food in the laundry. A couple of minutes later, Gabe returned with Jed at his side. The dog ambled across the kitchen and into the back room and began eating.

Relieved the hound was no longer taking up her couch, Lauren took a shallow breath. "Thank you...Gabe."

He looked a little amused by her sudden use of his name and the slight tremor in her voice. His mouth twisted fractionally, as if he was trying not to smile. "No problem... Lauren."

"Well...good night."

His glittering gaze was unwavering. "I'll see you tomorrow."

Her eyes widened. "Tomorrow?"

He grinned a little. "I told Cameron I'd take the dog to work tomorrow so he doesn't destroy your yard trying to escape...until you can make other arrangements, of course."

She hadn't spared a thought to how she would care for the dog during the day. "Oh, right," she said vaguely, thinking about how the darn dog had suddenly become a reason why she would be forced to interact with Gabe. She made a mental note to call her friend Mary-Jayne and ask her to help. Lauren knew one thing—she didn't want to turn up on Gabe's doorstep again. "I'll tie him in the back when I leave, and you can collect him from there. You don't start until ten tomorrow, right?"

Gabe frowned. "How do you know that?"

"Cameron left me the roster," she replied. "I said I'd work the Sunday shifts while he's away if I'm needed."

"You're the fill-in lifeguard?"

"Don't look so surprised."

"I'm just curious as to why your brother didn't mention you specifically."

She shrugged a little. "I may have told him that I thought you were an ass."

Gabe laughed. "Oh, really?"

"It was after the wedding, so who could blame me?"

He raised his hands. "Because I innocently overheard your deepest secret?"

"Well, that was before I…" Her words trailed. Before what? Before she realized he wasn't quite the ogre she'd pegged him for. Now wasn't the time to admit anything. "Anyhow…good night."

Once he left, Lauren forced herself to relax. She took a long shower and changed into her silliest short-legged giraffe pajamas and made a toasted cheese sandwich for dinner. She ate in the lounge room, watching television, legs crossed lotus-style, with plans to forget all about her neighbor.

And failed.

Because Gabe Vitali reminded her that she was a flesh-and-blood woman in every sense of the word. The way he looked, the way he walked with that kind of natural sexual confidence, the way his blue eyes glittered… It was all too easy to get swept away thinking about such things.

And too easy to forget why she'd vowed to avoid a man like him at all costs.

She'd made her decision to find someone steady and honest and ordinary. No powerful attraction. No blinding lust. No foolish dreams of romantic love. Just friendship and compatibility. It might sound boring and absurd to her

friends, but Lauren knew what she wanted. She wanted something lasting.

Something safe.

Since she spent most of the night staring at the ceiling, Lauren wasn't surprised when she awoke later than usual and had to rush to get ready for work. She fed the dog and then tied him on a generous lead to the post on her back patio and headed to the store. Her mother was there already, changing mannequins and merchandising the stock that had arrived Friday afternoon. Irene Jakowski had first opened The Wedding House twenty-five years earlier. Lauren had grown up around the gowns and the brides, and it had made her fall in love with weddings. During her school years, she'd worked part-time in the store, learning from her mother. When school finished, she'd studied business and accounting for two years at college before returning to the store, taking over from her mother, who now worked part-time.

Lauren dropped her laptop and bag on the desk in the staff room and headed to the sales floor. The rows of wedding gowns, each one immaculately pressed and presented on hangers, filled her with a mix of approval and melancholy.

"How's the dog?" her mother queried when she moved around the sales counter.

Lauren grimaced. "Missing his owner and slobbering all over my furniture. You know, like in that old movie *Turner & Hooch?*"

Irene laughed. "It's not that bad, surely?"

"Time will tell," she replied, and managed a rueful grin. "I don't know why he can't go into a boarding kennel like other dogs."

"You're brother says he pines when he's away from home," Irene told her. "And it's only until the house sitter returns, isn't it?"

"Yeah," Lauren said, and sighed. "Gabe is taking him to the surf club today, so at least my patio furniture is safe while I'm here."

Her mother's eyes widened. "Gabe is? Really?"

Of course her mother knew Gabe Vitali. She'd mentioned him several times over the past six months. Irene Jakowski was always on the lookout for a new son-in-law, since the old one hadn't worked out. The fact he'd bought the house next door was like gold to a matchmaking parent.

"Matka," Lauren warned, using the Polish word for *mother* when she saw the familiar gleam in her mother's eyes. "Stop."

"I was only—"

"I know what you're doing," Lauren said, smiling. "Now, let's get the store open."

By the time Gabe returned home that afternoon, he was short on patience and more than happy to hand Jed over to his neighbor. Damned dog had chewed his car keys, his sneakers and escaped twice through the automatic doors at the clubhouse.

When he pulled into the driveway, he spotted the fencing contractor he'd called earlier that day parked across the lawn. He locked Jed in Lauren's front garden and headed back to his own yard. He was twenty minutes into his meeting with the contractor when she arrived home. Gabe was in the front yard with the tradesman, talking prices and time frames, as the older man began pushing at the low timber fence that separated the two allotments and then wrote in a notepad.

She walked around the hedge and met him by the letterbox, eyeing the contractor's battered truck suspiciously. "What's going on?" she asked, looking all business in her black skirt and white blouse.

"A new fence," Gabe supplied and watched her curiosity quickly turn into a frown.

"I wasn't aware *we* needed a new one."

"This one's falling down," he said, and introduced her to the contractor before the other man waved his notepad and said he'd get back to him tomorrow.

Once the battered truck was reversing from the yard, she clamped her hands to her hips. "Shouldn't we have discussed it first?"

"It's only an estimate," he told her. "Nothing's decided yet."

She didn't look convinced. "Really?"

"Really," he assured her. "Although the fence does need replacing."

Her eyes flashed. "I know it's my responsibility to pay for half of any fence that's built, but at the moment I'm—"

Gabe shook his head. "I intend to pay for the fence, should it come to that."

She glared at him, then the fence, then back to him. "You don't get to decide that for me," she snapped, still glaring.

He looked at her, bemused by her sudden annoyance. "I don't?"

"It's my fence, too."

"Of course," he replied. "I was only—"

"Taking over? And probably thinking I couldn't possibly afford it and then feeling sorry for me, right?"

He had a whole lot of feelings churning through his blood when it came to Lauren Jakowski…pity definitely wasn't one of them. "Just being neighborly," he said, and figured he shouldn't smile, even though he wanted to. "But hey, if you want to pay for half the fence, go ahead."

"I will," she replied through tight lips. "Just let me know how much and when."

"Of course," he said.

She huffed a little. "Good. And have you been messing around with my gate?"

Ah. So the real reason why she looked like she wanted to slug him. "Yes, I fixed your gate this morning."

"Because?"

"Because it was broken," he replied, watching her temper flare as the seconds ticked by. *And broken things should be fixed.* He'd spent most of his adult life fixing things. *Fixing people.* But she didn't know that. And he wasn't about to tell her. "No point risking more splinters."

"I liked my gate how it was," she said, hands still on hips.

Gabe raised a brow. "Really?"

She scowled. "Really."

"You're mad at me because I repaired your gate?"

"I'm mad at you because it wasn't your gate to repair. I don't need anyone to fix things. I don't need a white knight, okay?"

A white knight? Yeah, right. But there was an edge of vulnerability in her voice that stopped him from smiling. Was she broken? Was that part of what drew him to her? Like meets like? He knew she was divorced, and at her brother's wedding she'd admitted her marriage hadn't been a happy one. But Gabe didn't want to speculate. And he didn't want to ask. The less he knew, the better.

"Okay," he said simply.

For a moment, he thought she might argue some more. Instead, she dropped her gaze and asked an obvious question. "What happened to your shoe?"

He glanced down. The back of his left sneaker was torn and the lace was missing. "Jed."

She looked up again, and he saw her mouth curve. "Was that the only damage?"

"Other than chewing my car keys and making a run for it whenever he got the chance."

She moaned softly. "Sorry about that. I'll get Cameron to replace them when he gets back."

Gabe shrugged. "No need. It's only a shoe."

She nodded, turned and walked back around the hedge. Gabe shook his shoulders and made a concerted effort to forget all about her.

And failed.

I really need to stop reacting like that.

Lauren was still thinking it forty minutes later when she emerged from the shower and pulled on frayed gray sweats. Her reaction, or rather her *overreaction,* to Gabe's news about the fence was amplified by his interference with her gate.

She didn't want him fixing things.

Lauren didn't want *any* man fixing things.

It was a road she'd traveled before. She knew what she wanted and white knights need not apply. Her ex-husband had tried to fix things—to fix her—and it had ended in disaster.

James Wallace had ridden into her life in his carpenter's truck, all charm and good looks. He'd arrived at The Wedding House to make repairs to the changing rooms, and she'd been unexpectedly drawn to his blatant flirting. An hour later, she'd accepted his invitation to go out with him that night. They ended up at a local bistro for drinks and then dinner, and by midnight he'd kissed her in the car park, and she was halfway in lust with him.

Three months later, she had a fairy-tale wedding.

Even though it was the wedding she'd planned to have to someone else.

To Tim. Sweet, handsome Tim Mannering. Her first love. Her only love. He had been her college boyfriend and the man she'd intended to marry. They'd made plans for the future. They'd talked about everything from build-

ing their dream home, taking an African-safari vacation, to how many kids they would have. They'd loved one another deeply and promised each other the world.

Except Tim had died three weeks before their wedding.

And Lauren walked down the aisle with another man less than two years later.

She swallowed the tightness in her throat. Thinking about Tim still filled her with sadness. And she was sad about James, too. She should never have married him. She hadn't loved him. They'd shared a fleeting attraction that had faded just months into their marriage. They'd had little in common and very different dreams. Within a year, James was gone, tired of what he called her *cold, unfeeling heart.* And Lauren was alone once more.

But she still hoped to share her life with someone. And she wanted the children she'd planned for since the day she and Tim had become engaged. Only next time, Lauren was determined to go into it with her eyes wide-open and not glazed over by romantic illusions. What she'd had with James wasn't enough. And what she'd had with Tim had left her broken inside. Now all she wanted was the middle road. Just mutual respect, trust and compatibility. No fireworks. No deep feelings. Lust was unreliable. Love was painful when lost.

There was nothing wrong with settling. Nothing at all. Settling was safe. All she had to do was remember what she wanted and why. And forget all about Gabe Vitali and his glittering blue eyes and broad shoulders. Because he was pure heartbreak material. And her heart wasn't up for grabs.

Not now.

Not ever again.

Chapter Three

Gabe went to his cousin's for dinner Wednesday night and expected the usual lecture about his life. Scott Jones was family and his closest friend, and even though he knew the other man's intentions were born from a sincere interest in his well-being, Gabe generally pulled no punches when it came to telling his cousin to mind his own business.

Scott's wife, Evie, was pure earth mother. She was strikingly attractive and possessed a calm, generous spirit. Gabe knew his cousin was besotted with his wife and baby daughter, and he was genuinely happy for him.

"How's the house coming along?" Scott asked over a beer while Evie was upstairs putting little Rebecca down for the night.

Gabe pushed back in the kitchen chair. "Fine."

"Will you stay there permanently?"

"I doubt it," he replied.

"Still can't see you renovating the place yourself," Scott said, and grinned.

Gabe frowned. "I can fix things."

Like Lauren's gate, which hadn't gone down so well. He should have left it alone. But she'd hurt herself on the thing and he didn't want that happening again. There was no harm in being neighborly.

"Job still working out?"

Gabe shrugged one shoulder. "Sure."

Scott grinned again. "And how's it going with your next-door neighbor?"

He knew his cousin was fishing. He'd told him a little about the incident at the wedding, and Scott knew he'd bought the house next door. Clearly, he'd told him too much. "Fine."

"I like Lauren," Scott said, and smiled.

Gabe didn't respond. He didn't have to. His cousin spoke again.

"You do, too, judging by the look on your face."

Gabe didn't flinch. "You know my plans. They haven't changed."

"Your five-year plan?" Scott's eyes widened. "Still think you can arrange life to order?" He looked to the ceiling, clearly thinking about his family upstairs. "No chance."

"I know what I'm doing."

It sounded good, at least. Pity he didn't quite believe it.

"You know she's divorced?" Scott asked.

"Yes."

Scott nodded. "Evie knows more about it than I do. And, of course, about the other guy."

His head came up. The other guy? "I don't—"

"He died about five years ago," his cousin said, and drank some beer. "They were engaged, that's all I know."

Gabe's insides contracted. So she'd lost someone. And married someone else. The wrong someone else. It explained the haunted, vulnerable look shading her brown

eyes. But he didn't want to know any more. Hadn't he already decided the less he knew, the better?

"Not my business."

Scott's eyebrows shot up. "So no interest at all?"

He shrugged again. "No."

Scott chuckled. "You're a lousy liar."

I'm a great liar. His whole life was a lie. Gabe stood and scraped the chair back. "Thanks for the beer."

He left shortly after, and by the time he pulled into his own driveway, it was past ten o'clock. There were lights on next door, and when he spotted a shadowy silhouette pass by the front window, Gabe fought the way his stomach churned thinking about her. He didn't want to be thinking, imagining or anything else. Lauren Jakowski was a distraction he didn't need.

And he certainly didn't expect to find her on his doorstep at seven the next morning.

But there she was. All perfection and professionalism in her silky blue shirt and knee-length black skirt. Once he got that image clear in his head, Gabe noticed she wasn't alone. Jed sat on his haunches at her side.

"Am I stretching the boundaries of friendship?" she asked, and held out the lead.

He nodded. Were they friends now? No. Definitely not. "Absolutely."

She chewed at her bottom lip. "I wouldn't ask if it wasn't important."

Gabe shrugged. "What's the big emergency?"

She exhaled heavily. "He chewed off a piece of my sofa and broke the table in the living room when I left him home on Tuesday. Then he terrorized my parents' cat when I left him there yesterday. Mary-Jayne said she'd take him tomorrow and Saturday. She's got a fully enclosed yard and a dog, which will keep him company. But today I'm all out

of options. I can't take him to the store and…and…I don't know what else to do."

Her frustration was clear, and Gabe knew he'd give her exactly what she wanted. Because saying no to Lauren was becoming increasingly difficult. "Okay."

"O-okay?" she echoed hesitantly.

"Yeah. Okay."

Relief flooded her face. "Thanks. I…I owe you for this."

Gabe shrugged again. He didn't want her owing him anything. Owing could lead to collecting…and that was out of the question. "No problem," he said, and took the lead.

"So dinner?" she asked and took a step back. "Tonight. I'll cook. My way of saying thanks."

His back straightened. "You don't need to—"

"I insist," she said quickly, and then looked as though she was itching to get away. "Say, seven o'clock?"

She left, and Gabe didn't go back inside until she disappeared around the hedge.

Dinner. Great idea. *Not.*
What were you thinking?
Lauren spent the day chastising herself and making sure she didn't let on to her mother that she'd somehow invited Gabe into the inner sanctum of her house, her kitchen and her solitary life. But she'd made the offer and it was too late to back out now. Besides, he was doing her a favor looking after the dog. Dinner really was the least she could do in return. He'd helped her out, and it was her way of saying thank-you. It was nothing. Just a simple meal between neighbors.

Only, simple seemed at odds with the way her nerves rattled just thinking about it.

She stopped by the supermarket on the way home, and by the time she pulled into the driveway, it was nearly six. She jumped into the shower, dried off, applied a little

makeup and changed into loose-fitting cargo pants and a red knit top. By six-thirty she was in the kitchen marinating steaks and prepping a salad. And ignoring the knot in the pit of her stomach as best she could.

The doorbell rang at exactly seven o'clock.

Jed rushed down the hallway the moment she opened the door, clearly eager to get to his food bowl in the laundry.

"Hi," she said, and stepped back.

"Hi, yourself," Gabe said as he crossed the threshold.

He closed the door, and she didn't linger. Instead, she pivoted on her heels and headed back to the kitchen. By the time she'd made her way back behind the countertop, he was by the door, watching her. She looked up and met his gaze. He looked so good in his jeans and navy T-shirt, her breath stuck in her throat. She noticed a tattoo braid that encircled one biceps peeking out from the edge of his sleeve. She'd never liked ink much, but it suited him. It was sexy. Everything about Gabe was sexy. His broad shoulders, black hair, dazzling blue eyes... The combination was devastating. And dangerous.

Be immune to sexy.

He moved and rested against the door frame, crossing his arms, and Lauren was instantly absorbed by the image it evoked.

"You know, you really shouldn't look at me like that," he said, and Lauren quickly realized she'd been caught staring. Or ogling. "I might start thinking you aren't serious about that vow of yours."

Her skin warmed. "Don't flatter yourself."

His lips curled at the edges. "I never do."

"I don't believe that for a second."

"Then what do you believe, Lauren?" he asked, and met her gaze.

"I don't know what you mean."

His stare was unwavering. "I think you do."

"You're talking about what you overheard at the wedding?" She shrugged as casually as she could manage. "I thought we'd agreed not to talk about that."

He half smiled. "Did we? You said you wanted a passionless relationship."

Her breath caught. She didn't want to talk about that with him. Not when her pulse was racing so erratically. She remembered how he knew her secrets. He knew what she wanted. "Yes," she replied and hated that it tasted like a lie. "Passion is overrated."

"Do you think?" he asked quietly, his intense gaze locked with hers. "And chemistry?"

"Even more overrated."

"That's a handy line when you're in denial."

She tried but couldn't drag her gaze away. "I'm not in denial," she insisted. "About…anything."

About you. That was what she meant. And he knew it, too.

"Good," he said, almost as though he was trying to convince himself. "Shall I open this?" he asked, and gestured to the wine bottle he carried.

Lauren nodded and grabbed two glasses and a corkscrew from the cupboard, laying them on the counter. "How do you like your steak?"

"Medium rare," he replied. "You?"

She shrugged. "Same. Did Jed behave himself today? No disasters? No sacrificial sneakers?"

He grinned and grabbed the corkscrew. "It was moderately better than the last time."

She laughed softly. "He's usually very civilized when Cameron is around."

"He's pining," Gabe said, and popped the cork. "Missing the people he loves most. It's natural he would."

Lauren nodded. "You're right. And it's only for a few more days. I heard from Cameron's house sitter this morn-

ing, and she's flying back into Bellandale on Sunday afternoon."

He passed her a glass of wine, and Lauren's fingers tingled when they briefly touched his. If he noticed, he didn't show it. "How long have you lived here?" he asked.

"Just over a year."

"It's...nice. My sister, Bianca, would love it," he said easily and rested against the countertop. "She's into decorating."

Lauren pulled a couple of plates from the cupboard. "Do you have one of those large Italian-American families?"

"There are four of us. Aaron is thirty five and the eldest. He's divorced and has twin four-year-old boys. And then there's me, three years younger." He grinned a little. "Then Luca, who's thirty and married to his IT job, and Bianca, who is twenty-six and the baby of the family."

She nodded. "And your parents?"

"There's only my mom," he explained, watching her with such blistering intensity, Lauren found it hard to concentrate on preparing their meal. "My dad died fifteen years ago."

Her expression softened. "I'm sorry. Were you close?"

"Very."

She nodded again. "What did he—"

"Lung cancer."

The awful words hung in the air between them, and an old pain jabbed between her ribs. She pushed the memory off as quickly as it came.

"I'm sorry," she said gently. "I feel very lucky to still have both my parents."

"And there's only you and Cameron?" he asked.

"Yes," she replied. "And he's actually my half brother. Our mother married my dad when he was three years old. I would have loved a sister, though. I mean, we're really close, but a big family would be wonderful."

His gaze absorbed hers. "You want children?"

She nodded. "I always thought I'd like to have three kids."

He raised a brow. "With Mr. No-Passion?"

A smile tugged at his mouth, and Lauren couldn't stop her lips from creasing into a tiny grin. "Maybe. Hopefully. One day."

He looked at her oddly, as if he wanted to have an opinion about it but was holding his tongue. When he finally spoke, he surprised her. "You'll make a good mom."

"I… Thank you." The air crackled, and she avoided eye contact by feigning a deep interest in the salad she'd prepared. When he spoke again, she looked up.

"Need any help?" he asked, and took both wineglasses to the table.

"No," she replied and plated the food quickly. "I'm nearly done. Take a seat."

A minute later, she placed the plates on the table and sat down. For one crazy second she thought…no, *imagined*… that the mood between them felt a little like a date. *A first date*.

Stupid. They were neighbors. Acquaintances. Nothing more. So what if he was the most attractive man she'd ever met? Attraction hadn't done her any favors in the past. She'd been attracted to James, and that had ended badly for them both. This would be the same. And anything more than attraction was out of the question.

"So did you have a similar job in California?" she asked, determined to steer the conversation away from herself.

"Not really," he replied vaguely and picked up the utensils. "I worked as a lifeguard part-time at Huntington Beach, near where I lived."

"Cameron said the place has never run so smoothly. Do you enjoy the work?" she asked.

"Yeah…sure," he replied casually. "I like the beach," he

said, and when she raised a brow indicating she wanted him to elaborate, he continued. "And I get to teach a few classes, lifeguard on the weekends and juggle paperwork during the week." He shrugged. "It's not exactly rocket science."

She was itching to ask him more questions. Cameron had told her he was clearly overqualified for the role at the surf club. She knew he didn't talk about himself much, and that suited her fine. Most of the time. But tonight she was interested. As much as warning bells pealed, she wanted to know more about him. She wanted to know what made him tick. She wanted to know why he'd moved his life from California to Crystal Point.

"Don't you miss your old life? Your friends, your family?"

He looked up. "Of course."

"I could never leave my family like that," she said, and knew it sounded like a judgment. She shrugged and sighed a little. "I mean, I'd miss them too much to be away for too long."

If it was a dig, he ignored it. Because he was so mesmerized by her sheer loveliness, Gabe couldn't look away. He shouldn't have come around. He shouldn't have thought he could spend an evening with Lauren and not get caught up in the desire that thrummed through his blood. She was tempting. And he was…tempted.

"You really are quite beautiful."

The words were out before he could stop them. She fumbled with her cutlery, and the steak portion on the end of her fork fell back onto the plate. He watched as she pressed her fingertips against her mouth and discreetly wiped away a little sauce.

"Um…thank you. I guess."

Gabe rested back in his chair. "You don't sound convinced."

"That I'm beautiful?" She shrugged. "I've never really thought I was. Attractive, perhaps."

"No," he said quietly. "You're beautiful."

She grabbed her drink. "Are you coming on to me?" she asked bluntly.

Gabe chuckled. "No."

She met his gaze. "Because I'm not your type?"

"I'm not coming on to you because you're exactly my type."

Heat filled the space between them, and a sudden surge of blinding attraction clung to the air. But it was best to get it out in the open. He wanted her. And he was pretty sure the feeling was reciprocated.

"Is that because of what I said about you...you know... at the wedding?"

"You mean when you told your friends you've thought about me naked?"

Color quickly flamed her pale cheeks. "Is that what I said?"

"Yes."

She shrugged and smiled a little. "Well, since you were there and heard the whole conversation, there's no point denying it."

Gabe laughed. He liked that about her. She wasn't serious all the time. Even without her natural beauty, she had an energy and humor that fascinated him. For a moment, Gabe wished he could wind the clock forward, to a time in the future when he could guarantee any promises or commitment he might want to make. But he couldn't. And wishes were for fools.

He pushed some words out. "I guess not. Your friends don't seem to approve of your plans, though."

"They don't," she said, and sipped some wine. "But they support me, so that's all that matters. You know how fam-

ily and friends can get sometimes…as if they know what's best, regardless of how a person might feel about it."

Gabe knew exactly. "You don't like weddings much?"

Her eyes widened. "Sure I do. Weddings are…my life."

"Really?"

She looked at him. "Well, maybe not my life. My job, at least."

He heard hesitation in her voice. "But?"

Her shoulders dropped. "Oh, you know, pretending the fairy tale exists on a day-in-and-day-out basis can be monotonous." She shook herself and picked up the cutlery again. "Sorry, I don't normally complain about it. But you're…" She stopped and looked at him. "Even though a week ago I was convinced you were simply another ridiculously handsome but conceited jerk, you're surprisingly… easy to talk to."

A good bedside manner is essential….

How many times had he heard that?

Gabe shook off the guilt between his shoulder blades. "Oh, I can be just as much of a jerk as the next guy."

She laughed, and the sound echoed around the room. "Well, thanks for the warning."

He placed his elbows on the table. "Don't thank me. I said I wouldn't make a pass. I didn't say it would be easy."

Her cheeks bloomed with color. "Oh, because I'm—"

"Because you're Commitment 101."

"And you're not?" she queried.

"Exactly."

"Have you ever been tempted? Or close?" she asked and pushed her barely eaten meal aside.

"Once," he replied and took a drink. "It didn't work out."

She stared at him, as if she was trying to figure out why. But she never would. He didn't talk about it. Ever. She took a second, swallowed hard and then spoke. "Did you love her?"

"It didn't work out," he said again, a whole lot quicker than he would have liked. "I guess there's your answer."

Her brows arched. "So you didn't love her? Not even a little bit?"

Gabe's mouth twisted. "I didn't realize there was such a thing as being a little bit in love. I cared for her, sure. But like I said, we didn't work out. There's no great mystery to it."

He wasn't about to tell Lauren that she was right—he hadn't really loved his ex-girlfriend. He'd done her a favor by letting her go. He was sure of it. And besides, Mona hadn't put up much resistance. Once she'd known she had an out clause, she'd left their relationship as quickly as she could.

Lauren bit her bottom lip, watching him. "So you got burned?"

He shrugged. "Not exactly."

"Then what, exactly?" she asked.

"We split up," he replied. "We went our separate ways. Neither of us was heartbroken."

"Which leaves you where?" Her eyes were full of questions. "Working at the surf club and having casual relationships and sex with women who are equally uninterested in commitment?"

"Ah…I suppose."

"Well, that sounds…like fun."

Not.

That was what she was thinking. Shallow and meaningless and hollow. Gabe thought so, too…even though he'd drilled himself to accept his present and future. But he suddenly lost his appetite.

"It is what it is," he said, and pushed back in his seat. "I'm not looking for…anything."

She watched him, her brown eyes darkening. "I've always believed that we're all looking for something…love

or sex, belonging, companionship. Or maybe something more complicated, like peace of mind…or even isolation."

Which one are you looking for?

That was the question in her words. Gabe shrugged a shoulder casually. She was so close to the truth. "Is that why your marriage didn't work out?" he asked, shifting the focus back to her. "Because you wanted different things?"

She gripped her wineglass. "My marriage failed because my husband and I had nothing between us but fleeting physical attraction. Which isn't enough," she added.

It explained why she wanted a passionless relationship… sort of. "And now you're looking for more?" he asked. "Or maybe less?"

"Sometimes less *is* more," she replied. "Which is why I'm determined to think with my head next time…and not my—" she paused, smiling "—libido."

Gabe tensed. Thinking of *her* libido didn't do his any favors. "Or your heart?"

She smiled. "Precisely," she said.

He remembered what his cousin had said to him the night before. She'd lost someone. She'd lost love and settled for sex. The fact that she now wanted a middle road made perfect sense. "Someone did get it, though?"

Her gaze was unwavering. "You mean my heart? Yes. Someone did."

"Who was he?"

Silence stretched between them. He shouldn't have asked. He shouldn't want to know. The more he knew, the harder it would be to stay away from her.

"My first love. My only love, I guess."

She said the words so quietly and with such raw honesty, his insides contracted. He didn't want to hear any more. "You don't have to—"

"His name was Tim," she said, cutting him off. "We met

in college. I was nineteen and studying business. He was across the hall in engineering. We fell in love. A few years later we got engaged. And then…"

Gabe knew what was coming, but he asked anyway. "And then, what?"

She drew in a sharp breath. "And then he died."

"Was it an accident?"

She shook her head. "No. He was sick."

Sick…

Gabe's stomach churned uneasily, and he forced the next words out. "What kind of illness did he have?"

"Primary glioblastoma," she replied. "It's a—"

"I know what it is," he said quickly and pushed his chair back some more.

Brain tumor…

An aggressive, unforgiving kind of cancer that usually left a patient with months to live rather than years. It was all he needed to hear. It was time to go. He needed to finish eating and leave.

"I'm sorry," Gabe said, and spent the following few minutes pretending interest in his food. Even though he felt sick to his stomach. He pushed the meal around on the plate, finished his wine and declined the coffee she offered to make.

"I need to get going," he said as soon as he felt it was polite to do so, and stood.

"Oh…sure." She got to her feet. "Thanks again for looking after Jed."

"No problem. Thanks for dinner."

Once they reached the front door, he lingered for a moment. He liked her. A lot. She was sweet and warm and funny and so damned sexy, he could barely think of anything other than kissing her perfectly bowed mouth. He wanted Lauren in his bed more than he'd wanted anything for a long time.

But he wouldn't pursue it.

She'd lost the man she'd loved to cancer.

And he'd bet his boots it wasn't a road she'd ever want to travel again.

He needed to forget all about Lauren. And fast.

Chapter Four

Spending the evening with Gabe confirmed for Lauren that since her divorce, she'd gone into a kind of lazy hibernation. She'd quit volunteering at the surf club, rarely joined her mother for the tai chi classes she'd always loved and avoided socializing regularly with anyone other than her two closest friends. It hadn't been a deliberate pulling away, more like a reluctance to go out and put on her happy face.

That needed to change.

Lauren knew if she was going to find someone to share her life with, she actually needed to start having a real *life*.

But that real life didn't include her sexy neighbor.

On Friday night she went to the movies with Cassie and Mary-Jayne, stayed out afterward for coffee and cake and got home by ten.

There was a light on next door. Lauren ignored the fluttering in her stomach and headed inside. As soon as she'd crossed the threshold, she heard Jed's whining. Minutes later she discovered her great plan of leaving him locked

in the laundry was not such a great plan. It was, in fact, a disaster. He'd somehow chewed a hole in the back door, and his big head was now stuck between the timbers. Lauren groaned, cursed her brother under her breath for a few seconds and then attempted to pull the dog free. But he was lodged. His neck was wedged around the cracked timber, and she didn't have the strength to pull him free.

Surprisingly, the dopey dog was in good spirits, and she patted him for a moment before she grabbed her phone. She could call her father? Or perhaps Mary-Jayne might be able to help?

Just get some backbone and go and ask Gabe.

She reassured the dog for a little while longer before she walked next door. The porch light flickered and she sucked in a breath and knocked.

Gabe looked surprised to see her on his doorstep.

"Lauren?" He rested against the door frame. "What's up?"

He wore faded jeans that were splattered with paint, and an old gray T-shirt. There was also paint in his hair and on his cheek. She wanted to smile, thinking how gorgeous he looked, but didn't. Instead, she put on a serious face.

"I need help."

He straightened. "What's wrong?"

"It might be better if you just see for yourself."

He was across the threshold in seconds. "Are you okay?"

"I'm fine. Jed, on the other hand…"

"What's he done now?" Gabe asked as they headed down the steps.

"Like I said, you need to see this for yourself."

A minute later they were in her house. They moved to the laundry and were facing Jed's bouncing rear end. And Gabe was laughing loudly. Really loudly. In fact, he was laughing so hard he doubled over and gripped the washing machine.

"It's really not that funny," she said crossly and planted her hands on her hips. "He could be hurt."

"He's not hurt," Gabe said, still chuckling as he moved across the small room and knelt down beside the dog. "The goofy mutt is just stuck."

"Exactly. He's wedged in and I can't pull him free."

He examined the door. "Do you have a hammer?"

"A hammer?"

"I need to knock a bit of this plywood out the way," he explained.

She nodded and grabbed the small toolbox under the sink. "I think there's something in here."

He opened the box, found the small hammer and got to work on the door. Jed whined a little, but Lauren placated him with pats and soothing words while Gabe made the hole large enough for the dog's head to fit back through. It took several minutes, but finally Jed was free and immediately started bounding around the small room, whipping Lauren's legs with his tail.

"Oh, that's good," she said on a relieved sigh. "Thank you."

"He looks okay," Gabe said, smiling. "But your door's not so lucky."

Lauren glanced at the door. The hole was bigger than she'd thought. "I'll need to call someone to fix it on Monday."

He nodded as he rose to his feet. "Sure. I'll board it up for you now so you'll be safe over the weekend."

Lauren's insides contracted. The way he spoke, the way he was so genuinely concerned about her, melted what was left of her resentment toward him.

Admit it...you like him.

A lot.

Too much.

"Ah—thanks," she said quietly and moved Jed out of the small room.

Gabe followed her. "Be back soon," he said as he strode down the hallway and headed out the front door.

He returned five minutes later with a large square piece of plywood, a cordless drill and a box of screws, and quickly repaired the hole. Lauren watched from her spot near the door, absorbed by the way he seemed to do everything with such effortless ease. Nothing fazed him. He was smart and resourceful and sexy and warmed the blood in her veins. Gabe made her think of everything she'd lost. And everything she was determined to avoid.

"Lauren?"

His voice jerked her back to earth. He was close. They were sharing the space in the narrow doorway, and Lauren's gaze got stuck on his chest and the way the paint-splattered T-shirt molded his chest. Her fingertips itched to reach up and touch him, to feel for herself if his body was as strong and solid as it looked. She remembered how he'd pulled her from the pool at the wedding and how his hands had felt upon her skin. It had been a long time since she'd felt a man's touch. Longer still since she'd wanted to.

Memories of Tim swirled around in her head. She'd loved him. Adored him. She'd imagined they would spend their lives together, loving one another, having children, creating memories through a long and happy marriage. But he'd never, not once, made her knees quiver and her skin burn with such blistering, scorching awareness. Even the fleeting desire she'd felt for James seemed lukewarm compared to the way Gabe made her feel. Her sex-starved body had turned traitor, taunting her…and she had to use her head to stay in control.

"I was…I was thinking…"

Her words trailed off when she looked up and met his blistering gaze. There was so much heat between them. Un-

deniable heat that combusted the air and made her stomach roll.

"Thinking?" he asked softly. "About what?"

Lauren willed some movement into her feet and managed to step back a little. "Your jacket," she muttered and turned on her heels and fled through the kitchen and toward the guest bedroom.

When she returned, Gabe was in the hallway, tools in hand.

"I forgot to return this," she explained and passed him the dinner jacket he'd given her the night of the wedding and which she'd since had dry-cleaned. "Thank you for lending it to me."

"No problem." He took the garment and smiled. "Well, good night."

"Ah—and thanks again for freeing Jed.... Your saving me from disaster is becoming something of a habit."

"No harm in being neighborly," he said casually.

Too casually. She knew he was as aware of her as she was of him. But they were skirting around it. Denying it.

"I guess not. Good night, Gabe."

He left, and Lauren closed the door, pressing her back against it as she let out a heavy sigh. Being around Gabe was wreaking havoc with her usual common sense. He wasn't what she wanted. Sure, she could invite him into her bed for the night. But that was all it would be. He'd called her Commitment 101, and he was right. He'd told her he didn't do serious. He didn't want a relationship. They were too different.

When she arrived at The Wedding House the following morning, her mother was there before her, as was their part-time worker, Dawn.

"You look terrible," her mother remarked, clearly taking in her paler-than-usual skin and dark smudges beneath her

eyes. Lauren wasn't surprised she looked so haggard—she hadn't slept well. Instead, she'd spent the night fighting the bedsheets, dreaming old dreams, feeling an old, familiar pain that left her weary and exhausted.

"Gee—thanks," she said with a grin. "Just a little sleep deprived because of Jed, but I'll tell you about that later."

Irene smiled. "Are you heading to the surf club this afternoon? Or do you want me to go? We have to have the measurements for the stage and runway to the prop people by Monday, remember?"

She remembered. There was a fund-raiser at the surf club planned for two weeks away, and although Grace was the event organizer, Lauren volunteered to help in her sister-in-law's absence. Since she was organizing a fashion parade for the night anyway, it wasn't too much extra work liaising with the staging and entertainment people and the caterers.

"I'll go this afternoon," she said, and ignored the silly fluttering in her belly. All she had to do was measure the area for the stage and change rooms for the models. It was not as if she would be hanging around. It was not as if she had a reason to *want* to hang around.

"If you're sure," her mother said, her eyes twinkling.

Her übermatchmaking mother knew very well that Gabe might be there.

"I'm sure," she insisted. "And stop doing that."

Her mother raised both brows. "What? I just want to see my only daughter happy."

"I want to see me happy, too," Lauren said, and instructed Dawn to open the doors.

"I'm concerned about you," Irene said, more seriously.

"I'm fine, Matka," she promised. "Just tired, like I said."

The models for the parade had started coming into the store for their fittings, and that morning Carmen Collins crossed the threshold and held court like she owned the world. They'd gone to school together, and the self-

proclaimed society princess made it her business to insult Lauren at every opportunity. But the other woman knew people with deep pockets, and since that was what the fund-raiser was about, Lauren bit her tongue and flattered Carmen about the tight-fitting, plum-colored satin gown she was wearing in the parade.

"I do adore this color," Carmen purred and ran her hands over her hips. "So are you modeling in the parade?"

"No," Lauren replied and saw her mother's raised brows from the corner of her eye. "I'll be too busy with the show."

"Pity," Carmen said with a sugary laugh. "You do look so sweet in a wedding dress."

Lauren plastered on a smile and pulled back the fitting room drapes. "Maybe next year," she said, clinging to her manners as though they were a life raft. "I'll have the dress pressed and ready for the show."

The other woman left by eleven, and her mother didn't bother to hide her dislike once Carmen was out the door.

"Can't bear that woman," Irene said, and frowned. "She was an obnoxious teenager and hasn't improved with age."

"But she married a rich man and knows plenty of people who'll donate at the fund-raiser," Lauren reminded her mother. "That's all that matters, right?"

Her mother huffed out a breath. "I suppose. Anyway, we've only got three more of the models to come in for a fitting and we're done. So off you go." She shooed Lauren and smiled. "I'll close up."

Lauren grinned, hugged her mother, quickly changed into gunmetal-gray cargo pants, a pink collared T-shirt and sneakers and then headed to the Crystal Point Surf Club & Community Center to measure the space she'd need for the catwalk.

The holiday park was filled with campers and mobile homes, and she drove down the bitumen road that led to the clubhouse. Almost a year earlier, the place had been gutted

by fire, and the renovated building was bigger and better with much-improved facilities. She parked outside, grabbed her tape measure and notebook and headed through the automatic doors on the ground level.

And came to an abrupt halt.

Gabe was there.

Wet, laughing and clearly having a good time in the company of a lifeguard, a young woman who Lauren vaguely recalled was named Megan.

"Lauren?" he said as he straightened from his spot leaning against the reception desk. "What brings you here?"

She held up the tape. "Benefit stuff," she said, and tried to ignore the way the safety shirt he wore outlined every line and every muscle of his chest and shoulders at the same time as the little green-eyed monster was rearing its head.

Snap out of it.

"Do you know Megan?" he asked and came toward her.

She nodded. "Hello."

"It's Mimi," the girl corrected cheerfully, showing off perfectly white teeth and a million-dollar smile to go with her athletic, tanned body. "No one calls me Megan except my parents." She laughed and gazed at Gabe a little starry-eyed. "And you." Then she turned her attention back to Lauren. "So Gabe said you might be filling in for Cameron while he's away if we get too busy. The beaches have been crazy today…. Gabe just pulled an old man in from the rip."

Lauren smiled and looked at Gabe. That explained why his clothes were wet and why he had sand on his feet. "Is the man okay?"

"Shaken up, but fine," he replied and smiled. "But I wouldn't call him old. He was probably only forty."

Perfectly toned and tanned *Mimi* laughed loudly. "Ancient," she said, and grabbed Gabe's arm, lingering a lot longer than Lauren thought appropriate. "Well, I'd better get back on patrol. See you."

She breezed out of the room with a seductive sway that Lauren couldn't have managed even if she'd wanted to.

"Do you need help with that?" Gabe asked, looking at the tape in her hand.

Lauren shook her head. "No."

"So you're organizing the benefit with Grace?"

She looked at him. "The fashion parade. Why? Are you interested in modeling?"

He laughed. "Ah, no thanks. I did promise your brother I'd help out setting up, but that's all."

Lauren placed the retractable tape at one end of the room, and when it bounced back into her hand, he walked over and held it out straight for her. "Thanks," she said, and pulled the tape out across the room.

"If you need models, perhaps Megan can help?" he suggested and came across the room.

"Mimi," she corrected extrasweetly, and placed the notebook on the desk. "And I think I have all the models we need." Lauren remained by the desk and raised a brow. "She's a little young, don't you think?"

He frowned. "No. She's a strong swimmer and a good lifeguard."

Lauren flipped the notepad open without looking at him. "That's not what I meant."

The second he realized her meaning, he laughed loudly. "She's what, nineteen? Give me *some* credit."

Lauren glanced sideways. "She's perky."

"And a teenager." He moved closer. "Why all this sudden interest in my love life?"

"I'm not interested," she defended, and shrugged as she faked writing something on the notepad. "You can do what you like. Although, everyone knows that interoffice romances can be tricky and—"

Lauren was startled when he touched her arm gently. Mesmerized, she turned to face him. Side by side, hips

against the desk, there was barely a foot between them. She tilted her head back and met his eyes. His gaze traveled over her face, inspecting every feature before settling on her mouth. It was intensely erotic, and her knees quivered. The hand on her arm moved upward a little, skimming over her skin, sending jolts of electricity through her blood.

Her lips parted...waiting...anticipating...

It had been so long since she'd been kissed. Too long. And she knew *he* knew that was what she was thinking.

"I'm not going to kiss you," he said softly, his gaze still on her mouth. "Even though I want to, and it would certainly stop you talking nonsense about Megan."

"All I—"

"Shh," he said, and placed two fingertips against her lips. "Keep talking, and I *will* kiss you."

Lauren knew she had to move. Because if she didn't, sanity would be lost, and she'd fling against him and forget every promise she'd made to herself. The fleeting attraction she'd experienced the first time they'd met six months ago had morphed into heady, hot desire that was slowly becoming all she could think about.

And it's not what I want....

Mindless passion was dangerous.

And if I'm not careful, I'm going to get swept up in it all over again....

"You promised," she reminded him on a whisper. "Remember? No making passes."

"I know what I promised," he said, and rubbed his thumb against her jaw. "I did warn you I could be a jerk, though."

Lauren took a deep breath. "You know what I want."

"And you seem to be of a mind to tell me what I want," he said, still touching her lips. "Which is not, I might add, a teenager with a silly crush."

"She's more woman than teenager, and—"

He groaned. "You really do talk too much."

If the automatic doors hadn't whooshed open, Lauren was certain he would have kissed her as if there was no tomorrow. And she would have kissed him back. Vow or not.

"Gabe," Mimi's squeaky voice called frantically from the doorway. "I need your help."

He dropped his hand and stepped back. "What's wrong?"

"There's a lady on the beach who's had a fall, and I think she might have broken her ankle."

Gabe moved away from her and grabbed the first-aid bag. "Okay...show me where."

He was out the door in a flash, and Lauren took a few seconds to get her feet to move and follow. By the time she reached the first crest of the sandbank, Gabe was already attending to the elderly woman. He was crouched at her side, one hand on her shoulder and asking her questions while Mimi unzipped the first-aid bag.

Lauren moved closer to assist. And took about ten seconds to realize that Gabe didn't need her help. He knew exactly what he was doing.

It wasn't broken, but his patient, Faye, had a severe sprain and probably tendon damage, and as he wrapped her ankle, he instructed Megan to call for the ambulance. The woman was well into her eighties, and her tender skin was bruising quickly. She needed X-rays and the type of painkillers he couldn't administer.

Gabe wrapped her in a thermal blanket to ensure she didn't go into shock and stayed with her and her equally elderly husband until the paramedics arrived. The beach was busy, and he sent Megan back onto patrol and remained with the couple...excruciatingly aware that Lauren was watching his every move.

Once the ambulance arrived, it was about a fifteen-minute process to get Faye from the beach and safely tucked inside the vehicle. Her husband chose to travel in the am-

bulance, and Gabe accepted the old man's car keys for safekeeping and was told their grandson would be along to collect the car within the hour.

His shift was over by three o'clock, but he lingered for a while to ensure the remaining bathers were staying between the boundary flags, as the water was choppy. Megan took off for home, and Gabe headed back to the clubhouse to lock up. He found Lauren in his office, sitting at the desk and writing in her notebook. He watched her for a moment, thinking that an hour earlier, he'd been on the brink of kissing her. It would have been a big mistake. Definitely.

"Did you get your work done?" he asked when he came into the room.

"Yes," she replied and collected her things together.

"I gather this benefit is important?"

She nodded. "It will raise money for the Big Brothers Big Sisters program. Cameron said you've been working with the program, too."

"A little," he replied, reluctant to tell her any more. Like the fact he volunteered his time to help coach an under-twelve's swimming and lifesaving team twice a week.

"You and Cameron put me to shame."

"How so?"

She shrugged and stood. "He's always been community focused. Not...self-focused. You're like that, too, otherwise you wouldn't be doing this job you're clearly overqualified for, or do things like volunteering with the kids from the Big Brothers program."

Discomfiture raced across his skin. So she knew. "It's nothing, really. Just a couple of hours twice a week."

"It's more than most people do," she qualified. "More than I do."

"You're helping with the benefit," he reminded her. "Raising money for the program is something important."

She shrugged again. "I guess. You know, you were

amazing with that elderly lady. Cameron was right about you…you have a talent for the first-aid side of things in this job."

Gabe's insides crunched. He could have told her the truth in that moment. He could have told her that she was right. But that it wasn't talent. It was experience. He could have told her that for ten years he'd worked as a doctor in the E.R. at the finest hospital in Huntington Beach. But if he did, she'd want to know why he left.

Why I quit…

And how did he tell her that? One truth would snowball into another.

And Gabe wasn't ready.

He wasn't ready to admit that an innocent woman and her baby had died on his watch.

Chapter Five

Lauren dropped Jed off at her brother's house on Sunday afternoon. The house sitter was back and would be in residence until Cameron and Grace returned from their honeymoon. It was past five by the time she got home, and by then she only had half an hour to shower, change and prepare an array of snacks for the girls' night she was having with Cassie and Mary-Jayne.

It was impossible to *not* notice the bright yellow car parked at the entrance of Gabe's driveway.

She'd spotted the same vehicle outside the surf club. Megan's car. Obviously.

So what? He can do what he likes.

But Lauren had to force back the swell of jealousy burning through her veins.

She'd never *done* jealous. Not even with Tim. And she certainly wasn't going to waste time thinking about her neighbor and the perky *Mimi* doing *whatever* over the hedge.

When her friends arrived, Lauren headed through the front door to greet them and immediately heard a woman laughing. She noticed that Megan and Gabe were now outside and standing by the yellow car, clearly enjoying one another's company. And her stupid, rotten and completely unjustified jealousy returned with a vengeance. She willed it away with all the strength she could muster. When Cassie and Mary-Jayne reached the porch steps, they must have noticed the scowl on her face, because they both had raised brows and wide smiles on their faces.

"Trouble in paradise?" Cassie asked and walked up the steps.

Her friends knew what had happened at the wedding. They'd called it fate. Kismet. *Providence.* The fact he'd moved in next door simply added fuel to their combined romantic foolishness.

Mary-Jayne blew out a low whistle. "That's some serious competition you have there."

Of course she meant Megan. Young, perky, chirpy… Everything she wasn't. Lauren's scowl deepened. Her friends were teasing, but she felt the sting right through to her bones. For Gabe's no-commitment, casual-sex-only lifestyle, the effervescent Megan was no doubt perfect. She was pretty and uncomplicated. She probably wasn't haunted by memories of a lost love. She almost certainly wasn't looking to settle down and raise a family. So, perfect.

"Glaring at her over the hedge won't make her turn to stone, you know," Mary-Jayne said, and grinned.

Worse luck.

She jabbed her friend playfully in the ribs. "I need a drink," Lauren said as she turned on her heels and followed the two other women back inside.

Ten minutes later they were settled in the living room, a tray of snacks on the coffee table and a glass of wine

in hand. Except for Cassie, who made do with sparkling grape juice.

"Have you heard from Doug?" Lauren asked her pregnant friend as she settled back in the sofa. "Has he warmed to the idea of the baby?"

The fact that Cassie's much older soldier boyfriend hadn't taken the news of her pregnancy very well had become a regularly talked about subject between them. It had been a month since Cassie had told him the news about the baby, and Lauren was concerned for her friend.

"He said we needed to talk about it," Cassie explained, her eyes shadowy. "I know he'll come around and consider this baby a blessing. But I don't want to distract him while he's on a mission."

"He's a total jerk," M.J. said bluntly, and tossed her mass of dark curls. "You know that, right?"

Lauren quickly took the middle ground. Something she often had to do. Cassie was a calm, sweet-natured woman who avoided confrontation and drama, while effervescent M.J. attracted it like a bee to a flower. Lauren figured she was somewhere in between. As different as they were, she knew they shared one common trait—unfailing loyalty to one another and their friendship.

"Perhaps we shouldn't judge him too quickly," she said, and ignored M.J.'s scowl.

"He should be judged," M.J. said, and grunted. "Do you even know where he is at the moment?"

Cassie shook her head. "Not really."

Lauren tapped Cassie's arm. "His brother might know. Perhaps you should—"

"Tanner's in South Dakota," Cassie said quietly. "And he and Doug rarely talk. Besides, Doug will come around. You'll see."

Lauren hoped so, for her friend's sake. And if not, she'd

be there to support Cassie, just as her friends had rallied around her when she'd needed them.

Cassie smiled. "So let's talk about you, not me. What's been going on between you and Mr. Gorgeous from next door?"

"Nothing," Lauren replied, and drank some wine. She wasn't about to tell them about the near-miss kiss at the surf club the previous afternoon. They'd be all over that information in a second. It wasn't as though she really wanted to exclude them. She knew they worried about her. They'd been her rocks after Tim died. And then again when James had walked out. But they didn't really understand her determination to avoid those kinds of feelings…even though they supported her. But Gabe was a complication she didn't need to discuss with her friends. The more time she spent with him, the less she felt she knew.

And she had to get him out of her system once and for all.

Only, she had no idea how she was supposed to do that when he had a habit of invading her thoughts…and her dreams.

It was ironic how much Gabe had come to avoid hospitals. At one time, the four walls of Huntington Beach's largest health-care facility had been his life. But then everything changed. Funny how some lingering fatigue and a small lump in his armpit could so quickly alter his fate.

Biopsy…cancer…surgery…chemo…radiation therapy…

The disease had been caught early, and with a bit of luck he'd been assured of a long life, but that didn't mean he could avoid the necessary follow-up examinations every six months. The specialist asked the usual invasive questions on his visit—questions he'd never considered invasive until he'd been on the other end of the conversation. Being a cancer patient had certainly altered his perspective on

having the right kind of bedside manner. If he did decide
to practice medicine again, he would do it with a renewed
respect for what the sick endured.

If...

Gabe missed his career more than he'd ever imagined
he would. Becoming a doctor had been his dream since he
was twelve years old, and getting into medical school had
been the realization of years of study and hard work. But
things changed. Life changed.

And then one arrogant decision had altered everything.

He'd gone back to work too soon. Everyone around him
said so. His family. His colleagues. His oncologist. But after
a bad reaction to the treatment and medication, and after
six weeks in bed chucking his guts up, he'd had enough.
He was determined to reclaim his life and return to the
job he loved.

Two weeks later a young mother and her baby were dead.

Perhaps technically not his fault, but he knew in his heart
that the blame lay at his feet. Nauseated and tired from that
day's round of treatment, Gabe had left a second-year resident alone in the trauma room for a few minutes and headed
for the bathroom. While he was gone, a patient had been
brought into the E.R. and the young doctor didn't have the
experience to handle the emergency. The young woman,
who was seven months pregnant, had hemorrhaged, and
both she and her unborn child died.

Plagued by guilt, after the inquiry, an undercurrent of
uncertainty had shadowed him and he'd stuck it out for
another month before he bailed on his career, his friends
and his family.

His life as he knew it.

And Crystal Point was as far away from all that as he
could get.

It was a place where he could wrap himself in anonym-
ity. A place where he could forget the past and not feel de-

fined by his illness or the tragedy of that terrible night in the E.R.

"Gabe?"

He stopped beneath the wide doorway of the specialist's rooms. Lauren stood a few feet away. Discomfort crawled along his skin. She was the last person he'd expected to see. And the last person he wanted to see outside the specialist's office.

"Hello," he said quietly, and wondered how to make his getaway.

She came to a stop in front of him. "What are you doing here?"

He took a second and considered all the things he wouldn't say. "What are *you* doing here?"

She frowned. "My friend Cassie works on reception in Radiology. I'm meeting her and Mary-Jayne for lunch."

She had a friend who worked at the hospital? One who might recognize him when he came in for testing? His discomfort turned into an all-out need to get away from her as quickly as possible before she asked more questions. Before she worked things out.

"I have to go," he said, and stepped sideways.

Her hand unexpectedly wrapped around his forearm and she said his name. Her touch was like a cattle brand against his skin, and Gabe fought the impulse to shake her off. Being this close didn't help his determination to stay away from her.

"Is everything okay?" she asked, and glanced up at the signage above his head. The word *oncology* stuck out like a beacon.

Any second now she's going to figure it out.

Dread licked along his spine. The thought of Lauren looking at him with sympathy or pity or something worse cut through to his bones. "Everything's fine."

She didn't look convinced. But Gabe wasn't about to

start spilling his guts. He wanted to get out of there as fast as he could.

She half smiled and then spoke. "I'm just surprised to see you here. Are you visiting someone or—"

"Last I looked I wasn't obligated to inform you of my movements."

His unkind words lingered in the space between them, and he wanted to snatch them back immediately. Even though he knew it was better this way. For them both. He knew she was struggling with the attraction between them, just like he was. He knew she wanted someone different... someone who could give her the picket-fence life she craved. And that wasn't him. She'd lost the man she'd loved to cancer. Of course she wouldn't want to risk that again.

"I'm...sorry," she said quietly. "I shouldn't have asked. I was only—"

"Forget it, Lauren," Gabe said sharply, and saw her wince as he pulled his arm away. "And I...I didn't mean to snap at you." The elevator nearby dinged and opened, and he wanted to dive inside. "I have to go. I'll see you later."

Gabe moved away and stepped through the doors. Away from her. And away from the questions in her eyes.

But by the end of the week, he was so wound up he felt as though he needed to run a marathon to get her out of his system. He needed to, though...because he liked being around her too much. He liked the soft sound of her voice and the sweet scent of her perfume. He liked the way she chewed her bottom lip when she was deep in thought. He liked how her eyes darkened to a deep caramel when she was annoyed, and wondered how they'd look if she was aroused. He wondered lots of things...but *nothing* could happen.

She'd lost her fiancé to cancer...making it the red flag of the century.

And Gabe had no intention of getting seriously involved

with anyone. Not until he was sure he could offer that someone a real future. He had a five-year plan. If he stayed
cancer-free for five years, he'd consider a serious relationship. Maybe even marriage. Until then, Gabe knew what
he had to do. He had to steer clear of commitment. He had
to steer clear of Lauren.

Cameron returned from his honeymoon midweek and
stopped by the surf club Saturday morning just as Gabe
was finishing off first aid to a pair of siblings who'd become entangled with a jellyfish. He reassured their concerned mother her children would be fine, and then joined
his friend at the clubhouse.

"Busy morning?" Cameron asked, looking tanned and
relaxed from his weeks in the Mediterranean, as he flaked
into a chair.

"The usual summer holiday nonsense," he replied. "Sun-
burn and dehydration mostly."

Cameron nodded. "Thanks for helping my sister out with
Jed. She told me what happened to her door."

Gabe shrugged. "No problem," he said quickly, and tried
to ignore the way his pulse sped up. He didn't want to talk
to his friend about Lauren. He didn't want to *think* about
Lauren. "Gotta get back to work."

Cameron stood and shook his head. "Thanks again. And
don't forget to swing by my folks' house tonight, around
six," he reminded him. "My beautiful wife is trying out her
newly learned Greek cooking skills in my mother's kitchen,
so it should be mighty interesting."

Gabe experienced an unexpected twinge of envy. His
friend looked ridiculously happy. Cameron had the same
dopey expression on his face that Scott permanently carried these days. He was pretty sure he'd never looked like
that. Not even when he'd been with Mona.

"Sure," he said, thinking the last thing he wanted to do

was spend an evening at Lauren's parents' home, because he knew Lauren would be there, too. "See you then."

When he got home that afternoon, he changed into jeans and a T-shirt and started painting the main bedroom. It kept him busy until five-thirty. Then he showered, dressed and grabbed his car keys.

When he reversed out of the yard, he realized that Lauren was doing the same thing. Their vehicles pulled up alongside one another at the end of their driveways. He stopped, as did she. Their windows rolled down simultaneously.

"Hi," she said. "Are you going to my—"

"Yes," he said, cutting her off.

"My brother mentioned you were coming. Probably foolish to take both cars?"

She was right. He should have offered to drive her. But he hadn't seen her since their meeting at the hospital. He'd behaved badly. Rudely. Gabe nodded. "Probably."

"So…" Her voice trailed. "Yours or mine?"

Gabe sucked in some air. "I'll drive."

Her mouth twisted. "Be back in a minute."

He watched as she moved her car back up the driveway, got out and came around the passenger side of his Jeep. When she got in, the flowery scent of her perfume hit his senses. She buckled up and settled her gaze to the front.

"Ready?" he asked.

"Yes."

He backed the car onto the road and then came to a halt. He had something to say to her. "Lauren, I want to apologize again for being so dismissive the other day." He invented an excuse. "I was late for an appointment and—"

She waved a hand. "Like you said, not my business."

Gabe was tempted to apologize again. But he didn't. He nodded instead. "Okay."

She flashed him a brief look. "Just so you know, when we turn up together my mother is going to think it's a date."

"It's not, though," he said, and drove down the street. "Right?"

"Right," she replied.

Gabe reconsidered going to the Jakowskis'. He didn't want Lauren's mother getting any ideas. Or Cameron. Whatever he was feeling for Lauren, he had to get it under control. And fast.

Lauren knew the moment she walked into her mother's kitchen that she was going to get the third degree. Irene had greeted them at the door, explained that Cameron had been called into work and would be joining them later and quickly shuffled Gabe toward the games room to hang out with her father.

Her mother ushered Lauren directly into the kitchen. Grace was there, standing behind the wide granite counter, looking radiant. Her new sister-in-law was exceptionally beautiful. In the past, she'd always considered the other woman frosty and a little unfriendly, but Lauren had warmed toward Grace since it was clear her brother was crazy in love with her, and she with him.

Lauren stepped in beside Grace and began topping her mother's signature baked lemon cheesecake, a task she'd done countless times. Her sister-in-law remained silent, but her mother wasn't going to be held back.

"It's nice that Gabe could join us this evening. He really is quite handsome," Irene said as she busied herself pulling salad items from the refrigerator. "Don't you think? And such a lovely accent."

Lauren's gaze flicked up briefly. *"Matka,"* she warned, and half smiled. "Don't."

But she knew her mother wouldn't give up. "Just stating the obvious."

"His ancestors are Roman gods," Lauren said, and grinned. "So of course he looks good."

Irene laughed softly. "That's the spirit…indulge my matchmaking efforts."

"Well, there's little point fighting it," Lauren said with a sigh. "Even though you're wasting your time in this case."

"Do you think?" her mother inquired, still grinning as she grabbed a tray of appetizers. "Don't be too quick to say no, darling. He might just be the best of both worlds," Irene said, and smiled. "When you're done decorating that cake, can you grab the big tureen from the cabinet in the front living room?"

Lauren smiled. "Sure," she replied, and waited until her mother left the room before speaking to her sister-in-law. "See what I have to put up with?"

"She just cares about you," Grace replied, and covered the potato dish she'd prepared. "And he seems…nice."

He is nice. That was the problem. He was also sexy and gorgeous and not the *settle-down* kind of man she was looking for. He'd said as much. And she'd had nice before. Tim had been the nicest, most sincere man she'd ever known. Even James had been nice in his own charming, flirtatious way. The kind of nice she wanted now didn't come with a handsome face and the ability to shoot her libido up like a rocket.

The best of both worlds…

What exactly did her mother mean? That Gabe was attractive, charming, funny and smart and just what any sensible woman would call the *perfect package?*

Too perfect. No one was without flaws. Secrets.

Lauren placed the cheesecake in the refrigerator and excused herself. The big living room at the front of the house was rarely used. It housed her mother's treasures, like the twin glass lamps that had been in their family for four generations, and the cabinet of exquisite crockery and dinner-

ware. Lauren stopped by the mantelpiece and stared at the family photographs lining the shelf. There were more pictures on the long cabinet at the other end of the room. Her mother loved taking pictures.

She fingered the edge of one frame and her insides crunched. It was a snapshot of herself and Tim. He looked so relaxed and cheerful in the photo. They were smiling, pressed close together, his blond hair flopping over his forehead. Had he lived, he would have been soon celebrating his thirtieth birthday. She looked at his face again. It was Lauren's favorite picture of him. Memories surged through her. Memories of love. And regret. And…anger. But she quickly pushed the feeling away. Anger had no place in her heart. Not when it came to Tim.

"You looked happy."

Lauren swiveled on her heels. Gabe stood behind her. Engrossed in her memories, she hadn't heard his approach. "Sorry?"

"In the picture," he said, and stepped closer. "You looked happy together."

"We were," she said, intensely conscious of his closeness. "That's…Tim," she explained softly and pointed to the photograph. "He was always happy. Even when he was facing the worst of it, somehow he never lost his sense of humor."

Gabe's eyes darkened. "Did he pass away quickly?"

She nodded. "In the end…yes. He died just a few weeks before we were due to be married."

"And then you married someone else?"

"Not quite two years later," she replied and immediately wondered why she was admitting such things to him. "It was a big mistake."

Gabe nodded a little. "Because you didn't love him?"

"Exactly," she said, and sucked in a short breath.

"There must have been something that made you marry him?"

Lauren's skin grew hotter. "Sex."

His blistering gaze was unwavering. "That's all?"

"I'd had love," she admitted, so aware of his closeness she could barely breathe. "And I'd lost it. When I met James, I thought attraction would be enough."

"But it wasn't?"

She sighed. "No."

"And now you don't want that, either?" he asked.

Lauren raised a shoulder. "I don't expect anyone to understand."

"Actually," he said quietly. "I do. You lost the love of your life, then settled for something that left you empty, and now you want to find that no-risk, no-hurt, middle road."

Middle road? Could he read her mind? "That's right. I married my ex-husband after only knowing him for three months. It was a foolish impulse and one I regret…for his sake and mine."

Gabe looked at the mantelpiece. "Which explains why there are no pictures of him."

"My mother was never a fan of James," she said, and felt his scrutiny through to her bones. "Once we divorced, the wedding pictures came down." Lauren looked down to her feet and then back up to his gaze. "Ah…what are you doing in here? I thought you were out on the back patio with my dad."

"I was," he replied, and grinned fractionally. "But your mother sent me on a mercy dash to help you carry some kind of heavy dish."

Lauren rolled her eyes and pointed to the tureen in the cabinet. "My mother is meddling."

He smiled, like he knew exactly what she meant. "To what end?"

Lauren raised a shoulder. "Can't you guess? I told you she'd think this was a date."

His gaze widened. "Should I be worried?"

She laughed a little. "That my mother has her sights set on you? Probably."

Gabe laughed, too, and the sound warmed her right through to the blood in her veins. He was so…likable. So gorgeous. And it scared her. With James, she'd jumped in, libido first, uncaring of the consequences. Still grieving the loss of the man she'd loved, Lauren had found temporary solace in arms that had soon left her feeling empty and alone. Although she'd thought him good-looking and charming, she'd realized soon after they'd married that they had very little in common. But the attraction she had for Gabe was different. The more time she spent with him, the less superficial it felt. Which put her more at risk.

"I shall consider myself warned," he said, and chuckled.

Lauren walked toward the cabinet and opened the door. "Thanks for being so understanding," she said, still grinning.

"I, too, have a meddling, albeit well-meaning mother who wants to see me…shall we say, *settled.* So I understand your position."

For a second, she wondered what else they had in common. He clearly came from a close family, as she did. "Doesn't she know you're not interested in commitment?"

His gaze locked with hers. "I don't think she quite believes me."

Lauren's breath caught. "Have you…"

"Have I what?"

She shrugged, trying to be casual but churning inside. "Have you changed your mind about that?"

Lauren couldn't believe she'd asked the question. And couldn't believe she wanted to know. Her elbow touched his arm and the contact sent heat shooting across her skin.

She should have pulled away. But Lauren remained where she was, immobilized by the connection simmering between them.

"No," he said after a long stretch of silence. "I haven't."

Of course, it was what she needed to hear. Gabe wasn't what she wanted. Because he made her feel too much. He made her question the choice she'd made to remain celibate until she found someone to share her life with. He didn't want what she wanted.

He's all wrong for me....

Even though being beside him, alone and in the solitude of the big room, seemed so unbelievably normal, she was tempted to lean closer and invite him to kiss her. His gaze shifted from her eyes to her mouth, and Lauren sucked in a shallow breath. Her lips parted slightly and he watched with such searing intensity, her knees threatened to give way. There was heat between them, the kind that came before a kiss. The kind of heat that might lead to something more.

"Gabe…" She said his name on a sigh.

"We would be crazy to start something," he warned, unmoving and clearly reading her thoughts.

"I know," she agreed softly.

Crazy or not, she was strangely unsurprised when he took hold of her hand and gently rubbed his thumb along her palm. He was still watching her, still looking at her mouth.

"Do you have any idea how much I want to kiss you right now?"

She shivered at his question, despite the warmth racing across her skin. Lauren nodded, feeling the heat between them rise up a notch. "Do you have any idea how much I want you to kiss me right now?"

His hand wrapped around hers. She was staring up, waiting, thinking about how she hadn't been kissed for such a long time. And thinking how Gabe had somehow, in a matter of weeks, become the one man whose kiss she longed for.

Chapter Six

Gabe could have kissed her right then, right there. He could have lost himself in the softness of her lips and sweet taste of her mouth. He could have forgotten about his determination to keep away from her and give in to the desire he experienced whenever she was near. And he would have. But a loud crash followed by an equally loud shout pushed them apart immediately. The dish from the china cabinet was quickly forgotten as they both hurried from the room.

When they reached the kitchen, he saw there was glass and water on the floor and also a pile of tattered flowers. Lauren's father was sitting on the ground, knees half-curled to his chest.

"Dad!" Lauren gasped as she rushed to his side.

Irene and Grace came through the doorway and stood worriedly behind Gabe as he quickly moved between them to settle beside the older man. Franciszek Jakowski was holding up a seriously bleeding hand, and Gabe quickly

snatched up a tea towel from the countertop and wrapped it around his palm.

"I knocked the darn vase off the counter," Franciszek explained as Gabe hauled him to his feet. "Cut myself when I fell."

"Can you walk?" Gabe asked, knowing he needed to look at the wound immediately.

Franciszek winced as he put weight on his left foot. "Not so good."

He looked at Lauren. "Hold your father's hand up to help with the bleeding, and I'll get him to a chair."

She did as he asked, and Gabe hooked an arm around the other man's shoulder and soon got him settled onto the kitchen chair. Blood streamed down his arm and splattered on Gabe's shirt. He undid the towel and examined Franciszek's hand. The cut was deep and would need stitches. Irene disappeared and quickly returned with a first-aid kit. Gabe cleaned and dressed the wound, conscious of the scrutiny of the three women hovering close by. Within minutes, he also had Franciszek's left ankle wrapped with an elastic bandage.

"The cut definitely needs stitches," he said, and wiped his hands on a cloth Lauren passed him. "And it looks like you've only sprained your ankle, but an X-ray wouldn't hurt just to be sure."

Irene extolled her gratitude and was on the telephone immediately, making an appointment to see their local doctor within the next half hour.

"I'll drive you," Lauren volunteered, but her mother quickly vetoed that idea.

"Grace can drive us," she said, and looked toward her daughter-in-law, who nodded instantly. "You can stay and clean up. And I need you to keep an eye on dinner. We won't be too long."

"That's for sure," Franciszek agreed cheerfully, although Gabe was pretty sure the older man was in considerable pain. He patted Gabe's shoulder. "Thanks for the doctoring, son. Much appreciated."

Gabe's stomach sank. Being reminded of who he was, even though no one but his family knew the truth, hit him like a fist of shame between the shoulder blades. He glanced at Lauren and then looked away. There were questions in her eyes. Questions he had no intention of answering.

It took several minutes to get Franciszek into the car, and when Gabe returned, Lauren was in the kitchen, picking up pieces of shattered glass from the floor. She was concentrating on her task, looking shaken and pale.

"Are you okay?"

She glanced up. "Just worried about my dad."

"He'll be fine."

Her small nose wrinkled. "Thanks to you," she said as she rose to her feet and walked around the countertop. "You might want to consider switching careers."

His gut sank. "What?"

"You'd make a good paramedic," she said, and grabbed a banister brush from the cupboard beneath the sink. "You clearly have a knack for it. You know, I have a friend who's an admin in emergency services. I could probably arrange for you to—"

"No…but thank you," he said, cutting her off before she said too much about it. "Need some help with this?"

She held his gaze for a moment, and then passed him the broom. "Sure. I'll get the mop and bucket." She propped her hands on her hips and looked at his blood-stained shirt. "I'll find you something to wear and you can pop that shirt in the machine before it permanently stains. I think Cameron has some clothes in one of the guest rooms. I'll go and check."

She disappeared, and Gabe stared after her. Guilt pressed

down on his shoulders. He wanted to tell her the truth about himself. But one would lead to another and then another. And what was the point? There were already too many questions in her lovely brown eyes.

When she returned with the mop and bucket, she placed a piece of clothing on the table. "I'll finish up here. You can go and change."

He met her gaze. "Okay."

Gabe left the room and headed for the laundry. Once there, he stripped off his soiled shirt and dumped it in the washing machine. He added liquid, cranked on the start switch and rested his behind on the edge of the sink. Then he expelled a long breath.

Damn.

He wanted to kiss her so much. He wanted to touch her. He wanted to feel her against him and stroke her soft skin. He wanted to forget every promise he'd made to himself about waiting to see if his illness returned before he'd consider being in a relationship. But it wouldn't be fair to any woman. More than that, it wouldn't be fair to Lauren. He couldn't ask her to risk herself. He *wouldn't*. He'd seen firsthand what it had done to his mom when his father had battled cancer for three years. He'd watched his mom lose the light in her eyes and the spirit in her heart. He'd watched her grieve and cry and bury the man she'd loved.

And Lauren had been there, too. He'd heard the pain in her voice when she'd spoken of her lost love. It should have been enough to send him running.

She thought he'd make a good paramedic? The irony wasn't hard to miss. There were questions in her eyes, and they were questions he didn't want to answer. But if he kept doing this, if he kept being close to her, he would be forced to tell her everything.

And admitting how he'd bailed on his life and career wasn't an option.

Pull yourself together and forget her.

He needed to leave. And he would have if Lauren hadn't chosen that moment to walk into the laundry room.

When Lauren crossed the threshold, she stopped dead in her tracks. Gabe stood by the sink in the small room with the fresh shirt in his hands. And naked from the waist up. He turned to face her.

It had been so long since she'd been this close to a man's bare skin. And because it was Gabe, he was thoroughly mesmerizing, as she'd known he would be. She'd known his skin would look like satin stretched over steel and that his broad shoulders and arms would be well defined and muscular. The smattering of dark hair on his chest tapered down in a line and disappeared into the low waistband of his jeans, and Lauren's breath caught in her throat.

His gaze instantly met hers, and she didn't miss the darkening blue eyes and faint pulse beating in his cheek. Somehow, she moved closer, and when Lauren finally found her voice, they were barely feet apart.

She dropped the bucket and mop. "I…I'm sorry…I didn't realize you were still in here."

Heat swirled between them, coiling around the small room, and she couldn't have moved even if she wanted to. She tried to avert her gaze. Tried and failed. He had such smooth skin, and her fingers itched with the sudden longing to reach out and touch him.

"You…" Her voice cracked, and she swallowed. "You were right with what you said before. We'd be…crazy…to start something…to start imagining we could…"

Her words trailed off, and still he stared at her, holding her gaze with a hypnotic power she'd never experienced before. Color spotted her cheeks, and she quickly turned and made for the doorway. Only she couldn't step forward because Gabe's hands came out and gently grasped her shoul-

ders. She swallowed hard as he moved in close behind her and said her name in that soft, sexy way she was becoming so used to. The heat from his body seared through her thin shirt, and Lauren's temperature quickly spiked. His hands moved down her arms and linked with hers. She felt his soft breath near her nape, and his chest pressed intimately against her shoulders.

His arms came around her and Lauren pushed back. One hand rested on her hip, the other he placed on her rib cage. The heat between them ramped up and created a swirling energy in the small room. Her head dropped back, and she let out a heavy sigh as his fingertips trailed patterns across the shirt. It was an intensely erotic moment, and she wanted to turn in his arms and push against him. She wanted his kiss, his touch, his heat and everything else. She wanted him to plunder her mouth over and over and then more. Flesh against flesh, sweat against sweat. She wanted his body over her, around her, inside her. She wanted *him*... and not only his body. Lauren tilted her head, inviting him to touch the delicate skin at the base of her neck with his mouth. But he didn't. Instead, Gabe continued to touch her rib cage with skillful, seductive fingers, never going too high and barely teasing the underside of her breasts.

She could feel him hard against her. He was aroused and not hiding the fact. Lauren moved her arms back and planted her hands on his thighs. She dug her nails against the denim and urged him closer. His touch was so incredibly erotic, and she groaned low in her throat. Finally, he kissed her nape, softly, gently, and electricity shimmered across her skin.

"Lauren," he whispered against her ear as his mouth trailed upward. "I'm aching to make love to you."

Lauren managed a vague nod and was about to turn in his arms and beg him to kiss her and make love to her when

she heard a door slam. The front door. Seconds later, she heard her brother's familiar voice calling out a greeting.

Gabe released her gently and she stepped forward, dragging air through her lungs. "I should go."

"Good idea," he said softly as he grabbed the shirt and pulled it quickly over his head. "I should probably stay here for a minute."

She nodded and willed some serious movement into her legs and was back in the main hallway seconds later. Cameron, dressed in his regulation police-officer uniform, greeted her with a brief hug and ruffled her hair.

"Hey, kid…what's happening?" he asked once they were in the kitchen and saw the pan of broken glass on the countertop.

She quickly filled him in about their father's mishap, and once she was done, he immediately called Grace. Her brother was still on the phone when Gabe walked into the room. Her body still hummed with memories of his touch, and their gaze connected instantly. If Cameron hadn't turned up, she was sure they'd be making love that very minute. And it would have been a big mistake. When the moment was over, there would be regret and recrimination, and she'd hate herself for being so weak.

When her brother ended his call, he explained that their father was being triaged, and that they'd be home as soon as he was released. In fact, they returned close to an hour and a half later. By then, Lauren had shuffled the men out of the kitchen and finished preparing dinner.

It turned out that Gabe was right. Her father had needed stitches for his hand, and his foot was only sprained. By the time they settled her dad at the head of the table, crutches to one side, it was nearly nine o'clock. Lauren was seated next to Gabe and felt his closeness as if it was a cloak draped across her shoulders.

Once dinner was over, she headed back to the kitchen

with Grace and began cleaning up. Gabe and her brother joined them soon after, and Grace tossed a tea towel to each of them.

"Idle hands," her sister-in-law said, and grinned when Cameron complained. "Get to work."

Lauren laughed and dunked her hands into a sink full of soapy water. Like with everything he did, Gabe ignored Cameron's whining and attended the task with an effortless charm that had both Lauren and Grace smiling. It would, she decided, be much better if he had the charisma of a rock. But no such luck. Aside from the insane chemistry that throbbed between them, Lauren liked him so much it was becoming impossible to imagine she could simply dismiss her growing feelings. Sexual attraction was one thing, emotional attraction another thing altogether. It was also hard to dismiss how her mother, Grace and even her brother watched their interaction with subtle, yet keen interest.

By the time they left, it was past eleven o'clock, and then a quarter past the hour when Gabe pulled his truck into his driveway. She got out, and he quickly came around the side of the vehicle.

"Well, thanks for the lift," she said, and tucked her tote under her arm.

He touched her elbow. "I'll see you to your door."

"There's no need," she said quickly.

"Come on," he said, and began walking down the driveway, ignoring her protest.

Lauren followed and stepped in beside him as they rounded the hedge that separated their front lawns. He opened the gate and stood aside to let her pass. By the time she'd walked up the path and onto the small porch, she was so acutely aware of him she could barely hold her keys steady.

Open the door. Say good-night. Get inside. Easy.

Lauren slid the key in the screen door and propped it

open with her elbow while she unlocked the front door. "Um…thanks again," she said, and turned on her heels. "And thanks for what you did for my dad. I'm glad you were there to—"

"Lauren?"

She stilled, clutching her tote, hoping he wouldn't come closer. Praying he wouldn't kiss her. "We…we need to forget what happened tonight," she said in a voice that rattled in her throat. "We agreed it would be crazy to—"

"Nothing really happened," he said, cutting her off. "Did it?"

Lauren took a breath. "Well, what *almost* happened. I've made a vow, a promise to myself…and it's a promise I intend to keep. And I'm never going to find what I want if I get drawn deeper into this…this attraction I have for you. We both know it won't go anywhere other than your bed, and I'm not prepared to settle for just sex. Not again."

He didn't move. But he stared at her. He stared so deeply, so intensely, she could barely breathe. The small porch and dim light overhead created extreme intimacy. If she took one tiny step she would be pressed against him.

"You're right," he said, and moved back a little. "You shouldn't settle for sex. You should find that middle road you want, Lauren, with someone who can give you the relationship you deserve."

Then he was gone. Down the steps and through the gate and quickly out of view. Lauren stayed where she was for several minutes. Her chest was pounding. Her stomach was churning. Her head was spinning.

And her heart was in serious danger.

Gabe knew he was right to leave Lauren alone. He hadn't seen her all week. Deliberately. He left for work earlier than she did and returned home before her small car pulled into

the driveway each afternoon. Not seeing her helped. A lot. Or more like a little. Or not at all.

Unfortunately, not seeing her seemed to put him in a bad mood.

Something his cousin took pleasure in pointing out on Thursday afternoon when Gabe dropped by the B and B.

"You know, you'll never get laid if you don't ask her out," Scott said with a wide grin, and passed him a beer.

"Shut up," he said, and cranked the lid off.

His cousin laughed. "Hah. Sucker. Just admit your five-year plan is stupid and that you're crazy about Lauren."

Gabe gripped the bottle. "I know what I'm doing."

"Sure you do," Scott shot back. "You're hibernating like a bear because you don't want to admit you like her. That's why your mom has been calling my mom and my mom has been calling me. You haven't been taking any calls from your family for the past two weeks."

"They worry too much," he remarked, and shrugged. "They think I'm going to relapse and die a horrible death. And maybe I will. All I know is I don't want to put anyone in the middle of that. Not anyone. Not Lauren."

"Maybe you should let her decide that for herself."

"Will you just…" Gabe paused, ignored the curse teetering on the end of his tongue and drank some more beer. "Stop talking."

Scott shrugged. "Just trying to see my best friend happy."

"I'm happy enough," he shot back. "So lay off."

His cousin laughed, clearly unperturbed by his bad temper. "You know, not every woman is going to run for the hills if you get sick again."

"Mona didn't run," Gabe reminded the other man. "I broke it off with her."

Scott shrugged again. "Another example of you needing to control everything, right?"

Tired of the same old argument, Gabe finished his beer and stood. "I have to bail."

"Hot date?"

Gabe grabbed his keys off the table. "A wall that won't paint itself."

"Sounds riveting," Scott said drily. "Renovating that house won't keep you warm at night, old buddy."

His cousin was right, but he had no intention of admitting that. He took off and was home within a few minutes. Once he'd dropped his keys on the hall stand, he rounded out his shoulders. Pressure cramped his back, and he let out a long breath. He needed to burn off some of the tension clinging to his skin. There was easily over an hour of sunlight left, so he changed into his running gear and headed off down the street.

Gabe reached The Parade quickly. The long road stretched out in front of him. He crossed the wide grassy verge and headed for the pathway leading to the beach in one direction and to the north end of the small town to the other. He vetoed the beach and headed left, striding out at an even pace and covering the ground quickly. It was quiet at this end of town. Without the holiday park, surf club and kiosk there was only a scattering of new homes, and the waterfront was more rock than sand. He spotted a pair of snorkelers preparing to dive close to the bank and waved as another runner jogged past.

Up ahead, he spotted someone sitting alone on one of the many bench seats that were placed along the line of the pathway. It was Lauren. He'd recognize her blond hair anywhere. He slowed his pace and considered turning around. But he kept moving, slowing only when she was about twenty feet away. She was looking out toward the ocean, deep in thought, hands crossed in her lap. An odd feeling pressed into his chest. As though he suddenly couldn't get

enough air in his lungs. God, she was beautiful. He stopped a few feet from the seat and said her name.

Her head turned immediately. "Oh, hi."

She was paler than usual. Sadder. The tightness in his chest amplified tenfold.

He stopped closer. "Are you okay?"

"Sure," she said quietly, unmoving.

Gabe wasn't convinced. He moved around the bench and sat down beside her. "I'm not buying. What's up?"

"Nothing," she insisted.

"It's four-thirty on a Thursday afternoon. You're not at the store," he said pointedly. "You're sitting here alone staring out at the sea."

She shrugged a little. "I'm just thinking."

He knew that. "About what?"

She drew in a shallow breath. "Tim."

Of course. Her lost love. "I'm sorry, I shouldn't have—"

"It's his birthday," she said quietly, and turned her gaze back to the ocean. "I always come here on this day. It's where he proposed to me."

Gabe immediately felt like he was intruding on an intensely private moment. Big-time. He got up to leave, but her hand came out and touched his arm.

"It's okay," she said, her voice so quiet and strained it made his insides twinge. "I could probably use the company."

"Do you usually?" he asked. "Have company, I mean?"

She shook her head and dropped her hand. "Not usually."

Gabe crossed his arms to avoid the sudden urge to hold her. He looked out at the sea. "You still miss him?"

"Yes," she said on a sigh. "He was one of the kindest people I've ever known. We never argued. Never had a cross word. Well, that is until he…"

Her words trailed, and Gabe glanced sideways. "Until he what?"

She shrugged again. "Until he was dying," she said, so softly he could barely hear. "It sounds strange to even say such a thing. But I didn't find out he was sick until a few weeks before the wedding."

"His illness progressed that quickly?"

She shook her head. "Not exactly. He knew for over six months. He just didn't tell me."

Gabe's stomach sank. But he understood the other man's motives. The unrelenting guilt. The unwanted pity. Gabe knew those feelings well. "He was trying to protect you."

"So he said. But all I felt was…angry."

The way she spoke, the way her voice cracked and echoed with such heavy pain made Gabe wonder if it was the first time she'd admitted it out loud. Her next words confirmed it.

"Sorry," she said quietly. "I don't ever whine about this stuff to anyone. And I don't mean to criticize Tim. He was a good man. The best. When we met we clicked straight-away. We were friends for a few months, and then we fell in love. Even though it wasn't fireworks and insane chem-istry and all that kind of thing."

"But it was what you wanted?" Gabe asked quietly, his heart pounding.

"Yes," she replied. "But then he was gone…and I was alone."

Gabe uncrossed his arms and grasped her hand, hold-ing it tightly within his own. She didn't pull away. She didn't move. Silence stretched between them, and Gabe quickly realized that despite every intention he'd had, his attraction for Lauren had morphed into something more. Something that compelled him to offer comfort, despite the fact he had to fight the sudden umbrage coursing through his blood when she spoke about the man she'd loved. He wasn't sure how to feel about it. He wasn't sure he should even acknowledge it.

Thankfully, a few seconds later, she slid her hand from his and rested it in her lap. Gabe sucked in some air and tried to avoid thinking about how rattled he'd become by simply sitting beside her.

"You don't like being alone?"

"No," she replied. "Not really. I guess that's why I married James. And exactly why I shouldn't have." She took a long breath. "I wanted the wedding I was denied when Tim passed away."

"And did you get it?"

She nodded. "Yes. I had the same venue, the same guests and the same themed invitations." Her voice lowered. "I even wore the same dress I'd planned on wearing two years earlier."

The regret and pain in her voice was unmistakable, and Gabe remained silent.

"When I was engaged to Tim, I was so wrapped up in the idea of being married," she admitted on a heavy sigh. "Up to that point my life, my world, had been about the store and weddings and marriage and getting that happily ever after. I was so absorbed by that ideal, I didn't realize that he was sick…that he was *dying*. When he was gone, I felt lost…and I turned that grief into a kind of self-centered resentment. Afterward, I was so angry at Tim for not telling me he was ill. And then James came along, and he was handsome and charming and…and *healthy*. Suddenly, I glimpsed an opportunity to have everything I'd ever wanted."

Gabe's chest constricted. Any subconscious consideration he'd ever given to pursuing Lauren instantly disappeared. She was looking for a healthy, perfect mate. Not a cancer survivor. "But you still want that, right? Even though your marriage didn't work out?"

"I want my happily ever after," she confessed. "I want someone to curl up to at night. I want someone to make me

coffee in the morning. And I really want children. It doesn't have to be wrapped up in physical attraction or even some great love story. In fact, I'd prefer it if it wasn't. It just has to be real…honest."

Her words cut him to the quick. "I hope you find what you're looking for," he said, and got to his feet. "I'll walk you home."

"That's okay," she said, and twisted her hands together. "I think I'll stay here for a while longer."

"Sure."

"And, Gabe," she said as he moved to turn away. "Thanks for listening. I needed a friend today."

He nodded. "Okay."

On the run back home, Gabe could think of only one thing. Lauren had needed a friend. The thing was, he didn't want to be her friend. He wanted more. Much more. And he couldn't have it.

Not with his past illness shadowing him like an albatross.

He was broken physically. She was broken emotionally.

And he was stunned to realize how damned lonely that suddenly made him feel.

Chapter Seven

With the benefit at the community center only hours away, Lauren really didn't have time to dwell on how she'd literally poured her heart out to Gabe just days earlier. It was better she didn't. Better…but almost impossible. Her dreams had been plagued by memories of all she'd lost. Of Tim. And more. She dreamed about Gabe, too. Dreams that kept her tossing and turning for hours. Dreams that made her wake up feeling lethargic and uneasy.

But she had to forget Gabe for the moment. Tonight was about the benefit. Her sister-in-law had done an amazing job organizing everything. It was a black-tie event, catered by the best restaurant in Bellandale. On the lawn outside the building, a huge marquee had been set up to accommodate a silent auction of items ranging from art to fashion and jewelry and a variety of vacation destinations. Under a separate marquee, there were tables and chairs set out for dinner, and a dance floor. There was also a band in place to provide entertainment. Inside the building, the runway

was decorated and ready for the models to begin the fashion parade. Lauren stayed behind the scenes, ensuring hair and makeup were on track before the models slipped into their gowns. She'd also changed into a gown—a stunning strapless silk chiffon dress in pale champagne. It was shorter at the front, exposing her legs to just above the knees and then molded tightly over her bust and waist, flaring off down her hips in countless ruffled tiers that swished as she walked. She'd ordered the gown months ago and had never had occasion to wear it. Other than Cameron's recent wedding, it had been too long since she'd dressed up. Too long since she'd felt like making an effort. But tonight was special. The money raised would help several children's charities, including the Big Brothers Big Sisters program that was so important to her brother.

She hadn't seen Gabe but knew he had been there earlier, helping out with the marquees and the staging setup. Avoiding him was her best option. Avoiding him made it possible to function normally. Avoiding him was what she needed to do.

"Lauren?"

She was alone in the foyer of the community center. She'd been checking the stage and working out the music cues with the DJ, who'd since disappeared. The models were upstairs; so were Mary-Jayne and Cassie, as they'd volunteered to help with the gown changes.

Lauren turned on her high heels. Gabe stood by the door. He wore a suit, probably the same one he'd worn to her brother's wedding, and he looked so gorgeous, she had to swallow hard to keep a gasp from leaving her throat.

"Need any help here?" he asked.

Her brows came up. "Changed your mind about strutting on the catwalk?"

He laughed. "Not a chance. But I hear you roped my cousin, Scott, into it."

"Not me," she said, and placed her iPad onto the stage. "He's Mary-Jayne's brother-in-law, so she did all the convincing."

Gabe's gaze rolled over her. "You should be modeling tonight…you look beautiful."

She shrugged. "What? This old thing," she said, and laughed softly. "Thanks. You know, you don't look so bad yourself."

He grinned in that sexy, lopsided way she'd become used to. "So, need any help?" he asked again.

Lauren shook her head. "I don't think so. Grace has everything under control. She's *very* organized."

He chuckled. "You mean the consummate control freak? Yeah, I kinda figured."

Lauren relaxed her shoulders. "Well, it's good to have someone like that at the helm for this kind of event. Actually, I…"

"You…?" he prompted when her words trailed.

"Oh…nothing…I was just thinking how I should apologize for the other day."

"No need," he said quietly.

"It's only that I don't usually talk about those things. It probably sounded like I was blaming Tim for dying. I wasn't," Lauren assured him, unsure why she needed to explain herself. But she did. "Sometimes…sometimes the grief gets in the way."

His eyes darkened and he nodded as if he understood. It struck her as odd how he could do that. It was as though he knew, somehow, the depth and breadth of the pain in her heart.

"I remember how my mom was after my dad died," he said quietly. "I don't think she ever really recovered."

"Sometimes I feel like that," she said. "I feel as if the pain will never ease, that I'll be grieving him forever. And then…and then there are times when I can't remember the

sound of his voice or the touch of his hand." She stopped, immediately embarrassed that she'd said so much. "I don't know why I do that," she admitted. "I don't know why I say this stuff to you. It's not like we're…" She stopped again as color rose up her neck. "The truth is, I'm very confused with how I should feel about you."

"You shouldn't be," he said softly. "We're neighbors. Friends. That's all."

If she hadn't believed he was saying it to put her at ease, Lauren might have been offended. She drew in a long breath then slowly let it out. "After what happened at my parents' house the other night, I think we're both kidding ourselves if we believe that."

"What *almost* happened," he reminded her. "There's no point getting worked up over something that didn't happen, is there?"

Annoyance traveled up her spine. He thought she was overreacting? Imagining more between them than there actually was? She pressed her lips together for a second and gave her growing irritation a chance to pass. It didn't. "Sure. You're right. There's no point. Now, if you don't mind, I have to finish getting ready for the parade."

He didn't budge. "You're angry?"

"I'm busy," she said hotly.

As she went to move past him, one of his arms came up to bar the doorway. "Wait a minute."

Lauren pressed her back against the doorjamb. He was close. Too close. "No. I have to—"

"I'm trying to make this easy for you," he said, cutting her off.

Lauren's gaze narrowed. "I think you're trying to make this easy for yourself."

He moved, and his other arm came up and trapped her in the doorway. "Maybe I am," he admitted softly. "Maybe I'm just crazy scared of you."

Scared? She wouldn't have pegged Gabe to be a man scared of anything. Especially not her. "I don't understand what you—"

"Sure you do," he said, and moved closer. "You feel it, too. Don't you know I can barely keep my hands off you?"

Lauren had to tilt her head to meet his gaze. "So it's just about attraction?" she managed to say in a whisper. "Just…sex."

Their faces were close, and his eyes looked even bluer. Lauren sucked in a shaky breath, feeling the heat rise between them against her will. She wanted to run. She wanted to stay. She wanted to lock the door and strip off her dress and tear the clothes from his body and fall down onto the carpet and make love with him over and over. She wanted him like she'd never wanted any man before.

"I wish it was," he said, and inched closer until their mouths were almost touching. "I wish I didn't like spending time with you. I wish I didn't keep thinking about you every damned minute I'm awake, and could stop dreaming about you every time I go to sleep."

The frustration in his voice was both fascinating and insulting. He wanted her but resented that he did. Thinking of his struggle ramped up her temperature. And it made her mad, too.

"Sorry for the inconvenience," she said with way more bravado than she actually felt.

"Are you?"

She glared, defiant. "You're an ass, Gabe. Right now I wish I'd never met you."

He didn't believe it. Nor did she. He stared at her mouth. Lauren knew he was going to kiss her. And she knew *he knew* she wanted him, too. There was no denying it. No way to hide the desire churning between them.

"My vow…" Her words trailed as she struggled for her good sense. "I promised myself I'd wait until—"

"Forget your vow," he said, cutting off her protest. "Just for right now, stop being so sensible."

A soft sound rattled in her throat, and Gabe drew her closer, wrapping his arms around her as he claimed her lips in a soft, seductive and excruciatingly sweet kiss. She went willingly, pressing her hands to his chest, and she felt his heart thunder beneath her palm. His mouth slanted over hers, teasing, asking and then gently taking. Lauren parted her lips a little as the pressure altered and the kiss deepened. Everything about his kiss, his touch, was mesmerizing, and Lauren's fingertips traveled up his chest and clutched his shoulders. He was solid and strong and everything her yearning body had been longing for. When he touched her bare skin where the dress dipped at the back, she instinctively pressed against him, wanting more, needing more. He gently explored her mouth with his tongue, drawing her deeper into his own, making her forget every coherent thought she possessed.

"Hey, Lauren, have you seen the—" Cassie's voice cut through the moment like a bucket of cold water. Gabe dragged his mouth from hers and released her just as Cassie came into view, emerging through the open doorway on the other side of the room. "Oh, gosh! Sorry."

Gabe stepped back, his breathing a little uneven. He stared at her, through her, into a place she never imagined she'd ever let any man into again. "Good luck with the show," he finally said to Lauren, and slipped through the doorway.

She watched him disappear then took a deep breath and faced her friend. Cassie's eyes were wide and curious. "Did you need me for something?"

Cassie grinned. "Ah, the models are getting restless. Especially Carmen Collins. I said you'd come upstairs and give them a pep talk before the parade starts."

"Sure," Lauren said, and grabbed her iPad.

Cassie cleared her throat. "Sorry about that…I didn't mean to interrupt. But the door was open and—"

Lauren raised a hand. "Please, don't apologize. I shouldn't have let it happen."

"Why not?" her friend asked. "You're single. He's single. You're awesome. He's gorgeous. You like him. He *clearly* likes you. You're friends. Neighbors. Sounds perfect."

Lauren's brows shot up. "Have you been watching *When Harry Met Sally* or *Love Actually* again?"

"Don't disregard old-fashioned romance so easily," Cassie said, and grinned.

"I don't," Lauren said. "But you know that's not what I'm looking for." *Gabe's not what I'm looking for.* But her lips still tingled. Her skin still felt hot where he'd touched her. Lauren ignored the feelings and smiled toward her friend. "Come on, let's get the models ready."

The fashion parade was a success. And Lauren was so busy for the next four hours that she didn't have a chance to think about Gabe. Or talk to him. Or remember his kiss.

The models did a splendid job, and by the time the last gown had been paraded up and down the catwalk and the entire cast returned for one encore lap, Lauren was exhausted. Her mother was on hand passing out business cards, and made several bridal-fitting appointments for the following week.

The silent auction was also a hit, and Lauren put a modest bid on a vacation up north and was outdone by her brother. Dinner was served underneath the huge marquee, and thankfully, she wasn't seated at Gabe's table. He was with Scott and Evie and some of Evie's family, while she spent the evening at a table with her brother and parents. Grace was a fabulous emcee and the auction raised thousands of much-needed dollars.

By the time dessert was served, several couples had taken to the dance floor. Lauren turned to Cassie, who

was seated beside her, and immediately took note of her friend's pale complexion.

"You know, you don't look the best."

Cassie shrugged one shoulder and drank some water. "It's nothing. I'm a little tired. It's just baby hormones."

Lauren frowned. "Are you sure?"

"Positive."

She was about to get started on her dessert when she noticed someone standing behind her. Lauren knew instinctively it was Gabe. He lightly touched her bare shoulder, and the sensation set her skin on fire.

"Dance with me, Lauren?"

She looked up and met his gaze, ignoring how Cassie bumped her leg under the table. "I really shouldn't leave Cassie alone."

"I'll be fine," her friend, the traitor, assured them. "Go ahead. I insist."

He held out his hand. She took it and got to her feet. He led her to the dance floor and drew her into his arms. The woodsy scent of his cologne immediately assailed her senses and she drew in a shuddering breath. His broad shoulders seemed like such a safe haven, and she was almost tempted to imagine for one foolish moment that they were *her* safe place. Hers alone. Where no one could intrude. The place she'd been searching for. But that was a silly fantasy. She knew the rules. She'd made them. She wanted commitment and he didn't.

Like with everything he did, he moved with an easygoing confidence, and Lauren followed his lead when the music suddenly slowed to a ballad.

"You can dance," she said, and relaxed a little.

"I'm half Italian," he replied against her ear, as though that was all the explanation he needed to offer.

She couldn't help smiling. "Are you one of those men who is good at everything?"

He pulled back a little and Lauren looked up. His mouth twisted. "I guess I'll let you judge that for yourself."

His words wound up her spine like a seductive caress. Suddenly, she sensed they weren't talking about dancing. With the beat of the music between them and the memory of their kiss still hovering on her lips, Lauren was drawn into the depths of his dazzling blue eyes. As a lover, she imagined, he'd be passionate and tender and probably a whole lot of fun. Of course, she'd never know. But still…a little fantasy never hurt anyone.

"I'm sorry about before," he said, and held her close.

He regretted their kiss? "Sure. Forget about it. I have."

His breath sharpened. "I meant that it was hardly the place to start something like that. I hadn't planned on kissing you for the first time while two hundred people were within watching distance."

"So you *planned* on kissing me at some point?"

"After what happened at your brother's wedding, and all the time we've spent together since, I really don't think we could have avoided it."

Her brother's wedding? Was he referring to what he'd overheard her say to her friends? How she'd thought about him naked? Conceited jerk. "You're not irresistible, you know."

"I'm not?" he queried, and rested a hand on her hip.

Lauren could feel him smile as her forehead shadowed his chin. "No."

He chuckled. "So I guess that means you won't want me to kiss you again?"

Her belly fluttered. "Exactly. You have to remember that we want different things."

"That's right. You're still looking for Mr. Reliable?"

"Yes. And not Mr. Roll-in-the-Hay."

"Too bad for me, then," he said, still smiling. "Incidentally, have I told you how beautiful you look tonight?"

"You mentioned it."

Lauren couldn't help smiling. Their banter was flirty and harmless. Nothing more would happen unless she wanted it to. Gabe was charming and sexy, but he also oozed integrity. And she might have been tempted to sleep with him. If she didn't like him. But she did like him. A lot. Too much. And with her heart well and truly on the line, a night in his bed wouldn't be worth the risk, despite how much she wanted it.

"You're easily the most beautiful woman here tonight."

It was a nice line, even if she did think he was being overly generous. The song ended and Lauren pulled back a little. "Thank you for the dance."

"My pleasure."

As he walked her back to her table, Lauren was very aware that her mother was watching them. She could almost see Irene's mind working in overdrive. Cassie wasn't at the table, and she immediately asked after her friend.

"I think she went inside to collect her bag," her mother explained, and then patted the vacant seat, inviting Gabe to sit down.

"Be back in a minute," Lauren said, and walked from the marquee.

She found Cassie in the clubhouse upstairs, sitting on the small couch in the corner of the same room the models had used earlier as a dressing room. There were rails filled with gowns along one wall and shoes were scattered across the floor. Her friend looked up when she came through the doorway.

"Everything all right?" Lauren asked.

Cassie had her arms wrapped around her abdomen and grimaced. "It's nothing. I'm sure it's nothing."

Lauren's gaze moved to Cassie's thickened middle, and she walked across the room. "Are you in pain?"

"I'm fine," Cassie replied, and then clutched at her abdomen with both hands.

Suddenly, her friend looked the furthest from fine that Lauren had ever seen.

"What is it?" she asked and dropped beside the sofa. "What can I do?"

Cassie shook her head. "I don't know…I don't know what's wrong. It might be the baby."

There were tears in her friend's eyes, and Lauren quickly galvanized herself into action. Falling apart wouldn't help Cassie. "You need to see a doctor. I'll get Cameron to carry you into my car, and then I'll take you to the hospital."

She turned on her heels and headed for the door. Evie, Grace and Mary-Jayne were at the top of the stairs talking. "What is it?" Evie, the original earth mother, asked, and stepped toward the room.

"Cassie's ill."

The three women were in the room in seconds, and Evie touched Cassie's forehead with the back of her hand. "She has a temperature."

Cassie doubled over and gripped her belly. "It hurts so much. I'm scared. I don't want to lose my baby."

"It's okay, Cassie, you'll be fine. I'll ask Cameron to—"

"Grace, M.J.," Evie said quickly, and cut her off. "You'd better go and find Gabe."

Gabe?

Both women nodded and backed out of the room. Lauren waited until they'd disappeared and turned her attention back to Evie.

"Evie, I'm sure Cassie would prefer my brother to get her to the hospital."

Evie shook her head. "She needs a doctor. Right now."

"I agree. But I can't see how—"

"Lauren, Gabe *is* a doctor."

When Gabe entered the room, he spotted Lauren stand-

ing by the narrow sofa, comforting her friend. She looked at him, and his chest instantly tightened.

She knows....

Damn. But he'd known it was bound to come out eventually.

He wavered for a second before quickly turning his attention to the woman on the sofa. He asked Cassie a series of questions, such as how severe was the pain, was it constant or intermittent, was she spotting. And as Cassie quietly answered, he felt Lauren's gaze scorching the skin on the back of his neck.

It was hard to stay focused. Memories of that terrible night in the E.R. flooded his thoughts, and panic settled in his chest. *Just do it.* That night another pregnant woman had needed his help, and he'd failed her. But he couldn't fail Cassie. Not when Lauren was watching his every move. This was Lauren's closest friend. She'd be inconsolable if anything happened to her.

It was all the motivation Gabe needed to pull himself together. Instinct and experience quickly kicked in, and he asked Cassie to lie back on the sofa. He gently tilted her to her left side and asked questions about the position and intensity of the pain. He then quickly checked her abdomen. After a minute he spoke. "Okay, Cassie, I need you to relax and take a few deep breaths."

Cassie's eyes were wide with fear. "Do you think it's the baby? I don't want to lose my baby. I can't...I just can't... Not when Doug is so far—"

"You'll be okay. Both of you," he assured her and patted her arm. "We'll get you to the hospital." He turned toward Evie. "Call an ambulance. Tell them we have a patient in her second trimester with probable appendicitis."

Cassie let out a sob. "Do I need an operation?"

He nodded and squeezed her hand. "It'll be all right. You and your baby will be fine."

By the time the ambulance arrived, Gabe had Cassie prepared, and they were ready to go. Lauren volunteered to collect some of her friend's things from her home and meet them at the hospital. Gabe spoke to the paramedics as they carefully loaded Cassie onto the stretcher, and then he followed in his truck.

By the time he reached the hospital, Cassie was already being transferred to the surgical ward and was being prepped for an emergency appendectomy.

He'd been in the waiting room for about forty minutes when Lauren walked through the doorway. She'd changed into jeans and a blue shirt and carried a small overnight bag in one hand. She came to a halt when she spotted him.

"Is she in surgery?" she asked quietly.

Gabe got to his feet. "Yes. Is there someone we should call?"

"Only Doug, her boyfriend," she replied and placed the bag on the floor. "He's a soldier on tour, and I don't know how to contact him. I guess I could check the numbers stored in her phone. She doesn't have any real family of her own other than her grandfather, and he's in an aged-care home and suffers dementia. Doug has a brother in South Dakota, so I could call him if anything…I mean, if something…" Her eyes shadowed over. "If something goes wrong with Cassie or the baby."

"She'll pull through this," he said, fighting the urge to take Lauren into his arms.

"Do you know what's happening to her?" she asked coolly.

"You mean the surgery?" He drew in a breath. "They'll probably give her an epidural or spinal anesthesia as it's safer than general anesthesia."

"And the baby?"

"The safest time for a pregnant woman to have surgery

is during the second trimester. Cassie is seventeen weeks along, so she and the baby should be fine."

"Should?" Lauren's brows shot up. "Is that your professional opinion?"

It was an easy dig. "Yes."

She dropped into one of the vinyl chairs and sighed heavily. "I feel like such a fool."

"Lauren, I wanted to—"

"It's so obvious now," she said, and cut him off dismissively. "That first night when I picked up Jed and I got the splinter. And the old lady on the beach. And then when my dad sprained his ankle." She made a self-derisive sound. "How stupid I would have sounded to you, prattling on about how you'd make a good paramedic. What a great laugh you must have had at my expense."

Guilt hit him squarely between the shoulders. She had a way of making him want to tell her everything. "I wasn't laughing at you."

She met his gaze. "No? Then why all the secrecy?"

Gabe shrugged one shoulder. "It's a little complicated."

"Handy cop-out," she said, clearly unimpressed. "I thought we were…friends."

I don't know what we are. But he didn't say it. Because he didn't want to be her friend. He wanted to be more. And less. He wanted to take her to bed and make love to her over and over. He also wanted to stop thinking about her 24/7.

"I lost a patient," he said, and heard how the hollow words echoed around the small room. "So I took some time off."

Her expression seemed to soften a little. "Oh…" He could see her mind ticking over, working out a way to ask the next question. "Was it because of something you did wrong?"

"Indirectly," he replied and sat down opposite her. "It was around midnight and I'd worked ten hours straight.

I left the E.R. for a while, and when I was gone, a young woman was brought in. She was pregnant and hemorrhaging, and a second-year resident treated her. Unfortunately, the patient and her baby died."

She stared at him. "How awful."

"Yes," he said, remembering the event like it was yesterday. "It was a terrible tragedy. And one I will always regret."

"You said you weren't there at the time," she said, and frowned. "Which means it wasn't actually your fault."

Guilt pressed down. "It was. Even though I wasn't the only doctor in the E.R. that night, I was the attending physician on duty, and I should have been there when I was needed the most. A less experienced resident was forced to handle the situation and because of that, a woman and her child died."

It wasn't an easy truth to admit. And it sank low in his gut like a lead weight. It didn't matter how many times he replayed it over in his mind. He should have been there. His arrogance and self-importance had been the reason he'd failed the patient. The blame lay at his feet. And his alone. If he'd followed his own doctor's advice, he wouldn't have returned to work so quickly. Instead, he'd ignored everything and everyone and done it his own way. With fatal consequences.

Her eyes widened. "Were you sued?" she asked. "Was there some kind of malpractice suit? Is that why you quit being a doctor?"

Gabe's stomach tightened. *Quitter.* He'd called himself that over and over. But it had been easier leaving medicine than swallowing the guilt and regret he'd experienced every time he walked through the hospital corridors.

"There was an inquiry," he said, and ignored how much he wanted to haul her into his arms and feel the comfort of

her touch, her kiss, her very soul. "The hospital reached a settlement with the woman's family. I wasn't implicated."

"And the other doctor?"

"She was suspended and left the hospital soon after."

Lauren twisted her hands in her lap. "Would you have saved the patient if you were there?"

Gabe took a deep breath. "I believe so."

"But you don't know for sure?"

He shrugged lightly. "Who can know anything for certain?"

Her gaze was unwavering. "But as a physician, wouldn't you be trained to deal with absolutes? Life or death. Saving a patient or *not* saving a patient. There are no shades of gray. It's one or the other, right?"

Her words cut deep, and he wanted to deny the truth in them. "I can't—"

"So tell me the truth," she said, and raised her brows. "Why did you really quit being a doctor?"

Chapter Eight

Lauren pushed aside the nagging voice in her head telling her to mind her own business. She couldn't. He was a mystery. A fascinating and infuriating enigma. She wanted to know more. She wanted to know everything.

Because…because she liked him. As hard as she'd tried *not* to, she was frantically drawn toward Gabe. The kiss they'd shared earlier that evening confirmed it. She hadn't planned on having feelings for him. But now that she had them, Lauren was curious to see where it might lead. He was attracted to her…. Perhaps it might turn into more than that. Maybe he'd reconsider his no-commitment position. Just as she'd begun to rethink her own plans for wanting a relationship based on things other than desire or love.

Love?

Oh…heavens. *I'm in big trouble.* The biggest. *Desiring. Liking. Loving.* Her once broken and tightly wrapped-up heart had somehow opened up again. And she'd let him in. Even if he didn't know it.

"I told you why," he said, and got to his feet.

Lauren watched him pace around the room. The tension in his shoulders belied the dismissive tone in his voice. "You told me you felt responsible for losing a patient that wasn't directly *your* patient. How is that your fault? How is that a reason to throw away your career?"

He stilled and stared at her for the longest time. Lauren knew she was way out of line. He would have been well within his rights to tell her to go to hell. But she knew he wouldn't. There was something in his expression that struck her deeply, a kind of uneasy vulnerability she was certain he never revealed. Not to anyone.

"Walking away from that life was one of the hardest things I've ever done," he said quietly. "I don't expect you or anyone else to understand my reasons."

Lauren drew in a shaky breath. "I'm sorry. I don't mean to sound like I'm judging you. I'm not," she assured him. "It's just that I…I guess I…care."

He didn't budge. His blue-eyed gaze was unwavering. Only the pulse in his cheek indicated that he understood her meaning.

"Then, don't," he said, and crossed his arms. "We've been through this before, Lauren. You want something else, something and someone who won't give you grief or pain or disappointment. That's not me. If you waste your heart on me, I'll break it," he said, his voice the only sound in the small room. "I won't mean to…I won't want to…but I will. I'm not the middle road you're looking for, Lauren."

Humiliation and pain clutched at her throat. But she wouldn't let him see it. "Sure. Whatever." She stood and grabbed the bag at her heels. "I'm going to check on Cassie."

She left the room as quickly as she could without looking as if she was on the run. Once she was back in the corridor, Lauren took several long gulps of air. Her nerves were rattled. Her heart felt heavy in her chest. She made her way

to the cafeteria and stayed there for the next hour. She was allowed to see Cassie when she came out of surgery, but her friend was groggy and not very talkative. By the time Lauren headed home, it was past midnight.

Gabe's truck was not in the driveway, but she heard him return about twenty minutes after she did. She didn't want to think about him.

If you waste your heart on me, I'll break it....

It was warning enough. She'd already had one broken heart when she'd lost Tim. Lauren wasn't in the market for another. He'd made his feelings, or lack thereof, abundantly clear.

After a restless night where she stared at the ceiling until 3:00 a.m., on Sunday morning, Lauren headed off to the hospital. Seeing Cassie lifted her spirits.

"You look so much better today."

"Thanks," Cassie replied, and sighed.

Lauren placed the flowers she brought on the small bedside table. "When are you getting out of here?"

"Tomorrow," her friend replied. "The surgery went well, and the baby is okay."

There was a huge look of relief on Cassie's face, and Lauren smiled. "I'm so glad to hear it. Did you manage to reach Doug?"

She shook her head. "But I left a message."

Lauren could see her friend's despair. "I could try to call him. Or perhaps you should contact Tanner, and he could try to get in touch with his brother."

Cassie sighed. "I haven't spoken with Tanner since the last time he came home, which was a couple of years ago. Last I heard, he was still horse whispering in South Dakota. Doug will call me," Cassie said assuredly. "He will. I know it. I left a message and said it was important. He'll call me," she said again.

Lauren hoped so. Doug's reaction to the baby had been lukewarm at best, and she knew Cassie hadn't heard from him since.

"So," Cassie said, and grinned. "About Gabe. I think—"

"Let's not," Lauren pleaded.

"Indulge me. I'm the patient, remember?" she said, and patted her IV. "I'm guessing you didn't know he was really a doctor?" she asked. "And a pretty good one, by the way he reacted yesterday."

"I didn't know," she admitted.

"I guess he had his reasons for keeping it a secret."

Sure he did. He was emotionally unreliable and therefore unattainable. She'd get over him soon enough. For the moment, he was just a distraction, and her fledging feelings would recover. Lauren was sure of it.

It didn't help that the object of her distraction chose that moment to enter the room.

With Mary-Jayne at his side.

Of course, she knew he was acquainted with her friend. He was Scott's cousin, and Evie was Mary-Jayne's sister. Still…a little burst of resentment flooded her veins.

She met his gaze. He looked so good in jeans and a black polo shirt, and walked with the easy swagger she'd come to recognize as uniquely his. Lauren tried to smile and failed.

"Look who I found outside," Mary-Jayne announced with a big grin.

"Ladies," he said easily, and stepped into the room. "Am I interrupting?"

"Not at all," Cassie was quick to say. "I'm so glad you're here. I wanted to say thank you for yesterday."

Gabe shrugged. "No thanks necessary. As long as you're feeling better."

"Much," Cassie said, and beamed a smile. "Are they for me?" she asked of the bunch of flowers in his hand. When

he nodded, her friend's smile broadened. "Daffodils are my favorite. Thank you."

Lauren fought back a surge of jealousy and drew in a deep breath. So he met Mary-Jayne in the hallway, and Cassie was a little starstruck? *It means nothing to me.* One kiss didn't amount to anything. She had no hold on him and shouldn't care that her friend might have a harmless crush on the man who'd potentially saved her and her baby. Besides, Cassie was devoted to Doug.

She hopped up from her chair and took the flowers, careful not to touch him. He said hello, and she managed to reply and then disappeared from the room in search of a vase.

"What's up with you?"

Lauren came to a halt and waited for Mary-Jayne to catch up. "Nothing."

Her friend grabbed her arm. "We met in the hall, that's all."

"I don't know what you mean."

Mary-Jayne's slanted brows rose up dramatically. "Sure you do. Dr. Gorgeous in there only has eyes for you."

"That's…that's ridiculous," Lauren spluttered. "We're just neighbors."

"You can deny it all you want, but I know what I see."

If you waste your heart on me, I'll break it….

His words came back again and sat like lead in her stomach.

The nurses happily obliged her with a vase, and when they returned to the room, Gabe was sitting beside Cassie's bed, and her friend's hand rested against his forearm. The scene looked ridiculously intimate. Resentment bubbled, and Lauren pushed it away quickly.

"I was just telling Gabe how grateful I am," Cassie said, and patted his arm one more time before she placed her hands in her lap and grinned at him. "Again."

He shrugged in a loose-shouldered way, but Lauren wasn't fooled. "I'll get going. Good to see you all."

Once he was gone, Cassie blew out a low whistle. "Boy, could you two be any more into each other and less inclined to admit it?"

Lauren colored wildly. "That's ridiculous."

"Yeah, right," Cassie said, and grinned. "I'm not the most observant person in the world, but even I can see that you have some serious feelings for him."

"And I think right about now is the time for me to leave," Lauren said gently, and grabbed her bag. She loved Cassie. But now wasn't the time to have a discussion about her feelings for Gabe. Feelings he'd made perfectly clear he didn't want and couldn't return.

"You know, I'm sure he had his reasons for not telling you he was a doctor," Cassie said, ignoring her indication to leave. "If that's what's bugging you. Some people don't like talking about themselves."

I know...I'm one of those people.

"I'll see you tomorrow. Make sure you let me know when you're leaving so I can pick you up. My mother is insisting you stay with her and my dad for a couple of days."

She hugged both her friends goodbye, and by the time Lauren arrived home, it was past midday. She got stuck into some cleaning and sorted through a few cupboards in the kitchen. It was menial, mind-numbing work that stopped her dwelling on other things. Or at least gave the impression. Later she did some admin work for the store and spent an hour in the backyard, weeding and repotting some herbs. Gabe wasn't home, and that suited her fine.

When she was done, it was well past five, and Lauren headed inside to clean up. She took a long bath and dried herself off before cozying into candy-pink shorts and matching tank shirt. She called Cassie and arranged to pick

her friend up the following morning. With that done and the store organized for next day, Lauren ignored the idea of dinner and mooched around the cupboards for something sugary. Being a usually health-conscious woman, the pantry was bare of anything she could call junk, and she made do with a bag of organic dried apples.

She was sitting on the sofa, watching television with her knees propped up and dipping in for a third mouthful of apple when the doorbell rang. Lauren dropped the bag and headed up the hallway. When she opened the door and found Gabe standing on her porch, Lauren took a deep breath. He looked tired. As though he hadn't slept for twenty-four hours.

Well, too bad for him.

"What do you want?"

He had an envelope in his hand. "I got the estimate for the new fence. You said you wanted to—"

"Sure," she snapped, and held out her palm.

He placed the note in her hand. "You're under no obligation to pay half. The fence is my idea and I'd rather—"

"I said I'd pay for it," she said, cutting him off.

He threaded his fingers through his hair, and she couldn't stop thinking how mussed and sexy he looked. "Okay. If you're sure. Check out the estimate and if you agree, I'll get the contractor to start work in the next week or so."

Wonderful. A great high fence between them was exactly what she needed.

"I'll let you know," she said through tight teeth.

He nodded, shrugged a little and managed a smile. "I'll talk to you later."

He turned and took a few steps. Lauren wasn't even sure she'd spoken his name until he turned back to face her.

"Yes, Lauren?"

She pushed herself out of the doorway, and the light above her head flickered. He was a few feet away, but she could still make out every angle of his handsome face. A question burned on the edge of her tongue. Once she had her answer, she'd forget all about him.

"Why did you kiss me last night?"

The words seemed to echo around the garden, and the sound of insects chorused the silence that was suddenly between them. He took a couple of steps until he stood at the bottom of the stairs.

"If you think this is such a bad idea," she went on, getting stronger with each word. "If you believe there's nothing going on here…why did you even bother?"

He let out a heavy breath. "Because I had to know."

She shivered, even though it was warm outside. "You had to know what?"

"I had to know what your lips tasted like just one time."

Her shiver turned into a burn so hot, so rampant, Lauren thought she might pass out. She grabbed the screen door to support her weakened knees. No man had ever spoken those kinds of words to her. Tim had been sweet and a little shy. James's flirtatious nature had been obvious and overt. But Gabe was somewhere in between. Not shy. Not obvious. He was a seductive mix of reserve and calm, masculine confidence.

"And that's all it was? Just…just a single kiss?"

"What do you want me to say to you?" he shot back. "Do you need to hear that I want to kiss you again? That I want to make love to you? Of course I do. I've told you that before. I've never denied that I'm attracted to you, Lauren. You're…lovely. You're smart and beautiful and the more time I spend with you, the more I want you. But I can't give you the kind of commitment you want. Not…not right now."

Not right now?

What did that mean? A possibility popped into her head.

"Are you married?" she asked. "Or separated? Is that why you—"

"Of course not," he cut her off tersely.

"I had to ask," she said, and sighed. "You're so hot and cold, Gabe. You say one thing to me and then do another. I'm confused, and it seemed plausible."

"Well, it's not. I've had three semiserious relationships and a few one-night hookups. But I've never been married. I thought about it when I was with my last girlfriend, but we never got around to making any firm plans. In between, I was busy with my career."

"A career you then gave up?"

His expression turned blank. And she'd never wanted to read him more. But couldn't.

"I have to go," he said. "Good night."

She watched him leave and waited until he rounded the hedge before she returned inside and closed the door.

On Tuesday morning, Gabe noticed five missed calls on his cell. Two from his mom. Three from Aaron. His brother had then reverted to text messaging.

What's going on with you?

He sent one back when he arrived at work.

Nothing.

Aaron responded immediately.

Mom's worried about you. Call her.

Sure.

Gabe knew his one-word replies would irritate his interfering older brother.

Ten minutes later, he received another message.

Just do it, Gabriel.

Gabe ignored the deliberate use of his full name in his brother's message and stuffed the phone in his pocket. Well-meaning relatives with advice he could do without.

Megan arrived, and he plastered on a smile. It would be best if he kept his lousy mood to himself. No one needed to know that he was so wound up, so frustrated, he could barely string a sentence together. She had her older sister with her, a remarkably attractive girl in her mid-twenties whose name he couldn't recall but who looked him over with barely concealed approval.

The teen dumped a few books on his desk. "Thanks for these," she said chirpily.

"They helped?" he asked, and pulled another medical textbook from the desk drawer.

"Yeah," she replied. "I sit the nursing entrance exam next week."

Megan had borrowed a few of his old medical texts to help with her studying and hadn't asked why he had them. Not like Lauren would have. She'd ask. She'd want to know everything. And the damnable thing was, he'd want to tell her.

"Well, good luck," he replied. "Just drop it back when you're done with it."

Megan grabbed the book and sashayed out of the room, but her sibling hovered in the doorway, brows raised suggestively. In another time, he might have been tempted to ask for her number, to take her out and get her into bed after a few dates. But he wasn't interested in the pretty brunette with the wide smile. Gabe cursed to himself. He was so

wrapped up in Lauren that nothing and no one else could shift his distraction. Nothing could ease the unexpected ache in his chest and the unrelenting tension cramping his shoulders. Kissing her had been like nothing on earth. And he wanted to feel that again. He wanted to take her in his arms and make love to her over and over and somehow forget he couldn't offer her the future she deserved.

The cell in his pocket vibrated again. It was another message from his brother.

You said you'd call. Get to it.

Gabe ignored the message and got back to work.

But by two he'd had enough, and since no one was booked in to use the upstairs rooms that afternoon, he locked up and headed home. Back at the house, there was painting to be done, drywall to replace and plaster, and the lawn needing mowing. But he ignored every chore. Instead, Gabe started unpacking some of the boxes in the spare room. The box marked Personal Items got his full attention. Gabe rummaged through the papers and soon found what he was looking for. His diploma of medicine. Still in the frame his mother had insisted upon. He looked at it, and shame hit him squarely behind the ribs.

Quitter...

Like he'd rarely allowed himself to think in the past eighteen months, Gabe wondered what would have happened had he stuck it out. What would have ensued had he ignored the guilt and regret tailing him around the hospital corridors? Would time have healed his fractured spirit? Would it have lessened the remorse? Would he have been able to practice medicine with the self-belief it demanded? Right now, he felt healthy. His last round of tests had come back clear. He was cancer-free.

Perhaps it was time to take his life back?

A first step. A giant step. But one he had to do if he was ever going to be truly happy.

Gabe shoved the diploma back in the box and resealed the lid.

He needed a run to clear his thoughts and stretch out the muscles in his back and limbs. He changed his clothes and headed out. When he returned, he showered, pulled on jeans and a T-shirt and grabbed his keys. If he wanted to take his career back, there was no time like the present to start.

He had a patient to check on.

Lauren sat on the edge of the bed in the spare room at her parents' house and chatted to her friend. It had been her bedroom once. Back then, the walls had been pink, and posters of rock gods had covered the walls. Since she'd moved out, her mother had redecorated in the more subtle tones of beige and white.

"This isn't necessary, you know, for me to stay in bed," Cassie insisted, and patted the mattress. "I feel fine."

"Good," Lauren said, and smiled. "But humor us all anyway, and rest for a few more days. You had surgery, and you need to take it easy."

Her friend had resisted coming to stay at her parents' home to recuperate. But since Lauren's dad was now retired, it meant that someone would be able to watch Cassie around the clock. Cassie meant a great deal to her family. She was like another daughter to her parents and as close to Lauren as a sister could be. She wasn't about to allow her friend to be alone.

"Okay," Cassie said, and grinned. "I'll be a model patient. As long as I know Mary-Jayne is looking after my dog, I'll relax."

"She is," Lauren told her. "I'll go and make some tea and bring it up with dinner."

"What time are your folks getting back?" Cassie asked.

Lauren checked her watch. It was just after seven. "Matka is at mah-jongg and will be back by nine-thirty, and Dad's helping Cameron supervise a bowling expedition with a group of kids from the Big Brothers program tonight. So you'll have to put up with me until then." She grinned. "But I promise I won't smother you."

Cassie chuckled. "Good. Um…I think I heard the doorbell. You might want to get that."

Lauren had heard it, too. She left the room and headed downstairs and was stunned to find Gabe on the other side of the door when she swung it back on its hinges.

"Oh…hi."

"Hey," he said, looking gorgeous beneath the overhead light. "I just stopped in to check on Cassie. I called her earlier, and she said she was here."

She did? Lauren needed to have a talk with her friend. She'd bet her boots Cassie had deliberately arranged this meeting. Her friend wasn't averse to a little matchmaking. Too bad it was pointless. "I didn't realize you had her number."

His mouth twitched. "I got it from Cameron."

"Oh, right. Well, she's upstairs…third room on the right."

Lauren turned on her heels and headed back down the hall. He could close the door. He could make his own way upstairs. She didn't want to spend any more time with him than was necessary. It was the only way she'd succeed in getting him out of her system.

But damn it if she couldn't hear them talking and laughing from her spot in the kitchen. The sound traveled down the stairway and managed to spur on her mounting jealousy and resentment.

She was about fifteen minutes into preparing dinner when she felt Gabe's presence in the room. Lauren looked

up and noticed him in the doorway, arms crossed and one shoulder resting against the doorjamb.

"How does she seem?" she asked stiffly, slicing cucumber as though it was the enemy.

"Good," he replied, and pushed himself off the door frame. "Recovering well."

"So nice of you to make a house call." She turned toward the sink. "You know the way out."

But he stepped closer. "Is every conversation we have going to be a battle from now on?"

She harrumphed. "Probably. I should have stuck to my guns that night at my brother's wedding and ignored you. My life was simpler then."

"We couldn't ignore one another if we tried," he said, and was suddenly behind the counter.

"Oh, I can try," she assured him. "And I will."

He turned and rested his behind on the countertop. "I don't know what it is about you, Lauren... You make me think about things. You have a way of getting under my skin."

"Like a burr?" She wasn't going to be nice to him. Lauren finished the salad and soup she'd prepared for Cassie and placed it on a tray. "I'm going to take this upstairs. When I come back down, I'd prefer it if you weren't here."

By the time she was upstairs, her knees were wobbling so much she had to quickly place the tray on the bed. She looked at her smiling friend.

"I figure this is your doing?"

Cassie shrugged innocently. "Maybe a little. I thought it was sweet that he wanted to make sure I was okay. He's very nice. You shouldn't give up so easily."

"I'm not giving up," she said, and propped another pillow behind her friend. "I'm just not going to waste time dreaming about something that will never happen."

She lingered in the room for a few more minutes, giv-

ing Gabe plenty of time to leave. But when she returned to the kitchen, he was still there, still standing by the counter.

She heard his phone buzz.

"I think you just missed a call."

"I didn't miss it," he said, and shrugged a shoulder. "I didn't answer it."

"Girl trouble?" she inquired, hurting all over just thinking about it.

He half smiled, as though he knew she hated imagining him with some faceless woman. "My mom," he explained. "Or my brother Aaron…checking up on me."

"Do you need to be checked on?"

"They seem to think so," he said, and pushed himself off the counter.

"Well, I guess it's natural for a mother to worry when one of her kids lives on the other side of the world. I don't imagine my mother would be any different. She likes that Cameron and I both live close by. It makes her feel as though everything is right in her world. I don't think it matters how old we get…she just needs to know we're safe and happy, because that makes *her* feel safe and happy."

His gaze darkened, and he looked at her oddly. "You know, I don't think I've ever thought about it quite like that before."

Lauren's knees wobbled again. She was trying hard to stay strong and ignore him. But staring into Gabe's brilliant blue eyes wasn't helping. Hearing the seductive tone of his voice wasn't helping, either.

She shrugged. "I don't think we ever fully understand how hard it is for parents to let us live our own lives. They want to protect us from being hurt and from enduring life's disappointments. Even though it can sometimes feel like being wrapped in cotton wool and then be overprotected."

"Is that what happened to you?" he asked quietly. "After Tim died?"

Lauren nodded. "And again when my marriage ended. With Tim… I think because it happened so quickly, I was in shock. One moment I was planning my wedding, the next I was dressed in black and standing beside his grave. There was no time to prepare…to say goodbye. I was so mad at him for shutting me out that I didn't spend time telling him the important things…like how much he meant to me and how much I would miss him."

"Maybe he didn't want to hear that," Gabe said, his voice soft and husky. "Maybe he couldn't have borne your sadness, and it was all he could do to control what was happening to him. Maybe he didn't want your pity and didn't want to witness your grief and your tears. And perhaps you being mad at him for shutting you out…well, maybe that made him feel *normal*…as though he wasn't defined by his illness. Like he was still the person you loved, still a healthy and strong man and not only a terminally ill cancer patient."

Lauren's throat burned. The raw truth in his words cut deep. Everything Gabe said made sense. Somehow, he knew how to reach into the depths of her soul.

She blinked to avoid the tears that threatened to spill. "Tim never got angry with me for reacting like I did. But *I* was angry with me. For a week I walked around in a daze. All I could think was how my wedding plans were ruined. I was so selfish."

"No," Gabe said gently. "Despair has many faces, Lauren. Focusing on your wedding plans was simply a coping mechanism. It's not so hard to understand."

She nodded, agreeing with him with her heart, even though her head told her to forget him and find someone who truly wanted her back. "I guess you would have seen grief like that before. I mean, dealing with patients and their families."

"I… Yes," he said quietly. "Of course."

His unwavering gaze was deeply intense and made Lau-

ren's heart race. Heat and awareness coiled through the space between them, somehow drawing them closer, even though they were two feet apart. They weren't touching, but Lauren *felt* his presence like a lover's caress.

Suddenly, the middle road she'd been longing for seemed passionless and bland.

And the man in front of her was the one man she wanted for the rest of her life.

Chapter Nine

"Has Gabe gone home?"

Lauren picked up the tray from Cassie's bedside table and ignored the way her heart beat faster simply at the mention of his name. He'd left with the barest of goodbyes, and she'd breathed a sigh of immense relief once he'd walked out the door.

"Yes," she replied. "But he said he'd check on you in a couple of days."

"That's sweet of him," Cassie said, and grinned. "Although I'm not sure he's actually dropping by to see me."

Lauren frowned. "You're as obvious as my mother."

Her friend began ticking off his attributes on her fingers. "He's handsome, charming, single and a doctor...what more do you need?"

Commitment and love...

She wanted exactly what she'd been saying she didn't want. And neither she was likely to get from Gabe Vitali.

"He doesn't want a relationship. He's commitmentpho-

bic." Lauren sighed heavily. "Looks, charm and medical degree aside, he's emotionally unavailable."

"I'm not so sure," Cassie said. "Maybe he's just been unlucky in love and is wary of getting close to someone again."

That's not it.

But there *was* something…some reason why he pulled back and made it clear he wanted to avoid commitment. And Lauren was sure it had nothing to do with a failed relationship. It was something else…something deeper. Something that was somehow wrapped up in the patient he lost, his decision to quit being a doctor and then choosing to move his life to Crystal Point.

"Perhaps," she said, and shrugged. "It doesn't matter anyway. He's not for me."

"Settling isn't the answer," Cassie said quietly. "I know you have this idea that you want an uncomplicated, painless relationship…but relationships *are* complicated. And they can be painful and messy. Just because things ended so tragically with Tim and then you married a man you didn't love, it doesn't mean you have to make do with ordinary."

But ordinary won't break my heart.

And Gabe would.

Hadn't he already told her as much?

"I don't believe in the fairy tale anymore," she said, and knew it was a lie. "You should rest. My folks will be home soon. I'll see you tomorrow."

She headed downstairs, and once the dishes had been done, Lauren made her way to the front living room. As always, the photographs on the mantel drew her closer. Dear Tim, she thought as she looked at his picture with a familiar sadness. Was Gabe right? Had Tim kept his illness a secret so she wouldn't pity him…so he wouldn't have to deal with her thinking of him as sick? As somehow less than a man? In the years since his death, she'd thought of

his reasons countless times and always ended up believing he'd wanted to protect her from the inevitable grief and loss. But what if it was more than that? Had she been so blind? So self-centered, she hadn't considered that Tim was protecting himself, too?

When her mother arrived home, she was still sitting in the front room, still thinking about the man she'd loved and lost. And she thought about Gabe, too…and wondered how she'd managed to develop feelings for someone she hardly knew. It was different to the way she'd fallen for James. Her ex-husband hadn't made her think…want…need. He hadn't stirred her mind and body the way Gabe did. James had been an escape from the terrible anguish of losing Tim. Nothing more. She was ashamed to admit it to herself. He'd deserved better. And so had she.

By the time she returned to her house, showered and changed and rolled into bed, it was past ten. There were lights on next door, and she wondered if Gabe was up late working on the renovations in the house. Once the work was done, she was sure he'd sell the place. What then? Would they see one another as infrequently as they had before he'd moved next door?

Sleep eluded her, and after staring at the shadows bouncing off the ceiling for most of the night, Lauren snatched a few restless hours before she pulled herself out of bed at seven, dressed and drove into Bellandale. She swapped her car for the store's van and then headed back to Crystal Point Surf Club & Community Center to collect the gowns that had been left there after the benefit. She'd borrowed Cameron's key and hoped she could get the task done before Gabe arrived for work.

No such luck.

He turned up just as she was trekking the third armload of gowns down the stairs.

He stood at the bottom of the stairway. "Need some help?"

Lauren brushed past him and clutched the gowns. "No, thank you," she said as she stomped through the doorway and loaded the dresses neatly into the back of the van. When she returned inside, he was still by the stairs.

"How did you get in?" he asked.

"I borrowed my brother's keys. I didn't think it would be a big deal."

"It's not," he replied, and followed her up the stairs. "Stop being stubborn and let me help you."

Lauren glared at him. "I'm not stubborn."

He raised one dark brow. "Yeah, right," he said, and held out his arms. "Give me what needs to be taken downstairs."

Lauren's mouth tightened, but she did as he asked. It only took another twenty minutes to get everything in the van, including the three metal hanging rails he quickly pulled apart and loaded in the back of the vehicle.

"Thanks. I appreciate your help," she said as she closed the back door to the van.

"No problem. Do you want me to follow you and carry this stuff back into your store?"

"Ah, no," she said quickly. "My mother will be there to help. Thanks again."

"Do you like working with your mom?" he asked unexpectedly, and followed her around to the driver's door. "And running your own business?"

"It's what I've always done," she replied.

"Which isn't exactly an answer, is it?"

Lauren shrugged. "My mother opened the store twenty-five years ago. I took over when I graduated from business college. Do I like it?" She sighed deeply. "It's all I know. I like it well enough."

But his glittering gaze saw straight through her facade. "Sometimes it makes you unhappy."

"Some days," she admitted. "Other days it's not so bad. When I was younger, I guess I was wrapped up in the romance of it all. The gowns…the tradition… Back then it seemed to have a purpose. Now…not so much."

Because Tim died, and I discovered that not everyone gets their happy ending….

His phone beeped, and he ignored it like he had before. Lauren's eyes widened. "So did you end up calling your mother and brother?"

Gabe stared at her for a second and then grinned a little. "Not yet."

Lauren grunted under her breath. "I didn't peg you to be the inconsiderate type."

"Inconsiderate?" He repeated the word and frowned. "I'm not."

"You might want to remind your family of that the next time you speak with them," she said, and smiled ultra-sweetly. "If you ever get around to it."

Lauren watched as his resentment grew. To his credit, he kept a lid on his rising annoyance. She wasn't usually driven to lecture someone she hardly knew. He'd accused her of getting under his skin…. The problem was, he did exactly the same thing to her.

And no one had ever made her so reactive.

Gabe challenged her thoughts and ideals. He made her really *think* about things. And he had, in a matter of weeks, forced her out of the self-absorbed routine she'd disguised as her life. Even her plans to find someone to share her life with had been tainted with the memories of all she'd lost. But who was she kidding? Settling for a passionless, loveless relationship was no way to live. And in her heart, she knew she could never honor Tim by settling for less.

Looking at Gabe, it was easy to get lost in his blue eyes and handsome face…but there was so much more to him than that. And that was what she found so hard to resist. He

was charming, certainly. And sexy. But he was also kind and generous, and despite her silly accusation, clearly considerate and helpful. Hadn't he come to her aid countless times? Like when she was forced to look after Jed. Or how he'd helped her dad after his fall. And he'd shown incredible concern for Cassie and her baby. There was something elementally *good* about Gabe. And that was what she was so attracted to. That was why her heart pounded whenever he was close.

That's why I've fallen in love with him....

She shivered, even though the breeze was warm.

Oh, God...it's true.

"Lauren?" His voice seemed to whisper on the wind. "Are you all right?"

She nodded, shell-shocked at the unexpected intensity of her feelings. How ironic that she'd done exactly the opposite of what she'd planned after her divorce. She'd derided attraction and desire and now found herself craving Gabe's touch more than she had ever wanted any man before. And love? She'd put it out of her head, too. Because it scared her so much to want love again.

"I'm...I'm fine," she stammered. "I have to go."

Another car pulled up just as she opened the door to the van. Two people emerged from the small yellow car. Megan and another equally pretty and sporty-looking woman in her mid-twenties. It took Lauren two seconds to notice how the other woman looked at Gabe as if she wanted to devour him.

"You could stay," he said with a grin as they approached. "For protection."

Lauren's mouth twisted. "I'm sure you're capable of protecting yourself."

"That's Megan's older sister," he explained.

"That's a woman with her eye on the prize," Lauren

said as she hopped into the van and drove off, drowning in jealousy.

And feeling like the biggest fool of all time.

It took Gabe twenty minutes to extract himself from the clutches of Megan's persistent sibling. She reminded him that her name was Cara and asked for his number. He avoided answering her, pleading a pile of urgent paperwork on his desk.

Once she left and Megan headed to the beach for her patrol shift, Gabe wrote a list of things he needed to do for the day.

Thing number one: stop thinking about Lauren.
Thing number two: stop dreaming about Lauren.

He snatched a glance at his cell phone on the desk. He really should call his mother. And Aaron. But he just wasn't in the mood to talk. Or to be talked *at*. His mom would know something was up. She'd dig and dig until he admitted that he'd met someone. That he *liked* someone. And that his beautiful next-door neighbor was driving him crazy.

Then Claire Vitali would want to know everything.

And he had nothing to say.

Lauren was broken emotionally. He was broken physically. It could never work. The more he knew her, the more it served to strengthen his resolve. Even though he could have easily talked himself into it. The way she looked at him, the way she'd responded to his kiss at the benefit, the way she argued and contradicted him at every opportunity… It was like pouring gasoline on a bonfire. Everything about Lauren drew him in. Her face, her body, the sweet floral scent of her skin…every part of her connected with every part of him.

Which was as inconvenient as hell.

Even more inconvenient was the sight of Megan's sister standing on his doorstep at seven o'clock that evening. He'd been home for several hours. He'd changed and gone for a run, then returned home to work on painting one of the guest rooms. He'd just emerged from showering and pulling on fresh jeans and a T-shirt when the tall brunette had arrived on his doorstep clutching the textbook he'd loaned to Megan. Returning the book had been her excuse for dropping by, and he made a mental note to query Megan about handing out his address.

His visitor managed to wheedle her way up the hall and into the front living room, and Gabe was just about all out of patience when he heard another knock on his front door. Gabe told Cara to stay put and headed up the hallway.

Lauren stood beneath the porch light. In a long floral skirt and pale blue T-shirt she almost stole his breath. Gabe quickly pulled himself together.

"Hey…what's up?" he asked.

She held out an envelope. "The estimate for the fence looks reasonable. There's a check in there with my half of the initial payment."

"Thanks for getting back to me," he said quietly and took the note. "I'll let the contractor know he can start as soon as possible."

She shrugged, and the T-shirt slipped off her shoulder a little. "Okay."

The sight of her bare skin heated his blood, and he swallowed hard. "If you like, I'll—"

"Gabe?"

Great.

His unwelcome guest chose that moment to come sauntering down the hall, hips swaying, calling his name. He saw Lauren's expression tighten. And as stupid as he knew it was, he didn't want her thinking he was entertaining some random woman in his home.

"Sorry," she said, breathing harder than usual. "I didn't realize you had company."

"I don't," he said, and her brows shot up instantly. It was stupid. They weren't together. They weren't dating. They weren't sleeping together.

One kiss...that was all it was...

And even though there was nothing going on with the unwanted woman in his hallway, Gabe still felt like an unfaithful jerk.

"You can do what you like," Lauren shot back, and swiveled on her heels.

She quickly disappeared down the garden, and Gabe let out an impatient sigh.

"You have to go," he said to the woman now at his side. "Good night."

Minutes later, after quickly packing Cara into her car and waving her off, Gabe walked around the hedge and tapped on Lauren's door. The screen was locked, but the door was open, and he could hear her banging pots in the kitchen.

He called her name. She responded with more banging. She was mad. And she was jealous. The notion made him grin stupidly.

"Lauren, come out here and talk to me."

"Go away."

"Not until you let me explain."

"I don't want to hear it," she said, and banged some more.

Gabe expelled a heavy breath and leaned against the door. "She was just returning a book I loaned to—"

"Yeah, I'm sure it's her reading skills that you like," she said loudly, cutting him off.

"I don't like anything about her," he said, and sighed. "I hardly know her. She was returning a book I loaned to

her sister. Now, will you come to the door so we can stop yelling?"

Pots banged again. "I said, go away."

Exasperated, Gabe straightened his back. "I hardly know her, like I said. You've no reason to be jealous."

The banging stopped. Gabe waited, but she didn't come to the door. The sudden silence was almost eerie. After a few minutes, he gave up and headed down the steps. He'd been back in his own house for about ten minutes when he heard the sharp rap on his front door. Lauren stood on the other side of the screen, cheeks ablaze, chest heaving.

He pushed the screen back and watched, fascinated and suddenly wholly aroused as she glared at him, hands planted on her hips.

"I. Am. Not. Jealous."

Oh, yeah, she was.

Gabe raised a brow. "No?"

Lauren pulled the screen out of his grasp and held it back farther. "No."

"I think you are."

"And I think you're an egotistical jerk," she shot back. "I've no interest in anything you do."

Every feeling, every ounce of desire he had for her rose up, and in that moment, Gabe was powerless to do anything other than smile broadly. "Then why are you on my doorstep?"

Lauren's resolve crumbled a little. Damn him. She shouldn't have let her temper get the better of her. Coming to his door was crazy thinking. "Because…we're arguing and I—"

"No, we're not," he said, and reached out to take her hand. "I think…" He paused, looking deep into her eyes. "I think this is more like foreplay than an argument."

Lauren flushed and pulled back. "Of all the conceited—"

"Let's not have this discussion on the doorstep, okay?" he said as he turned and walked down the hall.

Lauren stayed where she was for a moment. *I should turn around and go home.*

I really should.

Instead, she crossed the threshold, closed the door and followed him into the living room. When she entered the room, she saw he was standing by the sofa. And he was smiling. Lauren wasn't sure if she wanted to slug him or kiss him.

"Come here," he said softly.

She took a deep breath and stepped toward him. "You are the most—"

"That woman who was here earlier is Megan's sister, Cara. She returned a book I loaned to Megan," he said, cutting her off again. "Megan is sitting a nurse's entrance exam next week," he said quietly, cutting her off again. "And that's all. She may have had another motive, but I'm *not* interested in her…okay?"

Her heart raced.

Oh, sweet heaven. She tried to ignore the heat that traveled across her skin as well as the seductive sound of his voice. But failed. Every sense she possessed was on high alert.

"I shouldn't care what you do…" When he grasped her hand, she crumbled some more. "Gabe…I…I just…"

He lightly shrugged his magnificent shoulders and gently urged her closer until there was barely a whisper of space between them. "I can't fight this anymore," he admitted hoarsely. "I want to. I know I need to, for your sake, because you deserve more than the empty words of a future I simply can't promise you. And I've really tried to stop wanting you…but I can't."

There was such raw passion in his words, and Lauren's breath was sucked from her lungs. She moved closer and

they touched, chest against breast. Gabe wound his arms around her, urging her against him.

"I've tried, too," she said through a sigh.

Gabe touched her face and kept his gaze connected with hers as he rubbed his thumb gently across her chin. Lauren tilted her head back and smiled. In all her life, she'd never experienced anything like the sensation of being near Gabe, or his soft, mesmerizing touch.

Their mouths met, and Lauren's head spun. His kiss was like nothing on earth. His hands were warm against her back, his mouth gentle as he coaxed a response. Lauren gave it willingly. She would give him anything. Everything. And the revelation rocked her through to the core.

I am so in love with him. Completely, irrevocably, crazily.

She opened her mouth, tasted his tongue against her own, felt a rush of pleasure coil up her spine and across her skin. She whispered his name against his lips, and Gabe urged her closer. Lauren sighed deeply from that way-down place, which was fueled by need and longing and a powerful rush of desire.

"I want to make love to you," he whispered raggedly, moving his mouth from her lips to her cheek. "So much."

Lauren moaned, all resistance gone. *Just for tonight. I can have this. I can have him. I can pretend it will work out.* "I want that, too."

Gabe grasped her hand and led her down the hall and into his bedroom. He released her and flicked on the bedside lamp. The big bed was covered in a patterned blue quilt, and she swallowed hard as nerves spectacularly set in. His gaze never left her, and she felt the heat of his gaze through to her bones.

"So…here we are."

Lauren didn't move. "Here we are." She managed a tiny smile. "I'm a little nervous."

"You don't need to be."

There was desire and passion and tenderness in his eyes. He wouldn't rush her. He wouldn't coerce or manipulate her with empty words. He opened the bedside drawer, found a condom and dropped the packet on the mattress, and even that made her long for him all the more. He was sweet and considerate. He was everything she wanted.

"Lauren, come here."

She moved toward him and stopped about a foot away. Desire and heat swept through the room with seductive force. She wished she'd had a chance to change into something sexy and filmy. The skirt and T-shirt seemed way too ordinary.

She rested her hands against his chest and then trailed down to the hem of his shirt. "Take this off," she said boldly, and saw him smile.

Gabe pulled the shirt over his head and dropped it on the floor. "Better?"

Lauren nodded. "Much," she replied, and traced her fingertips down the middle of his bare chest and twirled her fingers through the dark hair. She noticed a faded crisscross of small scars near the curve of his armpit and instinctively reached up to outline a finger along the skin there.

He tensed instantly.

"What's this from?" she asked softly.

"It's…nothing," he replied, equally as quiet. "Forget about it."

"Gabe, I—"

"Shh," he said, and placed two fingers gently against her lips. "Later. Right now, let's forget about the past. Let's be in *this* moment."

Lauren's eyes widened as she slid out of her sandals. She liked the sound of that. She dropped her hands and deliberately took her time as she gripped the edge of the T-shirt and slowly lifted it up and over her shoulders. Then

she tossed it onto the foot of the bed and inhaled deeply. The white lace bra she wore was modest, but beneath the smoldering brilliance of Gabe's blue eyes, she felt as though it was the sexiest piece of underwear on the entire planet.

Heat charged between them, and she pushed past any lingering insecurity. He wanted her. That kind of look couldn't be faked. He had no agenda. She sucked in a breath and spoke. "Your turn."

He quickly flipped off his shoes and grinned in such a sexy way, her legs trembled. "Back to you."

She sucked in more air, willed strength into her knees as she unzipped her skirt and hooked her thumbs into the waistband. She heard his breath catch, saw the hot desire in his eyes. And waited. Took a breath. Then met his gaze head-on and slowly stripped the garment over her hips. She pushed it aside with her foot and rounded out her shoulders. Her briefs were white cotton and lace high-cuts. Not nearly seductive enough. Not the kind that aroused desire. Except Gabe looked hotly aroused, and it made her want him all the more.

"So," Lauren said, way more steadily than she felt. "You?"

Gabe's hands stilled on his belt, and his smile was pure sexual heat. He released the buckle and slid the belt from the loops. "Done," he said, and dropped it on the carpet. "Next?"

At a distinct disadvantage, Lauren smiled and backed up toward the bed. She reached around and slowly unclipped her bra, then eased herself from the shoulder straps and pulled the garment free. The bra fell from her fingertips and landed at her feet.

He looked at her and let out a ragged groan. Her nipples peaked instantly. "Okay...enough."

Lauren wondered what he meant for a microsecond, wondered if he found her lacking. But then he was in front

of her, reaching for her, wrapping his arms around her. His mouth hovered over her eager lips, waiting to claim, waiting for her surrender. She gave it, completely and wholly and pressed against his chest. He captured her mouth in a searing kiss and gently fisted a handful of her hair. There was no force, no reticence, only need and desire and the realization it was the perfect kiss. The perfect moment. And all other kisses were quickly forgotten.

They tumbled onto the bed, mouths still together, hands moving over skin. He cupped one breast, and Lauren moaned low in the throat. His fingers were firm yet gentle, his mouth hot against her as he trailed down her cheeks, to her neck and then lower still, to where she ached for his touch. There was magic in his hands and mouth, and Lauren experienced a surge of feeling so intense, so deep, that it warmed her through to her bones. For the first time in forever, she was exactly where she wanted to be, and she sighed heavily as she shook in his arms.

"What is it?" Gabe asked and looked up. "Are you okay?"

Lauren smiled and touched his face. "I'm fine. Don't stop," she pleaded, and grabbed his shoulders.

"I have no intention of stopping," he said, and kissed her hungrily.

It was what she wanted to hear. What she needed to hear. The kissing went on, soft and hard, slow and fast, mesmerizing and wholly arousing. Lauren pushed against him, felt the abrasive denim rub across her thighs. "You're still wearing too many clothes," she whispered, and placed a hand on the band of his jeans.

He smiled against her skin. "You, too," he said, and pushed her briefs over her hips in one smooth movement. The way Gabe looked at her was real and heady and made her spin.

Naked and without inhibitions, Lauren curved against

him and popped the top button on his jeans. She tugged at the zipper and laughed delightfully when he rolled her over and kissed her again.

"Please," she begged softly, and grabbed the waistband again.

"Relax, Lauren," he said, and curved a hand down her back and over her hip. "There's no need to hurry."

He was wrong. There was a need to hurry. She wanted him desperately. She wanted to feel his skin against her, taste his kiss over and over and have the weight of his strong body above her, inside her. It was a need unlike any Lauren had ever known. "I want you," she said against his mouth. "Now."

"Soon," he promised, and moved his hand between them, stroking her where she longed to be touched with skillful, gentle intimacy. Tremors fluttered across her skin, and Lauren responded instantly. The heat grew as her breath quickened, and she let herself go, up and up, shaken by a white-hot, incandescent pleasure so intense, she could barely draw breath. She'd forgotten that feeling—forgotten how good it felt to experience such powerful release. Gabe kissed her again and smothered her soft groans and whispered pleas.

She laid her hands on his jeans and felt him hard against the denim. "You really are wearing too many clothes."

He nodded and swung his legs off the mattress. As he watched her, the connection between them shimmered. Then he smiled that lovely smile she longed for more than any other. Seconds later, his remaining clothes were off, and once the condom was in place, he was beside her on the big bed. They kissed again, long, hot kisses, tongues dancing together, skin on skin. She touched him as she'd wanted to do for weeks—his thighs, his arms, his back. His smooth skin burned beneath her fingertips, and when his mouth found her breast and he gently toyed with the

nipple, she arched her spine off the bed. He moved above her and Lauren lay back, urging him closer. She wrapped her arms around his strong shoulders, opened herself for him and waited for that moment. He rested on his elbows, hovered above her and looked into her face with scorching intimacy.

The moment was achingly sweet and unbelievably erotic at the same time.

He nudged against her until finally they were together. Lauren sighed deep in her throat. She loved the feel of him. Being with Gabe felt right. He didn't move for a moment, didn't do anything other than stare deeply into her eyes.

"You're so beautiful, you take my breath away," he said softly.

It was a lovely, romantic notion, and Lauren absorbed his words right though to her heart. No one had ever spoken to her with such quiet tenderness. She blinked back tears and shuddered, feeling every part of him against her in a way she'd never experienced before.

He moved, and she went with him, up and over into that place where only they existed.

Chapter Ten

Gabe stirred, stretched out and took a deep breath. The soft scent of flowers played around in his memory. Lauren. He snaked an arm across the sheets, expecting to find her asleep beside him. But he was alone.

The digital clock on the bedside table read 4:00 a.m. A thin sliver of streetlight shone through a gap in the curtains, and he heard a dog barking in the distance.

Gabe swung off the bed, grabbed his briefs and jeans from the floor and pulled them on. He left the bedroom, padded down the hall and found Lauren in the kitchen, sitting at the table with a mug between her hands. Her tousled hair and T-shirt was enough to stir his blood. He could easily make love to her again. And again. And every day for the rest of his life.

Whoa.

He couldn't promise that. What if he didn't have a rest of his life? Only now. This moment. If his illness returned, he wasn't about to drag Lauren into what that would mean.

She'd been through enough. She already buried the one man she'd loved. How could he do that to her again?

She looked up when he entered the room and smiled. "Hi. Tea?" she offered, and tapped the mug.

"Sure," Gabe said, even though he didn't really care for the stuff. He watched her get up, move around the counter and flick on the kettle. "Couldn't sleep?" he asked.

She shook her head and grabbed a mug from the cupboard. "Not really. Sorry if I woke you."

Gabe walked into the galley. "Everything all right?"

"Sure," she said quietly, and popped a tea bag into the mug. "I'm not a sound sleeper. Comes from living alone, I guess."

"You're not alone now, though."

The kettle dinged, and she poured the water. "For the moment…no."

An odd twitch caught him behind the ribs. He stepped closer and touched her arm. "Lauren, forget the tea."

She inhaled and turned toward him. "You mean you want to have *the* talk? Before you skedaddle me back home?"

There was a familiar spark in her eyes, and it was a look he knew. She was annoyed with him. "I mean, forget the tea and come back to bed."

She twisted back to the sink. "I thought we'd have—"

"A postmortem?" He reached across and touched her cheek. Unable to help himself, he smiled. "Let's not do that. You think too much."

"I don't," she insisted. "And it's insensitive of you to laugh at me."

Gabe gathered her in his arms, kissed her forehead and spoke gently. "You're being a little ridiculous, you know that?"

She sagged against his chest, and he tightened his grip. "I know. I'm just not used to feeling like this. I'm not used

to *doing* this. We hardly know one another. I was looking for something else, and then you move in next door with your blue eyes and nice smile and I was…I was…"

He pulled back and softly grasped her chin. "You were what?"

She let out a long breath. "Done for."

Gabe's insides contracted. What was she saying? That it was more than a developing friendship and blinding physical attraction? That she loved him?

Sure, he had feelings for Lauren. A lot of feelings. And making love with her had been out of this world. But falling in love wasn't part of his plan. Hell, it was out of the question at the moment. Not when he didn't know if he actually *had* a future. He had a five-year plan and intended to stick to it. Lauren deserved more than empty promises. Or another casket to grieve over.

"Lauren, we're friends and I'd—"

"Friends with benefits?" she said, and cut him off as she pulled away. "I really hate that expression. It's a convenient line to avoid commitment."

Gabe bit back a frustrated sigh. "The only thing I'm trying to avoid is hurting you."

She blinked hard. "Well, you're not doing so great."

He knew that. There were tears in her eyes, and he'd put them there. "If I'd thought you wouldn't be—"

"Forget the condescending speech, Gabe," she said, cutting him off again. "I'm sorry I'm not able to take the emotion out of sex. Blame it on my traditional upbringing, but I've always thought that making love should mean exactly that."

She was right. It should. "I agree. And there was nothing casual about last night for me, Lauren. But I can't promise you more than this…." He paused and took a breath. "More than now. I can't say what the future will bring, and I don't know where I'll be."

She pulled herself from his embrace. "Are you leaving? Going somewhere? Are you going back to California? Is that why you—"

"No," he said quickly, and urged her close again. "Of course not."

"Then what do you mean?"

Guilt hit him between the shoulder blades. *Tell her the truth....*

But he couldn't. "Forget it. Come back to bed, Lauren."

Her eyes glistened, and she nodded.

Back in his bedroom they made love again. This time it was quicker, hotter, as though they had a need that had to be sated. Afterward, Lauren stretched and sighed and curved against him. And he was, Gabe realized as he drifted back to sleep, happier and more content than he could ever remember being before in his life.

At seven, Lauren rolled out of bed and met Gabe in the kitchen, wearing only a navy blue bathrobe he'd offered. He'd made pancakes, and she'd agreed to try them before she returned home to shower and change and head to the store. Despite her earlier display of emotion, there was an easy companionship between them, as if they'd done it before, as if they knew one another deeply and intimately.

Which they did, she figured, coloring a little when she remembered the way they'd made love just hours ago. Being with Gabe was like nothing she'd experienced before. He was an incredibly generous lover. He was thoughtful and attentive, and they were well matched in bed.

What about out of bed?

Was there enough between them to stand up to the test outside the bedroom? She hoped so. He'd made no promises, offered no suggestions that their relationship would go beyond one night together. But there was no doubt in her mind that what they'd shared was more than simply sex.

"Are you okay?" he asked, watching her as she mulled over her second mug of tea.

Lauren looked up and smiled. "Fine. Just thinking I should get moving. I have to open the store this morning, and if I'm late, my mother will ask a thousand questions."

He grinned. "Can I see you tonight?"

Lauren's insides jumped. "Are you asking me out on a date?"

"Yes."

Her brows arched. "That's quite a commitment. You sure you're ready for that?"

He came around the table and gently pulled her to her feet. "I guess we'll find out as we go."

He kissed her with a fierce intensity that had *possession* stamped all over it. And Lauren didn't mind one bit. They made out for a few minutes, and when he released her, Lauren was left breathless and wanting him all the more.

"I'll just grab the rest of my clothes," she said with a smile as she left the kitchen.

Back in his bedroom, she gathered up her clothes and quickly changed back into her underwear, skirt and T-shirt. She found her shoes at the foot of the bed and slipped into them before she walked into the en-suite bathroom to return the robe. She hung it on a hook and turned toward the mirror. Only to be faced with her pale complexion and mussed *bed* hair.

She moaned and finger combed her bangs. There were remnants of mascara clinging to her lashes, and she looked for a tissue to wipe beneath her eyes. When she found nothing on the counter, Lauren opened the overhead cabinet. And stilled immediately.

A long row of medication bottles caught her attention. Serious medication. Very serious. She'd seen similar medication bottles before. Along the same shelf, there were vitamins and several homeopathic tonics. Lauren's blood ran

cold. Why would a strong, healthy man like Gabe need so much medicine? It didn't make sense. She suppressed the urge to examine one of the bottles, but her mind continued to race. A rush of possibilities scrambled in her head. He was a doctor…perhaps it was something to do with that?

It's none of my business.

But she still longed to know.

Immediately embarrassed that she'd even noticed the bottles, she was about to shut the cabinet when she heard a sound from the doorway.

"Lauren?"

Gabe's voice. Marred with concern and query. She turned to face him and found his expression was completely closed off. Unreadable. Guarded.

Her mouth turned dry. "I was…I was looking for a tissue." She stopped speaking and looked at him. "I'm sorry, I shouldn't have opened the—"

He stepped forward and closed the cabinet door. "You should leave if you're going to open your store on time," he said flatly.

Lauren's stomach lurched. He looked solemn. He looked annoyed; he looked as though she'd invaded his privacy in the worst possible way.

"What's going on, Gabe?" she asked, stepping out of the en suite and into the bedroom. "Why are you—"

"I'll see you out," he said, and swiveled on his heels.

Lauren followed him out of the room and was halfway down the hallway when she said his name. He stopped and turned.

"What?" he asked.

"Exactly," she said. *"What?"*

They were now both in the living room doorway, neither moving. He was tense, on edge, and Lauren resisted the urge to reach out and touch him. He looked as if he wanted her gone. And the notion hurt through to her bones.

"It's nothing," he said quietly. "We should both get ready for work."

Lauren shook her head. "Don't do that. Don't shut me out."

Silence stretched between them like a piece of worn, brittle elastic. Somehow, the incredible night making love with one another and the lovely relaxed morning sharing pancakes and kisses had morphed into a defining, uncomfortable moment in the hallway.

All because she'd seen medication in a bathroom cabinet.

An odd feeling silently wound its way through her blood and across her skin. And a tiny voice whispered in the back of her mind. As the seconds ticked, the whispering became louder, more insistent. Something was wrong. Had she missed signals? Had she been so wrapped up in herself she hadn't really seen him? And without knowing how or why, Lauren suspected the answer was within her grasp.

Just ask the question.... Ask him.... Ask him, and he'll tell you....

"Gabe…" Her voice trailed off for a few moments and she quickly regathered her thoughts. "Are you…sick?"

Shutters came down over his face. She'd seen the look before—that day at the hospital when they'd met near the elevator. He'd been coming from the direction of the specialist offices. *The oncology specialist.* Lauren scrambled her thoughts together. Suddenly, she wasn't sure she wanted to hear his reply.

"No," he said finally.

"But…"

"I was," he said when her query faded. "Eighteen months ago."

A sharp pain tightened her chest. A terrible, familiar pain that quickly took hold of her entire body. It was hard to breathe, and she didn't want to hear any more. But she pressed on.

"What did you—"

"Hodgkin's lymphoma," he said impassively, cutting her off.

Cancer...

Lauren's knees weakened. He'd had cancer.

Just like Tim.

She swallowed the thick emotion in her throat. Every memory, every fear, every feeling of despair and pain she'd experienced with Tim rose up and consumed her like a wave. Tears burned the backs of her eyes, and she struggled to keep them at bay as a dozen questions buzzed on her tongue.

And then, like a jigsaw in her mind, the scattered pieces of the puzzle came together.

Gabe seemed to understand the despair she'd experienced at losing Tim. And he also seemed to understand the other man's motives better than she ever had. Gabe didn't want commitment. He wasn't interested in a relationship.

If you waste your heart on me, I'll break it....

She put her hand to her mouth and shuddered. It was too much. Too hard. Too familiar. And then she ran. Out of his bedroom. Out of his house. Out of his life.

By midday, Gabe was silently thanking Lauren for doing what he couldn't. For walking away.

For racing away...

It was better than facing what he'd expected—the reflection, the realization. *The pity.*

Of course she'd taken off. What sane, sensible woman wouldn't? It certainly hadn't taken Mona long to find the door once he'd given his ex-girlfriend an opportunity to bail on their relationship. She hadn't wanted to waste her life on a man with a death sentence.

And neither would Lauren.

Which is what he wanted, right? No involvement, no feelings, no risk.

Now he just had to convince himself.

Last night had been incredible. The best sex he'd ever had. But it had been a mistake. And wholly unfair to Lauren. From the beginning, she'd been clear on what she wanted, and Gabe knew he'd somehow ambushed that goal by allowing himself to get involved with her. He had a five-year plan, and he still intended sticking to it.

He got a text message from Aaron around two o'clock.

You still haven't called Mom.

He replied after a few minutes and got back to work.

I'll get to it.

When?

Gabe snatched the phone up and responded.

When I do. Back off.

He turned the cell to mute, logged off the computer and sat deep in his chair. He was, he realized as he stared at the blank screen, out-of-his-mind bored with his job. Shuffling paperwork during the week and attending to jellyfish stings and sunstroke on the weekends simply didn't cut it. He wanted more. He needed more.

During the night, in between making love with Lauren and holding her in his arms, they'd talked about his career. For the first time since he'd left Huntington Beach, Gabe admitted how much he missed practicing medicine. As he

sat at the desk that had never felt like his own, Gabe knew what he had to do.

It was after four, and he was just finishing a promising call with the human resources director at Bellandale's hospital when there was a tap on the door. It was Lauren.

She entered the room and closed the door.

"Hi," she said quietly. "Can we talk?"

Gabe's stomach tightened. She looked so lovely in her sensible black skirt and green blouse. She'd come to end it. Terrific. It was exactly what he expected. *And* what he wanted. They'd stay friends and neighbors and that was all. Perhaps *friends* was stretching it, too. A clean break—that was what they needed.

He nodded. "Sure."

Her hands were clasped tightly together. "I wanted to… I'd like to…"

Gabe stood and moved around the desk. "You'd like to what?"

She sighed and then took a long, unsteady breath. "To apologize. I shouldn't have left the way I did this morning. I think I was so…so…overwhelmed by it all, by what you told me…I just reacted. And badly. Forgive me?"

Gabe shrugged. "There's nothing to forgive. Your reaction was perfectly normal."

"Don't do that," she said, and frowned. "Don't make it okay. It's not okay."

"I can't tell you how to feel. Or how to respond to things." He perched his behind on the desk. "Considering what you've been through in the past, it makes sense that you'd react as you did."

"It's because of what I've been through in the past that I should *not* have reacted that way. I'm ashamed that I ran out this morning without asking you anything about it. But I'm here now. And I'd like to know." Her concerned expression spoke volumes. Gabe knew that look. He knew

what was coming. He waited for it. "Would you tell me about your illness?"

And there it was.

Pity…

His illness. As though it suddenly defined him. As though that was all he was. The ultimate unequalizer. Healthy people to one side. Sick people to the other.

Gabe took a breath. Best he get it over with. "There's not much to tell. I was diagnosed with lymphoma. I had surgery and treatment. And I still take some medication. End of story."

She nodded, absorbing his words. "And you're okay now?"

"Maybe."

She frowned. "What does that mean?"

"It means there are no guarantees. It means that my last round of tests came back clear. It means that without a recurrence within five years, I should be fine."

Should be. Could be. Maybe.

If she had any sense, she'd turn around and run again.

"And that's why you don't want a serious relationship?" she asked, not running.

Gabe met her gaze. At that moment, he didn't know what the hell he wanted other than to drag her into his arms and kiss her as if there was no tomorrow. But he wouldn't. "Exactly."

"Because you might get sick again?" Her hands twisted self-consciously. "Isn't that a little…pessimistic?"

"Realistic," he corrected.

She stepped a little closer. "Then why did you make love to me last night?"

Because I'm crazy about you. Because when I'm near you, I can't think straight.

"I'm attracted to you," he said quietly.

"And that's all?"

"It's all I can offer," he said, and saw her eyes shadow. He didn't want to hurt her, but he wasn't about to make any grand statements, either. She'd be better off forgetting him and resuming her search for Mr. Middle-of-the-Road. "You know what you want and that's not…me. I care about you, Lauren, too much to lead you on."

Her eyes widened, and she laughed shrilly. "You're joking, right?"

"No."

"That's a convenient line for a man who's *afraid* of commitment."

Gabe squashed the annoyance snaking up his spine. "I'm not afraid of—"

"Sure you are," she shot back quickly, and waved her arms. "You work here instead of the job you're trained to do, even though you're clearly a skilled doctor. You won't even commit to a phone call to your family. And let's not forget the meaningless one-night stands."

"That's an interesting judgment from someone who can't bear to be alone."

As soon as he said the words, Gabe knew he'd pushed a button. But damn, couldn't she see that he wanted to make it easier for her, not harder?

Her eyes flashed molten fire. "I *can* be alone. But I'd prefer to not be. And maybe you think that makes me weak and needy." She cocked a brow. "And you know what—perhaps it does. But I'd rather be like that than be too scared to try."

Gabe's gut lurched. He didn't want to admit anything. She was right when she said he was scared. But he couldn't tell her that. Because she'd want to know why. "You don't know what you're asking."

She shook her head fractionally. "I'm not asking anything. I never have. I like you, Gabe. I…I more than *like*

you. I wouldn't have spent last night with you if I didn't
feel—"

"You want a future, Lauren," he said, and cut her off before she said something she'd inevitably regret. "A future
that includes marriage and children and a lifetime together."
He inhaled deeply. "It's a future we all take for granted.
Until you're told you might not have it."

"But you said you were okay now."

"The cancer could still come back. I wasn't given a one
hundred percent chance of making it past five years," he
said, and ran a hand through his hair. "Not exactly dead
man walking, but close enough that I knew I had to make
a few decisions."

Her mouth thinned. "Decisions?"

"About my life," he explained. "About how I wanted to
live my life. I left my home, my career and my family because I'd had enough of people treating me as though I was
somehow changed...or that having cancer had changed me.
Because despite how much I didn't want to admit it, I was
changed. I am changed. And until I know for sure that I
have a future, I'm not going to jump into a relationship."
He stared at her. "Not with anyone."

"Jump?" She shook her head. "Most of the time I feel as
though you've been dragged into this by your ankles. So, I
guess *jumping* into bed with me doesn't count?"

"Of course it counts, and that's exactly my point," he
replied. "But I can't give you what you want. I can't and
won't make that kind of promise. It wouldn't be fair to you,
Lauren. I've had eighteen months to think about this, and
I didn't come to the decision lightly. I'm not going to get
involved here, only to…"

"To what?"

He sucked in a breath. "To die."

Lauren stepped back and wrapped her arms tightly

around herself. He knew she heard fear in his voice, and he hated the sympathy in her eyes. But she kept on, relentless.

"I don't need that kind of promise, Gabe."

He shook his head. "You do. You would. If we got serious, you'd want it. Hell, you'd deserve it. And I couldn't give it to you."

"How do you know?" she asked. "You're imagining the worst when—"

He made a frustrated sound. "Because I just know. Because I've lived with it for eighteen months. I know what being sick did to the people around me. As a doctor, I saw sickness every day and didn't have one clue what my patients went through until I found myself on the other side of the hospital bed."

"I wasn't one of those people."

"No, you weren't. But you know how this could work out." He raised a hand dismissively. "You've been through it, you grieved...you're *still* grieving for Tim and that life you'd planned for."

"This isn't about Tim," she said quickly. "This is about you. Tim had a terminal illness. An inoperable brain tumor. He was dying...you're not."

"I might," he said flatly.

"So could I. No one can expect that kind of guarantee."

"Isn't that why you married a man you didn't love?" he asked. "Because he was healthy and could give you that kind of assurance?"

"I was—"

"You were looking for your happily ever after," he said, frustrated and annoyed and aching inside. "You were looking for a man who could give you the life you'd dreamed about. I can't do that. Damn it, I don't even know if I could give you the children you want so badly."

Her face crumbled. "Oh, I hadn't thought about—"

"About the possible side effects of chemotherapy and radiation." Gabe expelled a heavy breath. "Well, think about this…there are *no* guarantees. And as much as you say you don't want them, we both know you do. Go home, Lauren," he said coldly, knowing he was hurting her, and knowing he had to. "Go home and forget about this."

Forget about me.

Seconds later, she was gone.

Chapter Eleven

Lauren left the store early on Thursday afternoon and arrived home to find two battered trucks in Gabe's driveway and one in hers. The fence between the two properties, which had long since been hidden by the overgrown hedge, was now in piles of broken timber on both front lawns. She maneuvered her small vehicle around the truck and parked under the carport.

One of the workers came around to her car and apologized up front for the noise they were making and said they'd be finished for the day within a couple of hours.

"But that tree has got to go," he said, grinning toothlessly.

The tree was a tall pine that sat on the fence line and often dropped its branches on her roof. It wasn't much of a tree, and her brother had offered several times to remove it for her.

"Oh, really?"

"The root system will wreck the new fence. We'll get started on it this afternoon, if that's okay?"

Lauren shrugged. "No problem."

Once inside, she changed into jeans and white T-shirt and set her laptop up on the kitchen table. She had invoicing and wages to do and preferred to do it without the inevitable distractions at the store. She poured a glass of iced tea and sat down to work.

By four-thirty, the contractors were still at it. And they were noisy. They were digging new post holes along the fence line with a machine that made a loud *clunk* sound with every rotation. And the buzz of dueling chainsaws didn't help her concentration.

Not that she was in a concentrating mood. For two days, she'd been walking around on autopilot, working at the store, talking to her mother, pretending nothing was wrong when she was broken inside.

Gabe's words still haunted her. His admittance that he might not be able to father children played over and over in her mind. In her heart, she knew that didn't matter to her. Sure, she wanted children. She longed for them. But she wanted Gabe more. Even though he didn't want her back.

At the store that day, she'd arrived early and took inventory on a range of new arrivals. When that was done, she'd dressed two of the windows with new gowns and played around with matching accessories. When she was finished, she'd stood back and examined the results. Not bad, she'd thought. How long had it been since she'd enjoyed her work? *Years.* Too long. After Tim died, she'd lost interest in the fashions and could barely tolerate the enthusiasm of the clients looking for their perfect gown. Her own fairy tale was over, and Lauren took little pleasure in anything related to weddings or the store. It had stopped being fun and instead became a duty.

Perhaps it was time to sell the business and try something new?

She'd once had dreams of taking a break from the store when she was married and had a family of her own. But Tim's death had changed everything, and now that dream seemed as unreachable as the stars around some distant planet. Because despite how much she'd convinced herself it was what she wanted, her plans for a loveless, passionless relationship were stupid. If falling for Gabe had shown her nothing else, Lauren now knew what she wanted. Along with friendship and compatibility, love and passion were vital. In fact, she wanted it all. Everything. A full and complete relationship.

Maybe a vacation was in order. She hadn't been on a holiday for years. Perhaps that would quell her discontented spirit. In the meantime, she'd talk with her mother about putting on another part-time employee so she could take some time off. She thought she might even go back to college.

And she'd get over Gabe. She had to.

Lauren was just about to get herself a second glass of iced tea when she heard an almighty bang, followed by several loud shouts and then a crash and the booming sound of timber cracking. Another sound quickly followed—this one a hollow rumble that chilled her to the bone. The roof above creaked and groaned, and suddenly parts of the ceiling gave way as tiles and branches came cascading through the gaping hole now in her roof. She dived under the table as prickly branches and sharp barbs of shattered timber fell through the gap. Plaster from the ceiling showered across the room in a haze of dust and debris, and she coughed hard as it shot up her nose and into her lungs.

When it was over, she heard more shouts and the sound of heavy boot steps on the roof. She coughed again and wiped her watery eyes. Still crouching, she shuffled back-

ward but quickly moved back when she felt a sharp sting on her left arm. A jagged branch had sliced her skin, and she clamped her right hand across the wound to stem the flow of blood. When that didn't help she noticed her T-shirt was ripped in several places, so Lauren quickly tore off a strip from the hem and made a makeshift bandage to wrap around her arm.

She moved forward and tried to make another exit point, but the branches were thick and too heavy for her to maneuver out of the way. Lauren swallowed the dust in her throat and coughed again. The kitchen table was completely covered in branches and debris from the ceiling support beams, shattered roof tiles and plaster. Her legs started to stiffen in their crouched position, and she stretched forward, looking for a way out from under the table. She tried to push a few of the smaller branches out of the way, but the sharp ends pinched her hands.

She could have been badly injured. Or worse. But she quickly put that thought from her mind and decided to wait for workers to come and help her. And finally, she heard a voice and heaved a relieved sigh.

"Lauren!"

Gabe. Her heart thundered in her chest when she heard footsteps down the hallway and then the sound of tiles crunching beneath his feet. She could see his jeans-clad legs through the twisted branches.

"Where are you?" he asked urgently, coming closer.

"I'm under here," she said, and rattled one of the branches. "Under the table."

"Are you hurt?"

"A few scratches," she replied, coughing again and ignoring the throbbing sting from the gash on her arm. "But I think I'm mostly okay. I have a cut on my arm."

"Stay still, and I'll be there as quickly as I can."

He immediately made his way through the room, eas-

ily hauling fallen plaster and timber out of his path. The branches around the table shook and swayed, and she heard him curse under his breath. Within seconds, he'd made a space large enough for her to crawl through. He crouched down, and relief coursed through her veins. She pushed back the swell of emotion rising up.

"Give me your hand," he said, and she reached out.

His fingers clasped around hers, warm and strong and lovely and safe. Lauren stifled a sob as he gently drew her out through the space and got her to her feet. And without a word, he folded her into his arms and held her close.

"I've got you," he whispered into her hair as he gently stroked her scalp. "You're okay now."

Relief pitched behind her ribs, and as Lauren glanced around, the enormity of the destruction struck her like a lash. The room was wrecked. Plaster and timber were strewn over the floor, and benches and dust from the shattered ceiling plaster covered every surface. The huge branch that had fallen through the roof covered the entire table, and there were broken branches and foliage everywhere.

"Oh…what a mess."

Gabe held her away from him. "Forget that for a minute. Let's check your injuries."

He quickly examined her and looked underneath her bandage. "I don't think it needs stitches, but you should probably see a doctor."

She smiled. "Isn't that what I'm doing right now?"

He stared at her for a moment, and then smiled back. "I guess so. I have a medical kit at home, so I can dress that for you. Now let's get out of here."

And then he lifted her up into his arms as though she were a feather.

"I can walk," she protested.

"Humor me, okay?"

Her legs did feel shaky, so she nodded. Seconds later, he

was striding down the hallway and out the front door. The contractors were all hovering by the bottom steps.

"I'm fine," she assured them when she saw their worried faces.

"Don't go inside," Gabe told the workers. "There could be structural damage. I'll be back soon, so wait here."

She smiled at his bossiness and then dropped her head to his shoulder. It felt nice being in his strong arms. When he rounded the hedge, she noticed how his front door was wide-open, as if he'd left the house in a hurry.

"I really can walk," she said once he'd carried her up the steps.

But he didn't put her down until they reached the kitchen. Then he gently set her to her feet and pulled out a chair. Once she was settled and he'd grabbed a first-aid kit, he undid the makeshift bandage and examined the wound.

"It's not deep," he said, and cleaned the area, applied a small bandage around her forearm and then circled it in plastic wrap. "That should keep it dry when you shower."

"Thanks," she said, and fought the urge to fall into his arms again. "I need to get back to my house and call my insurance company."

"Later," he said. "I'll go and check it out while you rest here."

"There's no need to—"

"There's every need," he said, and grabbed her hand. "You've just been through a frightening ordeal, and you're injured. Plus, there's a great gaping hole in the roof and there could be structural damage to the house."

Lauren ran her free hand down her torn T-shirt and jeans. "I need some fresh clothes, so I'll go home and change and then call the—"

"Stop being so damned obstinate," he said impatiently. "Let me check out the house, and I'll get your clothes while I'm there."

She pulled her hand free. "I'm not sure I want you rummaging through my underwear drawer. It's private and—"

"Lauren, I have seen you naked," he reminded her. "Remember? It's a little late for modesty. Go and take a shower, and I'll be back soon."

"A shower? I don't know why you—"

"Once you look in the mirror, you'll see why," he said, and smiled. "I'll be back soon."

He left the room, and Lauren tried not to be irritated by his high-handedness. She cradled her sore arm and headed for the en-suite bathroom. And worked out why he'd insisted she shower. She was covered in grime and plaster dust. Her face and hair were matted with the stuff, and her clothes were speckled with blood and dirty smudges.

Lauren stripped off the soiled clothes and stepped beneath the warm water, mindful of the plastic-covered bandage. She washed her hair as best she could, and by the time she emerged from the cubicle, wrapped her hair up in a towel and slipped into his bathrobe, she heard him striding down the hallway.

He paused in the doorway carrying a short stack of clothes. "Let me know if you need anything else," he said, and placed them on the bed.

She nodded. "Thank you. How does my house look?"

"Redeemable," he said, and half smiled. "I've told the contractor to tarp the roof so there's no more damage overnight. And I've arranged to have a certified builder assess the damage in the morning. Get dressed, and I'll make you a cup of that tea you like."

Lauren had to admit he'd done a fair job at choosing her clothes. Gray linen pants and a red collared T-shirt, a sensible black bra and brief set and slip-on sandals. As she stepped into the briefs, she didn't want to think about his lean fingers touching her underwear. Gabe's take-charge attitude should have made her as mad as ever, but she was

actually grateful for his kindness. What had been a frightening experience was eased by him coming to her rescue. When she was finished dressing, she headed for the kitchen. He'd made tea, as promised, and was staring out the long window, mug in hand.

"I think I inhaled a bucket of plaster dust," she said when she entered the room.

He turned and met her gaze. "If the cough keeps up, let me know."

"I will. Thanks for the tea." She saw her handbag, dusty laptop and house keys on the counter. "Oh, that's good. I wasn't sure the computer survived the tree crashing on top of it."

"It seems okay," he said quietly. "I found your bag but couldn't find your cell phone."

She shrugged. "That's fine. I don't need it, anyhow."

"So how are you feeling now?" he asked.

"Pleased I dived underneath the table."

"Me, too," he said, and set the mug down. "I'd just gotten home when I saw the pulley snap and then saw the branch nosedive into your roof."

"Apparently, that tree was going to mess with the fence," she said, and grinned. "They didn't warn me about what it might do to my house, though."

He chuckled, and the sound warmed her blood. "I'm glad you're okay. I was worried about you."

He sounded uncomfortable saying it, and Lauren tensed. He might have been worried, but he clearly didn't want to be. She'd accused him of being hot and then cold, and that certainly seemed to sum up the way he acted around her.

"Thanks for coming to my rescue," she said as flippantly as she could manage.

His mouth flattened, and he passed her his phone. "You can call your parents if you like. Or your brother."

She shook her head and placed the phone on the table. "They'll only worry."

"Well, they'll know something's up when you stay with them tonight."

"I'm not going anywhere," she said, and pushed her shoulders back. "I'm sleeping in my own bed, in my own house."

"No," he said quietly. "You're not."

"Ah, yes I am."

"I'm not going to argue with you about this, Lauren. You stay with your parents or your brother, or if you like I'll drive you to Cassie's. But you're not spending the night in a potentially compromised building that has a huge hole in the roof."

She crossed her arms. "You don't get to tell me what to do."

"Right now, when you're being stubborn and disagreeable, I'll do whatever I have to do to keep you safe."

His words had *ownership* stamped all over them, and the fact he had the audacity to say such a thing when he'd made it clear they had no future only amplified her resentment. He really needed to stop interfering. Sure, she was grateful he'd gotten her out from under the table, but that didn't give him open season on deciding where she would sleep.

"I'll be perfectly safe."

The pulse in his cheek throbbed. "No, you won't…so you stay with your family, or you can stay here. Those are your only options."

Of all the bossy, arrogant, bullheaded…

"Fine," she said quickly, and saw the startled look on his face. "I'll stay here."

No way…

Gabe's stomach landed at his feet. She wasn't staying with him when she had a bunch of perfectly good relatives

to rely on. She was simply being provocative. He was just about to say as much when the challenge in her eyes silenced any protests.

Instead, he called her bluff. "Okay…but you still have to call your parents and tell them what happened."

Her brows came up. "That's interesting coming from a man who won't pick up the telephone to call his own family."

"We're talking about you," he quipped, "not me."

She shrugged. "So where's my bedroom?"

"I'll sleep in the guest room. You can have my room. You'll be more comfortable there."

"Familiar surroundings, you mean?"

His body tensed. "I haven't finished painting in the guest room," he said, and grabbed his cell. "I can order pizza if you're hungry?"

She nodded. "Sure. No anchovies, please. And extra mushrooms."

He half smiled. "Why don't you rest in the living room, and I'll place the order."

She did as he suggested, and once the pizza had been ordered, Gabe grabbed a couple of ginger beers from the refrigerator and headed for the living room. He found her on the sofa, legs curled up, arms crossed, staring at the blank television.

"Everything all right?" he asked, and passed her a bottle.

"Just thinking about my wrecked house."

"It's a house, Lauren," he said quietly, and sat on the other end of the sofa. "Houses can be fixed."

"Not like people, right?" she shot back, and sighed. "Once broken, always broken."

The tremor in her voice made his insides contract. "Is that how you feel?"

"Sometimes," she admitted. "Lately more often than not. I think I just need to…make some changes."

"Changes?"

She raised her shoulders. "I was thinking of selling the store."

He didn't hide his surprise. "That's a bold move. Are you sure it's the right one?"

"Not really," she replied. "I'm not sure of anything. If I do decide to sell, I know my mother will be disappointed. But I don't know how much longer I can keep pretending that it makes me happy. I've been pretending since... since..."

"Since Tim died?"

She nodded slowly. "Yes. Some days I find it so stifling. And then other days I can't believe I'm having such ungrateful thoughts. I mean, what's not to like about being around people who are looking to create the perfect, most special day and then sharing in that joy? But all I feel is tired and weary of plastering on a wide smile every time a bride comes into the store looking for the gown of her dreams."

Her pain reached deep into his soul. "You've had a bad day...don't make a hasty decision when you might not be thinking clearly."

"Spoken from experience?" she asked softly.

"Yes," he replied.

She shrugged. "I won't."

The doorbell rang, and Gabe got to his feet. "Our dinner. Back in a minute."

They ate in the kitchen, and by eight-thirty were lingering over coffee.

"Are you okay?" he asked when he noticed her frowning.

"Tired," she replied. "And sore. I think I strained my back when I darted underneath the table. Which is a small price to pay considering what could have happened."

Gabe pushed his mug aside. "I don't want to remember what I thought when I saw that tree crash."

"I'm glad you were there to rescue me."

Was she? Was he? It seemed as though there was no escaping the pull that drew them together. It had a will of its own, dragging him back toward her at every opportunity.

"Nothing's changed," he said, and hated how cold his voice sounded.

"Everything's changed. I can't pretend and just switch off my emotions."

"Can't? Or won't?"

Her gaze was unwavering. "What are you so afraid of?"

Gabe sucked in a breath. "Hurting you."

"People get hurt all the time. You can't always control it."

"I can try," he said, and stood. "I won't mislead you, Lauren. I won't make promises I can't keep. I've told you how I feel about you and—"

"Actually," she said, cutting him off. "You haven't said how you feel about me at all…only how you feel about relationships and commitment."

Discomfiture snaked up his spine. "It's the same thing."

Her brows rose tellingly. "That's a man's logic," she said, and got to her feet. "And I'm a woman, Gabe. I think and feel deeply. And I know what I want. For the first time in a long time, I actually know what will make me happy. And who."

Guilt pressed onto his shoulders. "Don't pin your hopes on me, Lauren. I can't make you happy…because I can't promise you a future."

She stared at him, eyes glistening. "Is it because you think you might not be able to give me a baby?"

The burn in his stomach intensified. "You can't deny that's important to you."

"It was," she admitted. "It is. But there are other options, like IVF and adoption. I mean, no two people know if they'll be able to produce a child until they try. And you said it was a possibility, not an absolute."

Her relentless logic was butchering him.

"It's just one more complication, Lauren. One that you don't need."

"But I'm right?" she asked. "So now you're hiding behind this idea of potential infertility to keep me or any other woman at arm's length?"

"I'm not hiding. I'm laying out the facts."

"The facts?" she echoed. "You're like a vault when it comes to the facts. Right now, in this moment, you're well and strong and *here*...why isn't that enough?"

"Because it's not. Because it might not last," he replied, frustrated and angry.

"But you don't know what will happen...no one does."

"I know what the medical data says. I know what the odds are of it coming back. If I can stay healthy for five years and not relapse, then I'll consider my options. But until then—"

"Five years?" She cut him off and shook her head. "You can't organize feelings to order like that."

"I can. I will."

"So you plan to avoid getting close to anyone for the next few years just in case you aren't around to seal the deal? That's absurd. What made you so cynical?"

"Facing the prospect of death."

"I don't believe you," she said hauntingly. "There's more to it. You had a career where you saw death all the time, a career that obviously called out to you because you're mentally strong and compassionate and able to deal with grief and despair and hopelessness. I don't believe that all that strength disappeared because you were faced with the challenge of an illness you've now recovered from."

His chest tightened. "I can't talk about—"

"What happened to you?" she pleaded. "Tell me...what happened that made you so determined to be alone?"

Gabe's heart thundered, and he fought the words that

hovered on the end of his tongue. He didn't want to tell her; he didn't want to admit to anything. But the pained, imploring look on her face was suddenly harder to deny than his deep-seated determination to say nothing.

"My dad died when I was seventeen," he said flatly. "And I watched my mom become hollow inside. At first, I watched her become headstrong in her denial and refuse to admit the inevitable. I watched her use every ounce of strength she had to give him hope and keep him alive. I watched her argue with doctors and oncologists about his treatment and try every holistic and natural remedy she could to give him more time. And then when the treatment stopped working and he relapsed, I watched her care for him and feed him and bathe him, and then I watched her cry every day when she thought no one was looking. And when he died, part of her died, too. She was heartbroken. She was sad, and there was nothing anyone could do for her…there was nothing *I* could do for her."

He drew several gulps of air into his lungs. It was the first time he'd said the words. The first time he'd admitted how helpless he'd felt watching his mother fall apart.

"And I'm never going to put anyone through that…not ever."

She shuddered. "So instead you'll shut the world out?"

"Not the world," he said quickly. "Just…"

"Just me?" she asked, eyes glazed. "Or any woman who wants to be with you for more than a one-night stand?"

"Exactly," he said woodenly.

She shook her head. "It wasn't your job to fix your mother. No one can fix that kind of pain…only time can truly heal," she said quietly. "Believe me, I know. If your mother didn't recover, it's not your responsibility or job to question why. And it must be that your dad was the true love of her life."

"Like Tim was yours?"

Did he sound as jealous by that idea as he felt? He didn't want to feel it. Didn't want to think it. Didn't want to be so conflicted and confused that all he wanted to do was haul her into his arms and kiss her over and over and forget every other wretched thought or feeling.

Her mouth softened. "I did love Tim, very much. But I didn't honor that love when I married James. And when my marriage ended, I was determined to find someone who wouldn't make me feel anything that might dishonor those feelings again. And I tried," she said as tears filled her eyes. "And failed."

"And that's exactly why I won't do this, Lauren. That look you have when you talk about Tim... My mom had that same look. You've been through it, too. You know how it feels to lose someone you care about. Why the hell would you potentially put yourself through that again? It doesn't make sense. You need to walk away from this. And me."

"So you're doing this for me. Is that what you're saying?"

He shrugged. "I'm doing this for us both."

She inhaled resignedly. "I'm going to bed. Are you coming?"

Bed? He groaned inwardly. "No."

Her mouth twitched. "You're not going to make love to me tonight?"

Gabe's entire body tightened. She was pure provocation, and he wanted her so much, his blood felt as though it were on fire.

"No." It was close to the hardest thing he'd ever said.

Her eyes shadowed. "Would you just...hold me?"

Pain and longing sat in his gut like a lead weight. But she didn't know what she was asking. If he stayed with her tonight, there would be no turning back. He wanted her... he wanted her so much he ached inside thinking about denying that feeling. But Gabe wouldn't allow that wanting

to turn into needing. Needing meant giving everything. Everything meant loving. And that was impossible.

"I can't." His voice sounded hollow and empty. "I can't give you what you want."

She looked at him, and he saw the disappointment and regret in her eyes. She was hurt.

"No, I guess you can't," she said, and left the room.

Chapter Twelve

"And that's it?"

Lauren dropped her gaze to the floor. If she kept looking at Cassie and Mary-Jayne, they'd see the tears in her eyes. And she wouldn't cry anymore. She'd cried enough over lost love throughout the years. She'd cried for Tim. She'd cried when he'd finally told her he was dying and wouldn't be able to give her the future he'd promised. She'd cried over his grave and in the years since. She'd even cried for James when he'd walked out the door. She'd cried for lost dreams and for the children she'd never borne.

And not once, during all those tears and anguish, did she ever think she'd love again. Nor did she want to. She'd planned on friendship and companionship and then marriage and children to help ease her aching heart. And instead had tumbled headlong into something that was all desire and heat and a longing so intense it physically pained her. She loved Gabe. And she knew, deep down to her soul, that it was the one love she would never recover from.

But she had to try.

And she would.

"That's it," she replied, and pretended to enjoy the glass of wine she'd been cradling for the best part of an hour. She managed a smile. "Looks like I'm back to trawling ReliableBores.com."

Mary-Jayne made a huffing sound. "Did he give you a reason?"

Sure he did. But Lauren would never betray Gabe's confidence and tell them about his illness. Now she had to concentrate on forgetting all about her fledging feelings and put Gabe Vitali out of her mind. And show a little more enthusiasm for her friends' company. But she wasn't in the mood for a Friday-evening movie and junk-food marathon. She simply wanted to lick her wounds in private.

"Don't forget it's my sister's birthday party tomorrow night," Mary-Jayne reminded them. "I'll pick you both up."

Lauren nodded and noticed that Cassie, who still hadn't heard from Doug, looked about as unenthused as she felt. An evening with Scott and Evie Jones was one thing... knowing Gabe would be there, too, was another thing altogether. However, she was determined to put on a brave face and go. Avoiding Gabe was pointless. They shared several of the same friends and were bound to run into one another occasionally. She might be able to steer clear of him over the hedge that separated their homes, but becoming a hermit to her friends wasn't an option.

"How's the house look?" Cassie asked.

"The repairs will take the best part of the weekend, but I should be back in by Tuesday."

"Well, you can stay here as long as you like," her friend offered.

And she was glad she had such loyal friends. She'd gone to bed the night before with a broken heart and awoke with

more resolve than she knew she possessed. Gabe was gone by the time she pulled herself out of bed, and had left a cursory note telling her a builder would be at her house at seven-thirty to check for structural damage. By eight she was back inside her own house, cleaning up with the help of the fencing contractor and his crew, who'd arrived with sheepish faces and good intentions. And while the repairs to the roof were being done, she'd stay with Cassie and try to stop thinking about Gabe.

"Thanks, I appreciate it."

"That's what friends are for," Cassie assured her, then smiled. "You know, there's this man at work I think you might like."

Lauren groaned. "A blind date? Ah, no thanks."

"What's the harm? He's nice. He's in the pathology department. Want me to set you up?"

"No chance."

On Saturday morning, Lauren headed to the store early. She gave her mother an abridged version of what had happened with the house, leaving out how she'd stayed at Gabe's that night and only telling her she was bunking in with Cassie until the repairs were done. She didn't mention her thoughts about selling the store. She'd think about that later. When her heart wasn't breaking. When she was whole and was certain she'd finished crying wasted tears.

Late that afternoon, Lauren dressed in a pale lemon sundress in filmy rayon that tied at her nape. The garment fitted neatly over the bodice and flared from the waist. She matched it with a pair of silver heels and kept her hair loose around her shoulders. Mary-Jayne picked her up at six, and since Cassie had decided to give the party a miss, they drove straight to Dunn Inn. The big A-framed home was set back from the road, and the gardens always reminded

Lauren of something out of an old fairy story. There was a wishing well in the center of the yard, surrounded by cobbled paths and tall ferns, and it had been a bed and breakfast for over a decade.

Gabe's car wasn't out front, and she heaved a relieved sigh. She grabbed Evie's birthday gift from the backseat and followed Mary-Jayne inside. Evie was in the kitchen, as was Grace. Lauren had always envied the three sisters' relationship. They were as different as night and day and yet shared a formidable bond. Of course, she adored her brother, but sometimes wished she'd had a sister, too.

"Scott's running an errand," Evie explained, and Lauren wondered if she imagined how the other woman glanced in her direction just a little longer than expected. "He'll be back soon."

Mary-Jayne laughed. "Oh, with some big birthday surprise for you?"

Evie raised her steeply arched brows. "Well, it's certainly a surprise. Not for me, though. And since I'm not sure I really want to be celebrating the fact I'm only two years off turning forty, I'm more than happy about that."

"The gifts are all on the buffet in the front living room," Grace said as she cradled Evie's six-month-old daughter in her arms.

Her sister-in-law was glowing, and Lauren wondered if she was pregnant. It would certainly explain why her brother had sounded so chipper on the phone that morning when he'd called after hearing about her tree mishap from her mother. She was achingly happy for Cameron and knew he deserved every ounce of happiness that was in his life. But part of her envied him, too. He'd put his heart on the line when he'd pursued Grace, and it had paid off.

Not like me....

Her heart was well and truly smashed. Gabe was out of reach. As unattainable as some remote planet. He'd made

it abundantly clear that he wasn't interested. He'd rejected her, wholly and completely. And she had to stop wasting her energy hoping he'd come around. There would be no fairy-tale ending.

Lauren offered to take the gifts into the living room and left the sisters alone to catch up. The big room was formal and furnished with a long leather chaise and twin heavy brocade sofas. A collection of Evie's artwork covered the walls, and a thick rug lay in front of the fireplace and hearth.

She'd just laid the gifts out when she heard the wide French doors rattle. A second later, Gabe was in the room. In black trousers and white shirt, he looked so handsome, it was impossible to arrest the breathless gasp that escaped her throat. But he looked a little tired, too, and she wondered if he'd had as much trouble sleeping as she'd had. She almost wished sleeplessness upon him. She wanted to share everything with him...including her misery.

He didn't say anything. He only looked at her, taking his time to rake his stare from her sandaled feet to her freshly washed hair. A gust of awareness swept into the room like a seductive wind, and she couldn't have moved even if she'd tried. Heat coursed up her limbs and hit her low in the belly. In a flash of a second she remembered every touch, every kiss, every moment of their lovemaking. And she knew, by the scorching intensity of his gaze, that he was remembering it, too.

It was hard to stop from rushing into his arms. Because they were the arms she loved. She wondered how it had happened...how she'd managed to fall in love with a man who didn't love her in return. Who wouldn't risk loving her in return. A man who was everything she'd sworn off and yet was everything she craved. A man who openly offered her nothing but heartache.

"Lauren," he said finally, breaking the thick silence. "You look lovely."

She swallowed hard and shrugged. "Thank you."

"How are you feeling? Is your arm getting better?"

"Yes," she said, and touched the narrow bandage. "Healing well."

"How's the house?"

"Good," she replied. "Actually, I wanted to thank you for getting the builder to come around and assess the place. He's been very accommodating and will have the repairs finished by next week."

"No problem. He's the father of one of the kids in the junior lifeguard program at the surf club. He was happy to help out."

"Well, I appreciate your concern. I didn't see your truck out front so I wasn't sure you would be here today."

"I'm parked out back," he explained. "If you'd rather I left, then I'll go."

"No," she said quickly. "It's fine," she lied, dying inside. "It's Evie's birthday, and Scott is your cousin. You should be here with your family."

He stepped closer. "I've been thinking about you."

She shrugged. "I can't imagine why."

His gaze was unrelenting. "We left things badly the other day and I—"

"It's fine," she assured him with way more bravado than she felt. "You said what you had to say. I'm over it."

I'm over you....

Liar.

He nodded slowly. "That's...good. You know, I never planned on hurting you."

Humiliation coursed through her blood, and she had to dig herself out of the hole she was in. "You didn't, so spare yourself the concern. I'm perfectly okay. We had one night together. The sex was great. The pancakes were

not so great." She shrugged again and plastered on a tight smile as she counted off a few fingers. "And I'm back to day three of my new vow of celibacy."

"So…you're okay?"

Her smile broadened. "Never better. Don't worry on my account, Gabe. We had sex…it's not a big deal. People have sex all the time. We had an itch, we scratched it."

His mouth thinned. "An itch? Is that what it was?"

"Sure," she said, and shrugged. "What else? I mean, we really don't know one another very well, and we always seem to end up arguing. It's better we slept together early on rather than drag the whole thing out for an age. My plans haven't changed, and yours seem set in stone… so no harm done."

He stared at her, long and hard, and finally he crossed his arms and shook his head. "I don't believe you, Lauren. I think…I think you're saying what you imagine I want to hear."

She laughed loudly. "Maybe I just wanted to get laid… like you did."

"Is that what you think I wanted?" he asked quietly. "To get laid?"

"Sure," she replied, and shrugged. "You told me as much that night you came over for dinner, remember? You called me Commitment 101 and said you have casual and meaningless sex."

His brows came up. "I said that?"

"Words to that effect."

He smiled. "Well, I haven't had as much meaningless sex as you've clearly been imagining. And before you go accusing me of doing that with you, be assured there was nothing meaningless to me about the night we spent together. You told me you don't make love casually, and I believe that." He said the words with such arrogant con-

fidence, she wanted to slug him. "But I think you're hurt and I think you're angry. And I also think—"

"And I think you're the most conceited jerk of all time," she said hotly, cutting him off. A door closed in the house, and she heard voices, but Lauren pressed on, battling with the humiliating fury she felt in her heart. He didn't want her. He didn't need her. Why couldn't he simply leave her alone? "I don't care how much I want to get laid in the future, I will steer well clear of your bed. One night in the sack with you isn't enough to—"

Lauren stopped ranting when she heard someone clearing their throat and noticed that three people were standing in the doorway. It was Scott and two others. A man, tall and handsome with fair hair and blue eyes just like Gabe's, and a woman whose eyes were equally as blue and who looked to be around sixty. She heard Gabe groan as he turned on his heels and faced the group.

When he spoke, Lauren almost fainted on the spot.

"Hi, Mom."

Seeing Claire Vitali in the doorway, with his brother Aaron hovering close by, was enough to quell any urge he had to kiss Lauren's amazing mouth. Since he'd walked into the room and spotted her by the buffet, it was all he'd wanted to do. With her temper flared and her cheeks ablaze with color, he'd never seen her look more beautiful or more desirable. But she was hurting, too, and even though she denied it, Gabe knew he was responsible for the unhappiness in her eyes. He hated that he'd done that…even though he felt certain it was for the best.

The group moved into the room, and before he had a chance to make introductions, his mother was clutching at him in a fierce and long embrace. Once she'd finished hugging, she kissed his cheek and stepped back.

"It's good to see you, Gabriel," she said, using his full name for deliberate effect, and smiled.

Despite his shock, he was genuinely pleased to see his parent. "You, too, Mom."

His mother noticed Lauren immediately and held out her hand. "Hello, I'm Claire Vitali."

Lauren took her hand and introduced herself. "It's nice to meet you."

Gabe saw the gleam in his mother's eyes. "And you."

"Well, I'll leave you all to catch up," Lauren said, and moved across the room as if her soles were on fire. He noticed she smiled at Aaron and Scott on her way out but didn't spare him a glance.

"I'll go, too," Scott said, and grinned.

"Yeah," Gabe said. "Thanks so much for the heads-up."

His cousin shrugged. "Our mothers swore me to secrecy. And don't be too long. It's my wife's birthday, and there's cake."

Once he was gone, Aaron stepped toward him. "That's one pretty girl," his brother said with a grin, and went for a bear hug. Gabe ignored the comment about Lauren and hugged him back.

When the hugging was over and they were settled on the two sofas, he asked the obvious question. "So what are you two doing here?"

"I'm here because she insisted I come," Aaron said, and grinned.

"I wanted to see my son," his mother replied. "And since you weren't returning my calls…"

Gabe glanced at his older brother, looking his usually cocky self on the opposite sofa, and scowled. "I did text and say I was busy."

"Mom didn't believe me," Aaron said, and grinned again. "She wanted to see for herself."

He looked to his mother. "See what?"

"I needed to make sure you were okay," she said, and gave him a look of concern.

"I'm fine," he said. "As you can see."

His mother's mouth thinned. "Are you really? You can tell me if you're not."

"You came all this way because you thought I'd had some kind of relapse?"

She sighed crossly. "I came all this way because you're my son, and you and your brothers and sister are the most important thing in my life. I won't apologize for caring."

Guilt pressed between his ribs. "I'm sorry I worried you. But I'm fine."

"You don't look fine," she said, and frowned. His mother never was one to pull punches. "You look tired and annoyed, and you're clearly not happy that we've turned up unannounced. So what's going on with you?"

Sometimes Gabe wished he came from one of those families where everyone didn't know everyone else's business. Was there such a thing as caring too much? When he'd been diagnosed with lymphoma, his mother and siblings had closed ranks around him, almost to the point of smothering him with concern. And it hadn't taken long for resentment to set in. Since then, they'd treated him differently, and it irritated the hell out of him. It was as though they'd wanted to wrap him in cotton wool and *fix* everything.

"Nothing," he assured her, feeling about sixteen years old. "Everything's fine. I'm healthy. I have a job I like, friends… You don't need to worry, Mom. I'm a grown man, and I can take care of myself."

"I'll always worry," she said, still looking grim. "It's a given that a mother worries about her children, regardless of how old they are." She sighed and patted his arm affectionately. "But if you say you're fine…then I believe you. You still look tired, though."

"I'm just not sleeping great at the moment. Otherwise, I'm in perfect health and have the results of my latest tests to prove it. Please, stop fretting."

"So," Aaron said, and stretched back in the sofa. "You're fine. Which doesn't explain why you've been avoiding our calls for the past month or so." His brows rose questioningly. "What's the story with the pretty blonde with the big brown eyes who you clearly got into bed but who now wants nothing to do with you?"

"Aaron," their mother chastised. "That's enough."

Gabe's mouth pressed tight. "My relationship with Lauren is no one's business and I don't—"

"Relationship?" His brother laughed and cut him off. "Ha…of course. Now I get it." Aaron propped forward on the seat and grinned broadly. He looked at their mother. "Mom, he's not sick…he's *lovesick*."

Gabe found the urge to crash tackle his big-mouthed brother. "Shut up."

"Aaron." Their mom said his brother's name again, this time quietly. "Go and eat some cake. I'd like to talk to your brother alone."

"I'm right," Aaron said with a grin as he stood. "I know I'm right."

Once Aaron left, Gabe faced his mother's stare. "Is that true?" she asked gently.

"Is what true?"

She made a face. "Lauren… Are you in love with her?"

Gabe got to his feet and paced around the sofa. "No."

"But you're involved with her?"

"Not exactly. It's complicated," he said, and shrugged. "And I don't want to talk about it."

"Well, that's always been your problem, really…not talking," his mom said, and sighed. "Just like your father. Not talking about your illness…not talking about what hap-

pened at the hospital when you went back to work…not talking about why you broke up with Mona…not talking about why you needed to put an ocean between your old life and your new one."

His shoulders tensed. "You know why I left."

"Because you blamed yourself for that woman and her baby dying," she said gently. "Even though it wasn't your fault. Even though you weren't there."

"I *should* have been there. I was on duty."

"You were sick," his mother reminded him.

"Yes," he said hollowly. "I was. And I went back too soon. I did everything I would have told a patient to *not* do. I ignored what was best and did exactly what I wanted, and because of that a young woman and her baby died. I am to blame, Mom. It doesn't matter how many times I try to get it clear in my head, or how often I'm told the inquiry didn't find me culpable." He pointed to his temple. "In here I feel the blame. In here I see her husband weeping over her body. Because I was arrogant and thought I could trick my broken body into being what it once was." He sighed heavily. "But it's not. And it might never be. I won't pretend anymore. And I certainly won't drag anyone else into that place if I do end up back where I was."

His mother's eyes glistened. "You mean Lauren?"

"I mean anyone," he said pointedly. "I saw what it did to you, Mom…watching Dad slowly fade away. It was hard to sit back and for a time watch you fade away, too."

"Gabe, I didn't—"

"We should get back to the party," he said, and held out his arm. "Before that lousy brother of mine eats all the birthday cake."

She blinked a couple of times. They weren't done. But his mother knew not to push too much. Gabe led her into the dining room and noticed that everyone was there, standing

around the table as Evie prepared to blow out the birthday candles…everyone except Lauren.

Had she left?

He ducked out of the room and headed outside. She was in the front yard, standing on the cobbled pathway by the wishing well, partially hidden by large ferns, arms crossed and clearly deep in thought. Everything about her reached him deep down, into a place he'd never let anyone go.

Are you in love with her?

His mother's words came rushing back. He'd denied it. Because he didn't want to face what it would mean to truly love a woman like Lauren. Aaron had called him love-sick, and in a way that's exactly how he felt. He couldn't define it, couldn't put into words what he was feeling when he was around her. It was like a fever that wouldn't break. A pain that wouldn't abate. His chest hurt simply thinking about her. And his damned libido seemed to be on a kind of constant red alert.

Was that love?

He hoped not. He didn't want it to be. He was no good for Lauren.

"Are you making wishes?" he asked as he approached.

She shook her head. "I don't think I believe in them."

"You're going to miss out on cake," he said.

She turned her head sideways. "I'm going to skip the cake. And the party."

"Are you planning on walking home?" he asked, stepping a little closer.

"It's not far," she replied. "A few blocks."

"In those heels?" He stared at her feet for a moment. "I'll drive you home if that's what you want."

"No," she said quietly. "You should stay here with your family." She uncrossed her arms and turned toward him. "Your mother seems nice."

"She is nice."

"And clearly worried about you," she said, and smiled wryly. "I told you to call her."

Gabe shrugged. "I know you did. I should have listened. She was convinced I had...you know...relapsed."

"Well, she must be relieved to know you're fine. And I'm sorry if your mother and brother overheard our conversation before," she said, and Gabe noticed her cheeks were pinkish. "I shouldn't have lost my temper."

"My mom's cool. And don't worry about Aaron. He's a jerk, too," he said, and grinned a little. "You'd probably like him."

Lauren rolled her eyes. "I've decided to give up on handsome and charming men. Too much trouble."

"Maybe there's something safe in that middle road you were looking for."

"Maybe," she agreed. "Anyhow, I'm going home now."

Gabe reached for her instinctively. He took her hand and wrapped his fingers around hers. "I'm...I'm sorry, Lauren."

She didn't pull away. She didn't move. She only looked up at him, and in the fading afternoon light, he could see every feature. The morning after the night they'd made love, he'd watched her sleep, and in that time he'd memorized every line and curve of her face. He wanted to make love to her again. And again. He wanted to hold her in his arms and kiss her beautiful mouth. But she wasn't his to kiss.

"I know you are," she said so quietly, her voice whispered along the edge of the breeze. "I am, too. I'm sorry you think you're not worth the risk. And I'm sorry you think I'm not strong enough to handle whatever might happen. I guess after what happened with Tim, you have your reasons for believing that. But you're doing exactly what Tim did. He didn't trust me enough to try.... He didn't trust me enough to let me in and share the time he had...and you don't trust me, either."

Gabe's insides jerked. "It's not about trust."

"It is." She pulled her hand from his and reached up to gently touch his face, eyes glistening. "But do you want to know something, Gabe? I would have rather had five years, one year, one month with you…than a lifetime with someone else."

Chapter Thirteen

Lauren moved back into her house on Wednesday afternoon, and since the new fence was now complete, she had less chance of seeing Gabe. Which was exactly what she wanted.

She also made a few decisions. She talked with her mother about The Wedding House and agreed that they'd look to finding a buyer within the next twelve months if she was still keen to sell. In the meantime, Lauren had decided to cut back her hours at the store and return part-time to college to get her accounting degree.

And after much convincing from her meddling, albeit well-meaning friends, she agreed to go on a date with Cassie's pathologist on Friday night. She also made a commitment to walk Cassie's dog, Mouse, since her friend was still feeling the effects of her appendectomy, and at nearly five months pregnant, wasn't keen to be on the end of the leash of the huge Harlequin Great Dane. He was well mannered, though, and incredibly quiet and not unruly like Jed.

On Friday morning, she took him for a long walk, and was heading back along the pathway when she saw Megan jogging toward her. The teen's long limbs stretched out, and her tiny sports shorts molded her toned thighs. Lauren felt about as sporty as an old shoe in her baggy cotton shorts and sensible racer-back T-shirt when the girl came up to her.

"Hey, there," Megan said cheerfully. "Nice dog."

"Thanks," she said, and tried to be as equally cheerful.

"So," the other girl said, jogging on the spot. "Are you the reason why Gabe's in such a bad mood?"

Lauren's skin prickled. "I don't know what you mean."

She shrugged. "It was just something my sister said. But she can be pretty catty when she wants to be. She had this idea that you and Gabe were together."

"No, we're not."

Megan grinned. "Have you met his brother? He's hot. But then, I've always had a thing for blonds. Anyhow, if you're not the reason why he's in a bad mood, someone is, 'cause he's been unbearable all week." Megan laughed shrilly. "Gotta run. See ya!"

She watched the other girl jog away, and then turned Mouse back onto the path. She was about twenty feet from passing alongside the surf club when she spotted Gabe's brother outside the building, phone pressed to his ear. He was handsome, she thought, but not as classically good-looking as his younger brother. Lauren was hoping to pass by unnoticed, but he waved to her when he realized who she was.

Seconds later, he walked over. "Nice to see you again," he said, and smiled. "Although I don't think we were actually introduced. I'm Aaron. That's some dog you have there."

"He's on loan from a friend. So are you enjoying Crystal Point?"

"I like the scenery," he said, and grinned. "And nice weather. It's a lot like California."

She asked him about his twin sons, and was about to excuse herself when she saw Gabe standing on the second-story balcony, watching them. Or more to the point, glaring at them.

"Uh-oh," Aaron said, and waved to his brother. "He doesn't look happy. Can't figure why. Can you?" he asked with a devilish grin.

Heat seeped up her neck, and Lauren shrugged. "No idea."

"He can be a little uptight about some things."

She'd never considered Gabe to be uptight. Bossy and hardheaded, perhaps. And stubborn. And handsome and sexy, and she'd always thought him to be rather charming and easygoing. Stupidly, she didn't like that his brother was so openly criticizing him.

"I suppose we can all be like that," she said quietly. "Under certain circumstances."

He laughed loudly. "Ah, so you, too, huh?"

"Me, too, what?" she asked, puzzled.

He laughed again. "Nothing…just go easy on him, okay? He's been through a lot. And I don't think he quite knows what to do about you, Lauren."

Reject me…that's what.

She'd laid her heart on the line. She'd told him how she felt in the garden at Dunn Inn and he'd only turned around and walked away. No words. No comfort. No acknowledgment.

His silence had told her all she needed to know.

"Oh, I'm pretty sure he does. Nice talking with you. So long."

She walked off and felt Gabe's gaze follow her the entire way up the path until she disappeared from his view. He could stare all he wanted. She'd had nearly a week to

pull herself together and had so far had done a good job. He was out of her thoughts.

Now all she had to do was get him out of her heart, as well.

Gabe missed Lauren like crazy. He missed talking to her. He missed how the scent of her perfume always seemed to linger on his clothes for ages after they'd spent time together. And he missed kissing her.

And he hated that he'd hurt her.

I would have rather have had five years, one year, one month with you...than a lifetime with someone else.

Her words haunted him. They were honest and heartfelt and much more than he was worthy of. And he'd been so tempted to take what she offered. More than tempted. He'd wanted it. Longed for it. *Ached* for it.

He'd wanted to wrap her in his arms and hold her there forever.

Except...he might not have forever to offer her. And she deserved that. She deserved more than an empty promise and his broken, defective body.

He headed back downstairs and started work. It was mind-numbing admin stuff, but at least it kept him busy. And gave him a chance to stop thinking about Lauren.

"That's one seriously gorgeous woman."

Gabe turned around. Aaron was hovering by the door. He knew his brother was talking about Lauren. "Aren't you supposed to be packing for your flight tomorrow?"

"Change of plans," he quipped. "Mom and I were just talking... We're staying another week."

Gabe groaned to himself. Another week? He wasn't sure he'd cope with another week of his well-meaning mother and annoying older sibling. "Why? Don't you have a life and two kids to get back to?"

Aaron smiled, walked into the office and plunked into a

chair. "You know very well that my ex-wife has the boys, and my business partner is running things while I'm away. And anyway, I wouldn't miss this chance to see you squirm for anything."

Gabe called him an unflattering name and pretended to work.

"You didn't answer my question," Aaron said.

He stared at the paperwork on his desk. "It wasn't a question," he reminded his brother. "It was a statement. And I'm not squirming."

Aaron laughed. "Oh, you sure as hell are. And I must say she's very pretty and kind of wholesome looking…but sexy underneath that whole girl-next-door thing, if you know what I mean."

Gabe knew exactly what he meant. He jerked his head up. "Haven't you got somewhere else to be? Someone else to irritate?"

Aaron linked his hands behind his head and stretched. "Nope…just you."

"I'm working."

"You're ignoring my question…got it bad, huh?"

Gabe scowled. "What I've got is work to do and no time to waste. I'll see you tonight, around six."

His family was staying at Dunn Inn for the duration of their trip, since Gabe had insisted his house wasn't ready for guests, and the B and B was more comfortable. But he'd put off having them around all week until they'd invited themselves over for dinner that night.

His brother left shortly afterward, and Gabe spent the day moving from bad mood to foul mood and in no particular order. Not even the news that he'd been successful in his interview with the hospital had lightened his spirits. There were licenses and insurances to renew, but he'd been offered a job in the E.R. and would start the follow-

ing month. It meant he had time to hand in his resignation and help find a replacement.

By the time he returned home, it was well after five. He took a quick shower, dressed in jeans and T-shirt and was just marinating the steaks when he heard Scott's dual-cab truck pull up outside. He headed outside and walked down the steps. By the time he reached his brother and mother, another car had pulled up next door. He could see over the fence, and when he spotted Lauren walking down her driveway and then the male driver of the car get out, Gabe's body stilled. They were saying hello. She was smiling. The man opened the passenger door and she got into the car.

Aaron was now out of the truck and was also watching. He clamped Gabe on the shoulder and chuckled. "Looks as though you've got yourself some competition."

"Don't be an ass," Gabe said, and opened the door for their mother.

He greeted his mom and kept one eye on the car as it drove off down the cul-de-sac.

She's on a date....

It shouldn't have made him madder than hell. It shouldn't have made him feel anything. He'd made the rules. She'd opened her heart, and he'd refused to take it. But a date?

He was burning inside just thinking about it.

Over dinner, he stayed silent and let his brother and mom talk. Tension pressed down on his shoulders, and he couldn't quell the uneasy feeling in his gut. He'd told her to find someone else, and she'd done exactly as he'd suggested. It should have eased the guilt. But it didn't. It only amplified the confusion and discontent rumbling through his system and settling directly in the region of his heart.

When Aaron took a phone call and wandered off to the living room for some privacy, his mother cornered Gabe by the kitchen counter.

"So now that you've had a few days to calm down, would you like to tell me about Lauren?"

He shook his head. "No."

His mother sighed. "Do you know what I think? I think you're very much in love with her, and it scares you like you've never been scared before."

I'm not in love with her. I'm not in love with her. I'm not in love with her....

"Nonsense," he said, and started stacking plates in the dishwasher.

"Are you worried she'll leave like Mona did, should your health change?"

"Lauren is nothing like Mona," he replied, and continued stacking. "Actually, I'm concerned she'll do exactly the opposite."

His mother shook her head. "Gabe, isn't that her choice to make?"

"Not if I can help it." He straightened and placed his hands on the counter. "Please stay out of it, Mom. That means no interfering, no meddling... Promise me you'll just leave it alone."

"I can't do that," she said, and smiled. "When one of my kids is in trouble, I'll always interfere."

"I'm not in trouble," he insisted. "And I know what I'm doing. She's grieved for one man already. I won't be responsible for her having to do that over another."

"Another man? Who?"

He briefly explained about Tim. "Now, can we drop it?"

His mother nodded. "Yes, of course."

Gabe made coffee, and when Aaron returned, they sat around the table for a while, telling old tales about things they'd done as kids. Like the time Aaron got caught making out with the local minister's daughter, or when geeky, sixteen-year-old Luca got suspended from math club because he'd followed Gabe and Aaron and gotten a tattoo

on his arm. The stories made him laugh and put him in a marginally better mood. He waved them off at nine-thirty but was back on the porch fifteen minutes later when he spotted a car return next door.

She got out and walked up the driveway as the car pulled away. So her date didn't see her to the door. *Schmuck*. Mounting dislike and rage festered in his gut for a few more minutes, and before he had a chance to stop himself, Gabe was striding around the fence, the hedge and then through the gate and up the steps.

He tapped on the door and waited. He heard her heels clicking on the timber floor, and when she pulled the door open, she looked genuinely surprised to see him.

"Oh…Gabe."

He shifted on his feet. She was so beautiful. Her hair was down, framing her perfectly lovely face, highlighting the deep caramel eyes that haunted him. She wore a little black dress that flipped over her hips and made every ounce of desire and longing he possessed surge to the surface in a wave.

"Who the hell was that?" he demanded once she'd opened the security door.

She moved back a little. "You mean my date?"

"Yeah," he shot back, so agitated he could barely get the word out. "Your *date*."

She actually smiled. Like she thought him hilarious. Or the biggest fool of all time. Or both. "His name is Steve. Although I'm not quite sure how that's any of your business."

It wasn't. *She was on a date with someone named Steve.* Steve who? He hated the name, anyhow. *Forget about it… she can do whatever she likes. And with whomever she likes.* But be damned if the very idea of that didn't make every part of his flesh and bones ache.

"I was only…" He stopped, realizing nothing he could say would make him look like anything other than exactly

what he was—a stupidly jealous idiot. It was a sobering realization. Had he ever been jealous before? Had he ever cared enough about anyone to garner such an emotional response?

No. Never.

I think you're very much in love with her, and it scares you like you've never been scared before....

His mother's words beat around in his head.

She made an impatient sound. "Goodbye, Gabe."

He didn't move. He stared at her. Long and deep. And the more he stared, the more he knew her impatience increased. And before he had a chance to question why, he reached out and pulled her close. She looked startled for a microsecond and then tilted her head and glared up at him. Body to body, breath to breath, Gabe experienced a connection with her that was so intense, so acute, it almost knocked him unconscious. Had her date kissed her? Had another man kissed those lips he'd somehow come to think of as his own? His arms tightened around her frame, drawing her against him so intimately, he could feel every lovely rise and curve.

She shook her head. "Don't you so much as think about—"

He claimed her lips, driving his own to hers with blatant passion and little finesse. He found her tongue and toyed with it, drawing it into an erotic dance as old as time. It took her seconds to respond, and she kissed him back, winding her tongue around his, and the sensation pitched an arrow of intense pleasure from his mouth to his chest and stomach and then directly to his groin. He urged her hips closer and groaned. She felt so good, and he wanted her so much. He wanted to strip her naked and feel every luscious curve and dip of her body. He wanted to lose himself in her sweet loving and forget he couldn't give her what she deserved.

Gabe was about to ease them both across the threshold

when she suddenly wrenched free. She pulled away from him and stumbled back on unsteady feet, dragging in big gulps of air.

She pressed the back of her fingers against her mouth. "Don't do that again."

"Lauren, I—"

"Leave me alone, Gabe. Don't kiss me. Don't touch me. Don't come over. Don't call. Don't so much as leave me a note in my letterbox. I'm done. You got that? *Done*."

Then she closed the door in his face.

Lauren didn't sleep that night. She tossed in her bed and stared at the ceiling. How *dare* Gabe turn up on her doorstep and demand to know who she'd been out with. How *dare* he act all jealous and wounded. And how *dare* he kiss her like that! It was a kiss that had *possession* stamped all over it. And he didn't own her. Her broken heart had now turned into an angry one. He'd forfeited any rights she may have given him. She'd date whoever she wanted to. Even Steve, who had been the perfect gentleman over dinner and was polite and friendly and had done all the right things for a first date. And since he'd called her only ten minutes after dropping her off and asked if he could see her again, he was clearly emotionally available. Unlike Gabe, who obviously only wanted to kiss her and confuse her. So maybe Steve didn't make her pulse race…. He might, over time.

She finally dropped off to sleep after two and woke up with a headache. Saturday morning was busy at the store. Lauren had a gown fitting around ten and put on a smile when the exuberant client arrived with her wedding party. The dress was a beautiful concoction of ivory organza and lace, and it fitted the bride like a glove. By midday the last client had left, and Lauren closed the doors while her mother attended to the cashiering.

"Everything all right?"

Irene Jakowski was too smart to fool. Lauren had been on autopilot for most of the day, doing and saying the right thing, when inside she was confused and hurting and angry.

"Fine, Matka," she said when her mother repeated her question.

Her mother nodded and touched her arm. "There's someone special out there for you, I know it."

Lauren sighed. "I think I've already had my someone special."

"You mean Tim?" her mother asked. "Are you sure about that?"

She frowned just a little. "Of course. You know what he meant to me."

"I know," Irene said. "But you were young when you met, and teenage love can sometimes have you looking through rose-colored glasses."

"Are you saying Tim might not have been as perfect as I imagine he was?"

Irene nodded. "He was a nice young man, and I know you were compatible in many ways. And you might have been happy together. But sometimes easy isn't necessarily what will *keep* you happy. You married James on the rebound. All I'm saying is don't *settle* simply because you think you have to. And not when something wonderful might be within your reach."

She knew what her mother was suggesting. In her mother's romantic eyes, Steve was settling, and Gabe was Mr. Wonderful. "It was one date, Matka," she reminded her. "A nice date, but one date."

"That's how it starts."

No, it had started with heated looks, an argument and an unexpected fall into a swimming pool. Now she had to get him out of her system, her head and her heart.

"I'm not going to settle, I promise you. I've had enough of thinking I want the middle road. I told myself I would

be happy with that because I felt so guilty about marrying James. I mean, the way I did it, the way I had everything the same as when I'd planned to marry Tim, only the groom was different. *That's* when I settled, when I married a man I didn't love because I was so wrapped up in having a big wedding. And it didn't make either of us happy. If my brief relationship with Gabe has shown me anything, it's that I want to be *in love.* Truly, madly and deeply. Because I know what it feels like now, and anything less simply won't be enough."

There were tears in her mother's eyes when she'd finished speaking. "I'm glad to hear you say that. I'm glad to hear you want to be happy. After Tim's death and then with James…I wondered if you'd ever risk your heart again. But you did. And I'm very proud of you."

Lauren shuddered out a long breath. "I did risk my heart, Matka. He just didn't want it."

On Saturday night, Gabe paced the rooms of his house like a caged bear. She'd gone out again. The same car had arrived to collect her at six o'clock. It was now close to ten, and she wasn't home. He tried painting the last of the bedrooms to take his mind off Lauren and her date and imagining her doing who knows what. When that didn't work, he poured bourbon he didn't drink, ordered pizza he didn't eat and ignored the two calls from Aaron on his cell.

He fell asleep on the sofa and woke up at midnight with a cramp in his neck. The lights were off next door and the realization that Lauren might have decided to stay out all night cut through him with the precision of a knife. By morning, Gabe was so wound up that he pulled on sweats and sneakers and ran for a solid hour, only caving when he got a stitch in his side. He jogged home, showered and changed into worn jeans and T-shirt and downed two cups of strong coffee.

When his mother arrived at ten, minus Aaron, he knew he was in for a sermon. He sat in the kitchen, cradling a mug of coffee and waited for it.

And got it in spades.

"I've been talking with Irene Jakowski," she said so matter-of-factly, she got his immediate attention. "And we've decided that we need to knock some sense into the pair of you."

Gabe actually laughed. "Mom, I think you and Mrs. Jakowski should stop colluding and accept the inevitable."

"And what's that? You're unhappy. Lauren's unhappy. The only thing that's inevitable is that it's going to stay that way unless you do something about it."

"She's moved on," he said, and pushed the mug aside. "Which is how it should be."

"Stubborn as a mule," his mother said, and tutted. "Just like your father."

"Realistic and sensible," he replied, and half smiled. "Just like you."

"Gabriel," she said with deliberate emphasis. "I'm going to say something I never thought I would ever have to say to you." She drew in a long breath. "Stop being such a coward."

"Mom, I—"

"All your life you've done the right thing. As a child, you never got into any serious trouble. You did well at school. You studied hard. You stayed away from the wrong crowds. You really were a pillar of strength when your dad died. Afterward, you pulled the family together. You were the glue, Gabe. I was so very proud when you got into medical school and then even more so when you became such a wonderful doctor. But I was so busy being proud, I failed to see that I'd relied on you too much."

His throat thickened. "You didn't, Mom."

"I did," she said. "And all that responsibility took a

heavy toll on you. While Aaron was acting wild and chasing girls and Luca was sticking his head into a computer to avoid thinking about what we'd all lost, you worked hard and got on with things. And I think a part of you closed down because of that responsibility. Aaron is charming and says whatever's on his mind, and Luca is all moody and mysterious and cross…but you don't let anything or anyone touch you."

She sighed and reached across the table to grasp his hand. "You got sick. And you should have shouted and complained and blamed something or someone…but you never did. You kept it inside and locked everyone else out. We were all falling apart at the idea of losing you, and you kept us at arm's length. Then you went back to work and something terrible happened." She squeezed his fingers. "You're not to blame, son. But the only way you're ever going to believe that is if you talk about it and share it and forgive yourself. And to do that, you need to let someone in."

Someone. *Lauren.*

"I can't," he said quietly. "I can't do that to her. Not after what she's been through. I can't promise her everything and potentially leave her with nothing. Not like Dad—"

"Nothing?" his mom said, and cut him off. "Do you think your father left me with nothing?" Her eyes glistened. "Gabe, your dad left me *everything.* He left me four incredible children and the memories of a wonderful life. Do you honestly think our marriage was defined by those last few years?"

Did he? Had he been so wrapped up in making sure they still worked as a family that he'd forgotten what it was like before his father became ill?

"I don't, not for one minute," his mother said earnestly, "resent a single moment of the time I spent caring for your dad when he was sick. He was my husband and the father of my children. He was my rock. My center." Tears welled

in her eyes. "And I was honored that he trusted me when he was at his most vulnerable and let me care for him right up until the end."

Gabe swallowed the emotion in his throat. He remembered what Lauren had said to him about trust. She'd said Tim hadn't trusted her. She said he didn't trust her, either. And she was right. He didn't trust easily. Because he was afraid. Of being really seen. Of being considered less than strong and whole. Of being weak. And Lauren saw through that. She saw it all and had still wanted him. And like a fool, he'd pushed her away.

He looked at his mother. "You asked me a question a week ago, and I lied to you."

Her eyes widened. "What question?"

"You asked me if I was in love with her."

Claire Vitali smiled. "And are you?"

Gabe took a breath, felt the air fill his lungs and give him strength and nodded. "Yes, I'm completely and hopelessly in love with Lauren Jakowski."

Chapter Fourteen

Lauren was with a client on Monday afternoon and had finished lacing up the back panel on a beautiful beaded lace gown when a deliveryman arrived, carrying an extravagant floral arrangement. Her first thought was that they were from Steve, and although she considered it a bit too much after only two dates, flipped open the card and looked for his name.

Wrong.

No name. Just a message and an initial.

"Can we talk? G."

Not from Steve. He wasn't trying to change her mind about seeing him again. He'd texted her that morning to arrange another date. A text she'd put off replying to because she didn't want to lead him on. Then he'd called, and she'd declined his offer to go out that week. He was nice. But that was all. He'd taken her refusal easily and wished her well for the future.

She looked at the message again. Gabe. And he wanted to talk? As far as she was concerned, she'd said all she in-

tended saying. They were done and dusted. She tossed the note in the trash and told Dawn, the salesclerk, to take the flowers home.

There was a note pinned to her door when she arrived home. "I would really like to talk with you." More talk? She scrunched the note in a ball and tossed it over the hedge and onto his front lawn.

Flowers arrived again the following day. Her mother and Dawn thought it was incredibly romantic. So did Cassie, when she relayed the story to her best friend. Mary-Jayne called her, too. And Grace. But she wasn't going to be swayed. She didn't want to talk to him. He'd had his chance, and he'd blown it.

On Wednesday, the flower deliveryman had a huge smile on his face when he entered the store. Lauren sent the young man away, flowers in hand, and felt an odd burst of triumph that she'd stuck by her guns. Of course, when she arrived home and found Gabe sitting on her porch steps, flanked by Jed, who wore a silly white bandana around his neck while Gabe held up a tiny white flag, her icy reserve thawed for a brief moment. Until she remembered he'd pushed her away time and time again.

"What's this?" she demanded, and flung her bag over her shoulder.

Gabe smiled and patted the dog on the head. "I borrowed him from your brother. I needed an ally."

She raised a brow and looked at the ridiculous flag. "You're looking for a truce?"

"I was thinking more along the lines of a complete surrender."

Her heart pounded. It was a romantic notion. But she wasn't falling for it. "I hear your family's still in town?"

"Yes," he replied, and got to his feet. The dog followed and rushed toward Lauren. "My mother would very much like to meet you properly."

"I can't imagine why." Lauren laughed loudly. "Since I intend to forget all about you, there's no point."

"You'll never forget me," he said, and stepped closer. "I'll bet that you'll remember me for the rest of your life."

Lauren laughed again. Egotistical jerk. "Have you been drinking?"

"I'm perfectly sober. Why did you send my flowers back today?" he asked.

"Because I don't want flowers or anything else from you."

He reached out and touched her hair, twirling the strands through his fingers. "The flowers are just a place to start."

"A place to start what?" she asked suspiciously as she pulled back from his touch.

"Our courtship."

"Courtship?" She laughed at the old-fashioned word and thrust her hands on her hips.

He *was* drunk. There was no other explanation. And he looked as if he was thinking of kissing her. Which was out of the question. She stepped back and frowned. "Why on earth would I want to do that?"

Gabe smiled that killer smile. "How about because you're in love with me?"

She laughed again, because she didn't know what else to do amidst the madness. "You're out of your mind. I'm going inside. Don't even think of following me."

"You didn't deny it."

"Because…because it's too ridiculous, and because I'm tired of this conversation."

She raced up the steps and fiddled with the door lock. She looked around, hoping he was gone. But no such luck. He stood at the bottom of the steps. Her body shook thinking about how handsome he looked, even holding the silly flag.

"I'll be here tomorrow," he said quietly. "Just in case you change your mind."

She frowned. "Don't you have to work?"

"I quit," he said softly. "I'm going back to medicine. I start in the E.R. at Bellandale Hospital next month."

"Good for you," she said extra sweetly.

"Don't you want to know why?"

She shrugged. "It's not my business."

He stared at her and didn't bother hiding the wounded expression. But she had no intention of backing down. He didn't have the right to simply snap his fingers and expect her to come running.

"I want to be the best man I can be...for you."

"What's the point?" she said flatly.

"Because I...I..."

"Good night, Gabe," she said exasperatedly. She unlocked the door. "And incidentally, I think courtship is meant to start before two people sleep together. We've had this back to front from the very beginning, and that's all the sign I need. And stop sending me flowers. I don't want them or anything else from you." Then she headed inside without looking back.

"Have you tried talking to her again?"

Romantic advice seemed to come out of the woodwork, Gabe discovered, when it became obvious to everyone he knew that Lauren wasn't about to forgive him anytime soon. This time it was his mother, who'd decided to hang around in Crystal Point for another week and dispense counsel about his failures to get Lauren's attention at every opportunity.

"Maybe it's time I had a talk with her," she suggested, and pushed her tea aside.

"You need another approach," a voice said from the doorway.

It was Cameron. *Great.* He was in for the big-brother talk. "Your point?"

Gabe figured he'd tried every approach he knew. He'd been on her doorstep each afternoon for the past four days,

and she'd simply ignored him and gone into her house and locked the door. There were calls she wouldn't return, notes she wouldn't read and flowers she sent back. And he had a diamond ring in his pocket he wanted to give her, but was convinced she'd toss it in the trash. Total emasculation wasn't in his plans.

He'd wait. And hope she'd come around.

"No risk, no prize."

Cameron again. And this time, Scott and Aaron were behind him. Gabe looked up and scowled. "What?"

"Is she worth it?"

It was a stupid question, and with his patience frayed, Gabe dismissed the question with a barely audible grunt.

"Is she worth risking everything for?" Cameron asked again, relentless.

Gabe straightened in his seat. "Yes."

"Then tell her that."

In that moment, Gabe realized that he'd been so busy trying to woo Lauren with flowers and dinner invitations, he'd neglected to do the one thing he should have done an age ago.

Tell her the truth. Risking everything meant telling her everything. Like she'd told him time and time again. She'd trusted him. First with her past, then her body and then her heart. It was time he did the same. Because she knew what he'd been through and hadn't turned away. She accepted and wanted him. No questions. No prejudice. *No fear.* When, because of what she'd been through with Tim, she'd had every reason to run and not look back. But she hadn't. She'd put her heart on the line and he'd smashed it. Instead of applauding her courage and embracing that love, he'd brought up a whole load of excuses and reasons why they couldn't be together.

And one reason in particular.

Because he was scared of dying. Scared of living.

He let out a deep breath and looked at her brother. "So what's your big suggestion?"

Cameron grinned. "Well, asking her to forgive you for being a stupid ass hasn't worked, has it?"

Gabe thought about the flowers and the notes and the restrained effort he'd shown during the week. He talked about caring and wanting, and laughed at her attempts to ignore him. But he hadn't told her what she wanted to hear. "Not so far."

"Well, I reckon it's time for you to start begging and prove to her you'll do anything you have to do to win her heart."

And that, Gabe thought with a weary laugh, might just work.

Lauren was ever thankful that Saturday mornings were always busy at the store. It kept her mind away from thinking about anything else. Or anyone else. Or someone in particular.

A bridal party arrived at ten for their final fittings, and when the bride emerged from the changing room in her dress, Lauren set to work, fluffing the three layers of tulle and organza before she adjusted the straps and stepped away so the client's mother and attendants could admire her. When the fitting was complete and the bride was out of her gown, Lauren handed the client over to Dawn to process the sale and bag up the goods.

The bell above the door dinged and Lauren smiled when Cassie and Mary-Jayne entered the store.

"Hi, there," she said, and looked at her friends. "What are you both doing here?"

Cassie grinned. "Reinforcements."

"Huh?"

Her friend shrugged and kept smiling. "Trust me."

"You know I—" The door opened again. The bell dinged. And Gabe's mother walked into her store.

"Good morning, Lauren," she said before Lauren had a chance to move. "I'm not sure if you remember me from last week—I'm Claire Vitali." She grabbed her hand and squeezed it gently.

Lauren stared at the older woman. She had the same eyes as her son, the same smile. There was kindness in her expression and warmth in her hand. Her resolve to stay strong wavered. But she wasn't about to be easily swayed.

"It's nice to meet you," she said, and withdrew her hand. "I'd like to stay and talk but I have to—"

"It can wait," Mary-Jayne said with one of her famous grins.

The door opened again, and Grace and Evie entered.

Lauren frowned. "What's going on?"

"Reinforcements, like I said," Cassie explained.

Panic rushed through her blood. Something was wrong. "Has something happened? Is it my dad, or Cameron or—"

"You're father is fine," her mother said as she emerged from the stockroom.

"So is your brother," Grace added.

Lauren backed up. "I don't think—"

"That's just it, Lauren," Cassie said gently. "Stop thinking. At least, stop *overthinking*. We're all here because we care about you."

She stilled as realization dawned. "So this is, what, an intervention? That's why you're all here?"

"Actually, I think they're all here to stand point and make sure I do the right thing."

Gabe...

She hadn't heard him come through the door. He moved around Evie and Grace and stood near the counter. Lauren remained rooted where she was. Her legs turned to Jell-O. Her heart raced like a freight train. She looked at her family and friends. They were smiling, all hopeful, all clearly wondering what she would do next.

I wish I knew.

It was hard not to stare at Gabe. He looked so good, and she'd missed him. But he'd hurt her. And she didn't want to be hurt again.

"This isn't the right time or place to have this discussion," she said, and tried to politely ignore the bridal party hovering behind her.

"Since you won't talk to me, I reckon it's the only time," he said, and flashed her customers a breathtaking smile. "I'm sure everyone will understand."

The bride nodded, and before Lauren had a chance to protest, her mother had subtly ushered the bridal party from the store.

"What do you want?" she asked as stiffly as she could once the customers were gone.

He took a breath. "First, to apologize."

Lauren shuttled her gaze to her mother, Claire Vitali, Cassie and the other women and saw they were all smiling. Like they knew exactly what was going on. "Okay—apology accepted. You can *all* go now."

But they didn't move.

"I mean it," she said crossly. "Don't think just because you'd managed to swindle everyone into coming here today that I'm going to simply forget everything you've said and done and—"

"They volunteered," he said.

She looked at the sea of faces. "I don't believe it."

"You should. They care about you and only want to see you happy."

"Exactly," she said, and frowned. "Which has nothing to do with you."

"It has everything to do with me," he shot back. "I make you happy."

"You make me mad," she snapped.

"Well, I'd make you happy if you'd let me."

She forced her hands to her hips. "And how do you propose to do that?"

"I'll get to the proposing in a moment. Now, where were we? Oh, yes, I was—"

"What?" Her eyes bulged. "You're going to propose?"

"Well, of course I'm going to propose. But back to what I was saying. Oh, yes…and second," he said, and came a little closer, "I'd like to tell you a story."

"A story?" she echoed vaguely, certain she'd just imagined that he said he was about to propose. "I don't know what—"

"It's a story about a man who thought he was invincible." He spoke so softly she almost strained to hear, but she was quickly mesmerized by the seductive tone of his voice. "He thought nothing and no one could touch him. He went to medical school and became a doctor and spent his days trying to fix people who were broken. But underneath that facade of caring and compassion, he was arrogant and stubborn and always did what he wanted because he thought he knew best. And then one day he was told he was sick and everything changed. He wasn't strong. He wasn't healthy. Now he was broken but he couldn't fix himself. He had the surgery and the treatment, but because he was stubborn and arrogant, he went back to work before he should have."

Lauren's throat closed over. Her heart was breaking for him. His pain was palpable, and she longed to fall into his arms. She had been so attuned to him, she hadn't noticed that their mothers and friends had somehow left the store. Everyone was outside and they were alone. She could see them through the big front window. They were smiling. And suddenly, she almost felt like smiling, too. Right now, in front of her, lay her future. But she didn't smile. Because he was opening up, and she wanted to hear everything.

"Gabe, I—"

"I went back to work too early," he said, his voice thick. "I didn't listen. I didn't want to hear it. I just wanted to prove that I was the same. That I wasn't damaged and somehow less than the man I once was. Less than the doctor I

once was. But while I was in the bathroom throwing up from the side effects of the medication I was on, the woman and her baby came into the E.R. I wasn't there. And she died, along with her baby. All because I wouldn't admit that I *was* changed. That I was suddenly not just a man. Not just a doctor. I was a cancer patient. And it felt as though those words defined me, made me, *owned* me."

Her entire body shuddered. The raw honesty in his words melted her. "That's why you quit being a doctor? Because you believed that patient died because you were sick? Because you were somehow less than who you used to be?"

"Yes."

Her expression softened. "But you're not."

"I know that now," he said, and smiled. "I know that because when you look at me, I know you don't see a patient. You don't see a man who was sick. You just see…me."

He stepped closer, and Lauren swayed toward him. "Of course I do."

"Doesn't anything scare you, Lauren?" he asked, and took her hand. "After what you went through with Tim, doesn't the very idea of being with me make you want to run?"

"I've only ever seen you, Gabe. Not the doctor, not the patient. The man…the man who has listened to me and comforted me and makes me feel more alive than anyone else ever has. A man who's kind and considerate and has never judged me. And I'm not scared."

He pulled her gently toward him.

"The only thing I'm scared of is waking up and finding that this is a dream."

"It's no dream," he said softly. "You must know that I'm in love with you."

Did Gabe just say he loved me?

She shook her head, not quite prepared to believe him. "No, you're not."

"I am," he said, and touched her cheek. "I love you. I love

that you make me laugh. I love that you tell me when I'm being an egotistical jerk. And I love that you had the courage to let me into your heart when you had every reason not to."

Lauren blinked back tears. "But…you said you had a plan and wouldn't—"

"A stupid plan," he said, and grasped her hand. "I was wrapped up in self-pity and afraid to get involved, and you knew it. You saw through me, Lauren, and still…still wanted me. Even when you knew there was a chance it might not be forever, or I could get sick again. Or I might not be able to give you the children you want." He linked their fingers. "You talk straight and make the complicated simple. You told me how you felt and it spooked me. I'm not proud of my behavior these past weeks, and I promise I'll always be honest about my feelings with you from this day. You have such incredible strength…a strength you don't even know you possess."

Lauren swayed, felt his arms beckoning her. He looked solemn, sincere and wholly lovable. "I don't know…I'm not sure I can."

He squeezed her fingers. "You can, Lauren. Trust me…I won't hurt you again."

"Trust you?" She looked at the sea of faces peering through the windows. "Even though you dragged my friends and family here today to give you an advantage?"

He smiled. "It was Cameron's idea. He thought if I made a big enough fool out of myself in front of our families, you just might just show mercy and forgive me for being an idiot." He came closer until they were almost touching. "I love you, Lauren. I think I've loved you from the moment I pulled you from that swimming pool. And I'm sorry I haven't said it sooner."

He really loves me? Her legs wobbled, and he took her in his arms. "You're not going to completely ruin my reputation and kiss me in front of all these people who are staring at us through the window, are you?"

"I certainly am."

She heard whoops and sighs from the people outside, and Lauren laughed. It felt good. She thawed a little more. Gabe's love was what she wanted. *All* she wanted. And suddenly having the whole world know it didn't bother Lauren in the slightest. He was right—she was strong. Strong enough to open her heart again. And strong enough to cope with whatever the future brought them. He'd pushed past his fears to claim her, and she loved him all the more for it.

"But first," he said, and stepped back a little, "I have to ask you a question."

"What question is that?" she teased, and grinned foolishly.

Gabe dropped to one knee in front of her. "Marry me?" he asked, and pulled a small box from his pocket. The lid flipped open and she saw the perfectly cut diamond, which glittered like his eyes. "When you're ready, when you trust me enough, marry me, Lauren?"

Lauren touched his face and held out her left hand and sighed. "I think you've made a big enough fool out of yourself today for me to know I can trust you, Gabe. And my answer is yes. I'll marry you. I love you." She grinned. "And I kind of like the idea of being a doctor's wife."

Gabe got to his feet, slipped the ring onto her finger and kissed her. "I have you to thank for making me see sense, for making me realize how much I've missed my work. I was afraid to go back. I was afraid to try to recapture what I'd lost. But knowing you and loving you has made me stronger. You make me whole."

Lauren returned his kiss with every ounce of love in her heart. "You're the love of my life, Gabe."

His gaze narrowed. "I thought—"

"You," she said, and touched his face. "Only you. I did love Tim, but honestly, anything I've felt in the past feels a bit like kid stuff compared to the way I love you. And want you. And need you."

His eyes glistened. "Thank you. And while I may not be the first man you've loved, I'm honored to be the one you love now."

"Now and forever." She pressed against him and smiled. "But, Gabe, where are we going to live? Your place or mine?"

"How about neither?" he suggested. "How about we find somewhere new? A new home for a new beginning."

"I like the sound of that," Lauren said, and accepted his kiss. "And I'd like to get a dog," she said breathlessly when the kissing stopped.

He grinned. "Anything you want."

Lauren curved against him. "And babies?"

His arms tightened around her, and he smiled. "I'll see what I can do."

She sighed. "I'm not worried, Gabe. I want to marry you and have your baby. But if there's only ever us, that will be enough."

"You're sure?"

"Never surer."

She kissed him again, knowing she finally had her happy ending.

* * * * *

COMING SOON!

We really hope you enjoyed reading this book. If you're looking for more romance, be sure to head to the shops when new books are available on

Thursday
12th July

To see which titles are coming soon, please visit
millsandboon.co.uk

LET'S TALK
Romance

For exclusive extracts, competitions
and special offers, find us online:

f facebook.com/millsandboon

◎ @millsandboonuk

🐦 @millsandboon

Or get in touch on 0844 844 1351*

For all the latest titles coming soon, visit
millsandboon.co.uk/nextmonth